Praise for *Tr*

"This astounding and action-packed novel by a fifteen-year-old New York City student is sure to appeal to adolescents everywhere with its theme of brave students vs. oppressive educators. It's sure to be a big hit, just the kind of subversive tale YA's recommend to each other."

—*KLIATT* (starred review)

"It is a big, raw, sprawling action film of a book, combining martial arts, street fighting, midnight raids, rooftop flights, and a high body count. Action rules, and teen boys will swallow this book at a gulp, demanding more." —*VOYA*

"Many will hear—and embrace—the passionate critique of high school experience wrapped within the Truants' battle cry." —*Booklist*

"Fukui . . . has the makings of a literary career."

—*Wired.com*

"Fukui exhibits a fair amount of sheer writerly skills. His prose is clean and vivid. His characterization is sharp and his plotting propulsive. In short, this book is a fine foundation for a long career." —*SCIFI Weekly*

TRUANCY

ISAMU FUKUI

A TOM DOHERTY ASSOCIATES BOOK
NEW YORK
TOR®

This is a work of fiction. All of the characters, organizations, and events portrayed in this novel are either products of the author's imagination or are used fictitiously.

TRUANCY

A Tor Teen Book
Published by Tom Doherty Associates, LLC
175 Fifth Avenue
New York, NY 10010

www.tor-forge.com

The Library of Congress has catalogued the hardcover edition as follows:

Fukui, Isamu, 1990–
Truancy / Isamu Fukui.—1st ed.
p. cm.
"A Tom Doherty Associates book."
Summary: In the City, where an iron-fisted Mayor's goal is to perfect control through education, fifteen-year-old Tack is torn between a growing sympathy for the Truancy, an underground movement determined to bring down the system at any cost, and the desire to avenge a death caused by a Truant.
ISBN 978-0-7653-1767-4
[1. Totalitarianism—Fiction. 2. Education—Fiction. 3. Counterculture—Fiction. 4. Fantasy. 5. Youths' writings.] I. Title.
PZ7.F951538Tru 2008
[Fic]—dc22

2007035391

ISBN 978-0-7653-2258-6

First Hardcover Edition: March 2008
First Trade Paperback Edition: February 2010

Printed in the United States of America

0 9 8 7 6 5 4 3 2 1

I dedicate this story
to every student
who has ever suffered
in the name of education.

Contents

Prologue: Follow Instructions *9*

PART I: STUDENT

1: The Bell *21*
2: Testing Patience *33*
3: The Truancy *47*
4: A Rebellious Child *62*
5: The Report Card *75*
6: Tardy *87*
7: Expulsion *96*
8: When Life Gives You Lemons *110*
9: Zero Tolerance *126*
10: Final Exams *142*
11: Death *159*

PART II: MISCREANT

12: Rebirth *173*
13: A Show of Force *188*
14: The Aftermath *204*

15: Swords *219*
16: Without Mercy *234*
17: The Taste of Blood *250*
18: The Heat of Battle *266*
19: His Most Dangerous Student *288*

PART III: **TRUANT**

20: A Treacherous Threshold *305*
21: The Definition of Love *319*
22: A Student Militia *334*
23: Backed into a Corner *346*
24: At the Hands of a Pacifist *361*
25: No Regrets *378*
26: A Guilty Conscience *396*
27: The Fall *413*

PROLOGUE
FOLLOW INSTRUCTIONS

The man sighed and flipped his lighter open, light reflecting off its chrome finish as he slowly brought a thick cigar to his mouth and lit it. Gray ash flaked down to match his expensively tailored suit, though he made no motion to brush it off. Grunting, he shut the lighter with a resounding *click*.

Looking around at the other men seated at the mahogany table, he noted that more than one of them seemed to dislike the fumes that his recently acquired habit tended to generate. Still, it seemed to keep him relaxed, which was why he did it and why they didn't mind. Not that they would've complained anyway. Especially not today.

"So," the man said grimly as he extinguished the butt of the cigar on a polished marble ashtray, "it looks bad, doesn't it?"

The room was silent. Glaring at the other men fidgeting in their equally expensive and uncomfortable outfits, the man managed a humorless grin.

"Yes, it does look bad," he answered himself. "Especially for you."

There was more uncomfortable silence, and then one of the men spoke up foolhardily.

"Mr. Mayor, you can't blame us for this debacle."

The tension in the room suddenly increased, and the Mayor twitched as his eyes snapped towards the audacious man. His name was Mr. Caine, the Mayor recalled, vaguely recognizing his face. He had joined the Mayor's cabinet two weeks ago. Obviously, two weeks was not enough time to get a clear idea of how things worked in the Mayor's City.

The other cabinet members looked at the unfortunate individual with a mix of subdued approval and pity. The Mayor gripped his lighter as Mr. Caine held his gaze. The Mayor had always known that, sooner or later, one of them would end up talking back to him. It was just as well that he would be making an example out of someone new.

"Mr. Caine, do you know the first thing our teachers are supposed to do when they get ahold of a student?" the Mayor asked pleasantly.

"No, sir, I can't say that I do," Mr. Caine answered, frowning now, sensing something subtly dangerous in the Mayor's voice.

"They are told to see how well the students will follow instructions," the Mayor explained. "Students are to obey every command given to them, they are not to speak without permission, they may not eat without permission, and they cannot even perform bodily functions without our consent."

"What's that got to do with me, sir?" Mr. Caine asked, causing a few cabinet members to gasp audibly.

"Because, Mr. Caine," the Mayor said patiently, "in my presence, the City is just one very large class, and I am its teacher. You are to speak only when I allow you to, say only what I want you to, and do everything I tell you to."

Mr. Caine flushed red and for a moment looked as though he might argue, but the Mayor's withering glare quickly silenced him.

The Mayor had no sympathy for Mr. Caine; the new cabinet member had undoubtedly endured worse, having once been a student himself, as they all had been. The entire purpose of school in the City was to produce civil and obedient adults—apparently this Mr. Caine had thought that being an Educator, being among the few that not only governed but truly *controlled* the City, would make him exempt. Some lessons learned in school, the Mayor reflected, were forgotten entirely too easily.

"Now, I believe you were saying that I can't blame you, Mr. Caine?" the Mayor continued. "I recall having a meeting to discuss the Truancy just before last week's attack. I believe I was assured that this 'handful of desperate children, poorly armed, with little organization and no competent leadership,' would soon fall apart. It seems clear to me now that my entire cabinet has been playing me for a fool."

"Mr. Mayor, we didn't understand the breadth and scale of the problem," Mr. Caine protested again, causing the rest of the cabinet to shake their heads in admonishment. "The Truancy is comprised of mere children! It was impossible to take them seriously at the time!"

The Mayor flicked his lighter open in agitation.

"They've been running amok for nearly two years now! Have you forgotten that they demolished the District 1 School itself?" the Mayor snarled, and the entire cabinet winced at the mention of that event. "Your reports led me to believe that they had been diminishing since then, not *growing*!"

"As far as we knew, they were, Mr. Mayor," Mr. Caine argued. "They had lain relatively low, and it was assumed that they didn't have the tenacity to just stick around like that. It was hard to believe that they hate us *that* much, sir."

"It's our job to brand numbers on these children like cattle, shove them into our schools as one faceless herd, treat them like inferior beasts, and then cast them out to rot in the gutter if they don't obey." The Mayor shut his lighter. "They're angry, and understandably so! Did you think that after a while they would just return to the playgrounds, whining for someone to help push them on the swings?"

"No, sir," Mr. Caine conceded. "But the City's educational system has always proved to be successful in the past, and the vast majority of children have always shown remarkable submission to our methods. There was nothing to forewarn us of such a dramatic reversal—"

"Nonsense," the Mayor snapped. "You went through the schools. I went through the schools. We all did. Do you even remember what it was like? Tell me, what are some of the side effects of the recent programs we've tested on the students?"

"Well, before they're broken in and their brains fully mature"—Mr. Caine began ticking points off his fingers—"students typically demonstrate depression, anger, anxiety, insomnia, and sometimes, relatively rarely, of course, irrational violence."

"Correct. Not exactly the flawless acceptance that you'd

have us believe," the Mayor pointed out. "Remember, the City is strictly experimental. Perfect control through education, that is our ultimate goal, and we were getting close. But as with all experiments, there are bound to be setbacks. It took several generations and a number of other Mayors, but those setbacks are here at last."

"Yes, but we never predicted armed revolt," Mr. Caine argued. "The notion of children taking up arms against us is just absurd!"

"*Was* absurd, before the Truancy, at least to you," the Mayor rebutted. "Children were the most obvious individuals to expect failure from. Education is the harshest phase of every citizen's life. Only if the students view their entire future as relying on education can they be easily forced into obedience. We, as Educators, have to crush any rebellious thoughts by *denying them any alternative*."

Rising from the table, the Mayor began pacing around the dimly lit room, his hands folded behind his back.

"But now, our system has been undermined," the Mayor muttered. "The Truancy provides them with an alternative. They can choose to fight us instead of obeying us."

Mr. Caine seemed to fight an internal battle with himself. For a moment he wavered, but then he opened his mouth anyway. The other cabinet members stared at him, wondering if the man was suicidal, or just stupid. They knew that while the Mayor wasn't fond of petty revenge, he wasn't one to let disrespect go unpunished either.

"Mr. Mayor, the Truancy is still just an underground movement of isolated, outcast children," Mr. Caine pointed out. "We've kept a tight hold on the media, and the general populace doesn't even know a resistance exists yet. The experiment hasn't been compromised. School attendance rates remain as high as they were two weeks ago. There's little chance of students just rising up and becoming Truants."

"Yet they *are* rising up and becoming Truants," the Mayor said, flipping his lighter open. "And it's growing painfully hard to hide this from the public. People are not so stupid that they didn't notice the unseasonable power blackouts in the City. Soon they're going to wonder why."

"We've already explained it as a mechanical malfunction—"

"Some will buy that," the Mayor conceded. "But others are going to start to wonder."

"We got auxiliary power running quickly, though," Mr. Caine protested. "It wasn't quite the disaster it might've been, since the Truancy seems to have avoided a total blackout for some reason. This whole thing will just end up being forgotten in a week or two—we'll throw something out there to distract the people. Maybe news of another impending disease epidemic."

"That gives the Truancy plenty of time to plan its next attack," the Mayor snapped. "We still know next to nothing about them. How are they supplying themselves? Where are they holed up? How do they keep evading the Enforcers? And most important, who's leading them? These are things we need to know, and should have known a long time ago." The Mayor clicked his lighter shut. "We've been relaxed for too long. We have to start to become aggressive. We have to authorize unlimited use of lethal force."

"That goes against City code," Mr. Caine said weakly.

"Forget the code!" the Mayor growled. "Let's measure the

damage to our social institutions *after* the threat is eliminated. Generations have worked to build the City into what it is, and I'm not about to let a gang of kids destroy it." The Mayor halted and turned towards the table. "Do you understand?"

"Yes, sir," the cabinet replied as one.

"Good." The Mayor glanced towards the only one of them that seemed willing to hold his gaze. "And you, Mr. Caine. Since you were so unconvinced of the threat the Truancy posed, you are now officially appointed as a Disciplinary Officer. It's time that you get to know what you're dealing with."

Mr. Caine's eyes widened and his face drained of all color.

"But . . . Mr. Mayor . . ." Mr. Caine struggled to keep his voice under control. "The Truancy assassinated three Disciplinary Officers last month alone!"

"Short life expectancy comes along with the title. You should have remembered that before you earned it," the Mayor countered curtly. Mr. Caine seemed to visibly deflate. "Now, on to other business. During the attack last week, the Truancy left several districts with power. I want to know why. Give me the district numbers."

There was a mad scramble to be the first or at least not to be the last one to draw out the thick folders stuffed with information about the attack. The Mayor gritted his teeth as the six men fumbled with the papers until one of them finally found the proper sheet.

"Uhh . . . 'all the districts connected to the District 19 power grid retained electricity during and after the attack,' " the lucky cabinet member read hastily.

The Mayor froze at the mention of District 19. The Truancy had left *District 19* alone. That was an abandoned district, and there was nothing of any importance there except . . .

"*Him.* So they know about him after all," the Mayor breathed. "How interesting."

The Mayor walked quietly toward a set of red velvet curtains. Drawing them back, he gazed out the window at the sprawling cityscape beneath him. It was night now, but with the power restored, a sea of lights blinked at him from building windows, street lamps, and cars, creating a moving, glowing stream that flowed throughout the layers of streets and skyscrapers that formed the City. It was a society unlike any other, its people believing that they were free while, in truth, all of their fates were determined by the educational system. It was, in a word, perfect. And it was his to control.

"Well," he amended quietly, "most of it, anyway."

He sighed and turned slowly to face the cabinet.

"Gentlemen, I want all Enforcers and Educators to stay out of District 19. Under no circumstances will they enter that area."

The cabinet members stared at the Mayor, wondering if it was some sort of trap. As the silence lengthened and the Mayor retained his pensive look, they began to shift uncomfortably.

"Mr. Mayor . . . if . . . if we stayed out of there, wouldn't the Truancy use that district as a haven?" someone asked.

The Mayor shook his head gently, as if recalling some distant, nostalgic memory.

"No. If they know about *him,* then they know better than to trespass on his territory," the Mayor said. "And so do I, for that matter. The order stands. Meeting adjourned."

The cabinet members filed out of the room, leaving the

Mayor alone to think. None of them had any idea who *he* might be, but they did know that it wouldn't do any good to ask.

In the end, the general consensus was that the Mayor had been unusually easy on Mr. Caine.

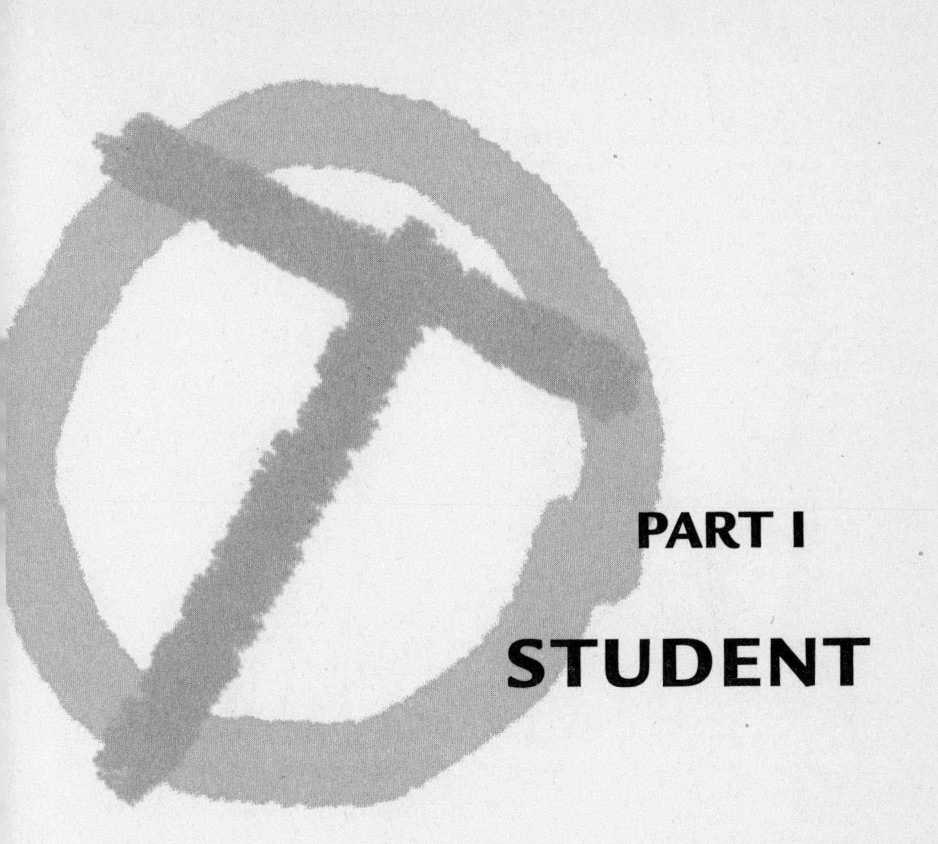

PART I

STUDENT

1

The Bell

"I hope that most of you will see this as a wake-up call," Mrs. Bean announced to the class, folding her arms haughtily. "If you got over an eighty-five, you've done tolerably. If you got lower than that, you should be concerned. If you got below a seventy, I'm going to *make* you concerned."

Tack gritted his teeth and clenched his test paper, wrinkling a good portion of it before he unceremoniously shoved the paper into his backpack along with his books and binder. Untamed brown strands of hair dropped in front of his eyes, obscuring his vision as he bent over to zip up his backpack and await the ending bell. Despite the cheerful sunlight streaming through the classroom's single window, an unmistakable aura of gloom emanated from the students around him, which Tack actually found to be oddly comforting. It meant that he wasn't the only one the teacher was going to "make concerned."

"There are a lot of you who can do better," Mrs. Bean continued, lifting her chin. "And there are a few who are beyond hope. If you don't work your butt off and if you don't follow instructions, that reflects on your tests. These test grades let me know how obedient you've all been. As you all know, that weighs heavily on your report card."

"Guess that means I'm out of luck," a boy to Tack's right murmured tiredly under his breath.

"Hey, is that *talking* back there?" Mrs. Bean spun about, glaring wildly around like a starved lioness with an appetite for students. Spotting Tack, who looked suspicious with his gritted teeth and packed bag, she quickly drew herself up into attack position.

"*You* of all people should be trying to do better!" she shouted, jabbing an accusing finger at Tack. "After your performance on this test I'd have thought you'd have learned to behave yourself!"

"M-me?" Tack sputtered haplessly.

At this point, Tack didn't even want to know how the teacher could've made such a huge mistake at his expense so much as he wanted to know how this class could possibly have gone any worse than it already had.

"Yes, you!" Mrs. Bean hissed. "You know what you did; you don't need anyone else to say it for you!"

"I didn't do anything!" Tack protested.

"Are you talking back to me?" Mrs. Bean stalked closer to Tack, lowering her voice menacingly.

"N-no, but—"

"No buts, you need to learn some respect, young man!"

"I . . . I . . ."

Still recovering from this latest misfortune, Tack quickly assessed his options. The teacher looked ready to sink her teeth into him, and the only thing that could save him now would be to rat out the real culprit, who was currently doing his best not to look involved. But being a rat simply wasn't an option; betraying a fellow student to a teacher would make Tack the enemy of all the other students. He simply couldn't afford that, as all the teachers were already by nature his enemies.

And so there was only one way that Tack could finish his sentence.

"I . . . I'm sorry."

Mrs. Bean purred contently. "Good. Now apologize to the class too. It was their time that you just wasted."

Tack felt an urge to stand up and tell Mrs. Bean that she was the one wasting their time by making such a huge deal over something so petty. Fortunately for Tack, he was quickly able to suppress that urge.

"I'm sorry, class," Tack mumbled, dropping his gaze.

"I don't think they can hear you," Mrs. Bean said.

"I said, 'I'm sorry, class'!" Tack nearly yelled.

"Better," Mrs. Bean said, resuming her prowl around the class.

Tack slumped in his chair, his stomach churning in humiliation and stress. The boy next to him, the real culprit, clapped him on the shoulder in a silent show of thanks, but Tack shrugged him off moodily. Eventually the bell rang, and the students began their silent mass exodus.

Tack stood up to join them, unconsciously tugging at the collar of his shirt. The gray school uniform felt annoyingly itchy and tight, no matter how many times he wore it. As he filed out of the classroom with the rest of the class, still adjusting his clothes, Tack couldn't help but wonder if they had been designed to be as unpleasant as possible.

Tack joined the gray river of uniformed students flowing neatly up and down the hallways, his stomach quickly forgetting the stress of the classroom as it began growling, reminding him that he had at least one good thing to look forward to in the immediate future: lunch.

All students looked forward to lunch, even if they weren't hungry. For one single period each day, students had permission to leave the school in search of nourishment and conversation, two luxuries that Tack noticed that adults of the City took for granted. Inside school NO EATING and NO SPEAKING were two rules that were rigidly enforced.

Of course, if any students displeased teachers, the teachers could revoke those students' lunch privileges for as long as they liked. Tack was glad that Mrs. Bean hadn't gone that far, at least.

"Hey, Tack!"

Tack froze in mid-step as the voice, barely a whisper, rose above the silent gray multitude that walked both around and into him. His heart racing frantically, Tack's first instinct was to look around for any teachers that might have noticed a student *speaking* his name. When he found none, his second instinct was to look for who it was that had nearly given him a heart attack. Looking up the staircase he was about to climb, Tack saw a younger girl with brown pigtails looking down at him with a lopsided grin.

"Suzie, what do you think you're doing?" Tack asked quietly, his face torn between worry and joy.

"Nothing much, Bro; Melissa is sick today, so I've got no one to eat lunch with," Suzie whispered back, causing more than a few passing students to stare at her.

At that Tack smiled and nearly forgot about the trouble

that his sister could land them both in by speaking. Suzie always ate lunch with her friends, so much so that she and Tack rarely ever saw each other except for the few hours that they spent at home.

"Wanna go grab something then?"

"Sure!" Suzie agreed so happily that Tack winced at how loud her voice had become.

A moment later, Suzie joined the flow of students descending the stairs, and together she and Tack made their way towards the lobby of the building. Much to Tack's relief, Suzie refrained from speaking aloud the rest of the way. Soon after they reached the lobby they came into sight of the armed guards that were manning polished metal turnstiles with scanners that inspected the arms of each of the many students filing in and out. It was very fast, very quiet, very orderly, very *clean,* almost unsettlingly so.

As they approached the nearest turnstile, Tack and Suzie rolled up the sleeves of their uniforms to reveal the nine-digit numbers and bar codes that had been imprinted upon their arms when they had first entered the City school system. The guards seized their arms, scanned them to make sure that the children were indeed allowed to eat lunch, shot them a nasty look in case they were thinking of breaking any rules, and then released them and turned their attention towards the next students in line.

Having finally cleared that last, oppressive hurdle, Tack and Suzie burst out of the large double doors, just two more students enjoying the feeling of the relatively fresh air of the City streets. As they strode upon the hard gray sidewalks under the looming shadows of steel-and-glass skyscrapers, Tack let out a quiet sigh as he allowed the thoughts of his test, Mrs.

Bean, school, and everything else that was wrong with the City to fade away.

"So what do you feel like eating today?" Tack asked. It felt a little odd to be able to use his voice again.

"I dunno; what're you hungry for, Tacky?" Suzie inquired.

"I'm not sure either. Maybe we should just get pizza," Tack suggested.

"That sounds good, Tacky." Suzie grinned.

"Don't call me that." Tack scowled.

"But it fits you!" Suzie said, shoving Tack playfully.

"No, it doesn't, and don't call me that," Tack said with mock annoyance, brushing her hand aside.

"You really are talky, Tacky."

"I'll poke you; I swear," Tack threatened in exasperation.

"No, you won't," Suzie said matter-of-factly.

"Why not?" Tack demanded.

"Because I'd tell on you." Suzie giggled.

"That's just below the belt," Tack complained.

The siblings laughed and continued to poke fun at each other until they reached their preferred pizza parlor. His stomach would have been just as satisfied at any of the other pizza places in the neighborhood, and while this one sported the typical yellow walls and dirty red floor tiles just like the rest, it always had plenty of seats available, as well as a large fan that kept the air circulating, along with a television hanging from the ceiling that was, unfortunately, always set to one of the City's news channels rather than anything Tack would've preferred to watch.

The man at the counter eyed Tack and Suzie suspiciously, as if the gray-clad students were vagrants in disguise. It wasn't uncommon for adults to treat students with suspicion, as each generation always accused the next of general disrespect and misbehavior. Tack thought that the generalization was somewhat unfair but didn't let it bother him as he drew enough cash from out of his pocket to pay for two plain slices of pizza. The squinty-eyed cashier seized the money and spent a few moments satisfying himself that the students weren't trying to rip him off. Meanwhile, the friendlier pizza maker, who seemed to recognize Tack and Suzie as regular customers, sliced up two pieces from a freshly baked pie and stuck them on a plate on a tray with a wink.

Tack grabbed the tray and led Suzie over to an empty plastic table. Tack's stomach was no longer growling but rather roaring with discontent. Suzie obviously felt the same as Tack. Even as they sat down, Tack tore into his slice, grease cascading down his chin. A moment later, Suzie followed suit. As Tack's stomach sated itself, he took the opportunity to concentrate on the broadcast that was blaring loudly from the television.

"Welcome back to CNC, the City News Channel," the brown-haired anchorwoman droned. "Today the Educators denied all rumors of human error concerning last week's catastrophic blackout, maintaining that the accident was solely the result of mechanical failure. This morning the Mayor himself issued a comment on the incident."

The broadcast switched to the familiar face of the Mayor as he stood on the marble steps of City Hall, surrounded by a sea of microphones. It was a face that every citizen of the City knew, from his salt-and-pepper hair to his glittering dark eyes, and the exaggeratedly large smile that always seemed plastered on to his face.

"Thorough investigation has concluded from the start that, popular speculation notwithstanding, this accident was just that—an accident," the Mayor said firmly. "Nothing has changed since. I promise you that measures are already being taken to prevent such an incident from occurring again. In the meantime, I urge every citizen of this City to do their part and work toward conserving electricity."

The brief message concluded, the image changed to show a series of test tubes, followed by coughing patients in a hospital ward.

"In our top story today, a terrifying new disease epidemic has taken the City by storm." The anchorwoman's voice took on a dramatic tone. "The new RAS virus has already been blamed for at least one death, with forty-two confirmed cases. The virus is airborne, and the three-week incubation period has City scientists fearing that many more people might be carrying the disease right now without even knowing it. No vaccine yet exists, and today the Educators issued a written statement asking citizens to take measures to slow the projected spread of the disease. Suggested preventive measures include avoiding large crowds and public transportation, as well as using a protective mask to cover the mouth and nose."

Tack stopped listening. Weird diseases were always ending up on the news, and while adults seemed to take the threats quite seriously, Tack figured that the lack of bodies dropping in the streets was a good sign. There were even times that he would have welcomed disease, in order to escape the torments of school, and he couldn't imagine walking around all day with a rag strapped around his face.

Reaching for a nearby shaker, Tack poured large amounts of powdered garlic onto the remnants of his slice to make it taste less like boring routine and more worth the money he'd spent. Suzie, he noted with affection, had already garnished her slice with liberal amounts of both garlic and red pepper, and was busying herself by piling on green herbs.

As he resumed eating, Tack's mind strayed to the Educators, idly wondering, and not for the first time, how they were chosen. The Educators essentially called all the shots in the City, and formed one of the two branches of its government. They made the City's laws and formed its policies while their subordinate branch, the Enforcers, enforced them. Educators presided over all matters of government in the City, especially, as their title suggested, education.

The Educators appointed principals and teachers, and had final say in the fate of any lowly student. Of course, there were various ranks of Educators. Tack knew that his own father had once had a minor position with them, but neither father nor son really liked to talk about that. As a matter of fact, Tack and his father rarely talked at all, as one or the both of them were usually busy with either work or school.

Other than his father, the only other type of Educator that Tack had ever seen in person was the Disciplinary Officers. These were special Educators, the inspectors of schools, and the only ones who could deal out the most serious punishment of expulsion. If a Disciplinary Officer ever showed up in a school for any reason other than a scheduled inspection, every student would instantly understand that someone must've *really* done *something*.

"So, Bro," Suzie said, finishing her slice and wiping her chin. "How's your day going?"

"Eh . . . I've had better," Tack admitted, choking down the last of his slice.

"What was it *this* time?" Suzie rolled her eyes.

"Science class. You know, with Mrs. Bean." Tack grimaced.

Suzie nodded wisely. "Oh, her. I heard she's awful."

"That's putting it lightly," Tack said bitterly, wiping his mouth on the gray sleeve of his uniform.

"Yeah, well, what can ya do?" Suzie shrugged.

Tack raised an eyebrow. "Rhetorical question?"

"Duh." Suzie rolled her eyes.

"Well, then we ought to be getting back to school before we're late and make a few more teachers act *awful*," Tack suggested, standing up.

"Don't you have Mr. Kiner next?" Suzie asked.

"Don't remind me," Tack groaned.

"Hey, don't sweat it, Bro; I heard he's not so bad until he starts shouting." Suzie elbowed Tack playfully.

"You hear a lot of things." Tack ruffled Suzie's hair.

Suzie grinned. "Yep."

"A lot of those things are true," Tack offered.

Suzie's grin widened. "Yep."

"We should still be getting back, you know," Tack said.

"Yep." Suzie's grin was now roughly the size and shape of a watermelon.

"Oh come on, you." Tack smiled in spite of himself, dragging Suzie along.

Tack and Suzie made their way back to the school, this time nagging at each other with each step upon the concrete. They drew close to the school, and quickly rejoined the herd of students marching back towards class. Reaching the doors, both siblings got in line and rolled up their sleeves, prepared to present their arms to the security guards. As they stepped into the queue, however, Tack and Suzie both hesitated briefly, knowing that they would now have to go their separate ways.

"Are you gonna be waiting for me today after school?" Suzie asked.

"You know I only have the time for that on Saturday," Tack said apologetically.

"And today is Wednesday, yeah yeah." Suzie's frown deepened. "Why do I have to get out a period later than you?"

"Because you get to school a period later than I do," Tack explained. "They have to make it equal, you know."

"That was a rhetorical question too, you know," Suzie teased as they drew closer to the glaring guards. "Anyway, Tacky, see ya later!"

Tack sighed as a guard seized his arm. "See you, Suzie."

The rest of Tack's classes passed by without much incident. After what had happened to him that morning, Tack took extra care to give his teachers no reason to focus their attentions on him. In math class, Mr. Kiner did throw a loud tantrum and call security upon finding two of his students exchanging notes in class, and his language teacher revoked the lunch privileges of a student who had spoken out of turn, but Tack wasn't either of those unfortunate victims, and so he didn't worry about any of it. One bad school experience a day was bad enough for him—and he hadn't even deserved that one.

When the 3:00 bell finally rang, Tack wearily made his way towards the front entrance, presented his numbered arm to the guard, who scanned him and waved him through with a dismissive gesture. Tack walked along with the other gray-clad students, making his way down the dull paths of concrete and across wide lanes of asphalt until he finally reached the nearest entrance to the City's underground subway. Making his way down the stairs that led into the station, Tack reached the turnstiles and allowed one to scan his bar code.

Having confirmed that Tack was a student and wasn't cutting class, the machine quickly allowed him to pass through with a curt beep. Another flight of stairs brought Tack into a filthy, cavernous area that constituted the subway platform.

As he stood patiently on the platform with other commuters, adults and students alike, Tack barely noted the earthshaking rumble of subway cars entering and leaving, but still managed to haul himself onto the appropriate train after it rumbled into the station and slid its doors open. Once inside, Tack sat down quietly with his eyes shut, the day's weariness catching up to him and furiously bludgeoning him upside the head in the form of a throbbing headache.

Unconsciously, he scratched at the number scarred onto his arm, the one that he never looked at or bothered to memorize, feeling suddenly like there was something, *something* unidentifiably wrong with his life, something that he just couldn't pin down.

At least, not for now.

2

Testing Patience

Tack lay on his bed in the darkness of his small room. The eerie glow of his tiny, muted television and computer cast his pale features into sharp relief as he tossed the thin white covers off of his body, hugging his knees to his chest. He was tired, but he couldn't rest—even in the sanctuary of his home, school found ways to keep him busy. Homework was the main culprit, though there were others, Tack's parents among them.

Lately, as school consumed more and more of his time and concern, Tack had been coming home to realize something unnerving; his parents, whenever he got to see them, seemed oddly detached, almost like strangers. What's more, they had started to look at him as though they didn't recognize him. And it didn't help that they were constantly pressuring him to do better with his schoolwork.

Sometimes they would yell.

Tack would yell back.

And no one would really end up happy.

He knew that his parents tried, and Tack genuinely believed that their hearts were in the right place, and he appreciated it. Tack liked to think that their distance was due wholly because he was too often away at school and his parents too often away at work, and indeed that was a big part of it—Tack's mother worked several different jobs, and was out of the house more often than not. Tack's father now worked as a City clerk, but having once held even a minor Educator position, he still maintained an infuriatingly authoritative air.

Suddenly, Tack jerked his head up. Soft, creeping footsteps were approaching his room. Tack paused for a second as he listened to the sound of the steps, and a wide grin unconsciously spread across his face. He had lived in that apartment, with its noisy wooden floorboards, all his life, and he could easily recognize the footsteps of each of his family members.

His parents had been strangers to him for some time now, but he never ceased adoring his sister.

"Suzie?" Tack called out as the steps halted in front of his door.

"Hey, Tack," Suzie whispered, pushing the door open a bit.

"Hey," Tack replied with a grin.

"What's up?" she asked in a hushed voice.

"Nothing," Tack said, sitting up slightly. "Why are you talking like that?"

"Mom and Dad said not to bother you," Suzie explained.

"Well, Mom and Dad say a lot of things, don't they?" Tack snorted.

"Yeah, but Dad told me that you should be working now." Suzie stepped into the room, frowning. "He said that if you didn't start trying harder, you might not even graduate."

Tack grimaced. His father *had* said that to him earlier that day. Among other things.

"I really can't stand it," Tack blurted out angrily. "I mean, interacting with Mom and Dad might be a little more tolerable if they didn't act so damn superior all the time."

"Aren't they, though?" Suzie cocked her head, playing the devil's advocate.

Tack thought about that for a moment. "I don't know. Is it right for *anyone* to be claiming superiority over anyone else?"

"I don't like it any more than you do, Bro," Suzie admitted. "But they make the rules, so what's the use in agonizing over it?"

That simple question, intended to cheer him up, instead brought home to Tack just how hopeless his situation was. Suddenly feeling very, very tired, Tack slumped over. Realizing that she'd struck a nerve in her brother, Suzie edged farther into the room and tugged on Tack's sleeve.

"Tack?" Suzie said.

"Yes?" Tack replied.

"Are you all right?" Suzie asked.

"Yeah," Tack said unconvincingly. "I think you should probably go before Mom or Dad comes along."

"Okay," Suzie said skeptically, turning to leave.

Tack waited for the sound of the door shutting behind her. It never came.

"Tack?"

"Yes?"

"Are you sure you're all right?"

"I'm fine, Suzie," Tack lied.

This time there was no response. Curious, Tack looked up. The next thing he knew, Suzie had wrapped her arms around him, pulling him into a warm hug. Tack instinctively hugged back, pressing his face to her shoulder. For several precious moments they maintained their embrace, and Tack could actually feel all his stress just bleeding away, replaced by a fluttery, warm, *pure* sensation. It was a strange thing, how reinvigorating it was to just hold someone and to be held. It reminded Tack that no matter how unfriendly the rest of the world might be, he could always count on at least one person's warmth.

Sometimes that was all the light he needed to get through dark days.

"Cheer up, okay?" Suzie said at last, withdrawing from her brother.

"You got it," Tack replied, reluctantly releasing his tight grip on her. "Hey, I know that we don't have time to do anything now, but why don't we got to the park this weekend?"

"Yeah, that sounds good!" Suzie said with contagious cheer.

"All right, now you should get going before Mom and Dad find out that you're bothering me and that I'm not working," Tack said with a weak grin.

"If you say so. See ya, Tacky!" Suzie smiled, prodding Tack in the belly affectionately before fleeing, just to make sure that she was meeting her sibling annoyance quota.

Tack fell back onto the bed, partly because of the hearty poke and partly because he knew that it would be his last respite before homework. Savoring the few empty seconds, he imagined that Suzie's arms were still around him, letting the warmth of her embrace thaw the monotony of his life. Eventually, feeling considerably better, Tack forced himself up and moved toward his desk. Flipping on the small black television that rested next to his work space, Tack set the volume low just for the sake of having something playing in the background while he tackled his homework.

"Welcome back to CNC, the City News Channel. Today the Educators announced a new City-wide attendance policy to benefit our youth by boosting school attendance rates," the anchorwoman announced. "The plan will impose harsher penalties upon students that cut class, and also call for increased Enforcer patrols in school neighborhoods that will locate and apprehend truants."

Tack glanced at the screen as it flashed to the Mayor's familiar figure.

"We believe these new provisions are absolutely essential," the Mayor proclaimed. "Our City-wide Exams continue to demonstrate that our after-school and weekend tutoring programs have us headed in the right direction. However, at the same time, Truancy rates have reached disturbingly high levels in this City. Maintaining the status quo is simply unacceptable, as this is our future, our children, that we're concerned about. We will do anything and everything we can to ensure that *every* child in the City gets the education that they need and deserve."

Tack shut the television off in disgust as he polished off another math problem. The actions of a few bad students would always result in consequences for them all. Every day a little more of his freedom slipped away. In a few years, what freedom would be left? What about in a few generations? What would the City look like then?

Slowly but surely, the Educators were taking control of every last step a student took. Every second not spent in a classroom had to be accounted for; every child walking down the street was a suspect—they would stop at *nothing* to keep control of *everything*.

Tack worked in silence, long past the time that the footsteps of his family had passed on their way to their own rooms. As time began to wear him down, Tack eventually surrendered to his weariness, changing quickly into white pajamas, brushing his teeth hastily, and plunging into bed.

His assignments included math, science, and language homework, not to mention that he had a social studies test the next day. Tack had managed to complete his math and science, but he'd go to sleep knowing that he hadn't written his language essay.

He was just that tired—so tired, in fact, that his sleepiness even outweighed the dread of the next day's tests and teachers.

Tack was jolted awake by the screeching alarm of his clock, a sound like a jackhammer pounding away at the concrete of sanity. Tack had heard that it was common practice for City students to leave their alarm clocks out of arm's reach. As he forced himself to sit up, he didn't find that rumor hard to believe.

Sitting on the edge of his bed, Tack enjoyed a brief moment of respite as he struggled to reach lucidity. Once he reached that elusive destination, however, he found that it offered few comforts. Recalling his unfinished paper, and realizing that he had a test to take, Tack briefly entertained the idea of feigning illness, but shook his head upon realizing that he'd only have to make up the test. The same reasons that he had to go to school were the same reasons that he wanted to stay out of it.

Tack struggled out of bed, back into his uncomfortable uniform, and finally to the dining table for a quick bagel before he solemnly marched out of the house and down into the subway. The absence of shoes at the doorway indicated that his parents had already left for work, which was just fine as far as Tack was concerned.

Half an hour later, Tack exited the subway and listlessly began walking towards his school. His was the District 20 School, belonging to one of the lower-middle districts. The City was comprised of fifty-seven different districts, each with its own school. All the kids in each district attended the same school, save for a few that were placed in advanced programs elsewhere. Not all of the District 20 students took the same route that Tack did, and so he mostly had the street to himself as he took each dreaded step closer to school.

As he paused for a moment at a curb, Tack's eyes idly followed a plastic bag that was fluttering with the wind and down the street. As he turned his head to watch its progress, he spotted a crude wooden barrier that had been erected to block the street off. That way led to District 19, Tack realized, and he couldn't help but stare sideways at the barrier for a few moments before continuing forward.

District 19 was an oddity, from what Tack understood. The houses visible above the fence were empty and showed every sign of abandonment—windows boarded shut, masonry crumbling from the façades. Tack couldn't remember a time the fence didn't surround the area. What's more, Tack had never seen anyone walking the streets of that district, not even the dangerous vagrants that the Educators warned overran abandoned districts.

Now, Tack knew that it wasn't uncommon for districts with low populations to fall into disrepair, and every so often the Mayor's Office would order these districts evacuated and sealed off for eventual renovation. But District 19 had not merely been long abandoned; none of the maps of the City produced in the past two years seemed to even acknowledge that it existed at all. District 19 was just one big blank spot, and no one knew why.

Teachers and even Educator announcements always insisted that students not go down that way, promising myriad punishments for disobedience, ranging from detention to expulsion. It was true that it was illegal to enter abandoned districts, but Tack had never heard of any other district so vehemently cautioned against. As a matter of fact, he couldn't see why anyone would care at all about the run-down District 19.

Some students had whispered rumors that the district was haunted, or that perhaps some crazed killer had made it its lair. Tack, however, had reasoned that District 19 must contain something interesting or dangerous, or perhaps both.

Either that, or maybe the Educators were just being pointlessly strict. More so than usual, even.

Tests. When compared to the time spent listening to a teacher lecture in a classroom, or even compared to the time spent doing the limited amounts of homework Tack could manage, tests were very brief. Almost trivial. Begun, and (hopefully) completed, all in one school period. And yet these scraps of paper carried more weight than any other aspect of a student's performance in the eyes of the Educators. Difficult tests and failure to perform well on them would mean that all the student's other achievements would be for naught. For students who didn't "test well," a test could be a death sentence.

Tack brushed a rebellious strand of brown hair out of his eyes as he sat outside the classroom. Another class was already inside taking the test, and students were still absolutely forbidden from speaking, even if they weren't in a classroom. Tack had heard that one student had recently been expelled for talking—not a fate that any student envied, and so they all kept their silence.

But that didn't stop them from finding ways to communicate.

Did you study? Tack read off the paper that one of his classmates, a girl, passed over Tack and to the boy sitting next to him.

The boy hastily scribbled his reply: *No, didn't have time. Did you?*

A bit, the girl wrote.

Well, all I know is that in five minutes, I'm screwed, the boy replied, completely resigned to his fate.

The girl dropped her pencil, looking thoughtful. Suddenly, she dug into her backpack, pulled out a few sheets, and began examining them, her eyes darting around madly.

Hey, can I borrow that? the boy wrote urgently, again using Tack as a go-between as he gestured towards the girl's paper.

No, I need it to study, came the cold reply.

Come on, you already studied, I need it more!

I didn't study, she replied.

You said you did! the boy countered triumphantly with his next note.

The girl paused, realizing that she'd been outmaneuvered. The boy looked at her desperately as precious seconds ticked by. The girl, however, made no move to turn the papers over, instead looking back down at them as she changed tactics.

Get your own, she wrote.

All right, I'll just look over your shoulder, okay? That's okay, right? the boy insisted.

Fine, just stop distracting me! The girl rolled her eyes as she passed her final message.

Tack shook his head as a number of other students, realizing what was going on, instantly formed a silent crowd around the girl to look at her papers. Tack knew that he was hardly ready for the test, but he wouldn't beg. To pass the few minutes that remained, he looked around, determined to see what his other peers were up to. Some, desperately trying to appear calm and collected, quizzed each other on paper about what questions they might have to face. Others looked like they were noiselessly convincing themselves that they *were* prepared and that they *would* ace the test.

Tack found it almost sickening, how a simple test could have come to affect their lives like this.

And then he remembered his own anxiety, and realized that he was no better himself. With that depressing thought in mind, Tack swallowed his pride, and pushed his way through the crowd to get a better view of the notes the girl had prepared. He was only able to catch a brief glimpse before the shrill sound of the bell echoed throughout the halls. The classroom doors swung open, and the previous class rushed out into the hallway, savoring the brief respite they'd earned. As they left, Tack's classmates, now free to speak for five minutes, rapidly fired questions, desperate to gain any sort of advantage they could before they entered the classroom themselves.

Tack filed into the classroom with all the other gray-clad students, sat in his assigned seat (no students were ever allowed to choose their own seating), and took out his pencils and paper. The teacher, with a carnivorous grin, wasted no time in passing out the papers. The test heading declared that the subject was Social Studies, and that the teacher's name was Mr. Niel. As Tack got his test he immediately felt relieved—it wasn't so bad. Just a brief essay question and some multiple choices. Certain that he'd have plenty of time, Tack immediately skipped to the essay question:

Describe life outside the City.

Tack began eagerly, writing all that he knew, describing the huge agricultural centers, the scientific outposts, and the unsettled areas that, amazingly, were not covered by buildings or roads or anything besides trees. Tack chewed on his pencil, briefly pondering the fact that he'd never seen any of these things for himself. There were other cities besides the one he lived in, he'd been told, though as far as he was actually concerned, *the* City might as well have been the whole world to him.

Social studies was a class that he had relatively little trouble paying attention in, so he was able to easily fill a page and a half of information before he started on the multiple-choice questions.

Then, all too soon, Mr. Niel broke the silence.

"You have two minutes left."

"What!" someone exclaimed, echoing the shock that Tack himself felt.

Tack turned to stare at the clock on the wall. That couldn't be right; the teacher must've made some sort of mistake.

"The period ends in fifteen minutes," Tack protested.

Mr. Niel glared at him. "Raise your hand," he snapped.

Tack raised his hand, feeling humiliated.

"Yes?" Mr. Neil nodded curtly at him.

"The period ends in fifteen minutes," Tack repeated.

"I know." Mr. Niel looked at him unpleasantly. "You have one minute left."

Tack was filled with a sudden fury. There were so many things wrong with what was happening that he could hardly think. All around him other students were thrown into a frenzy, filling in the answer bubbles on their tests as fast as they could. He looked down at his own test—his multiple-choice section was all but untouched. Finishing it within just one minute was *impossible*. Tack grudgingly began filling in the bubbles, guessing and sometimes even randomly picking answers. Even so, he had only finished half of them when Mr. Niel opened his mouth again.

"Pens down," he barked.

Most of the students obeyed, though disgruntled looks were exchanged.

"Tack, pens down!" Mr. Niel shouted this time.

Tack felt the fury in his gut begin to boil over. Even so, he dropped his pencil and glared determinedly at the blackboard. Satisfied, Mr. Niel began to walk briskly around the room, collecting the papers. The next fifteen minutes of class served only to let Tack's anger simmer dangerously. When the bell finally rang, and the other students filed out of the room, Tack walked up to Mr. Niel, who seemed about as open to discussion as a starving crocodile.

"Mr. Niel?" Tack said, trying to keep the anger out of his voice.

"Yes?" The teacher didn't look up, busy as he was with the test papers.

"I don't think that it's fair, how you told us that the test was going to end early when we had only one minute left."

"The other students seemed to do fine," Mr. Niel observed.

Tack ground his teeth together before responding. "I started with the essay because I thought we'd have the entire period."

"That was a bad decision then. I'm not having this discussion with you, Tack." Mr. Niel pushed the stack of papers aside and glared at Tack.

"We had the full period for all our other tests, and you didn't tell us this one would be any different!" Tack said, his voice growing louder in spite of himself.

Mr. Niel narrowed his eyes dangerously.

"If you have a problem, you come to me and discuss it calmly," the teacher growled. "You do not come to a teacher, start ranting, and expect to *get your way*!"

By this point Mr. Niel himself was ranting, specks of spit flying furiously from his mouth, punctuating each syllable. Tack knew a lost cause when he saw one, though his anger had hardly abated. Walking out the door, he cast one last, furious look at Mr. Niel, who glared back at him triumphantly. It would take more than just a few periods for Tack to forget his anger this time, he knew. As he stormed out of the class and through the halls, he couldn't help but wonder if he was the only one who hated school as much as he was beginning to.

He wasn't.

3

The Truancy

His name is Zyid," the Enforcer announced with the barest hint of pride.

"Zyid," the Mayor repeated.

"That's right, sir."

The Mayor shut his lighter loudly, his eyes never leaving the scene outside his office window. Lately he'd been spending a lot of time in his office, so much so that he sometimes felt that the Mayoral Mansion had no need for bedrooms. In addition to the usual tedium concerning budgets and school curriculum, he now had to hold regular meetings with the Enforcers to keep up with the latest news about the Truancy.

This particular Enforcer was leading the hunt for the Truancy leader, and after producing absolutely nothing for a long time, he had informed the Mayor that they had uncovered an important new lead. Never one to wait, the Mayor had secured a copy of the Enforcer's written report before meeting with him. Aside from the odd name, the report was really mainly padded with filler nonsense. The Mayor was experienced enough to recognize pointless padding—he had, after all, spent several years as a teacher grading essays in City schools.

"Is this all you know?" the Mayor asked scornfully. "And I don't want you to repeat the obvious facts you've used to dress up your report."

The Enforcer frowned, apparently having expected praise. "It's what we know at the moment, yes, but I'm certain that with more time and resources we could—"

"Three weeks. It's been exactly twenty-one days. You had a blank check. All of the City's resources. Everything was at your disposal," the mayor pointed out coldly.

"Yes, sir, and I've already shown you the results of our raids on Truant safe houses and storage sites," the Enforcer said, gesturing at a small pile of papers sitting on the Mayor's desk. "In addition to that memorandum signed by their leader, a wide variety of weapons, ammunition, chemicals, have been seized—"

"*Seized.* I like how you use that word. I assume you bravely fought off an army of kids to gather up these—when you say 'chemicals,' they were household cleaners again, I presume?" the Mayor asked, his voice dripping with sarcasm.

The Enforcer took a deep breath. "Sir, the Truants are able to manufacture effective explosives with compounds derived from—"

"I *know.* Were the sites you raided defended?"

"Aside from some booby traps, no, sir. The Truants rarely seem to use the same site two nights in a row, so there weren't any Truants present. However, capturing these places hurt their effort nonetheless—"

"They will rearm themselves," the Mayor said, flicking his lighter open. "They will find new holes to hide in. We've been playing this game with them for well over a year now. And while you were poking around uninhabited apartments, Enforcer, the Truancy assassinated two more Educators in the past three weeks."

"I know, I did read the report, sir—"

"Good, you're literate after all." The Mayor shut his lighter. "But I believe we're here to discuss this name you've discovered, not your reading habits. So then, to business—while it may be a blow to your ego, Enforcer, let me tell you that this ridiculous name that you labored so hard to produce is worth less than the paper you used to print it on."

The Enforcer looked confused, like a dog that had expected a treat but received a kick instead.

"The name isn't useless, sir—you can check the school files, the birth records, find out who this kid is, whether he has any living family. That's all classified *Educator* data, if I may respectfully remind you."

The Mayor snorted. "Brilliant idea. Or it would be, if Zyid were this child's real name."

"Excuse me, sir?"

The Mayor turned to glare at the Enforcer. It was rather like training a searchlight onto a mouse.

"This 'Zyid' is not stupid, and neither am I," the Mayor said matter-of-factly. "I checked the files already. Nothing. If he attended school in this City, he didn't do it as 'Zyid.' "

"And the birth records?"

"Again, nothing."

There was an unpleasant silence.

"Our options are running out," the Mayor said pointedly. "That means your time is running out. There are only so many ways to wage war against the Truancy while keeping it secret."

"I . . . I understand, sir."

"They are not ordinary criminals. They won't be satisfied with getting away with a single crime. They will strike repeatedly, until we give up, are dead, or have wiped them out. And thanks to your inept intelligence gathering, they may be planning an attack right now."

"We can't know that for sure, sir."

"And *that* is a problem. You will have to fix it."

"Yes, sir."

"I have your word. The next time we meet, I want to know more about this Zyid character. Something substantial, not more speculation. Understood?"

"Yes, sir."

"One more thing."

"Yes, sir?"

"We meet tomorrow evening."

The Enforcer gulped audibly. "Understood."

"Good. You're dismissed."

So, what's up?" Suzie asked, screwing the cap back on her water bottle.

Tack and Suzie lay on the soft grass, enjoying its rich, sweet smell, so rare in the City. It was Sunday, the only day of the week when students didn't have to don their gray uniforms and go to school. Tack had heard that there had once been a time when students had Saturdays off as well, but that had long since become history.

As they had agreed, Tack and Suzie were spending their day

in the Grand Park—District 20's only notable feature. The Grand Park was, as its name suggested, a massive park that spanned the entire length of the district. With its winding paths, masses of trees, decorative fountains, and fields of grass, it was the closest thing to nature that the City had. There were also a few playgrounds for the very young, though Tack and Suzie were both too old to be allowed entrance.

"I had a social studies test the other day," Tack said off-handedly.

"Oh," Suzie murmured, chewing on a blade of grass. "How did that go?"

"Badly," Tack said frankly, brushing a few stubborn strands of hair out of his eyes.

"Why's that?" Suzie asked sympathetically.

Tack frowned. Suzie continued nibbling away at her grass, patiently waiting for her brother to get more talkative. After a few minutes, Tack sat up and told her about how the test had been rigged against the students.

"That's messed up," Suzie observed.

"No kidding," Tack agreed.

"Ya know, I heard a few girls talking about a math test they took," Suzie recalled. "I think the same thing happened to them."

"Really?" Tack asked, incredulous.

"Yep," Suzie confirmed, finishing the last of her water.

"I thought Mr. Niel was just being his usual self," Tack muttered. "But why would two different teachers do the exact same thing?"

"Maybe they were told to," Suzie suggested.

"By who, the Educators?" Tack snorted. "Why would they waste time *trying* to piss us off?"

"I dunno; it's not like they need to put much effort into it." Suzie smirked.

"Whatever, all I know is that I'm not taking another test without asking exactly how much time we have," Tack declared.

"Good call," Suzie said. She eyed the waning sun, which had begun to cast an orange glow over the green park. "It's getting late."

"Yeah, it is," Tack agreed, frowning. "I guess we better be going home."

"All righty." Suzie gathered up her things.

As they made their way back home, Tack felt his spirit somewhat lightened, the fragrance of the park still heavy in his nostrils. He was ready to forget that the disastrous test had ever happened. Time spent with Suzie always cheered him up, though Tack had noticed that Suzie was subtly less cheerful herself. Tack was somewhat disturbed by that realization. School must be wearing down on her too, just as it was on him.

Is everyone in position?"

"Not only is everyone in position, but they've all been waiting for like an hour."

"Have you recounted the explosives?"

"Yeah, I have, all eight. Hell, I don't even need to count them. That backpack was so heavy, there's got to be more than enough in it."

"These pipe bombs are not light, nor are they to be taken lightly."

"My spine heartily agrees."

"Soon the Educators will as well. It's almost time. You'd better get to your position."

"Sure thing, boss. Can I ask a question though?"

"Make it quick."

"Why isn't that assassin of yours along for the ride? This attack's supposed to be big and important, right?"

"Noni has other duties to perform."

"Like what?"

"Suffice it to say that I've given a few more Educators failing grades."

"Ah, gotcha—the mark of death, eh?"

"If that's what you want to call it. Now get to your position; we execute in ten minutes."

"All right, I got your back, Zyid."

"Duly noted, Ken."

The Truant known as Ken ran towards a cement wall and crouched briefly, peering around the corner at the gatehouse to make sure that it was clear. He was clothed in black garments and a ski mask, as were all the other well-hidden Truants, numbering twelve in total. It was the dead of night—12:52, according to Ken's digital watch—and the Truants were all but invisible, moving shadows in this empty part of the City. There were no streetlights for blocks. In fact, the only light was the faint glow coming from inside the large building he was crouched near.

There was, in fact, a guard in the gatehouse in front of the large building. It was a middle-aged, overweight man that seemed more like a rent-a-cop than a true Enforcer. He looked like the epitome of boredom itself, leaning back in his chair lazily, with his feet up on the tiny desk inside the gatehouse. The guard was armed with a pistol, but hardly seemed prepared to use it. In fact, the night was rather hot and the guard had actually left the door open to let some air in.

Ken frowned. With security this bad, how important could the building be? He wasn't about to complain about an easy mission, but Zyid had told them so little that he was starting to wonder. He'd gathered that there was something inside that Zyid wanted to steal, but the building itself was odd. It didn't look like a warehouse, and stuck out as the only inhabited building inside an area of four abandoned districts. Well, *mostly* abandoned, as the Truancy had recently begun to make some use of them, hiding out and storing supplies.

Ken snapped back to reality as he saw a flashlight blink once to his left. That was the signal. He checked his watch. It was one in the morning, exactly. He looked around the corner again. The guard was still lying there, looking ready to doze off at any minute. Ken frowned. Zyid wasn't the type of person to be late with anything, especially his own plan.

Then the guard tipped his head to one side, facing the open door of the guardhouse. Something shot through the air, and hit its target with a dull *thunk*. Ken quickly darted toward the gate, where he was joined by ten other black-clad Truants. More than a few of them seemed transfixed upon the fallen guard, who looked as relaxed as he did a moment ago, except for his wide eyes and the knife that was embedded between then. For some of them, Ken knew, it was the first death they'd ever witnessed.

Zyid walked forward from the shadows, wearing the same nondescript black clothing they all did. He quickly inspected the body, removed the sharp knife, wiped it on his sleeve, and then replaced it in its leather sheath.

"Nice aim," someone murmured softly, voicing the general opinion.

"I enjoyed favorable conditions," Zyid allowed.

Though he was impressed at the skill Zyid had demonstrated, Ken couldn't pretend that he wasn't slightly disturbed at his indifferent attitude to death and killing. Ken frowned, fully aware of the uncomfortable way his companions were shuffling—they were probably thinking the same thing. He shook his head to clear his doubt. Zyid's was probably the only attitude that the leader of any army could afford.

"Paradoxically, it seems like the gatehouse doesn't actually open the gate," Zyid mused. "The controls must be inside."

Zyid paced along the length of the gates. "Too steep to climb, I believe. No shortcuts for us, we'll have to follow our original plan."

At this, two Truants stepped forward, placing a pipe bomb on either side of the gates, right below the hinges.

"Weapons at the ready," Zyid ordered quietly.

The Truants raised their guns in acknowledgment. Ken walked over to the fallen guard and retrieved the dead man's pistol.

"Shrapnel from pipe bombs can be nasty," Zyid warned. "Everyone except Ken and Steven take cover. You two, light the fuses before joining the rest."

As the other Truants took cover, Ken and Steven each stood over one of the pipe bombs, which resembled nothing more than plastic pipes sealed at both ends with firecracker fuses sticking out. Ken drew a lighter from his pants pocket, and watched Steven do the same. Bending down simultaneously, they lit the fuses and ran. Ken dived behind an old newsstand on the block, shutting his eyes and plugging his ears.

The lit fuses hissed and snapped angrily as the flames quickly traveled down them. As the sparks from the fuse came into contact with the densely packed saltpeter inside the crude bomb, the pressure of the explosion sent pieces of plastic shooting in all directions, and the force of the blast quickly separated the gates from their hinges.

The Truants sprang up from their hiding places and dashed onto what looked like a small parking lot for the building's workers. Spotting the glass doors that marked the entrance to the building, Zyid gestured towards it and broke into a brisk run. The other Truants followed, carrying duffel bags.

As they came up to the thick glass doors, Zyid gave a quick nod to one of the Truants holding a duffel bag. The Truant quickly produced a third pipe bomb and placed it down in front of the double doors. Zyid waved his arm in a wide arc, the signal for them to take cover. As they did so, Zyid produced his own lighter and lit the fuse, darting behind a parked car himself.

The pipe bomb exploded, shattering the glass doors. No sooner had the shards settled than Zyid had risen to his feet and dashed through their empty and battered frames, holding his shotgun in one hand and the duffel bag in the other. An alarm suddenly sounded, sending a loud shriek into the night. The other Truants picked themselves up and dashed into a large lobby. They paused as Zyid scanned the room. A security desk stood off to the right, with the chair overturned as if its occupant had very hastily left.

"There will be guards, and they will be armed," Zyid said. "The Enforcers are also likely on their way. Come, and quickly."

Zyid ran over to a floor directory, reading it as quickly as he could. Finding what he wanted, he gestured for the Truants to enter the large elevator, with two walking backwards to cover their rear. Suddenly, a gunshot rang out. One of the Truants crumpled. A guard, the one missing from the security desk, had taken cover behind a concrete pillar. One of the Truants dashed to check on his fallen comrade, while the others all determinedly fired at the pillar.

Zyid grimaced. He hadn't expected a casualty this early, and this firefight was only slowing them down. Reaching inside his duffel bag, he pulled out what looked like a glass bottle with a rag stuffed in its mouth. The liquid inside the bottle was a mixture of gasoline and motor oil. Lighting the rag on fire with his lighter, Zyid hurled the bottle at the pillar. It quickly burst, and sprayed what looked like liquid fire everywhere. There was a scream of pain, and the guard, all caution forgotten, desperately leaped from behind the pillar and began rolling on the ground.

Zyid allowed himself a satisfied grin. The motor oil stuck stubbornly onto surfaces, causing the fire to be very persistent. Ignoring the agonizing shrieks from the guard who was fast becoming a human torch, Zyid quickly moved to the downed Truant. As he did, one of them put the guard out of his misery with a single shot.

The Truants watched with bated breath as Zyid bent down and placed two fingers onto the side of the fallen Truant's neck. A moment later, Zyid removed the boy's ski mask. His own face, only half-covered by a neck-warmer, betrayed no emotion.

"It's Ken," he said, rising to his feet. "He's dead. We have to hurry, or more of us will join him."

"We're just going to leave him lying there?" one of the other Truants protested angrily.

Zyid turned to stare reprovingly at the speaker. "Our duties are to the living," he snapped. "Leave the dead."

The Truants, some of them reluctantly, began moving

towards the elevator. There would be time for mourning later. The Truants quickly filed into the elevator, adrenaline pulsing through their veins. Zyid entered last, and pressed the button for the fourth floor.

When the door opened, the Truants found themselves face-to-face with two surprised guards who had been waiting for the elevator themselves. Zyid didn't even need to aim as he brought his shotgun up and fired at point-blank range. The two guards crumpled. Zyid leaped atop a nearby stool and touched a fire sprinkler with his lighter—causing a new set of alarms to go off as all the sprinklers in the building sprayed water everywhere. Puzzled, but not willing to question their leader, the now-wet Truants approached a new set of opaque double doors. One of the Truants shot the lock off with his pistol, and Zyid kicked the doors open.

The room was large, square, and stacked to the ceiling with brown cardboard boxes. Zyid quickly began opening boxes and peering inside while the other Truants stood guard. As Zyid pulled out ceramic dishes and cutlery from the boxes, the other Truants became certain that there had been some sort of mistake. Zyid, however, remained emotionless as ever as he continued to open boxes.

Suddenly Zyid let out of a grunt of triumph. A few Truants gathered around to look at what he'd found.

"Ceramic kitchen knives?" One of them read the package in disbelief. "You're joking."

"I'm not," Zyid said evenly. "Pack as many as you can in the duffel bags—we destroy the rest with the remaining bombs."

"Won't they break if we jostle them?" Another Truant eyed the knives dubiously.

"No. The way they're made, they're tougher than steel," Zyid said, stuffing them into his own duffel bag. "And more important, they're invisible to metal detectors."

The importance of the kitchen utensils abruptly became clear to the Truants, and they quickly joined their leader. With all eleven of them working, they filled the duffel bags to bursting very quickly, leaving more than a few stacks of boxes. As they prepared to leave, Zyid's eye fell upon three longer but otherwise identical packages lying near the entrance. Moving over to them, he read the label on one.

"It says they're experimental," Zyid mused. "They must be for an aborted project if they're here." His curiosity piqued, Zyid opened the first package, and his eyes widened with delight at what he saw inside.

"Oh, excellent," he said softly.

"What is it?" one of the other Truants asked.

"Never mind," Zyid said briskly, shoving the three packages into his own duffel bag. "You'll find out when we get back. Right now, we destroy whatever's left."

Having already emptied the last two pipe bombs onto the floor to make room for knives, the Truants hastily left the room as Zyid lit the bombs.

They made their way back to the elevator, leaving the sound of shattering ceramic behind them. As the doors opened to reveal the lobby, the red and blue lights of Enforcer cars and fire trucks flashed from outside. The sprinklers, the Truants saw, had gone a long way towards extinguishing the results of the firebomb that Zyid had thrown earlier, though some stubborn flames licked at the walls where the water had not reached. Outside, the Enforcers and firefighters could be seen arguing heatedly over something.

"The Enforcers want to come inside and kill us, and the firefighters want to come inside to put out the fires," Zyid mused calmly. "Neither wants the other going in first. It'll take them a bit to figure out who's in charge of what."

The Truants stood around him, waiting for an order. Their only exit was blocked by an army of Enforcers, and yet they felt a lot calmer than they had any right to be. They all looked to Zyid, certain that he would have an answer. Sure enough, after a few seconds of thought, Zyid spoke.

"Alex and Gabriel, get that delivery cart over here," he ordered curtly. "Frank, give me your scarf. The rest of you, cover the doorway; shoot anyone that comes in."

As the two Truants quickly wheeled the cart over to Zyid, Frank unwrapped the black scarf he'd been using to mask his face. Zyid opened his duffel bag and took out the last item he'd saved. It looked like a white lump in the shape of a bread mold, with a fuse sticking out of it. He quickly wrapped it in the scarf. Loading it onto the cart, he lit the fuse and gave the cart a shove, aiming it towards the busted front doors.

"As soon as it goes off, run through, don't stop for anything, and scatter. Meet back at headquarters," Zyid ordered.

"What is that?" Frank asked, staring at the receding cart.

"Saltpeter melted together with sugar."

"Sugar?"

"Yes."

"What does it do?"

As if in answer to the question, extremely thick, white smoke began filling the parking lot. The Truants wasted no time in running through the doors and into the chaos outside. The smoke cloud grew larger and larger until it covered the entire block, and by the time the Enforcers organized a search of the area, all the Truants, except one, had vanished.

The Truant left behind was of no use to the Enforcers. The Truants would never betray each other, especially not in death.

4

A Rebellious Child

Several days had passed since Tack and Suzie's sojourn in the park, and it was now a Friday. Not any typical Friday, but the one day of the year traditionally set aside for "Freshman Friday," an event that was almost humorously named, despite its brutal nature. Freshman Friday was the day when upperclassmen were free to tackle, beat, and shove dirt into the mouths of freshmen, with the tacit approval of the Educators.

Tack wasn't a freshman and had nothing to fear for himself. Suzie, however, *was* in her first year of high school, and Tack was certainly afraid for her. Tack had survived his Freshman Friday two years ago with yolk from hurled eggs running down his face. He had been lucky—it was well-known that a few students every year were actually killed during Freshman Fridays.

Tack apprehensively wondered what the other students had prepared this year—eggs, water balloons, and rocks were among the less lethal things that he'd seen some of them carrying. Whatever it was, Tack was determined to protect his sister from it. Together, Suzie and Tack had come up with a survival plan earlier in the week.

"Thanks for waiting for me," Suzie whispered to Tack as they met in the lobby, under the shouts and screams coming from outside.

"It was no problem," Tack assured her quietly. With all the commotion going on right outside the front doors, he didn't think that there was much danger of the guards catching them talking. Still, he kept his voice down.

"How bad is it?" Suzie asked, looking towards the school doors, cringing at the distant noises of humiliation and pain.

Tack stated the obvious. "Looks and sounds pretty bad. A lot of last year's freshmen are out there having fun."

"They probably couldn't wait to start doing to others what had been done to them last year," Suzie pointed out, bitterness and anger in her voice. "Why is there a Freshman Friday at all?"

"It's a cycle. It's always been that way," Tack answered.

"But why do the new freshmen keep on becoming bullies? Why don't they change things when they're the bigger ones?" Suzie demanded.

"Because that's how people are," Tack snapped, steeling himself for what he knew would come next. "Come on. We'll go out with a large group of other students so we'll be harder to hit. We break off from the main group once they start attacking, and run straight for the subway."

"What if they come after us?" Suzie asked.

"Then you run, and I'll get them to follow me," Tack promised. "You just keep running for the subway."

Suzie frowned. "What if they catch you?"

"Then that's my problem," Tack said, more harshly than he intended.

Suzie's frown deepened. "Are you sure about this?"

"Yes," Tack confirmed, trying to convince himself that he was.

"All right," Suzie said, sounding unconvinced but resigned. "Then we might as well go out with that group."

Suzie pointed towards a moving clump of gray uniforms. A number of freshmen had huddled together for protection. Tack grabbed Suzie by the hand, and pulled her over to the back of the group, where they did their best to remain inconspicuous. The students waited until all their arms had been scanned by the guards, and then those at the front of the bunch pushed open the doors, and those behind quickly followed. The group nervously made their way down the street, remaining ominously unmolested.

As they turned the corner, a hail of loose bricks taken from the school building itself rained down upon them from the mob that had lain in wait.

Yelps of shock and pain erupted among the group, and Tack saw the girl in front of him go down bloody, having caught a piece of brick in the temple. Grabbing Suzie by the arm, he broke from the group, running as fast as he could towards the route he took to the train station—the one that bordered District 19, and the one that very few students ever took. Fortunately, it seemed that most of the group had had the same general idea as they, and they quickly scattered to take their own routes.

When Tack looked back, he found that none of the bullies were chasing them. As he and Suzie rounded another street corner and slipped out of sight of the ambush, they stopped to catch their breath, gasping heavily for air.

"We made it," Tack declared, clapping Suzie on the shoulder.

"No, we didn't," Suzie whispered, sounding horrified.

Looking up, Tack felt his heart leap into his throat. Standing in front of them were three large seniors, all grinning maliciously.

"I told you that some of them might come this way, Joe," the boy on the right said to the boy in the middle, who appeared to be their leader.

"Good thinking," Joe acknowledged, looking like he had never done any for himself in his entire life.

"Never miss an opportunity to teach them little kids some respect." The boy on the right grinned, cracking his knuckles.

"Why don't you assholes just leave us alone?" Suzie shouted suddenly.

Four pairs of eyes snapped towards Suzie. While the three bullies digested the fact that they had just been insulted by a girl less than half their size, Tack stared at his sister and wondered what had made her snap like that. He had never known Suzie to be so reckless.

"Looks like this one needs to learn to respect her elders!" Joe declared, as he advanced towards Suzie.

Tack made a split-second decision.

"Hey, you scrawny little bastards!" he bellowed. "Why don't you pick on someone who can kick your ass? Come here and try *me,* you cowards!"

The three bullies turned towards Tack. Realizing that he had a second at most before their shock wore off, he began to run. The three bullies plunged after him. Tack was not particularly athletic, though he was good at sprinting. Putting on a desperate burst of speed, Tack rounded the corner, and was brought up short by a sheer wooden wall. It was the barrier, Tack realized . . . the wooden barrier that separated District 19 from District 20.

District 19! The one place that no one would be crazy enough to follow him into! Seized by sudden, desperate inspiration, Tack gripped a plank jutting out from the crude wooden wall and scrambled over onto the other side.

The three bullies howled with outrage as Tack unceremoniously fell to the ground with an impact amplified by the weight of the backpack. Tack felt a mixture of pain and triumph, the former coming from the elbow that had taken the brunt of the fall and the latter coming from the fact that he'd escaped for now.

"Come on; let's get him!" Tack heard one bully say.

"No way, man, there're vagrants in there; don't you know anything?" Joe said, sounding terrified.

Tack quickly forced himself to his feet, thinking it prudent to get away as fast as he could while the bullies were still arguing. Taking a deep breath and swallowing his own apprehension, he began plunging deeper into District 19. Vagrants or no, he didn't have much of a choice now.

As he jogged along, Tack found himself glancing around frequently, looking for dangers lurking in the shadows. He found none, only more evidence that the district had indeed been long abandoned. There were no skyscrapers in the district, only rows of lonely houses and shops. Store display windows lay empty or broken, apartment buildings crumbled in disuse. An old movie theater had its box office windows boarded shut, and a café on a street corner had its tables and chairs all overturned. There was no sign that anyone had ever visited the district in years.

Feeling a little more confident that he wasn't in any immediate danger, Tack slowed to a walk, his breath gradually returning to normal. It was an odd place that definitely deserved to be labeled "abandoned," Tack thought, but he still couldn't imagine why exactly the Educators didn't want anyone to see it. As Tack rounded a street corner, however, he abruptly froze, certain that what he was seeing couldn't be real.

There, on the side of a street in front of a small brownstone building, stood a gray plastic folding table with a cardboard sign taped to its front and several items placed on top of it. There was a jug of pale liquid, stacks of paper cups, and a large blue and white plastic cooler. There was also a pair of metal folding chairs, one behind and another in front of the table. The one behind the table, Tack realized with a jolt, was occupied by a boy that looked to be around his age. Half-convinced that he had gone mad, Tack slowly walked forward.

As he did so, the boy looked up from a book he had been reading, dog-eared his page, and shut his book. Then he crossed his arms and calmly waited for Tack to approach.

The boy was peculiar in more ways than one. He had a faintly sallow complexion, which was rare in District 20. He certainly wasn't dressed for school. Instead of a uniform, he wore plain, khaki jeans that were slightly frayed, a plain polo shirt with a buttoned-up collar, over which he also wore a beige vest. The boy had put his feet up on the table, and Tack couldn't help but notice that he wasn't wearing any socks, just a pair of simple white sneakers.

The boy's sleek, shiny black hair had been parted down the

center into a neat, bowl haircut that looked strange to Tack. Something about the boy, however, immediately discouraged any thought of laughing. Perhaps it was his face, which was as perfectly placid as Tack could imagine a human's face being. Or maybe it was the opaque black sunglasses he was wearing that defeated any attempt to discern what was behind them.

Moving closer, Tack could see a bar code and nine-digit number tattooed onto the boy's arm. He was a student.

And yet he wasn't in uniform.

"Hello there," the boy said, lifting his legs and placing them back onto the ground. "It's been a long time since a stranger has come this way. I understand that students are specifically warned not to come here these days."

"Yeah," Tack managed, still not wholly certain that the kid wasn't some sort of stress-induced hallucination.

"Are you lost?" the boy inquired.

"Uh . . . I don't think I am," Tack replied, flustered.

"Well then, you must be here on purpose," the boy reasoned. "Care for a drink?"

The boy waved his hand at the metal folding chair that sat across the table from him, indicating that Tack should take a seat. Tack obliged without thinking, which was when he noticed what was written on the cardboard sign that had been taped to the front of the table. *"Lemonade—1 Bill,"* Tack read silently.

"Is this . . . your lemonade stand?" Tack asked incredulously.

"Indeed," the boy confirmed. "My name is Umasi."

"I'm Tack. So you . . . you just sit out here all day?"

"More or less, yes," Umasi agreed, taking some ice from his cooler and adding it to the large jug of lemonade.

"And you can make a living that way?" Tack asked in disbelief.

"No, not really." Umasi poured some lemonade into a paper cup. "I am very fortunate in that money is something that I do not have to worry about."

"Why not?" Tack asked.

"That, I'm afraid, is a secret," Umasi said lightly, pushing the cup of lemonade over to Tack. "Please, drink. You're sweating."

Tack wiped the sweat off his forehead and took a sip. It was good. Clearly homemade, not the bottled stuff sold by most stores in the City. Tack quickly gulped down the rest of it and placed the empty cup on the table. Unsure if he owed anything for the lemonade, he waited to see if Umasi would charge him.

Umasi didn't. Instead, he filled a second cup and nudged it over to Tack, who found that he *was* horribly thirsty after all the running he had done.

"So, why would a student of the City, who has signed all sorts of promises to obey the Educators, find himself here against their wishes?" Umasi asked, as Tack downed his second cup of lemonade.

"I was running from some bullies," Tack said dazedly, feeling as though it were all a dream.

"Ah yes." Umasi frowned, pushing a third cup of lemonade over to Tack. "Bullies—some of the Educators' most ingenious tools."

Tack paused with the filled cup halfway to his lips.

"Tools?" Tack repeated carefully.

"That's right." Umasi nodded. "Violent, aggressive students do the Educators' work for them. They work towards perpetrating an atmosphere of fear and pressure in school. They also keep the students hating each other, rather than blaming the Educators."

Tack contemplated that. It made sense, except for one thing. . . .

"Why would the Educators want to do that?" Tack asked.

Umasi froze, staring at Tack in a way that made him feel uncomfortable, as if he were a bug being examined under a magnifying glass. There was an ominous silence. Finally, Umasi seemed to come to a difficult decision, and began to speak.

"Tell me, Tack," Umasi said, stirring the jug of lemonade with a large wooden spoon. "Why do you go to school?"

Tack was thrown by the question. At first he stared at Umasi incredulously, sure that the strange boy was joking. Searching his face, Tack saw no signs of sarcasm. He decided to voice the obvious answer. But as he racked his brain for the obvious answer, he discovered that there was none.

"I go to school to learn," Tack invented wildly, saying the first thing that came to mind, though he knew in his heart that it wasn't true.

"Really?" Umasi raised an eyebrow. "Something tells me that you're not truly interested in learning what they teach you. Nonetheless, I'll entertain your proposition. Why do you want to learn?"

Tack frowned. It was as if they were engaged in a verbal duel and Umasi had the advantage of being able to read Tack's thoughts before he even had them.

"Because it's important," Tack said quickly, stalling for time.

"Why?" Umasi pressed.

"Because . . . because I want to be successful in life," Tack said, flustered at having to repeat what his parents and teachers always told him.

"That's not actually answering the question," Umasi pointed out. "Why is learning important?"

"To get a good job," Tack said mechanically.

"And don't you think," Umasi said, pouring himself a cup of lemonade, "that it's strange that you must go through these meaningless classes—that you must practice exceedingly complicated types of math, obscure minutiae of biology, aimless drawing, and more, all at the same time? Just to get jobs that, in all likelihood, would not involve even one of them, let alone all?"

Tack found that he had no answer to that, and it seemed like Umasi hadn't expected him to have one. Finishing his fourth cup of lemonade and finding his thirst quenched, Tack sat back and looked up at Umasi.

"But why?" Tack asked feebly. "Why make us waste our time?"

"Control," Umasi answered simply. "They keep you too busy to rebel, too downtrodden to protest being a second-class citizen, and too well-conditioned to challenge them when you reach adulthood. Indeed, many end up joining them so that they can do the same to the next generation. It's really a complicated form of bullying."

Tack thought he should be feeling more surprised than he was, but he wasn't. It was as if he had known it all along but had never had time to think about it. What he was surprised to find was that he believed every word that Umasi said. The mysterious boy couldn't be more than two years older than

Tack, and yet Umasi seemed almost omniscient. Something about the way he spoke made it impossible to doubt him.

"All I will say for school, Tack, is that it is less monstrous than some of the alternatives," Umasi said, taking a sip from his cup.

"Alternatives?" Tack inquired, sitting up in his chair.

"There are those in the City that fight the schools," Umasi said, his mouth curling down into a slight frown. "They fight the Educators. They are responsible for much destruction and death in the City."

"I've never heard of such people," Tack said, fascinated.

"You wouldn't have." Umasi's frown deepened. "The Educators' grip on the City is powerful, and it only grows tighter as others threaten to pry it loose. They've been careful to keep it covered up."

"So . . ." Tack thought quickly, his mind racing. "You say that neither side is very good, then?"

"I would not feel comfortable with the City under the control of either faction, no," Umasi agreed. "But my opinion matters little."

"Why?" Tack asked. Surely someone this knowledgeable and intelligent must have some kind of influence.

"Because I am merely an observer," Umasi said, taking another sip from his cup. "I am not involved with either side, and I do nothing to tip the scales either way."

"Why not?" Tack pressed.

"For reasons both complicated and private," Umasi said, finishing his lemonade in one big gulp.

Tack frowned. Umasi's tone of voice had made it very clear that there would be no further discussion of the topic.

"Tell me, Tack, did you once have a brother?" Umasi asked suddenly, peering at Tack intently from behind his sunglasses.

"No, just a sister," Tack replied, wondering what had prompted this change in the conversation. "Why do you ask?"

"You remind me of someone I used to know," Umasi said vaguely, his intense interest dissipating. "In any case, Tack, while I found our conversation most enjoyable, I'm afraid that time dictates that we save further discussion for another time."

Tack quickly looked at his wristwatch. 5:06, it read. He leaped to his feet in shock. Could he really have spent that much time in the forbidden district, just walking around, talking, and drinking lemonade?

"I have to go," Tack gasped. His parents would be livid, he still didn't know if Suzie had made it home safely, and he hadn't started on his homework.

"I know," Umasi said, the barest hint of a smile tugging at his lips. "You have more questions to ask, I think. If you ever find yourself thirsting for answers—or lemonade—feel free to return."

"I . . . we won't get in trouble?" Tack asked tentatively as he shouldered his backpack.

"I doubt it," Umasi said confidently as he picked his book up and resumed reading.

Tack wanted to ask how he was so sure, but stopped himself. Once he started asking questions, Tack was sure that he wouldn't be able to stop. How was this boy able to live comfortably, carelessly, here in a district that seemed to exist only for him? How did he seem to know everything about the City when all he did was sit at a lonely lemonade stand all day?

And, come to that, *why* did he just sit at that stand when there was only the slightest chance that anyone would come across it?

Shaking his head in confusion, Tack began walking back the way he came. His talk with Umasi left him with a lot more questions than answers, and yet the discussion had made him feel better. Something Umasi had mentioned had brought Tack some small measure of hope.

There were people in the City fighting for change. Tack hadn't heard of any such movement, but Umasi seemed so sure it was impossible to doubt him. Something was being done to make things different, and that lifted Tack's spirits in a way he'd never felt before. Maybe it was hope that he was now enjoying. Tack wouldn't know—he couldn't remember ever feeling hopeful before.

5

The Report Card

"So," the Mayor mused. "Someone new has been observed entering District 19?"

"Yes, sir, you made it very clear when I was promoted to this office that we should keep an eye on—," the Enforcer began.

"I know what I said," the Mayor interrupted impatiently.

"So sir, do you want to know who the child is?" the Enforcer asked.

"No, that won't be necessary." The Mayor opened his lighter. "At some point, there must be trust."

"Trust, sir?"

"Yes," the Mayor said. "You were briefed, I believe, on the boy that has made District 19 his home?"

"Yes, sir. There wasn't much in the report, but rumor has it that he is—"

"I have little patience concerning rumors." The Mayor snapped his lighter shut. "He doesn't like it when we do so much as approach his borders. Our previous surveillances of him haven't gone unnoticed. If he has made a new friend, I'm going to honor his wishes and leave him be."

"Sir, I confess that I don't fully understand—"

"Understanding is not a prerequisite for obedience."

"Yes, sir."

"I'm glad you're catching on quickly—Mr. Waters, is it? It gives me hope that you'll last longer than your predecessors." The Mayor smiled wryly. "As I'm sure you know, we've been going through a lot of Chief Enforcers lately. You are, I believe, the fifth in as many months."

Mr. Waters remained silent. After all, what was he supposed to say to that?

"Well then, if we're finished discussing District 19," the Mayor said briskly, "why don't you tell me how the war with the Truancy is going?"

Mr. Waters took a deep breath. This was the part he'd been afraid of—being Chief Enforcer these days meant being the bearer of bad news.

"Frankly, Mr. Mayor, it could be going a lot better. We still don't know why they attacked the ceramics lab, though I think it's safe to assume that they weren't after dinner plates."

Mr. Waters drew a notepad from his pocket and flipped a few pages. "The two Educators that were assassinated on the night of the attack may have been a distraction—they have good planning and coordination. The best that can be said is that our efforts to confiscate the Truants' supplies have been going relatively well. We've successfully raided five different locations this week alone."

"Have your men actually *seen* a live Truant yet?" the Mayor asked.

Mr. Waters flipped a few pages. "Yes, sir, we have. One was caught by an Enforcer patrol as he walked the streets during school hours. He was . . ." The Chief Enforcer frowned, knowing that the Mayor wouldn't like what came next.

"Killed resisting arrest?" the Mayor guessed.

"Yes, sir. One patrolman was badly injured. They feared for their lives."

"We're going to have to find some braver officers, then," the Mayor said. "If the cowards aren't jobless yet, make sure that they are by tonight. Live bodies are preferable to dead, and we've been getting too few of both lately."

"On the topic of bodies, sir . . ." Mr. Waters flipped another page of his notepad. "We've identified all of the dead Truants that we've recovered so far."

"Find anything interesting?" the Mayor asked.

"No, sir, there seems to be no connection. They come from different districts, attended different schools, and fit different social profiles."

"I expected as much," the Mayor said. "And what about this Zyid character?"

"We've learned next to nothing about him. Other than the fact that he appears to be something of a strategic genius."

"At least you don't waste my time," the Mayor said with mild approval. "Now, I have a hunch that this Zyid is what holds the Truancy together. If you remove him from the picture, all we have is a rabble of leaderless children."

Mr. Waters looked at the Mayor apprehensively. "Sir, are you suggesting . . ."

"I'm not going to expect him to be dead tomorrow." The Mayor flicked his lighter open dismissively. "But work on it. Dead or alive is fine. I would prefer alive, but I understand that that might be impractical."

"I'll get right on that, sir," Mr. Waters promised.

"Good. If there's nothing else that requires my attention, you may go."

"Yes, sir." Mr. Waters saluted, relieved that he'd managed to come away unscathed.

As the Chief Enforcer left, the Mayor shut his lighter and turned to his desk, where he sifted through a small mountain of paperwork. Stretching his back, he sat down in his brown leather chair and began reading the sheets at the top of the pile. There were maybe a dozen educational bills in the pile, the Mayor knew, and they weren't going to sign themselves.

Outside City Hall, the very building in which the Mayor sat secure in his domain, a group of four children loitered on the sidewalk, backpacks slung over their shoulders and ice-cream cones in their hands. They were the very picture of innocence, especially considering that it was after school hours. No one gave the bunch a second glance, and no one noticed that the group was looking particularly grim as they conversed in low whispers.

"Zyid, are you sure about this?" a pale, dark-haired boy inquired.

"Yes, Alex, I'm quite sure," Zyid said, pulling the hood of his gray sweatshirt farther over his head.

"I mean, I know that you kick ass and everything, but going into City Hall alone?" Alex pressed.

"I'll speak frankly. We lost Ken in last week's attack, and, most unfortunately, lost Frank to a random patrol three days later," Zyid said, his voice characteristically devoid of emotion. "Those losses have represented, as I'm sure you've noticed, a sizeable blow to morale."

The Truants all nodded at that. There was nothing that made you realize your own mortality quite like the death of a friend.

"As a result, I will not risk the death of another Truant. Not so soon," Zyid declared, remembering to take a lick at his ice cream.

"There's easily over a thousand Truants scattered throughout the City, and we'd probably need that many to attack City Hall. If you won't risk our deaths, why risk your own?" a dark-skinned Truant demanded, his ice cream untouched and melting.

"A valid question, Gabriel," Zyid conceded. "I would be lying if I said there was no danger."

"No danger? It's suicide," Alex said.

"That is certainly a defendable position," Zyid allowed. "But I believe that things are not so hopeless. Security in City Hall is relatively light—of all the places they might expect to be attacked, this is the last."

"Why now though?" Gabriel demanded, his hand now coated in melted ice cream. "They might be on edge after our last attack."

"Because morale works both ways," Zyid said, nibbling mechanically at his cone. "They are undoubtedly uncomfortable with our success at the ceramics lab, and we've assassinated a *lot* of Educators. They already fear for their lives, and an attack on City Hall itself would shatter whatever confidence they may have left."

"So you're not going to try to kill the Mayor or anything?" Gabriel asked.

Zyid paused, and something odd flickered across his face. A moment later, he returned to his normal, brisk self.

"No, it will mainly be a symbolic attack," Zyid said reassuringly. "We mean to make an impression, nothing more. They will, I do not doubt, greatly increase security here afterwards, which is fine since I do not expect to return anytime soon."

"But still, I don't know if even *you* can pull it off alone, Zyid," Alex said.

"I agree with you completely, Alex." Zyid allowed himself a smirk at the astounded looks on Alex's and Gabriel's faces.

"But . . . but you said—"

"He won't be alone," a new voice said quietly.

Alex and Gabriel both turned to the fourth member of their party, who had, up until then, remained completely silent.

"Noni here has offered to accompany me," Zyid said lightly, finishing off his ice-cream cone. "It is an offer that I will not refuse."

Alex and Gabriel eyed Noni carefully. The assassin's face was almost completely concealed by a hood identical to the one that Zyid wore, as well as a thin black scarf wrapped around the lower face. Noni was something of a legend in the Truancy for several reasons, and was second only to Zyid.

"Well," Alex said optimistically. "I wouldn't bet against Noni *and* Zyid, no matter how many Enforcers they've got."

"The two of you might stand more of a chance together," Gabriel conceded, not mentioning the fact that losing both Zyid and Noni would be a catastrophe.

"I'm glad that we all agree," Zyid said, opening his backpack and pulling a second black scarf from out of it. "I'm going to borrow Noni's fashion sense for today. I do not want to risk a security camera getting a good shot of my face."

"Why's that?" Alex couldn't help asking.

"Because," Zyid said simply, "the Mayor would recognize me."

Alex froze, staring at his leader as if seeing him for the first time. Noni even seemed to twitch slightly, though that might've been a trick of the sunlight. Zyid, seemingly unconcerned, wrapped the scarf around his lower face so that it covered everything from his chin to his nose, and then pulled his hood back over his head.

"The Mayor would do *what*?" Alex demanded, sure that he'd heard wrong.

"He would recognize me," Zyid repeated; this time his voice took on a very serious tone. "We have met in the past, and that is all there is to say on that topic." Zyid shot a warning look at Gabriel, who had just opened his mouth to speak.

"The time is now," Noni pointed out softly.

"So it is." Zyid glanced at his wristwatch. "I appreciate your escorting us up to this point, but you two should be far away from here when it starts. Wait for us back at headquarters."

"All right, good luck." Alex and Gabriel turned and made for the nearest subway station. They knew better than to question a direct order.

Zyid watched them go, and, once he was satisfied that they were a safe distance away, turned to face Noni.

"Well then, let us begin," Zyid suggested, nodding curtly at his partner.

Zyid and Noni made their way up the granite stairs towards City Hall's glass entrance. As they did, Zyid picked up a long, thin cardboard package that he had left lying to the side. Once through the open doors, they passed through a rectangular metal detector, which promptly beeped. Removing various metallic items from their pockets, including coins and a cell phone, they passed through the detector again for the benefit of the uniformed security guard that was watching them lazily. As they stepped inside the lobby, they were met by another pair of security guards. Zyid smiled beneath his scarf. Thanks to the Mayor, relatively few people in the City knew of the existence of the Truancy. These men weren't Enforcers, so they wouldn't be among those few.

"Hey there," the first guard greeted them. "What're you two here for?"

"School project," Zyid said casually. "Researching the City Hall and such."

"I'm his classmate," Noni said in a quiet voice muffled further by the scarf.

"Why the scarves?" the second guard asked suspiciously.

"It's the latest fashion," Zyid said. "It gets kind of warm, sure, but it looks cool."

"Kids and their fads these days." The first guard chuckled as his partner ran a handheld metal detector over them and their backpacks, just to be sure.

"Well, you two don't seem to be carrying anything dangerous," the second guard said, eyeing the metal detector readings. "Just don't wander off anywhere you're not supposed to."

"Oh, we won't," Zyid assured them. "We'll be on our best behavior."

Noni nodded vigorously in agreement.

"Right," the second guard said gruffly, turning back to face the entrance.

Zyid and Noni proceeded into the lobby, where they took a moment to look around. It was very lavish, like what one might expect to see in an expensive hotel. There were brownish-red leather couches and chairs scattered everywhere, all of them placed around polished wooden coffee tables. The floor was of green marble, with thick red and gold carpets covering most of it. There were some moderately sized chandeliers hanging from the ceiling, several potted trees, and in the middle was a large, white-marble fountain.

Zyid turned to Noni. "Make the call."

Noni whipped the cell phone out of her pocket and pressed the speed dial button. A few seconds later, somewhere in the mail room of the City Hall located two floors above the lobby, a bomb exploded. There were some distant shouts and screams, and seconds later Zyid and Noni watched as every Enforcer, security guard, and courageous bystander rushed towards the source of the commotion.

Zyid walked over to the fountain and gestured for Noni to follow. Using the confusion to their advantage, they each unloaded a pipe bomb at either end of the fountain. As they straightened up, a voice suddenly rang out.

"Hey, you two, what're you doing?"

Zyid's head snapped towards the voice, which belonged to an Enforcer that seemed to know exactly what they were doing. The Enforcer's hand reached for his gun, but as it moved, something white flew through the air and pierced his throat, causing him to crumple to the ground. Noni stood upright, two more ceramic knives clutched in either hand as Zyid opened his cardboard package and drew out a ceramic sword.

The weapon, one of the three recovered from the ceramics lab, was a risk that Zyid was taking. He wasn't sure exactly how well it would work—after all, only three were made before the project was scrapped.

"Our time, I'm certain, is running short," Zyid said, looking over at Noni. "Light the fuse."

Zyid and Noni each drew a packet of matches from his or her pocket. Lighting them, Zyid and Noni touched the flame to the fuses of the pipe bombs, causing the fuses to hiss and burn angrily. Turning away, the pair dashed behind a marble pillar as the pipe bombs exploded, sending chunks of the fountain flying everywhere. Drawn by the new disturbance, security guards and Enforcers began to rush to the scene.

One of the Enforcers passed by the column the pair had hidden behind. Noni grabbed the Enforcer's arm, used it as leverage to leapfrog over him, and then deftly twisted his head on the way over, snapping his neck. Noni dropped down behind the now-dead body and seized it, using it as a shield against a security guard firing from across the lobby.

Zyid leaped and dived behind an adjacent pillar, then dashed towards the security guard firing at Noni, plunging his sword into the guard's shoulder before he could turn to face the new threat. As he did so, another ceramic knife flew through the air and caught him in the temple. Zyid let the man's limp body drop to the ground as he seized his pistol, swinging it towards an Enforcer that had entered the wrecked lobby from the stairwell. Zyid's first shot missed, but the second brought the Enforcer down before he could bring his own weapon to bear.

Meanwhile, Noni had seized the weapon from the Enforcer

that she had killed by hand. Locating another security guard, this one crouching behind the security desk with a metal detector clutched uselessly in one hand and a gun in the other, Noni fired a well-aimed shot that buried itself in the guard's exposed arm.

Zyid, in the meantime, had been holding off several newcomers that kept coming in from the stairs. Glancing towards the row of elevators to one side of the lobby, Zyid noted that several elevators were on their way down, doubtlessly filled with more enemies. Turning towards the exit, he heard the lone security guard scream as Noni's bullet pierced his arm. Gesturing to Noni that they should leave, Zyid leaped up and, using the columns as cover, dashed over to the desk, jumped on top of it, and plunged his sword into the wounded guard's neck in one fluid motion.

Noni soon joined Zyid behind the desk, and he hurled several firebombs taken from his backpack that quickly ignited and discouraged pursuit. Before leaving, Zyid took a piece of paper from his backpack and dropped it onto the floor in plain sight. Then, stuffing their various weapons into their backpacks, Zyid and Noni dashed out the doors of City Hall. The pair of children ran through the crowd that had now gathered around the building, shed their sweatshirts and scarves, and soon disappeared into two separate subways.

No one tried to stop them. After all, they were just children.

It would take hours for the Educators to sort out what had happened, and by the time they realized that City Hall itself had been besieged by two lone Truants, all they were left with was a pair of sweatshirts, scarves, and the sheet of paper that Zyid had left behind. The paper, the Mayor had observed before he crushed it in his balled fist, was a blank report card, with a large "F" inscribed in blood.

The message could not have been clearer, and the Mayor's wrath had never been greater.

6

Tardy

"Well, well, well," Mr. Niel said softly as he leaned against one side of the doorway into his classroom. "Another latecomer."

Tack panted, too out of breath to explain himself. Besides him, another boy and a girl were also detained at the door, wearing extremely glum expressions.

The subways of the City did not have schedules, and the Educators made sure that arrivals, like the speed of the trains, were very inconsistent. Tack, having successfully escaped the bullies, had ridden the train home just fine the previous day, and had been relieved to find that Suzie had done the same. This morning, however, Tack had had the misfortune of being delayed because the train that he took to school didn't show up for nearly half an hour. As a result, Tack had arrived at school five minutes late and now stood exhausted outside his social studies class with Mr. Niel glowering at him.

"We are having a pop quiz today." Mr. Niel grinned unpleasantly at the three late students. "Really, it's all easy stuff; the problem is that if you're late, you aren't allowed to take the quiz."

"Why not?" Tack demanded.

"Because the entire purpose of the quiz is to punish students that come late to my class," Mr. Niel admitted. "If you're late, you can't take the quiz, and if you don't take the quiz, you get a zero."

"I was only two minutes late though!" the boy next to Tack protested.

"I don't really care." Mr. Niel smiled, clearly enjoying himself.

"I was here before class started!" the girl blurted out. "My backpack was here and everything; I just went to put my jacket in my locker!"

"Oh, well now that's a shame," Mr. Niel said with mock sympathy. "It's too bad that your backpack can't take your quizzes for you."

Tears began to form in the girl's eyes. Utterly indifferent, Mr. Neil turned and made to reenter his classroom.

"We will be doing this again, so I expect that you will all be very careful not to be tardy again." Mr. Niel shot them a venomous smile over his shoulder. "You can come back in after the quiz is over."

Mr. Niel laughed, and then slammed the door in their faces.

All right, what's up this time?" Suzie asked, looking up at Tack curiously.

"Nothing," Tack replied gruffly. He didn't intend to discuss the latest incident anytime soon.

"If you say so," Suzie said skeptically, turning back to the pizza counter.

It was lunchtime, and Suzie's friend Melissa was absent from school again. Tack had agreed to go to their usual pizza place for lunch, even though Mr. Niel's class had left him so angry that he didn't feel like talking to anyone.

"Whaddya kids want?" the squinty-eyed cashier demanded.

"I'll have ham on my pizza," Tack said grumpily, slamming a fistful of money onto the counter.

"I'll take sausage," Suzie chirped, adding her own cash to Tack's pile.

After collecting their money and counting it twice, the cashier elbowed the pizza maker in the belly, prompting him to cut up a slice from each of the appropriate pies and slide them onto dishes. Tack murmured his thanks and seized his plate, moving to an empty table, followed closely by Suzie.

As they sat down, Tack took a large bite out of his pizza so he'd have an excuse not to talk. He had a feeling that Suzie was going to be determined to cheer him up, but he had reached the strange level of anger and outrage where he didn't want to be cheered up at all. But he needn't have worried—Suzie seemed to be too hungry to want to bother with conversation either. She busied herself by tearing great chunks of pizza with her teeth and swallowing them with hardly any chewing. Meanwhile, Tack glanced up at the television. As usual, it was set to the City News Channel.

"The Mayor today held a press conference concerning the recent gas leaks and subsequent explosions that left eight dead at City Hall," the onscreen reporter intoned as the scene shifted to display a disgruntled-looking Mayor standing amidst a battalion of armed Enforcers.

"This incident is a monumental tragedy," the Mayor said. "My condolences go out to all the family members of the recently deceased. As you all well know, City Hall is a very old building, so in hindsight it is unsurprising that an accident like this occurred. A full investigation will be launched immediately to find out all the details, and we will of course keep the public updated as more information becomes available."

Tack frowned. Gas explosions in City Hall? It sounded kind of dodgy, but before Tack could think about it anymore, the scene onscreen shifted again.

"And now, in other news . . ." The anchorwoman paused for a dramatic effect. "Is the meat that *you're* eating safe? A woman in District 5 today has been diagnosed with Crazy Pig Disease! Crazy Pig Disease is an illness that originated from outside the City, and is always fatal. Enforcers quickly traced the contaminated meat to a local hot-dog stand, which in turn got its supplies from one of the biggest meat distributors in the City. The Educators now fear that a widespread breakout may be imminent. What's more, Crazy Pig Disease is unaffected by heat, so no amount of cooking can make sure that *your* food is safe!"

Tack frowned and looked down at the ham on his pizza. Suzie, meanwhile, hadn't taken any notice of the news and was now stuffing her mouth with warm crust. Tack considered the news about the Crazy Pig Disease for a moment. On the one hand, he was hungry and he loved ham. On the other, he certainly didn't want to experience any ham-induced deaths. But then again, strange diseases always kept popping up in the news, and nothing much really ever came of that.

Reassured by that thought, Tack forgot all about the broadcast and began attacking his pizza with renewed gusto. By the time he was halfway through his slice Suzie was already done and was watching him impatiently.

"So, anything interesting happen today?" Suzie asked, giving Tack a knowing look.

Tack quickly stuffed his mouth so full of pizza that his head resembled a blowfish.

Suzie laughed. "Well, if you don't want to talk about it, that's fine." Suzie tossed her plate into the garbage.

Tack quickly devoured the rest of his pizza, careful to keep his mouth full the whole way to avoid any further questioning. Suzie seemed to have gotten the message and made no further attempts to interrogate him. After Tack had disposed of his trash, the two siblings left the parlor and made their way back to the school. As they walked, Tack abruptly decided that he'd go back to the mysterious boy he'd met in District 19. Tack had put off returning to the abandoned district due to an abundance of schoolwork, but not a day went by when he didn't think about what he had learned there.

Tack briefly wondered why he was looking forward to visiting the district again, then realized that it was the only bit of freedom that he really had. Over there, without Educators, without Enforcers, he could ask whatever questions he wanted of someone who was both knowledgeable and young. Any answers that he got made sense and, in addition, made him feel more enlightened in a City where he was meant to be ignorant.

"Ah, Tack, welcome back." Umasi put down the letter he had been reading as Tack approached the lemonade stand.

"Hey, what's up?" Tack asked conversationally.

"While there are few people in this City with whom I maintain any correspondence," Umasi said, folding the letter and sliding it back into its envelope, "I actually just received some mail from an old acquaintance."

"I see," Tack said, mentally berating himself for being unable to say anything more interesting.

"You look significantly less rested since last we met," Umasi observed, filling two paper cups with lemonade from the ever-present jug.

"School's been tough lately," Tack said gruffly. Was it really that visible?

"I don't doubt it," Umasi said, sliding one cup over to Tack and raising the other to his lips. "Has anything in particular been bothering you?"

"Plenty of things," Tack said, trying hard to remember everything that had happened in the past week. "I can't really remember some of them, but they all piss me off anyway."

"Our minds are always eager to be rid of bad memories," Umasi said, taking a thoughtful sip from his cup.

"I'm getting really sick of school," Tack confessed as he drank from his own cup. "It's hard enough just to learn the stuff they teach you, but it's like every bit of school is specially designed to aggravate me."

"That's because it is," Umasi said, putting his cup down.

"What?" Tack asked dumbly.

"There is a board of Educators," Umasi explained, "with tremendous power and influence in the City. It focuses its efforts on making the school experience as mentally and emotionally draining as is possible without driving students mad or causing an alarming amount of dropouts."

"How does *that* help them control us?" Tack demanded, his cup of lemonade now forgotten.

"It's part of your conditioning." Umasi stirred his lemonade with a straw. "You are trained to obey even under the most terrible circumstances, so that you can emerge from the schools as obedient members of City society."

Tack pondered this momentous revelation. All the terrible things he was put through in school were *planned*?

"So really, we're just guinea pigs to them?" Tack asked bitterly.

"That is one way to put it," Umasi admitted. "The City is all about control. They believe by conditioning students while they are young and in their schools they can control them when they grow up."

"But . . . how can they . . . ," Tack sputtered, unsure of what he was even trying to say. He was more speechless than surprised by what Umasi was telling him. Somehow he knew there was just too much to hate about school for it all to be accidental.

"The Educators' plan *is* fundamentally flawed, however," Umasi mused, stopping his stirring. "If they cannot maintain control over the students before their treatment is complete, then they have a problem on their hands."

"But how would they lose control over the students?" Tack wondered.

"All it takes is one," Umasi said quietly. "And they already have begun to lose control. Remember that I told you that there were those that opposed the Educators?"

"They . . . they're *kids*?" Tack blurted in surprise.

"Yes," Umasi agreed solemnly. "Not unlike you or me. The difference is that they do not discuss their discontent. Instead, they express it through violence and killing. That approach can only lead to chaos and destruction for both sides."

"What should they do instead?" Tack demanded, wondering what else besides violence and death could make the Educators change their ways.

"They could wait," Umasi suggested simply. "The Educators will grow old, and they will die naturally. And then we will replace them. It's an idealistic hope, I know, but better than wholesale murder."

Tack paused. The idea made some sense, though it called for more patience than he thought he had.

"Enlightening the current generation," Umasi continued, "would be a bloodless victory. There is no need to fight the Educators. In time, we could *become* the Educators. It might take generations, but it would be done without loss of life."

Tack thought that over. Provided that he survived his school experience and ended up graduating, he could pursue a career as an Educator. If there were enough others like him, would they be able to change things? He didn't see why not.

"The problem with my idea, Tack," Umasi said with a sad smile, "is that it is unrealistic because it is unpopular. Why do you think that I stay concealed in this district? Patience is not a natural human trait. And it is unreasonable, perhaps, to expect enough students to remain unbroken by the Educators after they graduate."

"Well," Tack said slowly, noticing something else. "Your plan also doesn't do anything to help students in school now."

Umasi suddenly sat forward in his chair, staring at Tack meaningfully behind his dark sunglasses.

"It's true, there is little that I can do to make school less painful," Umasi admitted quietly. "But if I could help some students *understand* their pain, then they might find their pain more bearable."

That ended the conversation, and Tack returned home, rattled.

7

EXPULSION

Of all the punishments dealt out by the Educators, the most severe and feared was expulsion. Expulsion, unlike other punishments that could be put on a student's record to inspire future obedience, was final. Educators were normally reluctant to expel students—the moment students left the schools they became free from the Educators' direct influence. Expulsion, therefore, was reserved for students deemed a danger to school itself.

Expulsion was so significant that only an Educator could deal out such a punishment. Principals were, of course, able to request that a student be expelled, though they were not Educators themselves and could not make that most potent of decisions. In order to deal with the large number of students annually deemed unworthy for school, special Educators, the Disciplinary Officers, were exclusively assigned this purpose. It was they who ultimately weeded out the students unfit to bloom in the Educators' garden.

Students of the City tried not to think about expulsion too much, about simply vanishing from the schools, from the lives of their friends and classmates, and soon from memory. All people, especially children, fear the unknown—and being expelled, much like death, represented a great mystery for them. And so expulsion was feared, never understood, and no student ever thought to ask what really happened to those that were expelled . . .

. . . until one day, when Tack witnessed it for himself.

"So, did you hear that they caught the guy who messed up the bathrooms?" Suzie asked, idly kicking a soda can to the side.

Tack sat up suddenly. He hadn't caught much sleep the night before, and had skipped eating to spend his lunch period trying to rest outside in the shade of the Dumpsters behind the school building. It was a favorite spot of his, safe from both the guards and the bullies that Tack suspected might still be hunting for him. Suzie, having finished her own lunch, had found him there. For the last few minutes she had been unsuccessfully trying to wake him, though her last attempt was enough to bring Tack back fully to the realm of attentiveness.

"Really?" Tack asked, stifling a yawn and looking at Suzie expectantly.

"Yeah," Suzie said. "It was one of the tenth graders."

This was news to Tack. For the past week or so, several of the boys' bathrooms throughout the school had been vandalized. As the incidents grew more frequent and increasingly inconvenient, it had quickly become well understood that only one punishment would be severe enough to punish the culprit when he was caught.

"Has he been expelled yet?" Tack wondered.

"I heard he's been locked up in the principal's office," Suzie said, sounding pleased that she'd been able to wake Tack up. "The Disciplinary Officer is supposed to be coming soon, actually."

"Today?"

"Well, yeah, I mean it only makes sense since they've got the guy locked up and everything," Suzie said.

Tack was seized by a sudden excitement. He had always wondered what happened when a student was expelled—after all, it was the ultimate punishment and threat used against them. It seemed strange to Tack that no matter how unpleasant school was, being kicked out of it was considered the greatest punishment of all.

"If we went to the principal's office now," Tack said, "do you think we'd be able to see it happen?"

"You mean, see the guy get expelled?" Suzie looked up at Tack curiously. "Why would you want to see that, Tacky?"

Tack was willing to overlook the use of his annoying pet name, just this once. "I'm just curious," he said, keeping his voice casual.

"Well, I suppose we weren't doing anything else anyway," Suzie said, standing up. "If you really wanna, I suppose we'd have a good chance of seeing it."

"Great, what're we waiting for?" Tack leaped to his feet and slung his backpack over his shoulder.

It didn't take long for Tack to make his way around the building with a less enthusiastic Suzie in tow. As they reentered the school, they found that a small crowd had already gathered around the principal's office. Tack and Suzie quickly joined them, craning their necks to get a better look.

"Look, we just made it!" Suzie dared to whisper, speaking

low enough that no one would notice her breaking the "total silence" policy.

Tack nodded. In the midst of the crowd stood the principal. Next to her slouched a moody-looking, pale-faced blond boy. The boy had the air of a condemned person trying to hold on to some measure of dignity before his execution. The principal, meanwhile, looked as if she'd like nothing better than to order the students around her to leave—and she probably would have, were it not for the third, more formidable presence among them.

"Mr. Caine!" The principal greeted the Disciplinary Officer formally, offering her hand. "I'm glad that you could make it on such short notice."

"You gave every indication that it was urgent, so I came as soon as I could." Mr. Caine shook her hand.

Tack examined Mr. Caine with fascination. He looked like a normal person, albeit one crammed into a formal-looking suit that seemed almost as uncomfortable as their school uniforms. His features were utterly unremarkable, and had Tack seen him in passing, he would never have been able to identify him as an Educator, much less a Disciplinary Officer.

And then, as Tack examined Mr. Caine's face, he noticed something else that struck him as extremely odd—the man actually seemed *nervous*, though he was clearly doing his best to conceal it.

"It's a shame that we haven't had the chance to meet before," the principal said genially. "And I wish it could've been under happier circumstances."

"Well, I was only appointed to the job recently," Mr. Caine pointed out. "And as for the circumstances . . . ah, is this young Master Jones?"

Mr. Caine turned his gaze from the principal to the guilty child.

"That's my name," Jones confirmed quietly.

"Young man, this is Mr. Caine," the principal said sternly. "He is the new Disciplinary Officer for our school."

"What happened to the old one?" Jones muttered.

"He had a little accident." Mr. Caine smoothed his hair and frowned. "But that's beside the point."

"Mr. Caine, this boy is a miscreant," the principal said, sounding very formal.

"I can see that." Mr. Caine looked down at the boy. "So, Jones, I've heard that you've been waging a war against our . . . toilets."

"Yeah," Jones admitted boldly.

"You are aware that this school and everything in it is Educator property?" Mr. Caine asked.

"Something like that," Jones said.

"And you are aware, I hope, that destroying Educator property is illegal?" Mr. Caine continued.

"I guess," Jones said in a low monotone.

"You signed a number of documents promising to uphold our rules and abide by our laws," Mr. Caine pointed out, producing the folded documents from his coat pocket. "I have them here.

"I am afraid, given the magnitude of your crime . . . ," Mr. Caine continued, examining a few of the sheets he'd withdrawn, "and considering that you seem to have something of a history of troublemaking, I have little choice but to expel you from the City school system."

"Right," Jones said, keeping his voice level.

"I'm glad you're at least willing to accept responsibility for your actions." Mr. Caine folded the papers and replaced them in his pocket. "Your parents have already been informed. You won't be seeing them again. Now, come this way."

"Whatever," Jones said, trying his best to sound indifferent.

Mr. Caine placed his hand on Jones' shoulder, and led him firmly towards the school exit. The crowd knew better than to follow, and stayed rooted where they were, stunned.

The uneasy silence was broken by the principal. "All right, nothing to see here; clear out," she barked. "Show's over; get going!"

Reluctantly, the crowd began to disperse. Suzie led Tack away by his sleeve, and he allowed himself to be dragged, though his eyes and attention were focused on the retreating forms of Mr. Caine and Jones. What fate awaited him? What exactly happened to the expelled students after they were led out of the school by an Educator?

Every question Tack had ever asked himself about expulsion rose immediately to the top of his head, demanding answers. What made it worse was the fact that he knew that there was no one who could give him any answers, no one that he could ask—

No, that was wrong, wasn't it? Tack came to that realization with a jolt. There *was* one person he could ask.

So we know that the Truancy has been recruiting heavily from the vagrant population," the Mayor said, flipping his lighter open.

"Yes, sir. It seems that the vagrants prefer to try their luck as Truants, as opposed to starving. Observations indicate that, as a result, vagrancy levels are at an all-time low . . . ," Mr. Waters said.

"Leaving Truancy levels at an all-time high," the Mayor finished, clicking his lighter shut. "Let's get straight to the point, Chief Enforcer. I have a plan to deal with this problem."

"What's that, sir?" the Chief Enforcer asked, genuinely curious.

"Firstly, make it illegal for any expelled student to return to their homes or contact their parents and guardians after being expelled," the Mayor said as Mr. Waters took notes on a small pad. "In this way we can prevent the expelled students from ever seeing their parents. After that, we'll be free to execute them all quietly without anyone making any fuss."

The Chief Enforcer dropped his pen.

"Ex . . . execute them?"

"The vagrants were always just dead children walking," the Mayor said dismissively. "We used to be content to just let them rot and die slowly. But now they're becoming Truants, and we can't have that. So, let us preemptively put them out of their misery. I'll have the legislation done today. I want your Enforcers to begin executing newly expelled students within three days."

"But sir—," the Chief Enforcer began to protest.

"This is not a debate, Mr. Waters," the Mayor said coldly. "Remember, I took an oath to protect this City and its schools, and I intend to fulfill it by *any* means necessary. You Enforcers take a similar oath, and I expect the same from you. Do you understand?"

"Well, I . . ."

"I said, *do you understand?* It is not a complicated question."

"Yes, sir."

"Good. Oh, and one more thing."

"Sir?"

"Try to keep this quiet. I think it best that no one finds out about this."

"I agree, Mr. Mayor. I completely agree."

Tack ran as fast as his legs could propel him, his heart pounding in his chest. It had happened at last. Just as he had begun to forget about them, the bully Joe and his friends from Freshman Friday had spotted Tack on his way to District 19 after school and decided to finish what they'd started.

Tack knew that he could beat them to the barrier, but this time the three bullies were willing to follow, having seen Tack go over the fence and live to come back again. They wasted no time in scrambling over the fence after Tack. Tack still had a decent lead, but his chest was now burning with every step. Skidding around the corner, Tack had never been gladder to see Umasi sitting there, at his lemonade stand in his usual pose, book in hand with his feet up on the table.

He didn't know how he knew that Umasi would be able to help, but Tack was somehow confident that Umasi could solve *any* problem.

"Umasi, you've gotta help me," Tack panted, running up to the table.

Umasi put his book down and raised an eyebrow. "What's the matter?"

"Bunch of . . . jerks . . . chasing me . . . ," Tack gasped, pointing to the street corner he had just rounded.

"Why would they be doing that?" Umasi inquired.

"Because they're jerks!" Tack almost yelled in frustration, wondering why Umasi wouldn't appreciate the urgency of the situation.

Umasi was silent. A moment later, the three bullies rounded

the corner, spotted Tack and Umasi, and began approaching with menacing grins on their faces.

"Fools," Umasi diagnosed quietly.

"There you are. Get over here, punk," Joe ordered, pointing at Tack.

Umasi slowly lowered his feet from the table.

"You seem to take issue with my friend," Umasi said politely.

"Yeah, we do; you got a problem with that?" Joe challenged.

"Is there a reason that you wish to cause him bodily harm?" Umasi asked.

"The kid don't know when to keep his mouth shut and respect his elders."

Umasi sighed. "His words must have hurt your feelings very badly to provoke such a reaction."

Joe and his friends glanced at each other confusedly. Was the kid making fun of them? Who talked like that at their age anyway?

"You wanna fight?" Joe puffed his chest up and spread his arms.

"Not particularly," Umasi admitted. "Pounding a problem into submission was never my preferred solution."

"If you ain't gonna fight, then shut the hell up," Joe ordered.

"You misunderstand." Umasi frowned. "I would only *prefer* not to fight."

"Yeah, and whaddya think you're gonna do?" one of the other boys demanded.

"If you know what's good for you, you'll keep your mouth shut and stay out of this," Joe agreed.

"Please turn around and leave this district," Umasi requested, taking a sip of lemonade. "Otherwise, I must apologize in advance for anything I might have to do to ensure the continued well-being of my friend."

"Whatever," the third kid said. "Let's get him, Joe."

"Right." Joe grinned again, taking a few steps towards Tack, who was now sweating.

Joe moved as if to punch Tack, and what happened next happened so fast that Tack would never be sure about how it happened. All his eyes registered was a blur, and then came a sickly snapping noise. The next thing he knew, Umasi was grasping Joe's outstretched arm with one hand, his cup of lemonade still in the other, and had at the same time driven the heel of his foot into the side of Joe's knee joint so that the lower leg bent in strange directions. There was a moment of silence as everyone froze in disbelief. The silence was shattered by an agonized scream.

As Joe screeched and moaned, thrashing frantically on the ground, his buddies gaped at Umasi.

"It's nothing permanent," Umasi assured them. "He won't be kicking anyone with that leg for a while, but he'll be fine. Now, why don't you two see to your friend? Drag him back to school and have someone sort him out."

Anxious to get away, the two thugs grabbed their friend and started to drag him towards the corner, eliciting another loud scream as well as a long string of profanities. As they left, Tack was satisfied to see a look of utter bewilderment on their faces, noting that he wasn't the only one mystified by Umasi.

"So, I sense that something new is bothering you today," Umasi observed casually, regarding Tack as he sat down again. "Something beside bullies, that is."

Apparently, Umasi had come to know Tack a little better

during his increasingly frequent visits. On the other hand, Umasi had, throughout all the meetings, remained as mysterious and inscrutable as ever to Tack.

"Yeah . . . yeah, I had a question," Tack said, sitting down shakily, taking a drink from the proffered cup of lemonade to calm himself. The adrenaline coursing through his veins would take a while to wear off.

"Curiosity is a dangerous beast, Tack," Umasi mused, as though nothing had happened at all. "Speak, and I'll do my best to satisfy it—though in my experience the more it is fed, the bigger it gets."

Tack ignored the strange metaphor and looked up at Umasi, whose face was, as usual, expressionless. He took a deep breath, and asked the question that had haunted countless students over the years.

"What do the Educators do to expelled students?"

"Nothing."

Tack jerked his head up, unbelieving. "What?"

"Nothing is done to them, other than their removal from school," Umasi explained.

"But . . ." Tack stared, his head spinning. "Then why . . ."

"Because being removed from school is not the true punishment," Umasi explained. "It's what comes afterwards. As you know, the Educators control nearly everything in this City, either directly or indirectly. Students that are expelled are typically shunned by their families. Unable to find work, they inevitably end up prowling the streets as vagrants—a living, dreadful reminder to parents about what the consequences are if they do not groom their children to be obedient in school."

Tack digested this information.

"That's horrible," he said quietly.

"Indeed," Umasi agreed grimly. "Those condemned individuals usually wander for the rest of their short lives with no purpose. Occasionally they might get rowdy, in which case the Enforcers are sent in to . . . put them down."

Tack eyed the ground. So, being expelled was awful after all, although in an entirely different way than he had imagined.

"However . . . ," Umasi murmured.

Tack's head snapped up. There was something in Umasi's voice that told him that the other boy was considering revealing something secret.

"What?" Tack demanded excitedly.

Umasi adjusted his sunglasses and cocked his head. Tack couldn't help but feel slightly nervous as Umasi seemed to inspect him again, measuring his character. Finally, apparently having decided that Tack had passed the test, Umasi nodded slowly.

"Of late, expelled students have been given another chance at life," Umasi said.

"What? Are they being allowed back into schools again?" Tack asked eagerly.

"No." Umasi's face did not change.

"But . . . if they're not being allowed into school—," Tack began.

"They are being given the opportunity to fight it," Umasi said quietly.

"Fight . . . *fight* it?"

"Yes. You know, of course, about the children that fight the Educators. They welcome the vagrants into their ranks," Umasi explained. "The vagrants now fight against the system that disowned them. They fight because they might as well fight instead of starve. They also fight because they are deluded."

"About what?" Tack blurted.

"They typically believe that by fighting, they might improve their futures, but in reality all that they are offered is a more exciting death," Umasi explained quietly. "When it comes down to it, the only lucid ones are in it for the thrill, or for revenge."

Tack frowned. Imagining the bleak future that might await him if he was expelled, he knew that he wouldn't sit around idly, waiting to die. He'd want to fight the Educators. He'd want revenge; he would want excitement—if the expelled students were offered both when they would otherwise have *nothing*, could they really be blamed?

"I see that you do not completely agree with my evaluation," Umasi observed lightly. "That is understandable. Were I still attending school, I might disagree with it myself. But, having had the opportunity to spend years thinking about it, I've managed to convince myself that I am right." Umasi adjusted his sunglasses slightly. "Don't worry about it, Tack; I've yet to find anyone that agrees with me. At any rate, if you are lucky, you yourself will never have to make that decision."

"Which decision?" Tack asked, feeling that he was losing track of things.

"To fight the Educators, or not," Umasi reminded him. "In any case, it is getting late again. Let us conclude our business for today."

Wanting time alone to ponder what he had learned, Tack had no inclination to argue. He picked up his backpack, slung it over his shoulder smoothly, and began to make his way back home. He was no fighter, but Umasi was right about one thing, at least—if Tack were lucky, he would never have to worry about fighting. No, he'd just have to worry about homework, and tests, and keeping his sanity.

"I lose either way," Tack muttered to himself.

And he was right. After all, in the City, students were always the losers.

8

When Life Gives You Lemons

"And then my father heard about Mr. Niel's quiz, and he threw a fit and cut off my allowance!" Tack said angrily, flailing his arms in the air in an imitation of his father, forgetting that he was holding a cup of lemonade in his right hand. Lemonade splashed over the rim and onto Umasi's pants.

"Don't worry about it," Umasi said as Tack began to apologize. "The weather is getting warmer; I could do with some refreshment."

Tack noted that lemonade, being sticky on top of being cold, would hardly be comfortable no matter how warm the weather was. Still, he was grateful that Umasi was willing to overlook his clumsiness. He was also grateful for a lot more as well.

Following confrontation with the bullies, Tack had only ever seen the trio once at school, and they had quickly fled at the sight of him. Since then, Tack had made a habit of returning to District 19 to talk to Umasi, and to vent his frustrations. He was now visiting Umasi almost every day, even though his parents yelled at him for spending too much time with his friends and not enough time on his schoolwork. Tack didn't feel bad about lying to them, as in a way he was telling the truth. He regarded Umasi as a friend—though an extremely odd one.

"Please, continue," Umasi said. "I confess to succumbing to the human weakness of being fascinated by the troubles of others."

"Yeah." Tack tried to remember where he had left off. "So now they're barely giving me enough to buy lunch. It's like I'm in prison or something."

Umasi smiled slightly at that. "So, you're having a bit of a monetary difficulty?"

"Yeah," Tack acknowledged cautiously, wondering where Umasi was steering the conversation now.

"Well, I may be able to help you with that," Umasi said slowly, digging a small plastic card out of his pocket and placing it on the table. "I mentioned to you before that I have a healthy supply of money, and you asked how. I think I can answer *part* of that question now—this account card contains my substantial personal fortune."

"And you'd give me some?" Tack asked excitedly. He had only come to Umasi to talk; he hadn't expected the boy to share his seemingly endless riches.

"If you mean simply give it away, no," Umasi said bluntly. "But if you'd be willing to take on a job for me, you'd be well compensated."

"A job?"

"Yes," Umasi confirmed. "It's nothing dangerous or anything that might get you into trouble. I simply have some problems you might be able to sort out."

"What might that be?" Tack wondered aloud.

"If you accept the job, I expect you should find out," Umasi said.

Tack thought about it. Umasi struck him as an honest person, so whatever he had planned couldn't be awful. Really it just came down to one question.

"How much will you pay?" Tack asked.

"You will complete one task every day you can show up," Umasi said. "Upon your completing that task, I'll give you twenty in City currency."

Tack's eyes widened. That would add up to a lot of money in a hurry.

"And I can just show up any day?" Tack asked.

"Any day," Umasi agreed.

"How long do you think each task would take?" Tack asked.

"That would depend on you." Umasi gave a faint smile again.

"I'll do it," Tack said. It really sounded too good to be true. "Can I start tomorrow?"

"I was about to suggest that you do, actually," Umasi said casually. "Since we are of one mind, I will expect you here after school."

"Yeah, that's fine," Tack said. "Just one thing, could you tell me what the tasks are going to be?"

"No, Tack, they will remain surprises," Umasi said, which struck Tack as ominous. "Now, you should get some sleep. You might have a long day ahead of you tomorrow."

The comment did little to ease Tack's mind, though ultimately money concerned him more than Umasi's cryptic statements.

In all of District 19, only one street was inhabited—if having a single boy at a lonely lemonade stand qualified as "inhabited." The street itself was lined with old apartment buildings, generally of the brownstone variety, with balconies and fire escapes that formed a tangle of protrusions littering the exteriors of the buildings. Power still flowed through the wires of District 19, and so the orange streetlights still glowed at night, their eerie light casting strange shadows as it struck the buildings and sidewalk.

On most nights, the street was completely abandoned, as even Umasi had to sleep. For a long time, no one had ever violated the sanctity of the night in District 19. But this night was different. Umasi remained in his seat, at his stand, a cup of lemonade in his hand, patiently waiting for something. Finally, in the darkest hour of the night, it came—something even more unusual than Umasi's presence.

A second boy walked up the street, his large shadow cast onto the pavement by the street lamps. Umasi was aware of his presence, but made no move to acknowledge it. Undaunted, the second boy approached the lemonade stand and, without waiting for an invitation, sat down in the seat opposite Umasi.

"It has been a while, Umasi," the boy said, looking him up and down. "Isolation, I see, has not stunted your growth."

"I had thought that we agreed never to see each other again," Umasi said, ignoring the comment and getting straight to the point.

"Aren't you at least going to thank me for leaving you with power during the blackout?"

"I have little use for light," Umasi said dispassionately. "And again, I believed that we agreed never to see each other again."

"I do recall such an agreement being made, yes," the other boy admitted.

"And yet you have seen fit to break it," Umasi pointed out.

"You did not refuse my request for a meeting," the boy said. "And we have much to talk about."

"On the contrary, Zen, our discussion ended years ago. It ended in violence. We have nothing left to talk about," Umasi said firmly.

"I told you not to call me 'Zen' anymore. And this time I actually have a good reason." The boy frowned. "If the Educators were to get wind of my old name—"

"Your real name, you mean?" Umasi interrupted. "Yes, they'd find out who you really are, and that you're not dead like I told them you were. Would that be so bad? Do you intend to run from who you are forever?"

"I do not intend to run from who I *was,* as much as I intend to bury him," the other boy declared. "For all intents and purposes, 'Zen' is dead. Zyid has taken his place."

"Well, I am not prepared to waste energy arguing over a name, and courtesy dictates that I hear you out . . . Zyid," Umasi said. "So say what you came to say."

"Oh, but don't you already know what I came to ask, a brilliant prodigy like you?" Zyid asked with a mocking smile. "Things will be coming to a climax soon. I've come to ask what I asked of you years ago before we parted ways. I want your help."

Umasi leaned back in his chair, the light from the nearest street lamp casting his features into shadow.

"You want my help in murder and destruction," he observed, his voice dropping a few degrees.

"I want your help in casting down a corrupt system and freeing its victims," Zyid corrected, ignoring the chill in Umasi's voice. "Years ago you told me that we could never succeed, and yet now you can see for yourself that, even without you, we *are* succeeding."

"You measure success in the number of enemy bodies you pile up, do you?" Umasi asked coldly.

"I measure success in the power the Truancy is gaining and the Educators are losing every day!" Zyid said fervently. "Earlier today we managed to kill their latest Chief Enforcer! You never believed that there were people willing to die for this cause; yet they are fighting and dying now, with or without your help. You could save their lives, Umasi, since you value life so much."

"Save their lives by ending others'?" Umasi mused. "I wouldn't presume to value the lives of Truants over those of the Educators, Zyid."

"You still have sympathies for the Educators, after what they did to you?" Zyid raised an eyebrow. "Could it be that you are feeling sentimental?"

"And you aren't?" Umasi asked, surprised. "The Mayor, or so we now call him, has done nothing to provoke me since we left. And he has not, as you have, dared to approach me for help."

"Oh? Well, it just so happens that we've seen evidence that he's started to execute expelled students. Innocents." Zyid smirked as Umasi jerked up in his chair. "You look surprised. You shouldn't be, really—they're just showing their true nature."

"Only because you goaded them into it," Umasi retorted bitterly.

"Please, they've always been like this, and have always been growing steadily worse," Zyid said dismissively. "Our efforts only sped *their* schemes."

"Which is why I'll have nothing to do with either of you."

"So what will you do instead, continue to confine yourself in this abandoned dump, leaving your mind and body to rot while your talents are wasted?" A note of frustration entered Zyid's voice.

"My talents are my own, and mine to use towards whatever goals that I see fit," Umasi said defiantly.

"And what goals are those?" Zyid demanded.

"That, I'm afraid, is my business," Umasi said.

"You are intelligent, Umasi," Zyid hissed, placing his hands on the table and leaning forward. "Don't waste yourself here. Leave this district; come with me; with the both of us together, the Educators will fall within a year!" Zyid frowned. "Of course, I know full well that you're more likely to content yourself with being lazy, doing nothing."

"I never said that I would do nothing, Zyid," Umasi said. "I am, in fact, taking action—in my own way. You tend to gravitate towards the grand and the spectacular, but my accomplishments are more subtle and patient."

"I've seen no evidence of your accomplishments," Zyid said scornfully. "And if others cannot see and recognize anything you've done, what is the point of doing it?"

"Perhaps the point is simply that you've done it." Umasi shrugged. "I really can't tell you. In any case, as fascinating as our philosophical discussions always were, your purpose for coming here was to ask me a question, which you have done. Are we finished, or do you have any other requests for me?"

"No," Zyid said. "Just the one."

"Then I regret to say that my answer remains 'no,' and it is final," Umasi said. "It would be best if you do not ask me again."

"I will respect that wish," Zyid said, standing up. "But I hope, for old times' sake, that you will reconsider."

"Ah, old times," Umasi said reminiscently, tilting his head back. "We did have some fun, didn't we?"

"I won't deny it," Zyid admitted.

"And yet that fun was had as students," Umasi pointed out.

"If you're suggesting that we could go back to the way things were, or that things were better when we were students, you're wasting your breath," Zyid said quickly. "I, at least, have enjoyed freedom for too long, and seeing as how you are doing nothing else after all, I had hoped that you might consider joining me."

"I've had about two years, thus far, to consider that, Zyid," Umasi said wearily. "But if I ever change my mind, I will make it known."

"I don't doubt it," Zyid said, his voice suddenly softening. "Take care of yourself, Umasi."

"Oh, I will," Umasi assured him, warmth returning to his voice. "And don't get yourself killed out there."

"I don't intend to, just yet," Zyid said, sounding strained for the first time. "Farewell, Umasi. I don't foresee us meeting again for a while."

"Neither do I, Zen . . . or Zyid, rather," Umasi said. "But it was good to see you again."

"The same to you." Zyid turned and began to walk steadily away down the street. He never looked back, though his feet dragged along very slightly—the only sign of his regret.

Umasi, for his part, spent some time staring into the darkness that Zyid had vanished into, his cup of lemonade untouched in his hand, an unreadable expression on his face. After a few minutes had resolutely ticked by, Umasi shook his head and stood up.

"Well," he said to no one in particular, "there is work to be done."

You're kidding," Tack said, staring at the jar sitting in front of him.

"No, my friend, I'm quite serious," Umasi said, sounding oddly tired.

Tack had eagerly left school that day and had made a beeline for District 19, wondering all the way what sort of job Umasi would have for him. When he'd finally arrived, breathing heavily after his run, Tack had found that the job was nothing at all like anything he'd imagined. Umasi had set a jar upon the lemonade stand that seemed to be filled with some sort of gray powder. Umasi revealed, however, that the jar was actually filled with mixed salt and pepper. Tack's job, Umasi had said, would be to separate the salt and the pepper into two perfectly pure piles.

"But what's the point?" Tack demanded.

"Oh, I just need my salt and my pepper," Umasi said casually. "I think that your wages are more than reasonable."

Tack knew that there was no question about that. He was being paid an extravagant amount of money for such a menial task—for the same amount, Umasi could've buried his stand beneath salt and pepper. Still, the job seemed to define *tedious* for Tack, and he wasn't particularly eager to work at something that seemed to be utterly pointless.

"Couldn't you just—," Tack began.

"You do want the job, don't you?" Umasi interrupted.

Tack frowned. "Well, yeah, of course, but—"

"Then it would probably be best not to waste time asking questions," Umasi pointed out. "You'll need your energy: I have some exercises I'd like you to perform afterwards."

Tack shut his mouth, deciding that, on the whole, the amount he was being paid was worth not being able to ask questions. Without further ado, Tack sat down in his usual chair and unscrewed the jar lid. Across from him, Umasi nodded in approval, leaned all the way back in his chair, and actually seemed to drift into sleep. Tack sighed, and then emptied the jar out onto the table.

The job was worse that he'd imagined it would be—in his haste to finish it, Tack's fingers would slip and slide a grain of salt into pepper's pile, or a flake of pepper into salt's. Still, the task had a strange sort of appeal to it, the kind of basic pleasure that people get when confronted with a problem that they can overcome. It wasn't horrible work—just not the kind of thing anyone would ever bother doing without incentives. Tack tried to keep himself from going bored by humming to himself or imagining all the salt and pepper going up in flames. As Tack progressed, he occasionally glanced up at Umasi, who was still deeply asleep.

At long last, his eyes burning and his neck stiff from craning over, Tack finished sliding the salt and pepper into their appropriate piles.

"Hey, hey, Umasi!" he called loudly.

This produced immediate results, and Tack immediately decided that Umasi must've been in a very light sleep, or maybe was even faking, because the boy snapped back to full lucidity in an instant.

"Quite acceptable," Umasi said genially, leaning forward to inspect the separate piles. "Yes, this will do nicely, Tack."

Having satisfied himself with Tack's work, Umasi removed a bill from his pocket and handed it over to Tack, who accepted it gratefully.

"Now, before you leave," Umasi said, standing up and stretching, "there are a few things I'd like you to practice."

Tack paused, remembering that Umasi had mentioned something about exercises.

"Practice?"

"Yeah," Umasi said casually. "Physical exercises, you know. I prefer that my employees remain fit."

I think everyone knows why I've called this emergency meeting," the Mayor said, shutting his lighter wearily. "It's been confirmed that Chief Enforcer Waters has been killed by the Truancy. I don't know much more than that, and it's testing my patience. Someone explain to me how this happened."

"According to the Enforcer reports, he was with a patrol on a routine sweep through an abandoned district," one cabinet member said tentatively. "They found what they thought was just another uninhabited Truancy storage site. It turned out not to be as uninhabited as they thought."

"Great. Absolutely fantastic," the Mayor muttered sarcastically. "Announce to the public that he was killed in the line of duty, and don't bother getting any more specific than that.

Also, toss out that Bird Cold story that we've been saving for something like this."

"I'll draft the press release right away," another cabinet member declared, scribbling furiously on his clipboard.

"We have now gone through five Chief Enforcers since launching a full campaign against the Truancy just two years ago," the Mayor observed, his voice a blend of weariness and frustration. "I end up firing half of them for being too dull witted, and whenever we find someone halfway competent to take the job they end up getting killed. This needs to change. I'm open to suggestions."

The other men at the table looked nervously at each other, none of them willing to speak first. The Mayor was not a man that by nature gave the impression of being open to suggestion. The silence stretched on, until it was finally broken by one daring cabinet member.

"Sir," he said tentatively, "it's just a matter of personal security. If you can find someone fit for the job, simply assign him and other officials some bodyguards. For instance, we know that the Disciplinary Officers are being heavily targeted, and yet some of them still have virtually no personal security."

"I presume you speak of Mr. Caine, who occupied your seat before his assignment as a Disciplinary Officer." The Mayor flicked his lighter open. "Mr. Caine brought his position upon himself. As for Mr. Waters, he was apparently with a full Enforcer squad when he was killed—he was hardly unprotected."

"They ran into a whole nest of Truants," another man argued. "Reports indicate that there couldn't have been less than a dozen Truants there, and the Enforcers managed to kill four of them."

"Four of theirs for our Chief Enforcer is a bad trade, no matter how you spin it," the Mayor countered. "Mr. Waters shouldn't have been there in the first place. In fact, a new measure should be put in place—the Chief Enforcer is only to visit a scene if the area has already been deemed secure for a whole hour."

"It'll be law by tomorrow morning," one of the men promised, scribbling furiously on his notepad.

"Very good," the Mayor said. "We will also provide the new Chief Enforcer with a number of personal bodyguards. As for who that will be . . . we need someone creative, someone who can think like a Truant."

"How can we know what a candidate thinks like?" one man wondered aloud.

"Surely someone here must be able to make a recommendation," the Mayor said.

There was silence as the cabinet scratched their collective heads. It was broken by the wildest of suggestions.

"It sounds like we'd need a child, sir," a cabinet member said boldly.

There was a sudden silence as everyone in the room froze. The Mayor looked at the man in surprise.

"A child?" the Mayor mused.

"Yes, sir," the man said, now looking unsure if he had been wise to bring up the proposition. "Fight fire with fire and all that."

"A child . . . a prodigy . . . if we can control one . . . if we can use it . . ." The Mayor seemed lost in thought. "You are all briefed on the boy occupying District 19?" he asked suddenly.

A half-dozen heads all nodded around the conference table. The Mayor began to rub his chin in thought.

"It would be unwise to approach that boy himself for aid," the Mayor said, raising a hand to stop the men whose mouths had just opened in protest. "He has little reason to love us, and I do not wish to upset him. However, I know for a fact that he has made something of a hobby of teaching other talented kids in the past."

"So should we resume surveillance of District 19?" one of the men asked eagerly.

"No," the Mayor said firmly. "We don't want to provoke him, or he might decide to go over to the Truancy. Instead, I want you to pull up all the old surveillance files, find out who he used to see regularly, find out where they are now."

"That won't be easy," the man warned.

"I didn't say it would be," the Mayor countered, sounding heartened all the same.

"How do we know that recruiting one of his old friends won't anger the boy?" another man asked.

"I trust Umasi not to do anything drastic just because we approached one of his old acquaintances," the Mayor said, "for old times' sake, if nothing else."

The Mayor sounded so uncharacteristically sentimental that the cabinet members shot each other surprised glances.

"Well, now that that's settled, let us return to the subject of the Truancy," the Mayor said briskly. "The murder of our Chief Enforcer cannot go unpunished. It's time that we retaliate."

"Retaliate, sir?" A cabinet member spoke up cautiously. "But we don't know where they—"

"Yes, I know that," the Mayor snapped. "I don't mean attack the Truancy itself—let us instead hit them where they'll hurt. I've drafted a new proposition here that I want to become well-publicized law by tomorrow evening."

The Mayor pulled an official-looking document from an open briefcase at his feet. The entire cabinet eyed the paper apprehensively, and a few of them seemed to cringe as the Mayor slid it forward. One of the braver cabinet members reached for it and read the title out loud.

"The 'Zero Tolerance Policy,' " he read.

"Indeed," the Mayor said in satisfaction. "The Truants may have escaped our schools, but we still have hundreds of thousands of hostages—their friends. We can still harm their trapped peers. The Zero Tolerance Policy will provide for the interrogation and immediate expulsion of any student that commits any minor infraction. *Any* rule breaking, *any*thing that can be construed as a threat, will be severely punished."

"But sir, surely this is a bit extreme." One of the cabinet members spoke up bravely. "With your recent decree that all expelled students be executed . . . I mean, the students that stay in school are the ones that remain obedient! We should reward them, not punish them!"

"This will show the Truancy that we will not yield," the Mayor said. "Their morale will drop when they see what we can do to the friends that they are powerless to help. We need to assert our authority, prove that we are the ones in control."

The same cabinet member, seeming to forget the things that tended to happen to people who questioned the Mayor, opened his mouth to protest again. Another cabinet member, seeing the danger, suddenly headed him off.

"I think it's a great idea, sir," the man said quickly.

"Brilliant," another added.

"Show them who's boss, Mr. Mayor."

The Mayor shut his lighter as he stood up, turning towards his open window to look out at the City.

"Then it is unanimous. If we cannot punish the Truants, the students will just have to suffer in their place." The Mayor turned around, looking appraisingly at the men sitting at the table. "And I still want regular progress reports on finding a child from District 19. You are dismissed."

9

Zero Tolerance

"What the hell, it was just a joke!"

"I suppose you find killing funny then, eh, kid?"

Approaching the cluster of frightened students on his way to his next class, Tack soon discovered what the inexplicable commotion was all about. There was an adult arguing with a kid, and it was well-known that whenever an adult addressed a student outside of class, the student was usually in trouble. Curiosity getting the better of him, Tack joined the throng, shouldering his way past a smaller boy so that he could get a better view.

What he saw shocked him.

"I didn't do anything!" a dark-haired boy protested loudly as he was violently shoved against a wall by a security guard.

"You passed this note saying that you wished your teacher would die," a second security guard said, waving the paper aggressively as his partner grabbed the boy's arms and pulled them behind his back.

"That didn't mean anything!" the boy shouted as the second security guard slapped a pair of handcuffs onto his wrist. "This is a mistake!"

The sound of running footsteps echoed through the now-silent hallway, and Tack turned to see a half-dozen other guards racing to the scene.

"What happened here?" one of them demanded.

"Just enforcing the Zero Tolerance Policy," the first security guard explained, shoving the handcuffed boy onto the ground.

"What did he do?" The head guard pulled a notepad and pencil out from her pocket.

"Made a death threat against a teacher."

"I see." The guard quickly scribbled something down onto her notepad.

"That's a lie; I just made a joke!" the boy shouted from the floor.

"Is that so? Well, we'll see how funny you are after a few hours of interrogation."

"But he didn't do anything!" a girl protested suddenly, stepping forward. "He just passed me a note about classes. It was just stupid stuff; it wasn't serious!"

The security guards looked at each other decisively.

"So you were conversing with him about how his teachers should die, eh?" the head security guard demanded, bearing down on the girl.

"Well . . . yeah," the girl said, now looking uncomfortable.

"Sounds like conspiracy."

"Take her," the guard with the notepad ordered.

Ignoring the girl's shrieking protests, the other security guards cuffed her hands and shoved her onto the ground next to the boy.

"Now, was there anyone else here involved with this?" the head security guard demanded, glaring at the crowd of students, which immediately fell silent. Satisfied that there wasn't, the security guard turned back to her fellow guards.

"I don't think we should take any chances. Cuff their feet too; we'll bring out some stretchers to carry them out." She marched down the hall, the others in tow, leaving the two original guards to watch the prisoners.

"This is crazy!" the girl shrieked from the floor.

"You kids brought this upon yourself," one guard snapped, glaring at the pair of students restrained on the floor, then turning to address the crowd. "Things have changed. It looks like you haven't been informed about the Zero Tolerance Policy, so I'll warn you, just this once; if any of you are caught breaking any rules, making any threats, or showing any disrespect, you'll get the same that these two got."

"You can't do this; this can't be legal!" the restrained boy said angrily.

"Gag them too," the other guard suggested, kicking the boy in the belly, knocking the wind out of him.

Tack watched, horrified, as the guards produced a roll of duct tape and firmly taped over the two students' mouths. At this, the students thrashed so violently that it took both guards to hold each of them still so that their legs could be cuffed. By this time, the other guards had returned with stretchers. The guards lifted the struggling students onto them, and walked off, shooting threatening glances at the stunned students behind them.

As the students around him immediately burst into a flurry of note passing about the "Zero Tolerance Policy" and what it might mean, Tack stood still, his blood slowly reaching the boiling point. In all his time as a student, he had never witnessed anything so unjust, and it infuriated him. As he stood there, very nearly late for class, dangerous thoughts began to run through his mind, and he wondered for a moment if those thoughts might lead him to being handcuffed and dragged out of school.

The Educators were grasping for a new level of control, Tack realized. He wondered what that meant. Could the resistance that Umasi had told him about be gaining the upper hand?

I asked for a progress report on the search, not excuses," the Mayor said icily.

"Sir, before the observations were terminated, you ordered very specifically that the District 19 surveillances be discreet," one of the cabinet members protested. "It is unreasonable to expect—"

"It's not wise to tell me what to and what not to expect," the Mayor said, instantly silencing the speaker. "You want to warn me that I'm going to find whatever you've found to be less than satisfactory—duly noted. Now show me."

The six other men around the oval table quickly shuffled through their papers. One of them laid a number of fuzzy black-and-white photographs on the table while another quickly slid a thin folder containing several printed documents over to the glowering Mayor. The Mayor flipped through the folder, examining the photographs.

"Give me a summary," he ordered.

"Our cameras had caught a number of different potential

candidates on tape," one of the men said, pointing at each of the photographs in turn. "We've narrowed it down to three or four individuals that have visited the boy."

"Now, as you've probably noticed," another man spoke up tentatively, "the quality of the pictures is poor."

"Yes, I did notice," the Mayor said sardonically.

"We don't have a clear shot of any of their faces. We cannot even reliably determine gender. The best that we can do is distinguish between each of the individuals and the boy himself, though even in that there is some guesswork involved."

"So you're not certain about anything," the Mayor summarized coldly.

"No, sir, I'm not," the man admitted. "However, the folder I gave you contains written observations on a couple of individuals that we suspect came in contact with the boy. In every instance they outmaneuvered the Enforcers that encountered them, clearly displaying the types of characteristics we're interested in."

"How did you come by this information?" the Mayor inquired, looking over the papers with interest.

"I believe that you personally ordered in an Enforcer to spy on the district about two years ago," the man said cautiously. "It was just a matter of looking over the archives. The details should be somewhere in there."

"Ah yes, I remember that." The Mayor fingered his lighter idly. "He crawled back crippled, I believe. Shattered kneecaps, was it?"

"Yes, sir," the man confirmed, "all we ever got out of him was that a blond-haired male who appeared to be around fourteen or fifteen did it to him. It's the only physical description we have of any of the children that visited District 19, and it's a vague one, but it's all that we have to go on."

"No names?" the Mayor asked, still examining the photographs.

"None," the man confirmed.

"Well, it could have been worse, but it could have been a lot better," the Mayor muttered. The other men in the room were relieved to hear satisfaction in his voice. "I expect the matter to be given top priority. The sooner I have this blond-haired kid sitting in my office, the better. Now, on to other matters—let us proceed to the new report on Truant activity."

" 'We have been discovering an increasing number of abandoned areas that show signs of previous inhabitance.' " A new cabinet member spoke up, reading off a clipboard. "However, going against previous trends, the areas have been uniformly stripped of all supplies and anything useful. This seems to indicate that the Truants are beginning to consolidate into larger cells."

"So if we find one, we'll find the rest?" the Mayor asked.

"We think it unlikely." The man shook his head. "The Truants have always been exceedingly cautious, so we believe that the majority of them will still be divided into multiple cells—but at this point it is not unreasonable to believe that they are more tightly concentrated than before."

"They're planning something." The Mayor opened his lighter.

"The Enforcers suspect that, yes." The man nodded. "Not only have they begun to group up, but it also seems that all Truancy activity has ceased—there have been no attacks, no thefts, no assassinations, nothing so much as a misdemeanor."

"And do the Enforcers have any idea what they might be planning?" the Mayor demanded.

The man frowned. "No, sir."

"Typical." The Mayor clicked his lighter shut. "Well, if nothing else, I'm sure that our media coverage of the Zero Tolerance Policy will force their hand. Execute the first batch of expelled students today. We'll see what they're up to soon enough."

In one of the many abandoned districts of the City, there was a large, run-down office building. In better times, the building had been office space for a large company. Now, however, the desks had all long since been cleared out, the paint was peeling from the walls, and hardly any of the lights still worked—not that they would have been lit even if they could be, for the building was now a Truancy hideout, and lights shining in a supposedly abandoned district would be a bit of a giveaway.

The electricity and water in the building still worked fine, which was all that was needed to suit the Truancy's purposes. In one of the confined offices with boarded-up windows, a television had been plugged in. This particular television, one of several in the building, was reserved for special use—only two people were allowed into the office where it rested. That very evening, both of them stood there, their outlines silhouetted by the blaring television in the otherwise total darkness.

"The new Educator report released today shows an unprecedented and disturbing increase in classroom violence," the anchorwoman onscreen said. "To counter this trend, the

Mayor immediately signed into law a daring new set of countermeasures."

"We must identify the children in our schools that pose a threat to their peers, and we must do it before they strike," the Mayor declared from a podium in front of City Hall, his usual contingent of Enforcers almost obscuring him from view. "Only by dealing with these individuals harshly at the first sign of trouble can we ensure the continued safety of our children."

"Unbelievable," Zyid murmured as the figure next to him stirred uncomfortably. "He's going to kill them all."

"Along with the Mayor's announcement came a new warning to all students as a whole," the anchorwoman continued. "Students are cautioned not to joke in any way about performing any act of violence, nor are they to break any rules, as leniency will not be shown. Any student suspected of having any rebellious tendencies at all can be arrested, interrogated, and even expelled on the spot.

"The tough new policy went into effect this morning, and since then dozens of students have been detained, and dozens more are expected to be apprehended in the coming week. The Mayor's Office was quick to denounce any rumors of Enforcer brutality during interrogations as 'lies disseminated by the irresponsible families of these uncontrollably violent youths.' "

"I believe," Zyid said suddenly, "that I've seen enough. Unless you have any objections, Noni?"

"None, sir," the figure next to Zyid replied quietly.

Zyid reached for the television, shutting it off. The room was instantly plunged into total darkness, leaving the angry sound of Zyid's heavy breathing to fill the void.

"So," Zyid hissed. "He has decided to take this war to a new level of depravity. If he cannot get at me, he will instead destroy the ones I intended to save."

"They are not yet being destroyed, sir," Noni pointed out softly.

"It's only a matter of hours," Zyid said dismissively. "This slaughter is only the first step—he will have it escalate until he lures us out into the open."

"But of course you won't let that happen," Noni said passively.

"Indeed I won't," Zyid agreed briskly. "This may yet work to our advantage. The Mayor formulated this plot out of frustration and desperation—he evidently wasn't thinking clearly. There is an obvious flaw in this 'Zero Tolerance Policy.' "

"What's that, sir?" Noni asked emotionlessly.

"He's putting an unreasonable amount of pressure on the students," Zyid said in satisfaction. "It's too much, too quickly. He might've been able to get away with something like this if it were staggered in over time, but something this sudden will meet opposition. These are students that previously were complacent. The harder he pushes them, the more of them will decide to push back. Dropouts and runaways will increase, and when they drop and run, we will be waiting to catch them."

"You'll make this Zero Tolerance Policy the center of our recruiting effort," Noni observed softly.

"Essentially correct," Zyid affirmed. "Now, it looks like tonight will be busier than I anticipated. I must address the rest of the Truancy."

"They probably know already," Noni said. "They'll be watching the news too."

"They will need to know that there *will* be retaliation," Zyid said firmly, moving towards the door. "I promise you; very soon I will make the Mayor regret this move."

"I believe you, sir," Noni said quietly to Zyid's back as he opened the door and strode out of the office.

Yes, it is lamentable," Umasi said heavily, leaning back in his folding chair. "Justice is too often the first casualty of war."

"Why are they doing this?" Tack demanded, looking for an explanation for the madness from the only person who could give it to him. "Why don't they just kill us?"

At that, Umasi seemed to turn rigid, and Tack could sense that the boy was hiding something. He somehow looked sadder than Tack had ever seen him before.

"The Educators are getting frustrated," Umasi explained. "They are unable to retaliate against their true foes, so instead they lash out against the innocent students still under their control."

"But that makes no sense!" Tack raged. "What have we ever done to them?"

"You are not a perpetrator, Tack," Umasi said soothingly. "You are only a victim, as are all the students of this City. As for why, I can only guess that the Educators mean to strike an indirect blow to their enemy's morale."

"What's that mean?" Tack demanded, not in the mood to decipher Umasi's explanation.

Umasi looked at Tack carefully from behind his sunglasses. After a few uncomfortable seconds, Umasi began to speak. "The group in opposition to the Educators is known as the Truancy. The Educators believe that by making this move against the students, they will either cause the Truancy to despair or provoke them into rash action."

"Do you think it will work?" Tack asked, not fully appreciating the significance of what he'd been told.

"I doubt it," Umasi said thoughtfully. "The Truancy is competently led and organized. They will understand the Educators' intentions and very likely outmaneuver them."

"I wish them luck," Tack said with bitter sincerity.

Umasi cocked his head to one side. "You are, naturally, embittered by what has happened," Umasi said slowly. "But taking sides in this conflict will only lead you down a dangerous path."

"So what would you do?" Tack demanded.

"I would do nothing rash," Umasi said simply. "If you avoid doing things that might provoke the Educators, no matter what thoughts might run through your head, you will give them no reason to target you."

"So I should just roll myself out like a welcome mat, huh?" Tack asked, frustrated.

"No, you should roll yourself aside so that there will be no reason to tread on you," Umasi corrected gently. "Remember, Tack, the end of the school year is fast approaching. You will be studying for your final examinations very soon."

In the heat of all that was happening, Tack had forgotten about the end of the school year. Umasi was right—school *would* be ending in less than a month. Soon he wouldn't have to worry about the Educators, about homework, about his teachers or other students. Not for months, anyway.

"As you can obviously see," Umasi observed, "things are not quite as hopeless as you had begun to feel. There is always next year, of course, but that is still distant. Stand strong for just a little longer, and this school year will have passed into unpleasant memory."

"I guess I can do that," Tack conceded, his mind drifting off to plan his summer vacation.

"Excellent." Umasi beamed, pleased that he had succeeded in dousing Tack's anger. "Now, we've spent a long time on that discussion. Let's get our minds off of the . . . depressing news. I have some new work for you today."

"What's that?" Tack asked, snapping back to reality.

Over the past few days, Umasi always had the same work prepared for him. The jars of salt and pepper grew steadily bigger, but Tack was getting faster and more efficient at separating the salt and pepper to the point where it was almost easy. That left him with more time for the exercises that he was now actually finding interesting and rewarding.

The exercises were a mixed bag. Umasi had started at first with typical things like running through natural obstacle courses formed by the rubble of District 19, lifting heavy objects, and doing push-ups. As Tack grew more and more capable with those exercises, Umasi had begun teaching him some odd things like fighting hand to hand, and during breaks Tack threw darts at a board that Umasi placed on top of the lemonade stand. Tack found that it was all difficult to get a grasp of but somehow extremely rewarding when he did.

And that wasn't even really taking into consideration the generous payments Umasi gave him. Within a week Tack had amassed a small fortune . . . only to find that he was usually too busy to spend any of it.

"Your body builds muscle fairly quickly, and you're a quick learner when it comes to fighting," Umasi said, standing up and leading Tack over to a crude wooden target he'd set up in the middle of the road. "Your aim with the darts is likewise impressive. I think it's time that we moved you on up to throwing knives."

"Knives?" Tack repeated eagerly.

"That's right." Umasi nodded. "But first, as I alluded to before, I have a new type of jar for you to look at."

"What's in it?" Tack asked as Umasi placed a jar that seemed filled completely with white grains on the table.

"Sugar and salt," Umasi said, smiling slightly at the look on Tack's face as he said it.

"And I'm supposed to sort *those* out?" Tack asked, aghast.

"Yes," Umasi confirmed gravely. "Only afterwards will I teach you how to throw knives."

Tack frowned. Having come to know Umasi reasonably well, Tack concluded that the odd boy was not likely to elaborate, so he refrained from further questioning and instead turned his attention towards the jar.

He unscrewed the jar and poured the contents out onto the table. The salt and the sugar were so well mixed that he found it extremely difficult to tell them apart at all. However, the patience and attention to detail that had been instilled in him from his long experience with salt and pepper meant that Tack soon noted the small differences between them—the difference in size, how the light affected the different particles, the vaguest of color differences.

A few minutes later, Tack was industriously at work. His efforts, he knew, were far from perfect. On more than one occasion he knew for certain that he'd swept the wrong particles into the wrong pile, where they instantly became lost beyond recovery. The words *needle* and *haystack* immediately sprang to Tack's mind as he contemplated searching for a single grain of salt in his small mountain of sugar. But Tack was confident that his mistakes were small enough to pass unnoticed, and so he merely let them slide as he worked, and soon the salt and the sugar were sorted into two separate and neat piles, though Tack couldn't honestly vouch for their purity.

"Do you think that your performance is adequate?" Umasi asked as he shut his book and leaned forward.

"Fairly good, yeah," Tack said, hoping that it was true.

"People evaluate their work best only after they sample it," Umasi said gravely. "Which pile is sugar, Tack?"

Tack pointed at the pile that he was certain was mostly sugar, now feeling slightly discomfited by Umasi's ominous words. Without explanation, Umasi scooped up the pile of sugar into his hand and stood up.

"Please, wait here," Umasi said.

Tack sat in his chair obediently as Umasi turned and disappeared into the abandoned brownstone building behind him. When Umasi finally emerged, his left hand was empty and in his right hand he clutched a small glass of lemonade. Tack watched him approach in silence, and eyed him apprehensively as he sat down and placed the glass onto the table.

"This glass of lemonade," Umasi explained, "has been made from the pile of sugar that you presented me."

Tack cringed. He saw where this was going, and he didn't like it at all.

"If you did a good job," Umasi said, "consider it a refreshing reward. If, on the other hand, you did a bad job," Umasi continued, "consider improving next time. The lesson here is about consequences and responsibility. Learn it well."

Umasi pushed the glass across the table. Knowing what the gesture meant, and not feeling particularly up to protesting—it *was* fair, after all—Tack steeled himself and grabbed the glass. He brought it up to his mouth, tilted it back, and gulped it down as fast as he could.

The flavor wasn't as bad as he'd imagined it might be. Still, there was a definite trace of saltiness that did not go well at all with the sweet and sour flavor of lemonade.

"Well," Tack said, managing a small grin, "that wasn't so bad."

"Good," Umasi said in satisfaction, standing up and leading Tack over to a crude wooden target in the middle of the road. "And now it is time for the main event."

Tack could feel his excitement return as Umasi bent down to pick a knife out of a box he'd prepared. The idea of knife throwing felt somehow . . . *striking* to him.

"There are two ways to approach knife throwing," Umasi explained. "The first way is just for sport, and involves sending the knife spinning through the air. The problem with this is that in order to hit anything, you have to be either lucky or able to calculate the exact number of rotations the knife will make so that the blade and not the handle hits the target. This is best done under controlled conditions and can only be achieved with painstaking practice."

Tack nodded at that. "So what's the other way?"

"The other way is much more effective for actual combat." Umasi demonstrated, holding up a knife. "You hold it differently, like this, and you weigh the knife carefully before throwing it like a spear or dart."

Umasi abruptly spun around and flicked his arm forward. The knife shot through the air and buried itself cleanly in the head of the wooden dummy.

"The blade travels straight, and does not revolve. There's

no fancy nonsense with this method, but that doesn't mean that it doesn't take care and practice to master." Umasi handed Tack a knife by its hilt. "Here, you try."

Tack did so enthusiastically, having forgotten completely about the Zero Tolerance Policy.

But Umasi *hadn't,* and though Tack never saw his face as he receded into the shadows to watch, it was lined with untold worry and sorrow even as Tack's was plastered with a grin.

10

FINAL EXAMS

As the dreaded final exams approached, the students of the City tried not to think about the tests and the now thoroughly feared Zero Tolerance Policy. Instead, they looked hopefully towards the light at the end of the scholarly tunnel—that brief summer break during which the Educators planned the next year's curriculum, leaving them, at least for the moment, free.

As a result, exam fever had not quite caught on among the students, though it certainly held a tight grip on the teachers, who in turn worked the students harder than ever.

Which was why Tack had found it necessary to treat Suzie.

"Thanks for the ice cream, Tack," Suzie said, a smile plastered on her face as she accepted the proffered cone.

"It's no problem," Tack assured her. "Vanilla is your favorite flavor, right?"

"Yep," Suzie confirmed, licking her cone so voraciously that melted ice cream coated her nose and mouth.

"You should probably wash your face before we get back to school," Tack told Suzie.

"Yeah, maybe," Suzie replied, sounding utterly unconcerned as she took a crunching bite out of the cone.

Having already left the pizza parlor where Tack had piled both of their slices high with toppings, they had come across an ice-cream truck, which had strategically placed itself near the school in order to take advantage of the sweet-toothed students in the increasingly warm weather. This prompted Tack to idly suspect that the only reason that students were still allowed outdoors for lunch was to help contribute to the City economy.

"Hey, Tack," Suzie said suddenly, "how come you can afford this all of a sudden? I thought Mom and Dad cut off your allowance."

Tack willed his face to remain impassive, though inwardly the question instantly ignited a firestorm of doubt. The truth of the matter was, after all, very odd, so odd that he was sure that Suzie wouldn't believe him.

So what *should* he tell Suzie? Tack made a split-second decision.

"I got an after-school job," Tack said evasively.

"Doing what?" Suzie asked in mid-lick.

"Sorting out some stuff," Tack said. "It's pretty mundane."

"Oh, so that's where you disappear to all the time now?" Suzie asked, her ice cream momentarily forgotten.

"Yeah, that's right," Tack said, quickening his pace, hoping to make it back to school before Suzie asked one too many questions.

"So what do you sort out?" Suzie pressed.

Tack scowled. Suzie was just too sharp for convenience.

"Papers and stuff," Tack said quickly, hoping to change the subject. "So how's school for you lately?"

Tack cheered internally as Suzie made a sour face—the dangerous topic had been derailed, at least for now.

"It's not been very good," Suzie said, sounding like she had bitter medicine in her mouth instead of sweet vanilla ice cream.

"How so?" Tack asked, glad to have the opportunity to press Suzie about her scholarly woes, instead of the other way around.

"Well," Suzie began as they reached the school doors and leaned against the side of the building, neither of them willing to go inside until they'd finished their ice cream, "see, we had this big English paper due the other day."

"Uh-huh," Tack said, nodding sympathetically. In all the classes, big papers were actually more common than the small ones.

"And you know Melissa?" Suzie continued, looking up at Tack.

"I've never met her, but you told me about her," Tack said, remembering that Melissa was Suzie's best friend.

"Yeah, well, we both have the same teacher for English, Mr. Grant," Suzie said, taking another bite of her cone. "But Melissa and I are in different classes, and she hadn't done her essay by the night before it was due. And she's one of Mr. Grant's favorite students, she told me."

"Oh," Tack said sagely, seeing where the story was going.

"So I let her copy mine," Suzie said, "and so she turned in the same thing, word-for-word."

"You didn't get caught, did you?" Tack asked immediately,

suddenly worried that Suzie would be persecuted under the Zero Tolerance Policy.

"Nah." Suzie shook her head. "What makes me mad is that Mr. Grant gave me a lower grade than Melissa."

"You're kidding," Tack said, knowing full well that she wasn't.

"No, I'm not! She turned in the same paper as me, the one that I wrote, and she got a better grade!"

"What grades did you get?" Tack demanded.

"She got a ninety-five, I got an eighty-seven," Suzie said glumly.

"Well, eight-seven isn't bad," Tack pointed out thoughtfully.

"Yeah, but Mel shouldn't have gotten higher than me!" Suzie countered angrily. "How can the teachers just play favorites like that?"

Tack looked at Suzie sympathetically. He could understand her anger, but that didn't make him like it. He felt a sudden surge of hatred towards the Mr. Grant that he had never met, the one that had made his once-happy sister turn so bitter.

"Tack, are you all right?" Suzie asked suddenly, looking up at him worriedly.

Tack quickly made his face impassive, realizing too late that he'd let a look of unreasonable fury overtake him.

"Well, school isn't pleasant for anyone," Tack pointed out truthfully. "Don't let it bother you too much. And it wasn't Melissa's fault either," Tack added. "She didn't know that he'd give her a better grade than you."

"I guess you're right," Suzie said dejectedly.

Tack put his arm around her and tried to think of something comforting to say. Before he could, the shrill noise of the dreaded bell sounded. Looking at each other in panic, Tack and Suzie seized their backpacks and ran for the front doors, fear of the Zero Tolerance Policy heavy in their minds.

"This is a surprise, Noni. I've never known you to oppose any of my decisions," Zyid said dryly.

"I think only of your safety, sir," Noni replied quietly, standing motionless in front of Zyid's desk.

Zyid let out an exasperated sigh as he leaned back in the comfortable leather chair that had been left behind when its former occupant cleared out of the office. Zyid recognized that Noni was his most fiercely loyal subordinate—though really sometimes *too* fiercely loyal for his preference.

"I doubt very much that there will be much danger involved," Zyid said. "Or at least, there shouldn't be, provided that what you told me is true. You are confident about your observations, correct?"

"Yes, sir," Noni admitted reluctantly.

"Then I will take your word and trust that what you've told me about this Disciplinary Officer is right," Zyid said. "If his personal security is indeed lighter than the others', I will not miss the opportunity to retaliate for this Zero Tolerance nonsense."

"But sir . . ." Noni took a deep breath, as if preparing to cross a dangerous threshold. "Your life is more valuable than any of ours. Let me do it."

"It's not up to you to appoint such values, Noni," Zyid said, his voice suddenly so sharp that Noni cringed. "In any case, you will not be idle. I will make sure that the incident is loud and messy—in the meantime, while the Enforcers are busy looking for the person who killed their dear Disciplinary Officer, I want you to personally drop in on the two hangouts and make sure that the preparations are on schedule. I want them to be ready within three days."

Noni remained silent.

"Do you have confidence in my abilities?" Zyid asked suddenly.

"Of course I do, sir," Noni said quickly.

"Do you have confidence in my judgment?" Zyid demanded.

"Yes, sir," Noni replied.

"And do you trust me, Noni?" Zyid asked.

"With my life," Noni said without hesitation.

"Then I would have thought that you'd have no problem with my choosing to do this myself," Zyid pointed out.

Noni had no answer to that, nor did Zyid seem to expect one.

"Ideally," Zyid continued, "there would be another one of you or me to handle all that needs doing, but since there is not, I cannot supervise the entire Truancy all the time. Now, remind me, which Disciplinary Officer will be unlucky tomorrow?"

"Mr. Caine, sir," Noni said, "of the District 20 School. He has an inspection scheduled for tomorrow."

"Ah yes, District 20." Zyid frowned, muttering under his breath, "Closer to him than I would . . . actually it's practically on his doorstep . . . but nothing can be done about that. . . . I'm sure he will not interfere—"

"Sir," Noni interrupted Zyid's musings, "it might be a trap. The lack of security might be to bait you."

"Don't think I haven't considered that possibility, Noni." Zyid snorted derisively. "I'll be prudent, and anyway, the Educators are historically clumsy at setting up traps. I assure you, even if they anticipate my coming, the only one who will die tomorrow will be Mr. Caine."

"Your word is final, sir," Noni conceded.

"Thank you for the vote of confidence, Noni," Zyid said. "Now, tell me everything you've observed of this Mr. Caine."

Tack had found himself extremely busy not only with schoolwork but also with Umasi's training, which had intensified during those hectic weeks. To his great surprise, however, Tack found that the exercises and strange techniques actually helped him to relieve pre-exam stress, as did talking with the boy Tack had grown to respect as his mentor. Tack looked less favorably upon the new salt and sugar "jobs," but he had become efficient enough with them that he was now completely willing to drink any lemonade made out of his sugar piles, not to mention that he was being paid well for it. Besides, Umasi made it clear that it was also part of his training.

And all that training came to a head two weeks before final exams at school.

"So," Umasi said, looking evenly at Tack, who was busy tossing knives at a target that had been set up in the road. "The school year will be concluding soon."

"Yeah," Tack confirmed as he hurled the last knife into the bull's-eye with all the others. "Final exams are in two weeks."

"Your ordeal is almost over," Umasi observed.

"There's always next year though," Tack pointed out as he moved over to a crude punching bag made out of stuffed burlap sacks and began beating it.

"And the year after that," Umasi agreed as Tack frowned.

"Not much to look forward to then, huh?" Tack said, grunting slightly.

"Perhaps," Umasi allowed, "but fortune has a habit of surprising us all."

"I'm worried for my sister too," Tack confessed suddenly. "I think she's been . . . changed by school."

"So have you, Tack," Umasi pointed out. "Every student in this City is."

"Yeah," Tack grunted, deciding that he'd chosen a bad subject that needed to be changed. "So Umasi, are you ever going to tell me why you're really teaching me all this stuff?"

Tack asked the question casually, not for a second expecting to get an answer. To Tack's great surprise, however, Umasi was completely forthcoming this time.

"The main reason is that I want you to be prepared. The City is not a safe place these days, and I believe that it's only going to grow more dangerous in the coming months." Umasi shifted restlessly in his seat. "Another reason is that I do not like feeling inactive myself. You might say that I'm taking action through you."

"I see." Tack digested the answer as he started on his situps. "So how long are we gonna do this?"

"Actually, Tack," Umasi said, stretching his back, "I intend to give you your final exam now, before the Educators give you theirs."

Tack sat up and stared at Umasi.

"You're joking."

"No, I'm not," Umasi said cheerfully.

"Then what's the test going to be?" Tack asked eagerly.

"It's a two-part test. For the first part, I have yet another jar for you to sort out," Umasi explained as Tack grimaced.

"And what's the second part?" Tack asked.

"We are going to have a duel," Umasi said succinctly, standing up and stretching his back. "I can tell you're looking forward to that. But first things come first."

Tack looked disappointedly down at the table as Umasi pushed the jar forward and then casually began reading what looked like the previous day's issue of *The City Times.* After a few minutes of sifting through the mess, Tack frowned. He'd assumed it would be another salt and sugar mixture, but the entire thing looked like salt to him, and he couldn't find a single different grain. Tack looked questioningly up at Umasi, who was still intently reading his newspaper and paying no attention to Tack.

Tack bent so close to the grains that they slid out of focus. He prodded and shifted them with his finger, examined a dozen different ones individually, and did everything short of actually tasting the grains that looked for all the world like salt. Tack frowned in puzzlement, and then came to a decision. Looking up at Umasi again, he cleared his throat loudly.

"Yes, Tack?" Umasi inquired, putting his newspaper down.

"It's all salt, isn't it?" Tack said, grinning now.

"Very good, Tack." Umasi nodded in approval. "It took you less than five minutes to determine that it was a trick. Had you realized it from the beginning, however, you would have saved yourself those five minutes."

Tack frowned slightly. "Well, I just wanted to be cautious."

"That is commendable," Umasi conceded. "But were you able to see the lesson here?"

Tack scratched his head, something he wasn't in the habit of doing. "Go with your first instincts?"

"No, Tack." Umasi shook his head. "That would be a *bad* lesson. What you learned here today is not to let routines lure you into security—if a pattern you have come to accept for a long time is broken, you will be caught unprepared."

Tack pondered that and realized that Umasi was right.

"Well, I passed, didn't I?" Tack questioned Umasi.

"Indeed you did," Umasi affirmed. "And I know that you can't wait for part two. I won't keep you in suspense—follow me."

Tack followed Umasi numbly as he walked around the street corner and into a secluded alley that was empty save for a rusty old Dumpster. Tack couldn't help but be slightly apprehensive as they went—after all, having witnessed what Umasi was able to do in a fight when he put his mind to it, who wouldn't be? Still, the exercises had Tack feeling confident about himself, and he was pretty sure that Umasi didn't intend to cause him any permanent damage.

"We will be fighting with wooden swords," Umasi explained, gesturing towards a plastic bucket that held two polished wooden imitations of real swords. "At least until one or the both of us become unarmed."

"Sounds good," Tack said offhandedly, picking up the wooden sword and swinging it through the air lightly, getting the feel of its weight. Umasi had taught him a few tricks with the sword, and he was feeling pretty confident.

"As this is your final test," Umasi said, stretching his limbs, "I am afraid that you cannot expect me to hold back."

Tack stopped swinging his sword around and looked at Umasi strangely. Frankly, he didn't think he'd stand a chance if Umasi went all out, though he couldn't imagine Umasi killing him and wasting all of the time spent training him.

"I have a question," Tack said suddenly, his sword hanging limp.

"Ask it." Umasi took his own wooden sword out from the bucket.

"Is there anyone else in the City like you?" Tack asked.

"If you mean in knowledge and fighting talent, there *were* perhaps five others that I knew of who could compete with me," Umasi replied without hesitation. "As far as I know, only four remain, perhaps fewer by now. Unless you become the fifth, that is."

"That many?" Tack asked, surprised.

"Yes," Umasi said, his voice suddenly flatter than usual. "Three of them were former friends of mine. About two years ago, I worked with them one by one in a manner similar to how I am working with you now."

"What happened to them?" Tack asked apprehensively.

"One died, one left me, and the last one . . . ," Umasi began, looking up at the sky wistfully. "Well, the last one betrayed me. He attempted to kill me, though I'm pleased to report that he failed."

"I'm sorry," Tack said automatically.

"It's not a problem." Umasi waved his hand dismissively. "I expect that, someday, you might go your own way as well. People with strong wills will always seek to express individuality. This, above all else, irks the Educators."

Tack nodded. Who knew what his future might bring? He was lately enjoying a greater sense of possibility than he'd ever known before.

"But that's only three," Tack realized suddenly.

"Hm?" Umasi inquired distractedly as he ran his hand over his sword.

"You said there were five in the City like you," Tack pressed. "You only mentioned your three friends."

"Ah yes." Umasi frowned. "The last two would be Zyid, the leader of the Truancy, and Noni—the only one, as far as I know, that he ever taught."

"Do you know them?" Tack asked eagerly.

"We are acquainted," Umasi said simply. "I will leave it at that."

Tack nodded again, and then realized something.

"I have one last question."

"Very well." Umasi raised an eyebrow above his glasses.

"If all of your other friends failed you in one way or another," Tack began carefully, "then why do you trust me?"

"I'm usually not a bad judge of character," Umasi allowed. "And, as I mentioned when we first met, you reminded me of someone I used to know."

"One of your old friends?" Tack pressed.

"Yes." Umasi nodded.

"Which one?" Tack couldn't help but ask.

Umasi looked at Tack unflinchingly. "The one who died."

Tack suppressed a shudder and nodded, this time in acceptance. He was lucky, really, to have received as many answers as he had.

"If your thirst for information has been quenched," Umasi said, swinging his sword lightly, "then we should begin. Are you ready, Tack?"

"Yeah," Tack confirmed, raising his own wooden blade.

"Then before we start, I believe I should warn you," Umasi said, propping his sword up casually and leaning against it, "improvement only comes after suffering. I will drive you hard. It may be that I will beat you within an inch of your life."

"Yeah, all right," Tack said warily, though he still found it hard to imagine Umasi doing any such thing.

"You have talent, and I have given you technique," Umasi said, slinging his sword over his shoulder, behind his neck. "But when your life is threatened, will you have the nerve?"

Tack narrowed his eyes. It was a question that, he knew, would be answered here and now.

Umasi took a step forward, regarded Tack carefully from behind his sunglasses . . . and then lunged forward without warning, bringing his sword around in a powerful arc aimed at Tack's neck. Barely able to react in time, Tack swung his own sword up and to the left, parrying Umasi's blow. Not giving Tack any time to recover, Umasi slashed at Tack's legs. Tack jumped, avoiding the attack, and then seized his opportunity, jabbing his sword forward. Umasi sidestepped the attack neatly, then swung his weapon back again, landing a blow behind Tack's right ankle.

"Ouch!" Tack yelped, staggering backwards.

"You don't want to hit me," Umasi observed.

"What're you talking about?" Tack demanded. "I'm trying as hard as I can to hit you!"

"As hard as you can?" Umasi shook his head. "No. You do not wish to truly cause me harm, which is why you will fail to do so."

Umasi lunged forward again, swinging his sword towards Tack's middle. Tack stepped backwards, narrowly avoiding the attack, then frowned and swung his own sword up, aiming to cut a diagonal across Umasi's chest. Umasi brought his own sword down with terrible force, slamming Tack's wooden blade all the way to the ground. Taking advantage of the deadlock, Umasi shifted half his body forward and drove his knee up into Tack's gut.

"I will beat you hard, and then harder," Umasi said as Tack gasped in pain and doubled over. "You will learn to fight back out of necessity, if nothing else."

Umasi swung his sword at Tack's head. Tack blocked the attack feebly and tried to straighten up. Umasi knocked his sword out of the way with brute force and then proceeded to bring his weapon crashing down upon Tack's shoulder.

"You don't want to hurt others," Umasi said as Tack cursed and clutched his bruised shoulder. "There are people in this City that do not share your reluctance. If you stand against them, they will hurt you, and then they will kill you if you do not stop them."

Umasi parried another feeble blow from Tack, and then ruthlessly kicked his feet from under him.

"You cannot count on mercy—yours, Tack, or theirs!" Umasi shouted now, as he lifted his sword above his head and swung it down towards Tack, who lay groaning on the ground.

Tack's eyes snapped open, and he swung his sword up to block the oncoming attack. Rolling aside, Tack leaped to his feet and lifted his sword, breathing hard.

"You have spirit," Umasi observed, nodding in approval. "But you are not yet in control of your fear, Tack."

"I am *not* afraid." Tack glared at his mentor.

"Oh, but you are," Umasi insisted, raising his sword lazily. "You're afraid of being hit, and even worse, you're even afraid of hitting me."

Tack froze. Umasi was right, after all. Tack certainly didn't want to be hit, and he found it hard to seriously attack someone he regarded as a friend . . . though Umasi obviously held no such sentiments, Tack observed bitterly.

"When your enemy attacks—" Umasi spun, bringing his sword into a 360-degree arc aimed at Tack's left hip.

"—you must *know* that you will not be hit." Tack parried the blow and brought his sword down towards Umasi's outstretched arms.

"When you attack—," Umasi said, withdrawing his arms hastily as Tack's sword cut through the air they'd occupied a moment ago,

"—you must *know* that you will hit your target." Umasi rolled to the side, bringing his sword up to crash into Tack's belly, knocking the wind out of him.

"There is no room for fear," Umasi declared, slamming his elbow into Tack's face before he could recover, causing him to fall to the ground.

". . . or doubt . . . ," Umasi continued, bringing his foot down on Tack's right hand, which jerked and reluctantly released the sword it had been holding.

". . . or restraint!" Umasi concluded as he tossed his own sword away and placed a foot on Tack's heaving chest.

"And you can never give up, Tack," Umasi said quietly as Tack tried to catch his breath. "To give up in this City would be to throw your own life away. Life is one of the most precious things that exist in this world, and so even the rats, when backed into a corner, will fight to keep theirs."

"And what about your opponents and their lives?" Tack managed to ask, a trickle of blood running down his chin.

"There is time for mercy after they are defeated," Umasi explained quietly, increasing the pressure on Tack's chest, causing him to gasp painfully. "Do not seek to take life, Tack. Only seek to preserve it."

Tack's eyes flashed as Umasi pressed down on his chest even harder. Suddenly, he let out a roar and grasped Umasi's leg with both hands, throwing Umasi off-balance. Leaping to his feet, he snapped his wrist into Umasi's face, and then moved to deliver a punch to his waist. Umasi, more prepared now, twisted his body 180 degrees and grasped Tack's arm as it flew by. Using the arm as leverage, Umasi moved with practiced skill and hurled Tack over his head, throwing him onto his back, wedged between a brick wall and a rusted old Dumpster.

"Better," Umasi said in satisfaction as Tack nimbly returned to his feet. "You are backed into your corner."

Umasi turned his arms so that the palms of his fists faced upwards, and then drew them back under his shoulders. Assuming a defensive stance, he nodded slightly at Tack.

"I know that I will not let you land a blow," Umasi declared.

"And *I* know that I will hit you," Tack said, fierce determination shining in his eyes.

"One of us," Umasi reasoned, "will be proven wrong."

"Yes," Tack agreed, clenching his fists, "you will."

Tack lunged, pivoting on his left leg to snap a kick at Umasi's chest with his right. Umasi moved his right arm in a circle that brushed the attack aside. Not discouraged, Tack aimed a punch at Umasi's head, which was similarly brushed aside.

"Falling into a pattern invites defeat," Umasi warned as Tack moved as if to kick him again.

Seized by sudden inspiration, Tack stopped halfway

through his kicking motion and launched himself into a dive, caught the weight of his fall with his outstretched palms, and performed a somersault. Coming to a rest beside the wooden sword that Umasi had cast aside, Tack seized the sword, turned towards a surprised Umasi, and then hurled the weapon through the air the way he'd been taught.

The sword-turned-projectile caught Umasi right in the center of the chest. The sword fell to the ground and Umasi gasped, as much in surprise as in pain. As Tack smirked at him, Umasi grabbed his chest, stared at it for a moment, and then looked up at Tack.

"Well," Umasi said, a slow smile spreading across his face, "it looks like you pass the test in its entirety, Tack."

Tack grinned back, unsure of what to say.

"I've never been so glad to be proven wrong," Umasi said, walking over to Tack and clapping a hand on his shoulder. "I daresay we'll need to clean up some of your wounds before you return home."

"Yeah," Tack agreed, the adrenaline slowly leaving his body. "Just one thing . . ."

"Yes?" Umasi asked, raising an eyebrow.

"I'm thirsty," Tack declared.

"Well." Umasi laughed. "That can be easily remedied."

Together Umasi and Tack dusted themselves off and made their way back to the lemonade stand. Though Tack's body hurt in a dozen different places, he realized that he had never felt better. For that one afternoon, he felt invincible—ready to take the whole City. Tack had discovered that, as usual, Umasi was right:

Improvement only *did* come after suffering.

11

Death

Tack made his way towards the cafeteria. It was lunchtime, and though he wasn't feeling particularly hungry, he was hoping to meet Suzie there. She had made up with Melissa shortly after the incident with the copied paper, and Tack had been seeing less and less of Suzie. This worried him, in a nonspecific brotherly fashion.

Tack paused outside the large cafeteria doors as he heard a familiar voice echo through the otherwise silent hallway.

"Very well, the cafeteria seems to be in order. The food is no good by adult standards, of course, but the place is reasonably sanitary, and that's all that really matters."

"Thank you, Mr. Caine; we do pride ourselves on cleanliness in this school."

Recognition struck Tack like a punch in the face—it was the Disciplinary Officer that he had seen expel a student, standing again with the principal. Since it was nearing the end of the year, Tack immediately understood that the Disciplinary Officer must be performing his routine inspection.

"I expect you would like to sit through some of the classes?" the principal suggested.

"Naturally." Mr. Caine nodded, lifting a clipboard hastily to read something. "First, however, I'd like to look around the hallways a bit. We've had some trouble with students here under the Zero Tolerance Policy, I understand."

The principal frowned. "Well, yes, there were a few miscreants, but given the hundreds of well-behaved students that still remain, I'm sure that you understand that they were a small minority."

Tack and all the other students milling around knew that the principal was lying through her teeth. While cowed by the rumors of terrible punishments, most of the students at the District 20 School were now anything but well behaved. There was a restless anger simmering in the school, and in the past week alone, two dozen stink bombs had been set off in various classrooms and hallways, posters and notices taped to the walls had been torn down, and so many intentional messes had been made in the cafeteria that Tack was sure the janitors must have had to work overtime in order to make it clean enough to earn Mr. Caine's approval.

"And what's your name, young man?" Mr. Caine asked suddenly, causing Tack to jump. The Disciplinary Officer was looking right at him. "Don't worry about the rules for now; you may speak."

"Er, I'm Tack," Tack said nervously.

"Do you like it here at this school?" Mr. Caine asked.

"Oh, erm, yeah, it's pretty good," Tack lied.

"And what do you think of your teachers, in general?" Mr. Caine asked, twirling a pencil with his fingers.

"They're uh . . . good; they're good," Tack said lamely.

"I see." Mr. Caine sounded skeptical as he straightened up and turned away.

While Mr. Caine's back was turned, the principal shot Tack an angry glance, clearly displeased that he hadn't sounded more enthusiastic. Mr. Caine didn't notice, however, as he was busy scribbling something down on his notepad as he approached another student. Tack noticed a distinct increase in angry mutterings around him. Suddenly, as Mr. Caine marched over to interview another student, a high-pitched shriek issued forth from the crowd.

"How do you like *this* for Zero Tolerance?"

A second later, something shiny sailed through the air and landed near Mr. Caine's feet. Tack caught a glimpse of what looked like a tinfoil wrapper, just before it inflated and burst with a loud snapping noise. A foul odor spread swiftly throughout the corridor, prompting many students, Tack among them, to lift their shirts up to cover their noses. Mr. Caine stood frozen, which struck Tack as ominous, but the principal was now coughing in fury and looking wildly around at the students present.

"*Who did this?*" she shrieked.

Mr. Caine, however, had calmly surveyed the crowd with narrowed eyes. He suddenly stepped forward, shoving two boys aside to glare down at a girl with dark hair and a defiant expression upon her face.

"What's your name?" Mr. Caine demanded.

"Melissa," the girl said defiantly, looking up at Mr. Caine without fear.

"The stink bomb came from where you are standing," Mr. Caine said softly. "And your voice sounds like the one that shouted before it was thrown."

"Yeah, so?" Melissa said, still standing defiant. "You can't prove it was me."

"Expel her, Mr. Caine!" the principal said angrily. "We have no tolerance for this kind of—"

"Quiet," Mr. Caine ordered. "Now, Melissa, you are obviously a clever girl. You're right. I can't prove anything. Your mistake, however, is that I don't *need* to prove anything to expel a student."

Melissa seemed to deflate at this, breaking eye contact with Mr. Caine. Mr. Caine had the look of a predator that had cornered its prey. But before he could strike, someone called out from the back of the growing crowd.

"It wasn't her, Mr. Caine," the girl called. "It was me."

There were gasps of astonishment and an increased muttering as the students craned their neck to look at who had spoken. Tack couldn't get a glimpse from where he was standing. He thought that there was something very familiar about the voice, but before he put a face to it, Mr. Caine darted through the crowd. As Melissa stood there, seemingly struck dumb by her sudden rescue, a leaden weight of dread suddenly dropped into Tack's stomach. Melissa was the name of Suzie's best friend . . . no, it couldn't be. She wouldn't do something like this.

Tack shoved his way through the crowd after Mr. Caine. He saw Mr. Caine enter the stairwell, pulling a girl behind him by the scruff of her neck. *Suzie*. What the hell was she thinking?

Without bothering to wonder what *he* was thinking, Tack broke into a run and sprinted down the corridor. He slammed the stairwell doors open, and raced down the stairs after Mr. Caine and Suzie. All the while, Tack's mind was racing. Suzie, expelled? He wouldn't allow it; he couldn't allow it.

Remembering what Umasi had told him about the expelled students, about the hopeless fate that awaited them, Tack kicked the ground floor doors open and ran out into the foyer, just in time to see Mr. Caine and Suzie vanish through the school doors. Tack ground his teeth as he remembered what Umasi had said about doing nothing rash—but no matter what anyone said, he wouldn't roll himself aside so that Mr. Caine could step on Suzie.

Outside in the bright sunlight, Tack was blinded for a moment. Then he saw that the street outside the school was empty except for a few unoccupied cars and two lone figures at the end of the street. Tack ran after them, and suddenly saw Suzie turn to look at him. Mr. Caine stopped next to a black, unremarkable car.

"Suzie!" Tack shouted.

"Tack!" Suzie called back as Mr. Caine opened the passenger door and unceremoniously shoved Suzie inside.

"No!" Tack cried, still half a block away from the car.

Mr. Caine opened the driver's side door, slipped inside, and slammed it shut as Tack let out another shout.

Then, suddenly, a dark figure lunged from behind a parked car and hurled what looked like a fiery bottle inside the car that Mr. Caine and Suzie had just entered. Tack's mouth opened involuntarily as his eyes tracked the progress of the bottle, and in one fleeting moment he noticed that some kind of thick, sticky-looking paste had been smeared all along the other side of Mr. Caine's car, particularly near the fuel tank. Tack wanted to let out a warning, to somehow rush forward fifty feet and catch the bottle, to do *something* to stop what he knew was about to happen . . . but he couldn't. The bottle crashed against the side of the car, and then burst into flame.

Tack was overcome by a surreal sensation, watching as the flames leaped heavenward. In seconds, an angry fireball consumed the entire car. Mr. Caine had been expelled from the car by the blast, and now lay motionless on the sidewalk. But Suzie . . . where was Suzie?

Tack dashed forward, never once considering any danger. He plunged through the plume of smoke billowing from the car and to the passenger door, which he wrenched open with his bare hands, ignoring the burning-hot metal. His heart jolted up into his throat as Tack knelt down, and the dread that had already filled him multiplied a dozen times as his fears were confirmed. There in the backseat of the car, her body charred, lay Suzie. The world seemed to stop as he gently pulled Suzie's horribly unrecognizable body from the car and cradled her in his arms.

As if he were someone else entirely, witnessing the scene from far away as a spectator, Tack reached out mechanically to brush a blackened strand of hair out of Suzie's face. Hugging Suzie tightly Tack let out a great shuddering gasp and took a deep breath, heedless of the smoke and fumes flowing into his lungs. As tears began to run down his face, Tack could feel Suzie's body grow steadily cold in his arms, and he was suddenly seized by an urge to look at something, anything, else.

Hearing something move, Tack looked up. Standing above him was a boy who looked to be about Tack's age. Through the smoke, Tack saw that the boy's long black hair had been tied into a ponytail that flailed wildly in the fierce wind, the same wind that now blew smoke all around them. The boy wasn't wearing the gray uniform of students, but was clothed all in black—jeans, a leather belt, a long-sleeve shirt, a windbreaker buttoned around his neck so that it splayed behind him like a cape. The boy's left hand was clenched, and in his right he held a gun.

But what Tack noticed above all was the boy's face, faintly sallow complexion darkened by soot, expressionless, lacking compassion, fear, or regret. Tack searched desperately for any emotion, but could find none. For a moment, the two boys stood staring at each other, one the killer of the other's sister, and in that moment Tack somehow found the strength to speak just one word.

"Why?" he asked, his voice cracked and pleading.

The boy that had so calmly killed Suzie looked back at Tack evenly, his face not so much as twitching a muscle.

"She was collateral damage," the boy said coldly. "Nothing more."

And with that, the boy spun around and walked away, his windbreaker fluttering behind him. Tack watched him go, stunned by what he had seen and what he had heard. Then, as he looked down at his dead sister again, reality came crashing back down on him, and without knowing what he was doing, an unearthly shriek ripped from his chest.

A new impulse seized control of his brain. *Run,* it told him. *Run.* He didn't want to see others find Suzie like this, he realized; he didn't want to be there when they found her. He didn't want them to see him; he would've vanished off the face of the earth if he could. Tack stood up, and Suzie's body fell from him. He looked at his clothing, now thoroughly stained with Suzie's blood. He tore off the bloodied gray jacket of his school uniform and cast it aside.

Leaping to his feet, Tack ran. He ran so fast that the whole world seemed to be a blur to him. He didn't know where he was running or for how long. The aches and pains in his legs seemed distant to him, and the whole experience was so surreal that for a moment, Tack felt as though he were running through a dream.

And then it was over. Tack came to a stop, his head spinning, his legs burning, and his lungs screaming for relief. Without so much as looking around to see where he was, Tack collapsed onto the ground.

So, Noni, did you complete your task?" Zyid asked, shooting a glance at the assassin.

He removed his windbreaker and tossed it onto his desk. He'd arrived back at the Truancy hideout to find Noni there already waiting for him, which he took as a sign of his being behind schedule. He had been delayed a couple hours, as he had taken several detours, including one into a crowded mall arcade, to assure that he wouldn't be followed on his return. However, in retrospect the assassination had been so easy that he was probably being overly cautious.

"Yes, sir," Noni confirmed quietly. "And you?"

"I was successful, yes." Zyid gave a slight nod. "There were some complications, however."

"Complications?" Noni asked.

"It's nothing to be worried about," Zyid said dismissively. "A girl happened to get caught in the blast that ended Mr. Caine's life. Apparently the late Disciplinary Officer was in the process of expelling her when I got him."

"Civilian casualty," Noni said softly.

"Yes." Zyid nodded. "Also, a male acquaintance of hers apparently saw me do it."

"Someone saw you?" Noni asked hesitantly. "Shouldn't you have killed him, sir? He might go to the Educators as a witness."

"No, Noni." Zyid shook his head. "I draw the line between us and the Educators at the harming of students . . . whenever possible, at least. Sometimes it can't be helped or foreseen, as with the death of the girl, but otherwise I avoid it if I can. The boy probably won't be able to tell the Educators anything useful, at any rate—there was so much smoke that I could hardly see him myself."

"Yes, sir," Noni said.

"What time is it?" Zyid asked suddenly.

"Almost five thirty by my watch, sir," Noni replied dutifully.

"Time—there's never enough of it in this City." Zyid scowled. "Enough about my performance. Tell me how the hideouts are faring."

Tack awoke in the dark with a bad taste in his mouth, and he spent his first few moments of semiconsciousness spitting the foul taste out. As he grew more lucid, he moved to get to his feet, but felt a sudden pain stab through his legs. Tack tried again, and this time managed to stand, though the pain still lingered. Rubbing his legs, Tack wondered why they were hurting so badly. As a particularly sharp jolt of pain shot through his sinews, Tack suddenly remembered something about running. Running . . . yes, Tack realized, he had been running a lot. Running from what, though?

Then the memories came rushing back, and the next thing he knew, Tack was back on his knees with tears running down his face. Knowing that Suzie was dead was like being punched in the stomach, except the feeling persisted until Tack felt short of breath. Suzie wouldn't want him to be like this, Tack knew, but no matter how hard he struggled not to think about her, not to think about how she would never laugh again, never tease him again, he only managed to dredge up more memories, each plunging a sharper knife of emotion than the last into his chest.

Desperate to concentrate on something else, Tack forced himself to his feet again and looked around. He was standing on a rickety wooden pier overlooking the West River, the wide, unforgiving body of water that isolated the City on one side. Glancing around at a battered-looking warehouse with broken windows standing near some adjacent piers, Tack realized that the area had been abandoned. It was nighttime now, and the street lamps along the edge of the water were still lit, and in the distance Tack could see the busy, twinkling lights of the inhabited City.

Here, as far from the place he'd run from as he could have wished, Tack knew he should have felt better, should have felt freer, and yet as he looked out at the placid, black waters of the river, calmly mirroring the lights of the City, Tack only felt worse as he realized that there was no true escape. The City was just a cage, and no matter how hard people fought over it, in the end they were all still trapped inside it. The enormous breadth of the river seemed to gaze back at him gloatingly, wallowing in its perpetual victory.

"Let me out!" Tack suddenly screamed at the river, which made no response but to stir about in mocking calmness.

Tack seized a chunk of wood broken off from the pier and hurled it at the river, desperately wishing to cause the vast, dark entity some harm. The wood landed on the water with a splash, bobbed beneath it for a moment, and then rose to the surface, where it floated along the current of the river. Tack glared at the wood like it had betrayed him.

"Fine, go along with the stupid river!" Tack shrieked maniacally. "Maybe I will too! Then I'll be dead, dead like her!"

Tack clenched his fists and felt a wholly new level of rage bubbling in his gut. The kids were fighting the adults over control of the City and didn't care how many people they killed while they did it. Collateral damage, and nothing more? Tack stared angrily into the darkness of the river, which in turn seemed to stare deeper back into him. He remembered how the boy had turned his back on Suzie's dead body, and he felt his sorrow melt away into sweet, addictive anger. *Let the river do the mourning,* Tack thought. He wouldn't let sadness tear him apart; he would hate Suzie's killers instead. As Tack leaned against the rickety wooden railing along the side of the pier, he remembered the name. The Truancy, Umasi had called them. It was they that had killed his sister.

Tack had always been sympathetic to the Truancy, no matter what Umasi said, no matter what he had cautioned. Only now that the Truancy had ended one that he cherished did Tack truly appreciate the value of life. Suzie was dead, and her killer, who had so easily written her off as collateral damage, now walked free. The bubbling rage in Tack's gut spilled over, and he began to yell. Tack channeled all the emotion built up in his chest, and he yelled, screaming vague threats and promises into the night for what seemed like hours. No one was around to hear him except the dispassionate river, which swallowed his cries and made no response.

Finally, his energy all spent, Tack stumbled off towards the adjacent piers, but he didn't get far before sheer exhaustion forced him to simply lie down and give in to unconsciousness. He slept deeply, for as he lay there on the docks, he was as motionless as his poor sister, who would never sleep again. Meanwhile, the river continued flowing steadily, pitilessly, and the chunk of wood floating on its surface drifted slowly out of sight.

PART II

MISCREANT

12

REBIRTH

"Man, Zyid seriously wants us gone by tomorrow; why are we still messing around out here?"

"I'm supposed to check out the docks, remember?"

"Gabe, dude, come on; we're out here risking our necks just to look at some wrecked piers?"

"Stop acting like it's so bad; just look around. There's probably plenty of useful stuff lying about. And that warehouse over there, we can store the spare explosives in it."

"If you say so, Gabe, but let me tell ya—checking it up close is just gonna be a bigger waste of time."

"Zyid doesn't think it's a waste of time."

"Well, how hard does the guy want us to look? Should we crawl over every inch with a microscope? Hey, why not? That's a good idea. Let's start with this rusted nail I almost stepped on; I bet it'll be real useful!"

"I'm not in the mood, Steve."

"You're the one that dragged me out of bed, Gabe."

"I'd do it myself, but it's not safe to go around alone. Look what happened to Frank."

"Right, but seriously, Gabriel, there can't be any Enforcers for miles."

"You were the one talking about risking our necks."

"Cut me some slack, man; that was a joke."

"You're the joke."

"That was just uncalled-for. Look, here's an old tire, really useful, don't you think?"

"You know, if you actually tried being helpful instead of trying to prove your point, we could probably fill half an arsenal in ten minutes."

"Fill it with what, dirty river water? I'm telling you, man, there's nothing use—oh crap."

"What? What is it?"

"Look, over there!"

"Where? I can't see what you're pointing at."

"By the other pier, on the ground near the railing!"

"Son of a . . . think he's still alive?"

"Only one way to find out, Gabe."

Tack awoke to find something pointy jabbing him in the ribs. Still too weary to do anything about it, Tack squeezed his eyelids shut and turned on his side, hoping that the jabbing would stop.

"Hey, hey, Gabe, he just moved!" an excited voice exclaimed.

"Looks like he's alive after all. Poke him harder," someone said.

Tack felt another jab to his ribs, this one sharper and more painful than the others. Groaning, he turned over, one hand instinctively reaching to rub the bruised spot. None of this was helping him get back to sleep.

"Yep, definitely alive," the first voice declared.

"Lemme 'lone," Tack mumbled.

"He can talk too," a second voice observed.

"Yeah, looks like he was just taking one hell of a nap," the first voice said. "What should we do with him, Gabe?"

"It's a little late for recruiting, but he looks like our type. Wake him up, give him the introduction, and drag him off to the hideout," the second voice replied. "He can decide where to go after that."

"Should I poke him again?" the first voice asked eagerly.

"No, I've got a better idea. Give me your water bottle."

The next thing Tack knew, something very cold was splashing all over his face. His eyes snapped open as he sat up, sputtering. Light poured into his eyes, and he blinked as trickles of water ran down his face. Only then did Tack become fully aware that he wasn't alone.

"The stick would've worked just as good, Gabe."

Two unfamiliar faces loomed over him. One belonged to a dark-skinned boy with a cleanly shaven head who was looking Tack up and down curiously. The other belonged to a pale boy with freckles and dirty blond hair parted down the middle. In his right hand, Tack noticed with a frown, he clutched a long, thin piece of wood.

Noticing what Tack was looking at, the boy hastily dropped the stick, which looked to Tack as if it had been broken off from the pier upon which he was sitting. Completely unabashed, the boy offered his hand, which Tack accepted cautiously.

"Hey, I'm Steve; how're you doing?" the boy asked. "This is Gabriel, my boss." Steve pointed at the boy standing next to him.

"Don't call me 'boss,' Steve." Gabriel scowled.

"Gabe is very modest," Steve said cheerfully. "He's a real natural leader type. Pulls us peons out of bed like he's been doing it since he was born."

"I'm Tack—," Tack started to say, then realized that it might not be such a good idea to give his real name, especially if these two strangers were who he was beginning to suspect they were. "Takan," he corrected quickly.

Gabriel raised an eyebrow.

"Well . . . Takan . . . it's nice to meet you," Gabriel said politely.

Tack looked over the two boys and noticed what looked unmistakably like pistols sticking out of both Gabriel's and Steve's pockets. That was all the confirmation that Tack needed to know that they were Truants, though he had the sense not to voice his conclusions.

"So, what're you guys doing out here?" Tack asked, keeping his voice casual.

"We were actually about to ask you the same thing," Gabriel said.

"Actually, I was going to ask what happened to your shirt." Steve smirked.

Tack remembered that he was bare chested, having torn his jacket off the previous day when . . . he flushed in sudden fury as a memory of fire, of blood, of murderous eyes and a soulless face, flashed through his mind.

Coming to his senses, Tack quickly willed himself to remain calm. He couldn't afford to lose his cool, not in front of these two particular strangers who were now looking at him with surprise. Tack quickly decided on a lie that would satisfy Gabriel and Steve.

"I was expelled and I ran away. I was trying to sleep here," Tack said.

Gabriel and Steve glanced at each other.

"What'd you get expelled for?" Steve asked interestedly.

"I set off a stink bomb during a Disciplinary Officer inspection," Tack lied.

Gabriel whistled softly.

"Nice, what made you do that?" Steve asked, sounding impressed.

Tack got to his feet gingerly, rubbing his ribs. "You know, Zero Tolerance Policy and all that. I got fed up."

"Yeah." Gabriel nodded sagely. "I hear that a lot these days."

"So, what about you two?" Tack asked, though he was sure he knew the answer already. "You got expelled too?"

"Yeah, I sprayed a few teachers with deodorant. They needed it," Steve said lightly. "But Gabriel was a good boy; he just ran off by himself a couple years back."

"So why are you out here?" Tack asked, this time genuinely curious.

"That's what I want to know." Steve shot a sideways glance at Gabriel.

"We're here to scout out the piers," Gabriel said. "We're waging a little war against the Educators, you see."

"More than a little, if Zyid gets his way," Steve added.

Tack willed himself to be calm, though his heart was now racing. So his first suspicions were right—these were members of the Truancy. Just like the one that had killed Suzie, the one that had turned his back on her body even as it grew cold in Tack's arms. Tack clenched his fists, then, with immense effort, relaxed.

"A war?" Tack asked, feigning surprise. "What do you mean?"

"You know all those Educators and Enforcers that keep going missing?" Steve asked. "News reports make a little of 'em every once in a while?"

Tack nodded gravely, remembering Mr. Caine's body burning on the sidewalk.

"And all those explosions and blackouts that no one can explain properly?" Gabriel added. "That's us too."

"Just you two?" Tack asked calmly, knowing full well that it wasn't.

"Nope." Steve grinned. "There are hundreds of us. We're called the Truancy."

Tack was torn. One part of him felt like he could do Suzie some justice by killing these two Truants right where they stood. He knew that he had a decent chance of succeeding; he had learned quite a bit from Umasi.

But on the other hand, Tack couldn't bring himself to be angry at these particular two boys. There was no soullessness etched on their faces, no murderous intensity in their eyes, none of the monstrousness that Suzie's killer possessed.

But if they aren't to blame, Tack thought, *maybe they can lead me to the guy that is.*

"Can I join your Truancy?" Tack asked suddenly, prompting Gabriel and Steve to look at each other in surprise.

"Uh, well, I suppose we—," Gabriel began, blinking rapidly.

"We could always use more help, Takan," Steve finished affably.

For one confused moment, Tack had forgotten about the false name he'd introduced himself with, but he quickly recovered before either Steven or Gabriel could notice.

"So, do you guys have a house or something?" Tack asked quickly.

"Well, it's not quite a house, per se." Steve grinned.

"But it's good enough," Gabriel said, shooting a glance at Tack. "We can take you there right now."

"Sure, why not," Tack said, his heart racing.

"Come on then; follow us," Gabriel said, turning around.

"Try to keep up!" Steve said cheerfully.

Tack followed a few feet behind Steve and Gabriel as they led the way, giving him some time to think. As they turned from the docks to walk down a street strewn with crumbled masonry, Tack noticed that his fists were clenched, and he quickly opened them, looking down to see that his nails had dug into his palms hard enough to draw blood. Tack was fixed upon only one thought: Suzie's killer. He had a feeling that he was being led to the Truancy hideout, and that was as good a place as any to begin his search.

So, what do you think?" Gabriel muttered to Steve.

"Seems like our kind of guy," Steve replied as he picked his way through the spilled contents of an overturned trash can. "He looks pretty fit too. I wish I looked that good."

"Did you see that look on his face when you asked him about his shirt?" Gabriel whispered, glancing back at Tack, who was now examining his hand gloomily as he walked straight through the trash.

"Maybe the shirt killed his family or something." Steve

yawned, stepping off the street and onto the sidewalk to avoid the remains of a wrecked truck.

"And those stains on his arms and pants?" Gabriel continued, his voice heavy with suspicion. "They looked like blood to me."

"Maybe he cut himself somewhere," Steve suggested. "What, you think the guy's a murderer?"

"I think that there're some big, bad secrets that he's keeping," Gabriel said darkly.

"Well, not all Truants have glorious pasts," Steve said, causing Gabriel to smile grudgingly.

"I don't think any of them do, actually," Gabriel agreed, kicking an empty garbage can out of his way. "All right, you sold me. There's no time to put him through training, but we'll give him a chance to learn through experience."

"Yeah, might as well," Steve said. "I can't remember anyone who was that enthusiastic about joining up so quickly."

"Right," Gabriel said, turning around. "Hey, Takan, hurry up!"

"Gonna go straight to the hideout then?" Steve asked, jumping over a cardboard box.

"That's right," Gabriel confirmed.

"Great, no place like home." Steve grinned. "And since you dragged me out of bed early, I'm going straight back in as soon as we get there, and I'm not waking up until tomorrow."

"Lazy bastard." Gabriel scowled.

The hideout that Gabriel and Steve led Tack to was a large, abandoned apartment complex deep inside the district that was also home to the piers—District 13, Gabriel had told Tack on the way. The building was filled with cramped, cookie-cutter apartments that had been inhabited by the poorer citizens of the City before the district was abandoned. The boys walked under the tattered green awning and right in through the cracked glass front doors. The Truancy had kept the simple, dimly lit foyer relatively clean, though Steve told Tack that the elevators had broken down long ago, and that there was no hope of fixing them. He pointed Tack towards a stairwell instead, the door to which had been propped open by what looked like a stack of old textbooks.

"If you like privacy when you get around to sleeping, most of the apartments on floors six and up should be empty. The water still runs too, if you want to take a shower," Steve said pointedly as he handed Tack a copy of the master key to the building. "Dining apartment is on the third floor, if you're hungry. General supplies are on the second floor. Ask whoever's around there for a shirt; they'll give you one. The bar's also there. That's where most of us hang around when we don't have anything to do."

"The bar?" Tack asked, surprised.

"Yeah." Steve shuffled his feet uncomfortably. "Zyid's against it. 'You can't fight with a hangover!' he says. The other day Noni came to check and told us that we're supposed to get rid of the stuff by tomorrow."

Tack frowned. The names that Steve had used, Zyid and Noni, were familiar, though for the moment he couldn't remember where he'd heard them before.

"Who are Noni and Zyid?" Tack asked.

"Oh, that's right; you're new," Steve said as if reminding himself. "Well, Zyid, he's our leader; he started the whole thing. Toughest, smartest guy I've ever seen. But he's not the kind of guy you can get close to, you know what I mean? Dangerous kid; I'm glad he's on our side."

Then it all clicked for Tack. Umasi had mentioned them, on that day that they had dueled. *Zyid, the leader of the Truancy, and Noni—the only one, as far as I know, that he ever taught.*

"And Noni?" Tack asked, waiting for confirmation.

"Ah, Noni." Steve grinned suddenly. "Never met a girl like her. Hot, you know; she doesn't take any nonsense. Cold-blooded killer, she is, assassinates people left and right. Really loyal to Zyid though, but I don't think there's anything going on between them. She's like his assistant, or something."

"I see." Tack frowned. *Cold-blooded killer* seemed to describe Suzie's murderer perfectly, though Tack was positive that the culprit had been male, ponytail notwithstanding.

"Well, if that's all you need to know, I'm gonna go catch some sleep." Steve yawned to punctuate his point. "Gabriel is in charge of this hideout; he dragged me out of bed at six to search the piers; pain in the ass, and we didn't find anything but you. Say, where did Gabe go anyway?"

Tack looked around the foyer. It was completely empty.

Steve let out a sigh. "Well, seeing how he snuck off, I will too." He nodded at Tack as he turned to walk up the stairs. "Looks like you could use some sleep also—try and get some; there's big things planned tomorrow."

Tack nodded vaguely, not bothering to ask what the big things were. As soon as the echoing sounds of Steve's footsteps faded, Tack lunged up the stairwell to the second floor. He had no intention of getting any sleep just yet. Steve had said that all the Truants in the building hung out at the bar when they weren't busy, so if there was anywhere to start looking for Suzie's killer, it would be there.

On the second floor, Tack found a dull hallway with white walls and gray carpeting. A door halfway down the hall was open, and there were sounds of laughter and loud conversation issuing forth from it. Assuming it was the bar, Tack walked towards it. Just as he reached it, the door opposite swung open, and Tack turned to see Gabriel closing the door behind him. The word *SUPPLIES* had been crudely written across the door in bold black marker.

"Here, I found you a shirt," Gabriel said, tossing Tack a plain, spotless gray T-shirt. "You still seem to have the pants from your school uniform, so you should stick with those for now. All the supplies have been packed up for tomorrow; I had to go through some sealed boxes to get the shirt, and it's new, so don't lose it."

"I won't," Tack promised as Gabriel gave him a nod.

Tack slipped the shirt on quickly, then followed Gabriel into the bar. He stopped and sniffed the air, which smelled distinctly of tobacco smoke. Tack looked around. The room wasn't very big. In one corner a stack of what looked like wooden bookshelves had been lined up, with stools in front of it, to form a sort of bar. Behind it, a chubby boy sat upon stacks of boxes filled with bottles of what looked to be cheap beer. A refrigerator hummed behind him. The forgettable tan wallpaper was peeling off in places, but the room was crowded with kids of various ages standing around in clusters or sitting at the bar.

"Charles!" Gabriel snapped suddenly, over to a redheaded kid sitting against a wall with a cigarette in his mouth. "You're smoking again."

"Sorry, Gabe," the redhead said, looking up guiltily. "I can't help it; it calms my nerves, you know?"

"You're addicted," Gabriel said harshly, grabbing the cigarette out of Charles' mouth and crushing it beneath his feet.

"If Zyid finds out that you've been wasting Truancy money on cigarettes . . ."

"Don't tell him!" Charles begged, his eyes widening. "Please, Gabe, I'll stop, I swear; just don't tell Zyid!"

"Right." Gabriel stared down at Charles, looking deeply skeptical. "You're not getting any more allowance. Eat in the dining apartment from now on."

"You got it," Charles said sadly.

"And you know what, I think I'm going to go check your room, to make sure you're not hiding anything," Gabriel said, turning to leave the bar. "Again."

As soon as Gabriel left, Charles looked around frantically, and, spotting Tack, seized hold of the new kid and pulled him close.

"Quick, take these!" Charles hissed, reaching into his pocket and pulling out a pack of cigarettes and a lighter. "Gabe's gonna search me after he finds what's in my room, and if he finds these on me, I'm toast! Toast, man!"

And with that, Charles pressed the items into Tack's hands, leaped up, and scampered out of the bar. This left a confused Tack clutching a half-full pack of cigarettes and a lighter in his hand, the rest of the room's occupants looking at him with interest. Not knowing what else to do, Tack quickly slipped the pack into his pocket. As he did the same with the lighter, he was suddenly reminded of fire, of hungry flames. . . .

Tack shook his head furiously to shake the thought off, but now grimly remembered why he was there. As casually as he could, Tack examined the face and hair of every boy in the bar, but none of them stood out like he knew that the killer's would. Just as Tack was about to give up, the chubby boy behind the bar called out, “Hey, you! New kid!”

Tack turned towards the bar in surprise. “Me?”

“Yeah,” the boy called. “I haven’t seen you around here before.”

“Uh, I just got here,” Tack explained, approaching the bar.

“Oh, lucky you,” the bartender said. “You came just in time—tomorrow would’ve been too late! Has Gabriel told you about that yet?”

“He mentioned something about tomorrow but didn’t say what it was.”

“Well, then forget I mentioned it,” the bartender said hastily. “But since you’re new, why don’t you help yourself? Everything here is on the house—we need to get rid of it anyway.”

“No, I don’t think—,” Tack began.

“Come on; it looks like you’ve had a hard time,” the bartender interrupted, squinting at Tack. “Relax a bit; it’ll do you some good.”

Tack hesitated, and in that brief moment of weakness, the failure of his search brought back to him memories of Suzie, of warm blood and a cold body. . . .

“Give me a beer,” Tack ordered abruptly, shaking his head.

The bartender smiled, his fat cheeks bulging. He reached into the refrigerator and drew out a glass bottle filled with a gold liquid. Tack twisted open the cap with his new shirt, took a deep breath, and then downed a large gulp of beer. A moment later he was coughing violently—the alcohol left a sort of burning sensation in his throat that he wasn’t used to, and the beer itself tasted rather bitter. Still, Tack determinedly gathered himself together and a minute later had finished the entire bottle.

"More," Tack requested quickly, and the bartender hastened to oblige.

Halfway through his second bottle, Tack started shaking. He felt a tear running down his cheek, which he quickly wiped away on his sleeve. Realizing with a bit of panic that more tears were imminent, Tack suddenly remembered what the redheaded kid, Charles, had said. *It calms my nerves, you know?*

Desperate to wash away the painful stains from his mind, Tack removed the cigarette pack and lighter from his pockets and took one of the white cylinders, and inserted it into his mouth.

"Those aren't good for you, you know," the bartender said, looking worriedly at Tack. "You don't want Gabriel to see you with that if you got it from Charles."

"Shut up," Tack said harshly, his voice raspy as he blinked back tears.

Tack clumsily got the lighter to ignite, and quickly lit his cigarette. As he took a puff from it, his lungs were filled with a foul smoke that he quickly coughed out violently. Tack ignored the initial awfulness of the cigarette and quickly took five more quick puffs. Finishing up the rest of his beer in the hopes of washing away the bad taste in his mouth and throat, Tack suddenly felt a burning sensation in his face, followed shortly by a horrible throbbing, dizzying sensation in his head. Realizing vaguely that he'd just drunk more alcohol than he ever had in his life, on an empty stomach no less, Tack stumbled over to a corner of the room and collapsed onto the hard floor.

Tack heard concerned mutterings from all around him

now, which didn't help his headache at all. In the brief moments that followed, feeling like he'd been poisoned, Tack heard only one distinct sentence, spoken close by his head, and he thought he recognized the voice of the bartender.

"Man, he's a lightweight for sure."

And then he passed out.

13

A Show of Force

Tack awoke feeling worse than he ever remembered feeling in his entire life. The taste permeating his mouth and throat was so foul that he tried desperately to cough it out, only to find that his throat was too dry, causing him to spasm horribly. Involuntary tears streamed from his shut eyes as he rolled onto one side and gasped desperately for air. All the while, a horrible, intense headache unlike any he'd ever had before raged inside his head. It was like a sledgehammer was driving a blunt nail into his brain each time his heart beat.

Then he heard a voice.

"You've got a hangover, Takan; drink this."

Tack felt a plastic cup being raised to his lips, and bizarrely half-expected it to contain lemonade, but when he drank he recognized the taste of orange juice.

"You'll have to take these painkillers too; just swallow them," the voice commanded.

Tack felt two pills being forced into his mouth, and he

quickly downed them with another gulp of orange juice. Feeling slightly better, Tack gulped down the rest of the juice and opened his eyes blearily to see Gabriel crouched over him with a carton of orange juice clutched in his right hand.

"Are you good?" Gabriel asked.

"Yeah . . . yeah, I'm okay," Tack lied, shutting his eyes.

"Zyid is right. We need to get rid of that stuff," Gabriel muttered. "Listen, Takan. You weren't told yesterday, but we're clearing out the entire hideout today. We're meeting up with Zyid and then heading to the main hideout."

Tack knew that what he was hearing was important somehow, but the relentless pounding in his head wasn't allowing him to properly grasp what it was. He let out a groan.

"It's around five in the morning right now," Gabriel said. "We're set to leave at noon. You have about six hours to rest; that should be more than enough to get you back on your feet. We can't wait for anyone, Takan, so be ready by then."

"Okay," Tack mumbled, opening his eyes a crack.

"Here, take these." Gabriel shoved a jelly doughnut into each of Tack's hands. "You'll need to eat to keep your strength. And I'm leaving the orange juice here; one less thing to carry anyway, even if you don't drink it."

Tack nodded gratefully, then shut his eyes again. As the sound of Gabriel's footsteps died away, Tack lay on the floor breathing steadily, waiting for his headache to come under control. As soon as he was able to, Tack began to consider what Gabriel had said. Everyone was meeting up at the main hideout—where else would Tack have a better chance of finding the murderer if not at the Truancy's main base?

Briefly Tack's mind strayed back to his old life. What were his parents, the ones he felt no affection for, thinking now?

And his teachers, the ones that he had hated so much? And Umasi, the boy that he'd respected and learned so much from?

Then Tack remembered the bloody school jacket he had cast off at the scene of the explosion—*his* bloody jacket. Those people probably all thought him dead by now. There was no question of going back; there was nothing for him to go back to. Only one thing remained to drive his life forward—his determination to get revenge. Tack would work with the Truancy; he would walk among them until he found the boy that had killed his sister. Tack would find him, and then he would kill him.

Tack absentmindedly brought a jelly doughnut to his mouth and bit into it, enjoying the squishy pastry and the taste of gooey raspberry that spread throughout his mouth. It was funny, Tack thought suddenly, that the small pleasures of life still remained, no matter what kind of tragedies life inflicted.

Have the scout reports been confirmed?" Zyid asked as he paced about the rooftop upon which he and Noni stood.

"Yes, sir," Noni replied quietly.

"So, the Educators really are having helicopters patrol all the abandoned districts," Zyid mused. "Massively expensive for them, I don't doubt, and unfortunate for us."

"Sir, the first hideout will leave at noon," Noni pointed out. "That will be in twenty-three minutes. There is a good chance that the aerial patrols will see them."

"Yes, I know," Zyid said curtly. "There will be no rescheduling. We can turn this to our advantage; all we have to do is massacre the Enforcers. Helicopters will complicate matters, but they are hardly invincible."

"Yes, sir," Noni replied unquestioningly.

"Gabriel will have to be informed," Zyid muttered, drawing a cell phone from his pocket. "Alex's group leaves at midnight, so he will have more time to breathe."

Zyid quickly dialed a number.

"Gabriel? There's been a change of plans. Educators are flying helicopters over all abandoned districts. I want you to proceed directly to the ambush point."

There was a pause as Zyid listened intently to a reply. "I *want* you to be spotted," Zyid answered. "Don't worry about ground pursuit; if they want to see a show of force, I won't disappoint them." Another brief pause. "If the helicopter itself gives chase, you have my explicit permission to use the rockets."

Zyid inclined his head slightly as he listened to the response. "Leave at the scheduled time," he ordered, "unless you hear helicopters overhead. If you do, you may leave early at your discretion; we will be ready for you. Good luck."

Zyid jabbed a button on the cell phone, folded it shut, and turned to face Noni, who hadn't moved an inch the whole time.

"We have an appointment to keep," Zyid said imperiously. "Gather up the team; we're heading to the ambush."

"Yes, sir," Noni said obediently, bowing her head.

By eleven thirty, Tack had consumed the rest of his breakfast, gotten to his feet, stretched a bit, and decided that he was finally ready to face the day. Remembering what Gabriel had told him about leaving at noon, Tack left the bar to find the second floor hallway completely deserted. The door to the supply room opposite the bar was ajar, and Tack could see that the room had been emptied.

Tack didn't have a watch, but he recognized that all the

signs pointed to his being late. He dashed down the steps to the foyer, where dozens and dozens of Truants were bustling all over the cramped area like ants, moving cardboard boxes and wooden crates out the cracked front doors. Tack noticed that some of the Truants were standing grimly in a corner near a pile of what looked like the contents of an arsenal, picking through various guns and strange-looking white knives. Everyone was working in silence, which struck Tack as ominous.

In one corner of the room, Tack saw Gabriel standing with a group of Truants including Steve, deep in low conversation. Tack made his way towards Gabriel, and had almost reached him when the melodious sound of a cell phone echoed throughout the room. Almost reflexively, dozens of heads turned towards the source of the sound, which seemed to be inside Gabriel's pocket. Gabriel himself froze, and then quickly removed the phone from his pocket.

"Yeah, it's me; go ahead, Zyid," Gabriel said apprehensively. "Helicopters? What if they spot us and send ground support?" There was a sudden and total silence as Gabriel listened to the reply, nodding slightly as he did, which Tack took to be a good sign.

"And the helicopter?" Gabriel asked. Whatever reply Gabriel got seemed to please him; Tack noticed that his face had visibly relaxed. "So when should we leave? . . . All right." A moment later, Gabriel shut off the phone and closed it. "We'll need it," he muttered to himself as he slipped the cell phone back into his pocket.

"Well," Gabriel said loudly, addressing the gathered Truants, "as you probably overheard, the Educators are having helicopters fly over all the abandoned districts, and the chances are they'll pass over here soon."

The worried muttering that Tack had noticed when Gabriel had been on the phone quickly returned. Tack, for his part, found that he wasn't bothered by the news at all; the idea of death no longer seemed of terrible concern to him.

"Our orders," Gabriel said, "are to attract attention and lure any Enforcers into an ambush that Zyid has set. We leave in ten minutes, possibly less, so we need to hurry."

There was a brief pause, during which the Truants, some of them standing still as they clutched boxes and crates, looked at each other uncertainly.

"You heard him; get going!" Steve snarled.

The Truants returned to work with doubled vigor, shouting frantic instructions to one another. Stacks of crates and labeled boxes began to vanish out the door at a furious pace. Unsure of what to do, Tack stood there helplessly for a moment until Gabriel made his way towards him clutching a heavy-looking wooden crate.

"I see you're finally up, Takan! Take this outside." Gabriel shoved the crate into Tack's arms. "Charles!" Gabriel shouted as he seized another box. "You better not have that thing in your mouth when we meet up with Zyid!"

Tack turned around halfway to the door and saw the embarrassed-looking redhead quickly remove a cigarette from his mouth and throw it aside.

Soon Tack was swept out of the building by a flow of Truants, and once outside he couldn't help but gape in amazement. Overnight, the street had been filled with all sorts of vehicles that formed one long convoy that stretched down the entire block. There were old, rusted cars that might've been salvaged from the dump, shiny new trucks that looked fresh from the dealership, a couple of SUVs that Tack guessed had been taken without permission, a few white nondescript vans, and even an Enforcer patrol car.

The trunks and back doors of all the cars were wide open, and Truants were swarming all over the street, cramming the crates and boxes into the various vehicles. Most of the engines were already running, and already Truants were piling into the cars. Tack quickly went over to the nearest van and lifted his crate up to a waiting Truant who seized it and stacked it with the others. As he did, the last of the Truants poured outside and filed into each vehicle in so orderly a manner that Tack concluded that they'd each been assigned to a vehicle beforehand. It was impressive organization.

Tack was feeling slightly left out when suddenly an odd hush fell over the block, and he became aware of a heavy humming sound cutting through the air. Over fifty pairs of eyes rose up to look at the sky, where the faint shape of a black helicopter came into sight, forming a dark blot upon the midday sun. There was a moment of suspended awe, and then a furious voice rang out.

"What the hell are you bastards waiting for? *Move!*" Gabriel bellowed.

The Truants didn't need to be told twice; in a matter of seconds, everyone on the block was inside a vehicle except for Tack. At a bit of a loss, Tack looked around frantically for an open spot when he felt a hand grip his shoulder.

"You'll ride in my truck, Takan," Gabriel said, guiding Tack over to the front of the convoy. Waiting there was a red pickup truck, the engine running and Steve at the wheel. The passenger seat was occupied by boxes, but bizarrely it seemed like the back of the truck was empty. As Tack was pushed by Gabriel up onto the back, however, he fell onto a small mound of jagged things that he realized, with a jolt, were guns and boxes of knives. A second later, Gabriel himself climbed up to join Tack.

"All right, go, go, *go*!" Gabriel shouted at Steve.

The truck lurched forward, flinging Tack onto his back. Gabriel, however, remained sitting and was furiously sifting through the pile of weapons. As Tack lifted his head up, he saw that the entire convoy was now in motion, all of them following the truck at a furious pace.

"Straight to the ambush, right?" Steve called, sticking his head out of the window as the truck veered to the left.

"That's right!" Gabriel called back, still digging furiously through the mound. "Now keep your eyes on the road!"

The heavy beating of the helicopter grew monstrously loud, and Tack looked up to see the black shape descending upon them, the pilot apparently wanting to get a better look at a find that was too good to be true. Tack uneasily noticed that the sound was affecting Steve's driving; the truck was now jerking left and right erratically.

"What ambush?" Tack asked urgently as the helicopter swept down almost close enough to touch the rooftops.

"Zyid was prepared for something like this; he set a trap!" Gabriel shouted over the noise of the helicopter, which was gamely keeping up with the convoy.

"Think we'll live to see it?" Tack asked seriously, his eyes following the helicopter, which was now swooping towards their speeding truck.

"Let me worry about that, Takan; you keep your head

down!" Gabriel yelled as the truck banked a hard right, rattling the pile of weapons violently.

Tack decided that it would be best to do as he was told, and he crouched down in the back of the truck as Gabriel overturned some boxes of the odd white knives. As he did, the truck turned left at an intersection so sharply that the tires screeched and Tack and Gabriel were slammed against the side of the truck.

The helicopter banked left to follow, and suddenly Tack saw a dark figure lean out of one side of the helicopter holding a pistol. As Steve sped the truck straight down a street, heedless of the traffic lights that still glowed red, the helicopter swooped down on them and two shots rang out over the din, one missing completely and the other shattering a backlight of the truck.

"Don't worry about that; it was a lucky shot!" Gabriel said, still scrabbling around the pile for something.

Acting purely on instinct, Tack's hand blindly reached for a box, drew a white knife from inside it, and, after testing the weight, took aim and hurled it through the air just like Umasi had taught him. The knife landed right in the gunman's fleshy arm, which promptly dropped the pistol in shock. Over the sound of the beating propellers, Tack thought he could hear a scream of outrage, and the man withdrew into the helicopter.

"Nice aim!" Gabriel exclaimed, staring at Tack in surprise. "You throw as good as Zyid!"

"Looks like it's drawing back!" Tack shouted, pointing at the helicopter.

Indeed, seemingly awakened to the dangerous position it

was in, the helicopter had ascended to watch from where the pilot clearly thought it was safe.

"That's not good!" Gabriel shook his head. "Scared him away! Should've waited for me to find the real firepower!"

Tack was about to ask what the real firepower was when the truck swerved dangerously, jerking him around again. As they sped forward, Tack raised his head and looked back to see that they, and most of the other vehicles in the convoy, had very narrowly missed crashing into what looked like a fallen chunk of masonry.

"You didn't tell me there was so much junk on the roads!" Steve complained, yelling out the window.

"I didn't know there was; get your head back in there and drive!" Gabriel shouted as Tack helped him dig through the pile of weapons, assuming that he'd know what they were looking for when he saw it.

"Anything else you don't know about this route?" Steve shouted, viciously, spinning the wheel to take a left.

"We're going to have to find out, aren't we?" Gabriel bellowed, delving through a stack of ammo. "And watch where you're going!" he added, as Steve ran over an upturned trash can, which crashed and clanged noisily behind them.

"Backseat driver!" Steve retorted loudly, careening onto the sidewalk and then back onto the street.

"You do your job, and I won't have to!" Gabriel countered, and then let out an excited shout. "*Yes,* I found it!" Gabriel announced triumphantly as the truck smashed right through an old wooden traffic barricade.

Tack crawled up to look over Gabriel's shoulder. Hidden under some pistols of all shapes and sizes was what looked, at first glance, like large rifles with large bulges sticking out of their barrels.

"Rocket-propelled grenade!" Gabriel explained to Tack, seizing hold of one.

"Looks like it's coming back!" Tack warned, pointing up at the sky where the predatory shadow was growing steadily larger, the sound of its beating propellers intensifying angrily.

"That means his friends are near!" Gabriel said grimly. "But if the cocky bastard comes too close, I'll smoke him!"

"Enforcers!" Steve called out suddenly.

Tack's and Gabriel's heads both snapped forward. Sure enough, three Enforcer patrol cars had emerged from a side avenue, sirens blaring, and were now driving parallel with the convoy. A moment later, another patrol car joined them from another avenue, along with an armored vehicle that looked like it housed an entire assault team. Emboldened by these new arrivals, the helicopter again swooped down low enough to scrape the rooftops.

"We are the Enforcers, and you are all instructed to pull over!" a voice blared out from the helicopter through a megaphone. "Pull over or we start shooting!"

"No nonsense from them!" Tack observed as he looked over at Gabriel, who was now holding the rocket-propelled grenade upwards and grinning as he took aim.

"This is your last chance!" the voice from above declared. "Pull over, or we start—"

"Shooting?" Gabriel finished as he pulled the trigger.

There was a loud noise, and the rocket burst up from the launcher, leaving a trail of smoke behind. The rocket impacted the belly of the helicopter at what was practically point-blank range. A burst of fire bloomed in the middle of the helicopter; then it swayed dangerously before finally careening to the side and crashing into a row of buildings, where it exploded and sent pieces of metal raining down upon the convoy.

Uncomfortable similarities to Suzie's death immediately came to Tack's mind, but to his surprise, instead of feeling angry at Gabriel, he found himself cheering with him and clapping him on the back. The Enforcers were his enemies, Tack quickly reasoned as he watched the smoldering wreckage of the helicopter recede. The helicopter had been trying to kill him. It was different.

A large succession of shots rang out. Bending over one side of the truck, Tack looked back at the convoy, which was now being shot at by the Enforcer patrols that were obviously enraged at the loss of their helicopter. Truants began to fire back from the windows of the vehicles, creating a sort of high-speed parallel shoot-out that didn't look like it was going to end well for either side.

"Steve!" Gabriel called out as he reached for a semiautomatic rifle on the pile and jammed a clip into it.

"Don't worry; we're almost there!" Steve shouted back. "It's just around this corner!"

Upon hearing the word *corner,* Tack braced himself by grabbing a firm hold of the right side of the truck. Sure enough, the truck made another sharp turn that flung Tack into the side that he was grasping. Before he could recover and look up, he heard a sharp intake of breath next to him.

"Get off the road; park on the sidewalk!" Gabriel yelled at Steve. "We do *not* want to get hit by that!"

• • •

"If the noise is any indication," Zyid said sarcastically as the distant sound of sirens and gunshots grew steadily louder, "we will be entertaining company very shortly."

Noni, standing in the middle of the street, next to Zyid, nodded as the ten other Truants standing in front of them shifted restlessly. Those ten Truants had been arranged into two rows of five, and each of them was armed with a rocket-propelled grenade. About three hundred yards in front of them, a large white mass shaped like the pot it had been mixed in rested on the ground, a long trail of oil leading straight from it all the way to Zyid's feet, next to which rested a shotgun. In alleys far to either side of the white mass, a dozen well-equipped Truants all stood at the ready. The trap had been well designed; all that was needed now was the bait.

"First row, kneel," Zyid ordered suddenly, as the noisy commotion drew closer. "Prepare to fire."

The first row of Truants hastened to obey, holding their launchers at the ready.

"Well, well," Zyid said softly. "Here they come."

Around the corner swerved a red pickup truck, which quickly lurched forward up to the white mass, then braked and banked left to come to a stop on the sidewalk. Soon a dozen other vehicles followed suit, all of them taking care to stop far to the side. Even as they shut off their engines, three Enforcer patrol cars and an armored vehicle burst around the corner in pursuit, recklessly driving forward down the street before noticing that their quarry had come to a stop.

Zyid drew a lighter from his pocket, clicked it on, and then tossed it down to the trail of oil at his feet.

"First row, fire," he ordered, pocketing his lighter.

A line of rockets burst from their launchers and pummeled towards the hapless Enforcer cars. The rockets slammed into the oncoming cars and brilliant fireballs erupted, engulfing the first two cars instantly. The two vehicles behind them braked too late and slammed into the burning wreckage, pushing it mostly out of the way.

"Second row, you know what to do," Zyid said almost lazily.

After the second row of rockets obliterated the existing wreckage and created some more, the doors to the surviving vehicles swung open, and out poured dozens of angry-looking Enforcers, some in normal uniforms and others wearing more serious suits and helmets. But even as they brought their weapons up, the flames licking at the trail of oil finally reached the white mass placed in the middle of the street.

A second later, thick, white smoke burst into the air, filling the block in seconds. Taking this as their cue, the groups of Truants waiting in the alleys rushed forward into the smoke, firing at the places they had last seen the Enforcers. These Truants were soon joined by the massive number of Truants from the convoy, some of whom rushed forward into the cloud without so much as a weapon.

"Now we clean up the mess, Noni," Zyid said, picking the shotgun up from the ground and breaking into a run, Noni following closely behind him.

Zyid and Noni dashed forward into the smoke cloud together. As they did, Noni removed two ceramic knives from her belt while Zyid unsheathed his ceramic sword from a new scabbard that hung at his side. Once inside the thick smoke cloud, Noni vanished off to the side, but Zyid went straight, diverting his path only to make his way around a burning wreck of an Enforcer patrol car that cast an eerie orange glow through the smoke.

Hearing something moving behind one of the fiery wrecks, Zyid stealthily made his way towards it, his movements masked by the smoke and the chaos all around him. As he came around the wreck, he saw the outlines of two large figures crouching—definitely Enforcers. A point-blank shotgun blast later, both figures had crumpled to the ground and Zyid had proceeded deeper into the cloud. As Zyid made his way toward the spot he knew the armored vehicle would be, a helmeted Enforcer rushed forward through the smoke and actually bumped into him, letting out a yelp of surprise. Zyid acted reflexively, dropping to the ground before the Enforcer could fire, and then stabbing upwards with his sword. As the unlucky Enforcer let out a piercing shriek, Zyid leaped up behind him, brought his sword to the Enforcer's neck, and promptly slit the man's throat.

Meanwhile, Noni had darted through the smoke and lunged into the midst of a pack of four Enforcers that had been trying to take cover behind an old abandoned newspaper stand. She dropped low and slashed furiously at their legs, her knives working so fast that her victims had barely registered that there was an enemy present before they were incapacitated. As they screamed, Noni lithely returned to her feet and delivered a few stabs into the back of each of the crippled-but-armed Enforcers, and they dropped, leaving Noni to stealthily vanish back into the smoke, her braided ponytail swinging behind her. A minute later, another Enforcer taking cover behind a mailbox had his neck snapped, and by the time his companion noticed, a few stabs to various vital organs had already sealed his fate. Noni dispassionately wiped her knives on their clothes, and then slipped away as smoothly as if she herself were part of the smoke.

At the same time, Tack was doing well for himself. As the truck was engulfed by the smoke, he quickly seized the box of knives from the pile as well as a pistol, which he soon discovered was unloaded. Tack and Gabriel made their way into the smoke together, coming upon three Enforcers from behind. Tack unceremoniously plunged a knife into the first one's back, while Gabriel executed the second with a shot to the head. But even as they did so, the third reacted quickly, spinning around to take aim at Gabriel, whose attention was still on the Enforcer he had killed. Tack hurled his knife through the air, and it caught the Enforcer in the throat, causing him to crumple to the ground. Gabriel clapped Tack on the shoulder.

"Saved my life!" Gabriel shouted over the din.

"No problem!" Tack shouted back, and he meant it. For some strange reason, he felt a sense of comradeship with these Truants. Maybe it was because they treated him as one of them, or maybe it was because he had now fought and killed the same enemies beside them, as one of them.

Whatever it was, in the midst of a raging one-sided battle, with screams of both pain and triumph echoing around him, Tack took a moment to look down through the smoke at the bodies of the men he had killed. As he did, full realization struck him; he had killed Enforcers, and was prepared to do so again, so that Truants would live.

14

The Aftermath

"So, how many of ours?" Zyid asked, leaning against the armored Enforcer vehicle, which had a smoking hole in its side.

"Three dead," Noni replied quietly, standing next to him. "Fifteen wounded, mostly with minor injuries."

"Not particularly bad," Zyid observed, toeing a uniformed body aimlessly. "How many of theirs did we get?"

"We haven't been able to count the ones in the cars for certain," Noni said, gesturing towards the overturned and smoking remains of a nearby patrol car. "But we think around thirty, plus the helicopter."

"Fair trade," Zyid muttered, pushing himself away from the armored vehicle and straightening himself up. "Gather everyone up. It won't take the Educators long to figure out what happened, and when they do, every Enforcer in the City will be converging on this spot. We need to be long gone by then."

"Yes, sir," Noni said, turning to spread the message.

As Noni darted off, Zyid looked around to survey the carnage. All of the Enforcer vehicles had been wrecked beyond the point of salvaging, and some were still burning freely in the street, smoke plumes rising into the sky. The ground was littered with bodies, most of them in uniforms. Red blood stained the gray asphalt all over and trickled down to the gutters. There had been no Enforcer survivors; by the time enough smoke had cleared to allow visibility, not a single one was left moving. There had been, unavoidably, some friendly fire, though as far as Zyid knew none of it had turned fatal.

"Zyid!"

Zyid snapped out of his calculations and spun around to see Gabriel approaching him, picking his way through the bodies.

"What is it?" Zyid demanded.

"There's a guy you should meet when we get to the hideout," Gabriel said enthusiastically, coming to a halt in front of Zyid. "His name is Takan; the guy saved my life. We picked him up at the piers yesterday. He's surprisingly skilled—niftiest knife throwing I've seen since . . . well, you."

"Really?" Zyid raised an eyebrow. "You couldn't have possibly put him through even basic training during that time."

Gabriel nodded.

"Interesting," Zyid mused. "Very well, bring him to me after we return to the hideout now. For now, get your people back to their vehicles; they have permission to leave as soon as they can. Go."

"All right." Gabriel nodded, turning to navigate his way back through the wreckage and bodies.

"Everyone is ready and moving, sir," Noni said suddenly, having come up behind Zyid silently. "Should we go as well?"

"Yes, yes, we should," Zyid replied, not turning around or

even showing any surprise at Noni's appearance. "Let us join them."

Having already learned that the Truancy used what they could get, Tack wasn't surprised to see that the Truancy's main hideout was an abandoned office building that seemed to be something like fifteen stories high. Painted black, with filthy windows and glass doors that were intact, it certainly looked big enough to house hundreds, if not thousands. Next to the hideout on the right was a burger place, and through the glass storefront Tack could see Truants moving around inside it, no doubt taking advantage of the abandoned equipment.

Tack leaped down from the red truck expecting to enter the building with all of the other Truants. But as he took a step forward, he felt a hand on his shoulder.

"Zyid said he wanted to meet you," Gabriel said with a congratulatory grin, as though Tack had won the lottery.

Tack allowed himself to be led to what looked like an abandoned flower shop to the left of the hideout. The word *Florists* stenciled on the window had been partially scraped off, with a red symbol crudely spray painted over it. As Tack reached the door of the flower shop, he turned his head to get a better look at the symbol. It was the letter *T* turned slightly clockwise, contained inside a circle. In the meantime, Gabriel had already opened the door to the shop, and quickly ushered Tack inside.

The floor of the shop was wooden and moldy. The dim lighting came exclusively from a naked lightbulb hanging from the ceiling. Empty pots and sacks of soil lay strewn around, and a row of large glass-door refrigerators that Tack guessed had once held flowers stood against one wall. Tack eyed these with interest; they were filled with all kinds of food and drink ranging from milk to turnips. As Gabriel stepped forward into the roomy area, Tack's attention was suddenly drawn to a plastic folding table that had been erected in one corner far from the lightbulb and window, along with some metal folding chairs. Sitting at the table were two shadowed figures, their features too dark to see.

Gabriel addressed the taller of the two figures. "This is the guy, Zyid."

"I see; thank you for bringing him," the shadow murmured in a voice that Tack found, somehow, to be chillingly familiar. "Leave us now."

"Sure thing," Gabriel said, giving a respectful nod as he left.

Tack kept his eyes fixed on the two dark figures. The taller figure seemed to regard him for a moment, and then stood up and began to walk forward. Tack felt his heart start to beat furiously. So, he was about to meet the legendary Zyid, the one that Umasi had named as an equal, the leader of the Truancy, and the boy that all the other Truants regarded with such respect and even fear. But as Zyid walked under the lightbulb and his face came into view, Tack felt his racing heart stop suddenly.

A soulless face. Faintly sallow complexion and a long, dark ponytail. That intense glare Tack had come to associate with death. A black windbreaker buttoned around his neck like a cape. A nine-digit number and bar code on his arm indicating that he had once been a student. An aura that was at once cold, dark, and malicious.

Tack stared blankly, as if unsure of what he was seeing, and even more unsure of what to do. Zyid, however, looked him up and down carefully, and Tack had an uncomfortable feeling, like he was on an autopsy table being dissected.

"Your name is Takan?" Zyid asked suddenly.

Tack became aware that his mouth was slightly agape. Shutting it quickly and forcing his own face to remain as emotionless as Zyid's, Tack nodded. He felt somehow empowered by his lie—this Zyid knew nothing of him. Zyid couldn't know his intentions; he didn't read minds. Tack had an advantage, which was a comforting thought in the presence of this very formidable person that Tack now knew was his enemy.

Zyid looked very closely at his face, and Tack suddenly felt squeamish. Tack had recognized Zyid in an instant, but surely Zyid couldn't recognize him? After all, Tack had been covered in soot, tears, and blood a few days past when they had both borne witness to Suzie's death.

Tack cursed himself silently. He knew that he should be feeling anger right now, anger enough to strike out at Zyid, strike out at the killer he'd sworn revenge against. But somehow, under that fierce gaze, Tack couldn't muster the rage, or the will, to attack—both had been overwhelmed by fear and awe.

"You're physically capable in appearance and in rumor," Zyid observed at last, and Tack felt immense relief at having avoided recognition. "How did you get that way?"

"I exercised," Tack replied quietly, averting his gaze.

"While attending school?" Zyid asked shrewdly, raising an eyebrow.

"I wasn't a good student," Tack said, which was true.

"I hear that you are skilled in throwing knives," Zyid said. "Where did you learn this talent?"

"It was a hobby," Tack murmured.

"Do you have any other hobbies?" Zyid demanded.

"I can fight," Tack answered dutifully.

"Hand to hand?" Zyid pressed.

"And with swords and knives." Tack was finding it difficult to conceal anything under Zyid's gaze.

There was a sudden silence as Zyid seemed to ponder Tack's answers.

"You joined the Truancy only yesterday, correct?" Zyid asked.

"Yes, sir," Tack replied, and the shadow in the corner shifted for the first time.

"Why did you join?" Zyid demanded.

"I had nowhere else to go," Tack said quietly, which was also true.

"Fair enough." Zyid crossed his arms. "Are you willing to fight for the Truancy?"

"Yes, sir," Tack said honestly.

"And are you willing to die for it?" Zyid asked.

Tack hesitated for the briefest of seconds. "Yes, sir," he answered finally, though with little conviction.

"Good." Zyid nodded, and the shadow in the corner seemed to budge uncomfortably. "Are you curious about the Truancy, Takan?"

"Yes," Tack answered truthfully; he could think of a hundred questions about the Truancy that he'd love to have answered.

"Very well, I'll personally give you the tour," Zyid declared, now turning his head slightly back. "Noni."

The shadow in the corner got to its feet and walked forward into the light. As Noni's face became visible, Tack noticed with some discomfort that she was glaring daggers at him with icy blue eyes. Her skin was pale, contrasting starkly with her sleek black hair that was tied back into a long braid. Her lower face from the nose down was thoroughly wrapped with a thin black scarf, which struck Tack as odd considering that the weather was quite warm. She wore a tight-fitting black T-shirt with a denim vest over it, as well as blue jeans that seemed to have been hacked off right above the knees. Her very being seemed to exude a sort of hostility towards Tack, which made him unconsciously shuffle his feet in discomfort.

"Noni, this is Takan. Takan, this is Noni," Zyid said, sounding slightly amused as his eyes traveled from one to the other.

"Hi," Tack said lamely.

Noni said nothing, but her fierce blue eyes narrowed in suspicion. Tack was forcibly reminded of what Steve had told him. *Too bad she doesn't take any nonsense.*

"So, now that you're acquainted, let's head next door," Zyid suggested, leading the way. "There is much you need to be shown, Takan. Feel free to ask any questions as they come to mind."

Noni swiftly followed Zyid out the door, and Tack hastened to keep up. The three of them marched out of the flower shop and over to the large office building that was their hideout. A number of Truants were now busying themselves by moving the crates and boxes from the parked vehicles and into the building, with each emptied vehicle quickly driving off. As they reached the glass doors, several Truants called or waved at Zyid, who waved back without looking.

Inside, Tack found himself in an official-looking lobby with a marble floor, decorated walls, and a guard desk behind which several Truants were lounging. They quickly sprang to their feet as Zyid walked in, and Zyid gave them a curt nod as he led Tack and Noni over to a stairwell. Apparently the elevators in this hideout were also broken.

"We've consolidated the bulk of the Truancy here to better coordinate attacks of a larger scale, in preparation for summer," Zyid explained as they walked up the stairs. "We still have scattered cells around, but they're not nearly as common as they used to be."

Tack was finding it much easier to think for himself now that Zyid's dissecting gaze was off of him, and having been given approval to ask questions, he voiced the first one he could think of, convincing himself that he was only building up the courage to avenge Suzie.

"How do you feed everyone?" Tack asked, thinking of the amount of food it would take.

"When you gather hundreds of people together, you can be sure that there will be a wide variety of talents among them," Zyid said. "Cooking, fortunately, is one of them. We prepare massive meals twice a day, but mostly to get food Truants must go to the inhabited parts of the City."

"How do they pay?" Tack asked quizzically.

"Mostly, Takan, they eat free," Zyid answered. "Many of the supplies we receive, in fact, are donations."

"Donations from who?" Tack asked, bewildered.

"Surely, Takan, you don't think that you can't be a Truant while still at school?" Zyid laughed. "There are some still attending school that sympathize with us. The ones who know how to keep their mouths shut are occasionally recruited. Many of them have parents who run businesses. They don't have to fight to help—some pass us boxes of wholesale clothing; some give us buckets of day-old bread; others even just pass a hungry Truant a free hot dog from their father's stand."

"How do you recruit these people?" Tack asked with genuine curiosity.

"Most of that goes on during the summer," Zyid explained. "The summer is when we're most active. The students are out of school, so we can move more freely and blend easier. We can talk to and recruit new members. Also, children tend to help their parents out during the summer more than any other time of year."

"So *everything* you get is from donations?" Tack asked disbelievingly.

"You're very sharp, Takan," Zyid said, casting him an approving look as Noni scowled. "No, I personally pay for much of this."

"How?" Tack pressed.

"I am very fortunate in that money is something that I do not have to worry about," Zyid said lightly.

Tack suddenly remembered being told the exact same thing by Umasi, and he had a feeling that he wouldn't get much of an answer if he asked Zyid *why* he didn't have to worry about money. Instead, Tack thought up another question as he glanced back and became uncomfortably aware that Noni's eyes were drilling a hole into the back of his head.

"Why do you spend your money on this?" Tack asked.

"Because, Takan"— Zyid looked at Tack out of the corners of his eyes—"money is a trivial thing. How you spend it is nothing compared to how you spend your life."

They came to a floor where Zyid stopped and showed Tack around a room that was filled with cubicles. Sleeping bags had been rolled out in each, and Zyid explained that each Truant slept in a cubicle. Zyid quickly ran through what was on each floor, including which floors Tack could find a television on. Zyid also showed Tack where the water fountains and bathrooms could be found, and explained that most of the provided meals were now being served next door at the abandoned burger place. All the while, Noni stalked behind them agitatedly. Finally, Zyid led them back down to the lobby.

"I hope you found that enlightening," Zyid said to Tack as they stopped near the reception desk. "Do you have any more questions?"

Tack shook his head, having indeed exhausted every question he could think of.

"Excellent." Zyid rubbed his hands together. "Now, Noni, what time is it?"

"Six forty-three," Noni replied quietly, lifting her furious gaze off of Tack long enough to glance at her silver wristwatch.

"We have about five hours until Alex's group is scheduled to depart." Zyid said. "How about I take you two to dinner?"

"Erm . . . ," Tack began, unsure of how to reply.

"Yes, sir," Noni said quickly.

"Good," Zyid said approvingly. "Follow me; I know just the place."

Explain this to me again," the Mayor said in a deadly voice. "A helicopter, five Enforcer patrols, and one armored vehicle housing an entire attack squad, all lost?"

"By the time reinforcements got there, the vehicles were all wasted and the men dead," a cabinet member said, gulping. It was dangerous to be the bearer of news this bad. "No Truancy bodies were found, though there's evidence that at least a few of them were killed."

"*How* did this happen?" the Mayor asked, flicking his lighter open.

"We don't know, sir; it seems that they fell into some sort of an ambush," another cabinet member offered.

"I'm really looking forward to explaining this one to the public," the Mayor snarled. "And you tell me that there is no sign of the allegedly huge Truancy convoy that these Enforcers were chasing?"

"None, sir," the same cabinet member said nervously.

The Mayor slammed his lighter down onto the oval table, causing the cabinet members to jump in fright.

"I want to know how the Truancy managed this," the Mayor said, his voice now deadly calm. "And I want to know today. They've never fought back this hard before; always they ran whenever we found any of them."

"It's probably because they're now working in larger groups," a third cabinet member suggested. "They're more willing to resist."

"The next time they stand their ground, I want them crushed," the Mayor growled, clenching his fist to illustrate the point. "I want a full Enforcer task force on the standby at all times, ready to go if we see anything, *anything*."

"Consider it done, sir," a cabinet member assured, scribbling hastily onto a notepad.

"And you know that aerial surveillance?" the Mayor asked, earning some furious nods from all around the table. "Double it. And find some pilots with brains that don't chase after Truants armed with rockets."

"Pilots with brains, yes, sir," the scribbling cabinet member said, adding a few lines onto the notepad.

"Now get out of my sight." The Mayor shut his lighter.

The cabinet didn't need to be told twice; they clamored to leave the room, one of them clutching his notepad in his mouth. The Mayor rubbed his temples and moved to his desk, where he took out a clean sheet of paper and seized a pen from a mug on his desk. As he began to write, the Mayor found, to his chagrin, that the pen ran out of ink after five words.

"Nothing ever goes right around here." The Mayor breathed as he reached for a pencil.

Peter, it's been a while!"

A boy dressed in an uncomfortable-looking suit, leaning against a registration stand in one of the City's many fancy restaurants, who had been poring over the list in his boredom, looked up suddenly, and a wide grin spread across his face.

"Zyid!" the boy exclaimed, walking forward. "It *has* been a long time; what's up? Are you hungry?"

"Yes, that's why I'm all the way out here," Zyid said amusedly. "I think you've met Noni before? And this here is Takan, one of our very distinguished new members."

"Nice to meet you!" Peter said with a grin, immediately outstretching his hand.

Tack shook it embarrassedly. He didn't feel very distinguished wearing his gray sweatshirt, accompanied by Noni and Zyid, both of whom hadn't bothered to change into anything less casual before coming to this fancy restaurant, in one of the living districts, no less. The trio had already attracted a few curious looks from some of the restaurant's adult patrons, but no intense scrutiny yet.

"Big things went on today." Zyid had leaned forward to whisper to Peter, his eyes darting around to spot potential eavesdroppers. "Keep an eye on the news tonight."

"Ah, I gotcha," Peter said, nodding sagely, his grin never fading. "You're here to celebrate, then?"

"That's correct." Zyid returned the grin.

"Great. Come this way; you can have one of the private rooms," Peter assured them, ushering Zyid, Noni, and Tack over to a side hallway, around a corner, and through a set of large double doors into a lavishly decorated room that was safe from the eyes and ears of the other patrons.

"Any preference tonight?" Peter asked as they sat down.

"I'll leave the menu selection in your very capable hands, Peter," Zyid said, causing Peter to beam delightedly.

"You won't be disappointed," Peter promised as he bustled out of the room.

They weren't. Less than twenty minutes later, Tack was feasting on crispy duck cooked with pineapples, fried rice, and sweet-and-sour pork ribs. They drank plain water. Tack had no complaints, however; the food was delicious, the crispy duck being Tack's favorite, as the meat had a unique sort of richness that went very well with the taste of pineapple.

The meal was eaten mostly in silence, though Tack couldn't help but notice that after Noni loosened her scarf, she kept glaring at him over her glass of water, which bothered him more than he thought it should have. Determinedly focusing on his duck, away from Noni's gaze, Tack was mostly successful in preventing himself from thinking about the fact that he was now eating dinner with the murderer that had killed

Suzie. There were a few times that Tack gripped his fork and knife particularly hard, but they didn't last long; the duck *was* really good, after all.

After the dishes had been cleared away by Peter, Zyid folded his hands on the table and stared intently at Tack. Tack again got that uncomfortable feeling like he was on the operating table and under the knife.

"You're astute, strong, and skilled, Takan," Zyid said. "That is a rare combination. I think you are, in fact, more skilled than you let on. Tell me, who taught you what you know?"

Tack's mind was racing. It was like Zyid knew, but he couldn't possibly know about . . . and then Tack remembered Umasi saying that he *had* been acquainted with Zyid. What exactly was their relationship? Could Umasi have told Zyid anything about Tack? After a briefest moment of indecision, he steeled himself and decided to lie, hoping fervently that Umasi could keep secrets from other people beside him.

"I learned from tutors," Tack said steadily. "My parents wanted me to have extracurricular activities on my résumé, so they sent me to a variety of different training programs."

Tack willed his face to stay emotionless, which was something he was growing better at. Zyid looked at him for a few more moments, then spoke.

"How confident are you in your abilities?"

Tack frowned. It wasn't a question he'd ever thought about before.

"Pretty confident," Tack said slowly. "I think I can handle any job you want me to do."

"Really?" Zyid mused. "That's good, because I think I have the perfect test for you."

Zyid's gaze shifted to Noni, who had clenched her fists.

Tack turned to look at her, and saw for the first time a crackling eagerness glittering in her icy eyes. As Tack's mind deduced the obvious, he felt a sudden sinking sensation in his stomach, and it had nothing to do with the meal.

15
Swords

"This is a ceramic sword," Zyid announced, running his hand over the sheath. "I have one myself, and I've noticed that Noni has had her eyes on it for a while."

Tack looked at Noni out of the corner of his eye; she was staring down at her feet, looking embarrassed.

"For the record, Takan, the ceramic these are made of is stronger than steel and undetectable by metal detectors because, naturally, it is not metal," Zyid continued. "This ceramic sword is a prize. It will go to whoever can put it to better use."

Noni lifted her head, her icy eyes gazing covetously at the sword. Tack, for his part, didn't want the weapon half as much as Noni obviously did, but he didn't think that saying so would go over well with Zyid, so he kept his mouth shut.

The three of them were standing in the center of the flower shop. Pressing up against the walls of the room were a large number of Truant spectators that Tack guessed had been invited by Zyid. Night had fallen, and so the only light in the room issued forth from the single lightbulb hanging from the ceiling, the rest of the room, and the spectators, cloaked in shadow. Tack thought he recognized Gabriel among the milling shadows, but like the others he remained silent.

"I have here two wooden swords," Zyid said, pointing to a bucket at his feet. "Noni, Takan, these will be your weapons. The first person to land a killing blow wins. It's quite simple; I assume you both understand?"

Noni nodded and tightened the scarf around her neck. As she did, Tack noticed with a certain amount of discomfort that she looked ready not only to fight, but her eyes suggested that she was prepared to *actually* kill him. For the life of him he couldn't figure out what he had done to offend her. Tack, for his part, wasn't particularly eager to duel, especially not with an assassin that had a reputation for being a cold-blooded killer. But before he could think about protesting, Zyid had turned his gaze on him again and Tack found it impossible to refuse.

"Yeah, okay," Tack said meekly.

"Very good." Zyid nodded, snatching up both swords and tossing one each to Tack and Noni. "Let's not keep the spectators in suspense."

Tack had barely caught his sword when Noni lunged forward, bringing hers downwards, aiming for his head. Tack felt a jolt of surprise surge through his spine, but then, as he gripped the wooden weapon and felt the familiar feel of a wooden hilt, it was suddenly as if he weren't in control of his body, as if it were acting on its own accord.

Tack nimbly leaped back a few paces, narrowly dodging

Noni's attack. Ignoring the murmurs from the crowd, Noni was undiscouraged as she surged forward again, the end of her scarf and her braidtail trailing behind her. Tack saw that the attack was aimed at his heart, and as he stared into her icy eyes, he felt the familiar sensation of being backed into a corner, with no choice but to fight. As that thought passed through his head, he bizarrely heard Umasi's voice in his head, repeating words that he'd heard before.

You will learn to fight back out of necessity, if nothing else.

Tack dived and rolled to the side, coming up into a crouch as Noni missed him. She turned her increasingly furious gaze onto him and then lunged forward again. Tack found that he was making no motion to strike back, and as she swung at his legs he jumped backwards again. With a snarl of frustration, Noni brought her sword up and tapped it downwards sharply, hoping to hit Tack's shoulder with the swift blow. Tack merely sidestepped the attack and proceeded to back up.

"Coward," Noni muttered from behind her scarf.

Tack felt his eyes narrow.

You're afraid of being hit, and even worse, you're even afraid of hitting me.

Tack surged forward suddenly, catching Noni completely by surprise as he slammed into her with the full weight of his body. As she staggered back, he swung his sword in an arc at her neck. Noni ducked just in time, but Tack brought his sword swinging back the way it came, forcing her to block the blow with her own sword. They locked blades for a minute, and then sprang apart, regarding each other in a new light as the muttering from the crowd increased.

Falling into a pattern invites defeat.

Noni lunged forward again, but this time Tack met the attack head-on. As she brought her sword up, Tack jumped slightly into the air and kicked the oncoming blade with all the strength and momentum he had. Noni managed to prevent her own weapon from slamming into her face, but only just barely. Tack took the opportunity to deliver a snap-kick to her stomach, driving her backwards.

You do not wish to truly cause me harm, which is why you will fail to do so.

Tack strode forward, but even as he prepared to deliver a finishing blow, Noni recovered and swiftly brought her weapon swinging around at Tack's thigh. Tack managed to block the attack, but couldn't prevent Noni from driving her foot into his gut. As the wind was knocked out of him, Tack staggered backwards as Noni lunged forward, her blue eyes glowing with triumph. Without knowing what he was doing, Tack suddenly reached behind him and felt his fingers close on a metal folding chair near the table. Swinging the chair around with one arm, he brought it crashing into the oncoming Noni, who let out a cry of shock and anger as she was knocked to the ground, the chair falling on top of her.

There is time for mercy after they are defeated.

Without thinking, Tack stepped forward and kicked at Noni while she was down. He heard disapproving gasps from the crowd, and a yelp of pain from Noni, but as the chair fell off of her, he brought his sword down at her neck anyway. Noni unexpectedly shot up from the ground, and while Tack was in mid-swing she barreled into him, one hand closing around his throat while the other brought her sword back in preparation for a powerful thrust.

There are people in this City that do not share your reluctance.

Tack's hand shot up to grab Noni's arm before it could bring the sword down on him, and as he felt his windpipe being crushed, Tack brought his own sword around at Noni's neck. Seeing the danger, Noni immediately let go and sprang backwards, leaving Tack to gasp for air. The crowd had gone deathly silent, and Tack stopped gasping long enough to block a series of furious hammering blows aimed at his head that rattled his arm so roughly that it ached. It could not be clearer that Noni was determined to win, and as Tack looked into her blazingly icy eyes, he wondered for a moment if he might just let her.

And you can never give up, Tack. To give up in this City would be to throw your own life away.

The thought of surrender was gone as suddenly as it came. Tack looked to his left and saw the plastic folding table still standing there. As Noni came at him again, Tack, to the vocal amazement of the crowd, dropped his sword and jerked forward to seize ahold of Noni's arms. Slamming her against the edge of the table, Tack was seized by a sudden, mad inspiration and reached out to tug at Noni's scarf before she could recover, pulling it off of her lower face.

There was a moment of suspended revelation as Tack suddenly froze. The crowd gasped, and Noni's blue eyes widened in panic. Tack saw now why Noni had worn the scarf in the first place; a long, ugly scar ran all the way from the bottom of her chin and across her left cheek, marring her otherwise pretty features. Tack wondered for a moment if she would lash out at him, but the next thing he knew she had dropped her sword, covering her face with her hands as she sank to the floor.

Well, it looks like you pass the test in its entirety, Tack.

Tack suddenly became very aware that the crowd's mutterings had intensified, so that the room was now filled with the buzzing sound of conversation. Looking down at Noni's curled body, Tack felt a sudden stab of guilty pity for her, and he was about to act on it when Zyid caught his eye. Zyid's reproachful gaze reminded him of what he had to do, and so Tack reluctantly bent down to pick up Noni's dropped sword, and then touched it gently to her throat.

Zyid immediately walked forward, and all conversation stopped.

"Well done, Takan," Zyid said, presenting Tack with the sheathed ceramic sword.

Tack said nothing, but took the ceramic blade and dropped the wooden one. As the wooden sword clattered to the ground, Zyid crouched down, removed Noni's hands from her head, and carefully wrapped the scarf over her scarred face. He gave her a rough pat on the back and straightened up again, turning to nod approvingly at Tack. Noni shakily returned to her feet a moment later, and Tack noticed that she was no longer glaring at him, but avoiding his gaze completely.

"What time is it, Noni?" Zyid asked without looking at her.

"Ten forty-two, sir," Noni said in a voice so small that Tack thought it might vanish if it grew any softer.

"It's time that we head out to witness Alex's arrival," Zyid declared, turning to Tack. "Takan, I would like you to come with me."

Tack couldn't help but notice that Noni had been left out, something that she obviously hadn't missed as well; she was now staring at Zyid like he'd slapped her. Feeling more sorry for Noni than ever, Tack was about to refuse when Zyid turned his gaze on him again.

"Yes, sir," Tack replied quietly.

I don't know who you are, how you got the Educator clearance for this, or why this can't wait until morning, but I've brought her. And by the way, I was in that corridor when she threw that stink bomb, and I know she did it. Erasing that from her student profile in exchange for a midnight interview—"

"I understand that you're uncomfortable with the deal, but it's very important for me to find out what happened as soon as possible—I only just heard about it, you see. Where is she now?"

"She's waiting outside the office. And by the way, this is cutting into my sleep too."

"Thank you for your sacrifice. Please show her in."

"All right, but I'm warning you; you won't learn much. I told you already, the boy is dead. Tragic, but that's life."

"I appreciate your opinion, but as you know, it is often difficult to accept a friend's death. I'd just like some . . . closure, that's all."

"Well, I hope you get it, whoever you are."

The principal of the District 20 School opened the door to her office and held it open, calling out in a constricted voice as she did so.

"Melissa, the young man inside would like to speak to you. Answer any questions he has, and we'll . . . overlook your little incident. Oh, and be honest, please."

Without another word, the principal slipped wearily out of

the office, allowing an apprehensive and tired-looking girl with dark hair to enter. As the door closed behind her, she shook off her sleep and boggled at the sight of the odd boy seated behind the principal's desk, who now adjusted his pair of black sunglasses and straightened up in the principal's chair.

"Hello, Melissa," the boy greeted her. "My name is Umasi."

"Hi," Melissa replied tentatively. "The principal told me you wanted to talk to me."

"Yes, that's right." Umasi nodded. "It's about Tack. You see, he was a . . . friend of mine, and I understand that you were among the last to see him before his death."

Melissa bit her lip. "Yeah, yeah, I did."

"I want to know what happened that day," Umasi said. "It's okay to tell me; everything you say here is off-the-record. As a matter of fact, your record will be wiped clean anyway, so there's no harm in telling the truth."

Melissa peered blearily at Umasi for a moment, as if considering whether to trust him or not. After a few seconds, she'd apparently satisfied herself and straightened up.

"Well," she began, "Suzie and I, one of our friends got dragged away the week before."

"Under the Zero Tolerance Policy?" Umasi asked.

"Yeah." Melissa nodded. "I heard the Disciplinary Officer was around to inspect, so I thought I'd protest. I threw a stink bomb at him."

"What happened then?" Umasi asked gently, drawing his hands together.

"Suzie took the blame for me," Melissa said, her voice cracking a little. "And Mr. Caine took her away."

"And her brother saw this?" Umasi asked quietly.

"Yes." Tears started rolling down Melissa's face. "Suzie took the blame and so she got killed; it should've been me. I just stood there and watched her go."

"But Tack didn't just stand there, did he?" Umasi pressed as Melissa wiped her eyes with her sleeve.

"No." Melissa sobbed. "He ran after them. He chased them. I should've chased them too."

"It is natural to feel guilty, whether it is justified or not," Umasi said gently. "But my next question is very important, and I will need an answer."

Melissa nodded miserably, and Umasi leaned forward on the principal's desk.

"Did you see how Tack died?" Umasi asked.

"No." Melissa shook her head, wiping more tears from her face. "He went out of sight, with them, and we thought we heard a noise, and later they told us the gas in the car blew up."

"They said . . . the gas in the Disciplinary Officer's car blew up? By itself?" Umasi repeated.

"Y-yeah," Melissa said tearfully. "Why?"

"It's nothing," Umasi said quickly. "Thank you for coming here at this time of night, Melissa; you may go now. And when you're done blaming yourself, remember that it wasn't your fault."

As Melissa left, dabbing at her eyes with her shirt, Umasi leaned back slightly in the principal's chair and, once he was alone, voiced the name of the person whose fault he knew it was.

"Zyid," Umasi muttered. "So, Tack and his sister got caught up in a Truancy assassination. But they don't have your body, Tack, and that means that you're not dead . . . so where are you?"

• • •

A little under two hours after the duel, Tack was standing at Zyid's side atop an abandoned brownstone building whose ground floor had once been a Laundromat. Before they arrived, Tack expected Zyid to have prepared a trap similar to the one that had saved Gabriel's convoy. To Tack's surprise, however, Zyid led Tack through a forest of old washing machines and up to the roof on which they stood, where only five Truants were waiting, sitting on top of wooden crates with two rocket-propelled grenades resting at their feet. The streetlights below had either all been broken or been shot out by the Truancy, so that the whole block was under the cloak of total darkness.

The sound of gunshots and sirens had been audible for almost a whole minute, and Tack was now growing nervous as Zyid leaned casually over the edge of the building while the sounds grew louder and louder. Suddenly, from around the corner, the convoy of Truants appeared, like a collection of used vehicles. Tack watched in growing anxiety as the approaching Truants below sped desperately down the narrow street in their ragtag cars and trucks.

Tack came very close to asking Zyid why he wasn't doing anything about it, but he stopped himself before his mouth was properly open and instead watched the scene unfold below. Following closely behind the convoy emerged no fewer than a half-dozen Enforcer patrol cars, all of them in hot pursuit. The street was very narrow and the Enforcers were forced to line up one after another in order to pass through, but their equipment was quite obviously better and faster than anything the Truants had. As soon as the Enforcers passed the street and the road widened, Tack knew, it would be all over.

Tack shook his head. The loss of the vehicles alone would hurt, and how many Truants were down there inside them? How many would walk away from this? Gritting his teeth, Tack turned to look at Zyid, who was still calmly surveying the situation. Tack now felt sure that Zyid had made some sort of a mistake, that he'd led the Truants below to their doom. As Zyid continued to look downwards with mild interest, Tack had to restrain a sudden mad urge to simultaneously push Zyid off the edge of the building and rush down to the street to do something, anything to help the convoy. Revenge on Zyid, Tack resolved, could wait until he saw how this ended.

Tack was about to disregard all caution and open his mouth to say something when Zyid held up two fingers, and lightly gestured forward. Immediately, two of the Truants got up off the crates, picked up a rocket-propelled grenade each, and walked over to the edge of the building to flank Zyid on either side.

"It's a shame to cause the deaths of so many Enforcers," Zyid mused. "But we must act without mercy, as we have a responsibility to our friends."

Tack stared at Zyid, who continued to watch the approaching vehicles with an amused calmness, but his face was set and deadly serious, and Tack realized he wasn't joking. The situation looked impossible to Tack, but Zyid seemed to know what he was doing. Tack glanced down again; the Truants were now almost directly beneath them, with the Enforcers close behind. Whatever Zyid was planning, he'd have to act fast.

Tack didn't have long to wait. As soon as the Truants passed by and the Enforcers drew under them, Zyid made his move.

"Destroy the leading Enforcer vehicle."

One rocket burst from the launchers, cutting through the air to slam into the first Enforcer patrol car in the line. An angry smoke trail marked the rocket's path as it flew downwards, and a moment later Tack's jaw dropped in realization as the car leading the chase burst into a twisted metal fireball. Now he understood; the cars behind the wreckage, still pummeling forward at breakneck speed, crashed into the wrecked car and then into each other. As the damage piled up, the other Enforcer cars finally stopped and began attempting to back up.

"Now take out the last vehicle," Zyid said casually, hands clasped behind his back.

A second rocket sailed downwards at an angle, smashing through the windshield of the car at the back of the convoy. There was a moment's pause, and then an explosion and burst of flame as that car also blew up. The confused surviving cars still attempted to back up, comically smashing into each other until the drivers finally realized that they were trapped. But now the car doors began to open, and out of them issued forth a number of shadowy figures, all of them carrying guns.

Almost instinctively, Tack, Zyid, and the two rocket-carrying Truants backed up a few steps. A moment later, a hail of bullets came flying wildly upwards, smashing into all the buildings on the block, chipping off bits of masonry, or else zipping viciously through thin air.

"What now, sir?" Tack asked quietly, looking at Zyid with a new, grudging respect.

"Now we clean up the mess." Zyid gave Tack a rare grin, and then turned to the Truants behind him, all of whom were already pushing the wooden crates forward.

"Bring out the incendiaries."

The Truants worked quickly, picking up black crowbars that Tak hadn't noticed on the ground. Working together, they swiftly pried open the lids, revealing a padded interior filled with . . .

"Water balloons?" Tack asked incredulously.

"Why, yes." Zyid smirked, handing one to Tack. "Join us, will you?"

As the Enforcers below continued the barrage, Zyid and the five other kids began lobbing the water balloons over the edge in all different directions with great gusto. Almost unable to take the situation seriously, Tack feebly dropped his balloon off the edge. But as the gunfire below began to subside in favor of confused shouting, and then frightened yells, Tack suddenly realized why Zyid had called the water balloons "incendiaries."

"These balloons, what are they filled with?" Tack asked, looking up at Zyid.

"All sorts of things," Zyid said offhandedly, hurling the last of the balloons off the edge. "Lighter fluid, propane, motor oil, gasoline, there's even some confiscated vodka in there somewhere—anything flammable will do."

Tack grimaced, sparing a look down at the doomed Enforcers.

"That's an awful way to die," he said bitterly, averting his gaze.

"Perhaps," Zyid conceded softly. "But it's us or them."

Tack looked at Zyid and was surprised to find what looked like genuine regret flash across the Truant leader's face. But just as soon as it came, it was gone, and in an instant Zyid had returned to his usual brisk manner.

"They seek to consume our lives, and so fire will consume

theirs," he said, drawing a bottle out from his pocket that had a cloth jammed into its neck.

Lighting the cloth, Zyid turned and tossed the firebomb off the edge just as casually as he had treated the balloons. Almost reflexively, Tack rushed to the edge to watch the bottle fall towards the car, and suddenly he remembered a similar bottle flying through the air, crashing into a car, producing a burning, writhing body, the unbearable stench of sizzling flesh, and a dead girl lying bloody and charred in his arms. As the vision ended, he saw the fiery bottle fall in slow motion through the night, as if time itself took note of the event, and as it dropped Tack wondered if the Enforcers might look up and recognize their own death approaching.

It was the only thought Tack had time for before the bottle burst a few feet above the ground, spewing its fiery contents everywhere. A moment later, the streets, soaked in combustibles, lit up like a lantern. Smaller fires touched off bigger ones until the whole block took light. Gasoline inside the tightly packed cars ignited, causing a chain of explosions to ripple throughout the streets. Through the blazing inferno, terrified and pained screams ripped through the air, and angry red tongues of flames stabbed upwards into the darkness. As fire devoured the lives below, Tack shut his eyes and turned away. Opening them again, he saw that the other kids were all also determinedly averting their gazes, instead staring up at the twinkling starry night.

Except for Zyid. Of them all, only he still gazed down at what he had wrought. His eyes were wide and intensely determined as they mirrored the flames below, but as Tack glanced at him, looking for more reasons to hate the boy, Tack instead saw pain, an incomprehensible pain twisting Zyid's face as he stared unflinchingly downwards. That pain, more than anything else, made it even more difficult for Tack to imagine avenging himself upon his sister's killer.

Whatever it was that Zyid saw there in that street on that night he forever kept to himself. When Zyid finally looked away and silently led all the Truants back to the hideout, Tack took another look at the leader's face. Seeing only the usual emotionless expression, Tack found it hard to imagine that the pain was ever there.

16

Without Mercy

You cannot count on mercy—yours, Tack, or theirs!

We must act without mercy.

Tack sighed and leaned against the tiled wall. Mercy—it was the only thing that his new mentor and his old seemed to agree on. Tack had spent the past few weeks as if in a trance, spending most of his time trying to sort out the mess that his life had become. In between confused episodes, he felt as though he were a limp puppet made by Umasi, with Zyid now pulling the strings. Ever the master puppeteer, Zyid had spent much time filling Tack's head with advice and instructions that conflicted deeply with Umasi's teachings. Tack felt torn on the inside; he had come very close to accepting Umasi's words before joining the Truancy, but Zyid's tended to be overwhelmingly persuasive. Tack had spent an entire dazed afternoon trying to figure out how to fit "do not seek to take life" alongside "restraint is a weakness" and not feel some confusion.

Tack looked briefly through the glass front doors of the school; the evening sky was just beginning to darken outside. He shifted restlessly. For the past half hour he had been crouched outside the door of a principal's office in a school that he had never been to before. Ever since the bulk of the Truancy had grouped together Zyid had been pulling Tack's strings with increasingly frequency, sending him on all sorts of unsavory missions, most of which involved ending the life of any Enforcer or Educator Zyid might name. And Tack had done so flawlessly.

And yet, every time Zyid told Tack what a good job he had done, some suppressed corner of his mind rose up and asked him why he obeyed.

Tack never could find an answer.

He knew that he wouldn't be experiencing any less horror if he hadn't become Zyid's puppet; Truant parties went out regularly now, and skirmishes with Enforcer patrols were becoming more common every day. Tack didn't see much of his old Truant acquaintances anymore; Zyid always kept him close. This in particular made Tack feel uncomfortable; the feeble conscious part of him felt like he was betraying Suzie, but no matter how hard he tried, he couldn't stop serving the Truancy.

Tack sighed again, his thoughts shifting. His discomfort had been compounded by the fact that Zyid wasn't keeping Noni as close as he used to, something she obviously blamed Tack for. Not only did she avoid looking at him, but she avoided his presence entirely. Tack really wasn't entirely sure why that bothered him, especially when it was the least of his worries, but the aftermath of their duel had left him feeling immensely guilty.

Tack suddenly rummaged around in the pocket of his jacket absentmindedly, more for the sake of concentrating on something material than anything else. His hand gripped the bottle inside his pocket firmly when it found it. The particular mission that Zyid had sent him on was very unusual, and Zyid had impressed upon him that it was especially important. For the first time since Tack had entered Zyid's service, he was being asked to capture a target alive, and even more unusually, the target wasn't an Educator but merely the principal of the District 6 School. Tack wasn't sure what Zyid wanted the man alive for, but he had a feeling that it wasn't anything pleasant.

Tack looked around the ground floor of the school, checking idly for signs of other people. There was relatively little security here after hours; the Educators had begun to devote lots of resources to protecting their own and no one else. There had been only one guard present behind the circular security desk, and he had remained fast asleep even when Tack shot the lock on the front doors and entered the school. Tack had used his sword to make sure that the guard wouldn't be waking up, just in case, and then had proceeded to the room whose number Zyid had provided. Zyid had told him that the principal for this school would be working late, and sure enough, light issued forth from the thin crack under the door, and faint sounds of movement could be heard.

Tack had decided that the best course of action would be to wait for the principal to leave the office himself, and so he waited, crouched outside the door, with a brown glass bottle in one hand and a cloth in the other. Suddenly, the sound of activity inside the room increased, and Tack decided that the principal was finally preparing to leave. Tack gingerly unscrewed the bottle he held and soaked the cloth with the liquid contained inside. Avoiding breathing the fumes in, Tack screwed the cap back on the bottle and then held the cloth in his right hand, keeping it a safe distance away from his nose and mouth.

A few tense moments passed, and then the light under the door went out. Tack stiffened and prepared himself as the sound of footsteps approached the door. Then the door swung open, and the short, squat figure of a man stepped out, clutching a suitcase. Tack immediately sprang forward, using his left arm to bring the man into a headlock, and then using his right to smother the man's face with the towel. The man dropped the suitcase, struggled and yelled into the cloth for a few moments, and then went still. Tack acted quickly, tossing the bottle and cloth aside, and then dragging the man's rather heavy bulk behind him. Fortunately for Tack, the principal's office was on the ground floor, not too far from the main doors. Pushing open a door with his foot and grunting slightly as he heaved the man outside, Tack dragged his burden over to a black car that was parked nearby.

The backseat door swung open, and Zyid stepped out. As they silently lifted the principal into a sitting position in the backseat, Zyid murmured quietly.

"Did the ether work?" he asked, rather unnecessarily.

"Yes, sir," Tack answered quietly.

"Good." Zyid nodded. "Get in the passenger seat."

Zyid opened the passenger seat door and ushered Tack inside. Tack sat down, buckled himself in, and then shut the door. As he turned to look at the driver, he froze; Noni sat next to him stiffly, gripping the wheel, determinedly looking forward. Tack noticed that her scarf was wrapped tighter than ever around her lower face.

"We've picked up our guest." Zyid clapped a hand on the unconscious principal's shoulder, ignoring the tension in the front seats. "Now let's prepare to entertain him."

Tack knew better than to ask what the "entertainment" would be or where they would be performing it, but Noni had apparently been briefed, at least on the latter, since she turned the keys and hit the gas without hesitation.

"Once he is restrained at the site, I will need the two of you to keep a watch on him," Zyid said briskly, rolling down his window so that he could enjoy the rushing air. "When he wakes up, I want you to call me."

Zyid nodded at and tossed a cell phone over to Tack, who caught it and quickly slipped it into his pocket.

"Where will you be going?" Tack asked.

"For a bike ride," Zyid said, his voice suddenly taking on uncharacteristically weary tones. "I feel like visiting an old friend."

Tack turned to look back at Zyid carefully. The Truant leader had an almost sickly look, as if he was preparing to do something horrible. But as soon as Zyid noticed Tack looking at him, his face quickly smoothed out again. Tack glanced over at Noni, who he knew couldn't have seen what he had but must be as skeptical of Zyid's last pronouncement as he was. Tack understood, however, that they both knew better than to question Zyid about it.

Noni suddenly shifted in her seat, and Tack realized that his attention seemed to be making her uncomfortable. Tack tore his gaze from her and looked forward, leaning back in his seat. He wasn't sure that Zyid really had any friends. For that matter, he wasn't sure that anyone inside that car did.

Except, perhaps, for the principal, who was still resolutely asleep, blissfully unaware of his companions and what they had in store for him.

Well, now this is a most unexpected visit, Zyid," Umasi said, shutting his book and looking up from his seat behind the lemonade stand.

Zyid ignored Umasi's inquisitive look and slid neatly off of his bike, which he left lying on its side in the street. He walked forward to the front of the stand, directly across from Umasi. It had been fifteen minutes since he'd left Tack and Noni behind in a safe place far from District 6.

"Before you get defensive, Umasi, I'm not here as the leader of the Truancy," Zyid said wearily.

"Really?" Umasi raised an eyebrow. "Then what are you here as?"

Zyid took a deep breath and shut his eyes, as if bracing himself for a life-threatening experience.

"Your brother."

Suddenly the entire atmosphere changed, and Umasi's expression grew cold and furious. There was a moment of frozen silence; then Umasi reached up and swept the sunglasses from his face, regarding Zyid through narrowed, dangerous eyes. Zyid looked back calmly, having clearly expected such a reaction.

"You aren't my brother anymore," Umasi said harshly. "You yourself told me that years ago."

"I admit I've done little to deserve the title." Zyid sighed.

"But you only truly appreciate things when you lose them; you know that. I've missed you."

"Since when have you ever been sentimental?" Umasi asked scornfully.

"I must be getting old," Zyid said flippantly, prompting a bark of laughter from Umasi.

"You blew up a Disciplinary Officer only a few blocks from here," Umasi said viciously. "What kind of message does that send me?"

"That I have responsibilities to my people?" Zyid suggested. "I'm not here to argue, Umasi; I just want to talk."

"So you stroll in here, claim to be my brother again, and expect to be welcomed with open arms?" Umasi demanded. "And don't try giving me the look; it stopped working since we left school."

"I wasn't going to," Zyid protested.

"If you're my brother, tell me the truth," Umasi demanded. "There's a purpose to everything you do. You'd never come all the way out here just to tell me you've missed me. Why are you really here?"

Zyid shifted uncomfortably as Umasi glared at him relentlessly, sunglasses still in hand.

"I'm in the neighborhood on business," Zyid said finally. "I really did want to see you, and I'm due to meet up with my two assistants in a nearby district soon. I just decided to stop by to see how you were doing."

"You're meeting with assistants? Who's dying today?" Umasi asked sardonically.

"No one, though I won't deny that you wouldn't approve of what we're going to do." Zyid frowned, now looking vaguely anxious.

"Well, I'm not going to give you an excuse to detail your acts of depravity," Umasi said. "And I thought your only assistant was Noni. What happened? Did she become expendable?"

"Noni is still in my employ, but my new assistant is just as good, perhaps even better," Zyid said, glad for a new topic of conversation. "He joined recently, and he didn't even need training. His name is Takan, if you'd care to know."

Umasi froze. As his eyes scanned Zyid, he quickly composed himself, extinguished his anger, and put his sunglasses back on.

"Takan?" Umasi repeated carefully.

"Yes," Zyid said, suddenly suspicious. "Why? Do you know him?"

"No, I can't say that I do," Umasi lied smoothly. "I was just under the impression that Noni was irreplaceable, at least as your most valued subordinate."

"No one is irreplaceable," Zyid said stiffly.

"Even you?" Umasi raised an eyebrow.

"Even me. Why? Thinking about taking my place?"

"Yes, yes, that's exactly what I'm thinking about," Umasi said sarcastically. "You know how much I *love* the Truancy."

"That I do," Zyid mused.

Suddenly, a melodious tone issued forth from Zyid's pocket, and annoyance flitted across his face. Withdrawing his cell phone, he flipped it open and thumbed it on before bringing it to his ear.

"Is he, already?" Zyid murmured into the phone. "All right, I'm on my way."

Zyid switched the cell phone off and then turned again to Umasi, who was now observing him with visible interest.

"Well, dear brother, as good as it was to see you"—Zyid

gestured resignedly towards his pocketed cell phone—"I'm now running late."

"Please, don't stay on my account." Umasi waved his hand dismissively. "I suppose you're free to come back whenever you want, considering you'll do so anyway if you really want to. That said, I don't expect I'll see you soon."

"Oh, you never know," Zyid said wistfully, turning to grab his bike. "Good-bye, Umasi."

"Take care of yourself, Zyid," Umasi called.

Umasi watched as Zyid mounted his bike and rode around the corner, and out of sight. As he did, Umasi bent his head deep in thought, muttering quietly to himself.

"Well then, he's no longer my responsibility," he murmured. "I wonder if Zyid will find him any easier to control than I did."

Thank you for helping to keep watch, Noni; you may leave now," Zyid said loudly, drawing immediate attention as he slid down into the massive pit of a construction site.

Tack looked quickly at Noni, who was now staring at Zyid with hurt in her eyes. Tack was almost glad to see it there, since they had been completely empty for a long time. She and Tack had stood guard together outside the concrete room, one of many, under the tangle of piping and support beams that were the beginnings of the basement for an incomplete building. Having nothing to look at except shadowed plumbing, the unconscious principal, and the others, Tack had inevitably noticed that Noni's eyes were not icily intense, as they used to be, but uncharacteristically dull.

The next thing Tack knew, Noni averted her gaze and

climbed swiftly out of the pit. Zyid strode over to Tack and gestured for him to follow as he entered the crude room that he'd been guarding. Tack obligingly followed, shooting one last look at Noni's retreating form. As he turned his attention towards the room they were now in, the first thing Tack noticed was the dim lighting, which was just enough to illuminate the filth and rust caking the surface of the entire room. The second thing he noticed was the principal he'd abducted earlier.

Zyid had taken no chances with the prisoner before he left to supposedly visit his friend, Tack saw. The man was blindfolded and strapped down onto a stretcher, directly underneath a rusty water pipe. The man stiffened as he heard footsteps, and Zyid cast him an unusually grave look. He closed his eyes and took a deep breath, as if preparing himself, and then gestured Tack towards a valve in the corner. Tack understood and immediately took his place there, silently gripping the valve. Zyid nodded in approval, then walked to stand beside the captive.

"Hello, Mr. Flint!" Zyid said cheerily, as if greeting a favorite teacher.

"What is this? Who are you?" Mr. Flint demanded, turning his head towards the voice.

"My name is Zyid, sir, and you might call this my classroom," Zyid said in a voice filled with irony.

"Just what do you think you're doing?" Mr. Flint asked, struggling to maintain his brave face.

"Oh, I just brought you here to have a little pop quiz on current events," Zyid replied, walking over to Mr. Flint's side. "Look at me when I'm talking to you, Mr. Flint."

Zyid removed the man's blindfold. Mr. Flint blinked a few times, adjusting to the dim light. His eyes widened as they spotted Zyid.

"You're just a kid!"

"Not the kind that you're thinking of," Zyid said cheerfully.

Mr. Flint looked suddenly relieved. Kids. That's all they were. He could deal with kids.

"Young man, you'd better untie me right now or you'll be in serious trouble," he warned, assuming his most authoritative voice.

The cold chuckle that came in reply was not what he'd expected.

"You're incorrigible, Mr. Flint," Zyid said icily. "However, as I said, we have a test to take, and if you leave now you'll get a zero. And we both know what happens to people who get zeroes on their tests, don't we? They are . . . disciplined."

Mr. Flint looked surprised. This child's satirical response was disturbing to him. The idea that performance on a test could affect his very immediate life felt strange to him, and yet it was vaguely familiar nonetheless.

"Mr. Flint, I expect you to answer quickly and accurately," Zyid lectured. "Of course, I will not tolerate dishonesty. Dishonesty on a test would make you a cheater, and the harshest punishments of all are reserved for cheaters."

At this cryptic statement Mr. Flint seemed genuinely spooked. The child who was so imperiously giving him commands was entirely unlike any other he'd ever dealt with, despite his many years of experience, and that was . . . unsettling. But still, a kid was a kid. He'd handled rowdier students than this. Mr. Flint was spooked, but not yet scared.

"Look, kid, just cut the crap and let me go," he ordered harshly.

Zyid narrowed his eyes, then sighed. Turning to Tack, who had been observing the interrogation impassively, he gave a sharp nod. Tack almost reflexively twisted the valve he had been gripping rather tightly, and immediately wondered what he'd just done.

A drop of water slowly congealed in the mouth of the pipe on the ceiling, falling down to splash upon Mr. Flint's forehead.

"What the hell?" Mr. Flint exclaimed, caught off-guard.

"Witness what dedicated research can accomplish, Mr. Flint," Zyid said as another drop of water fell upon the principal's head. "Today's lesson will be about water torture. I stumbled across this in a book. How it works is that I will continue to drip drops of water onto your head."

"Yeah, so?" Mr. Flint demanded, with just a hint of doubt.

"So, as the drops slowly continue to fall, your mind will begin anticipating and even dreading the next drop. After a mere few hours, your own brain will begin to betray you. Each drop will feel like a hammer blow to the head, slowly but surely robbing you of your sanity. I can wait for days, Mr. Flint."

"You're crazy." Mr. Flint gasped as another drop slid down his face.

"Perhaps. But you're not a guidance counselor, and you're in no position to diagnose me, Mr. Flint," Zyid pointed out coolly. "Now, you have wasted enough of my class time already. We have a test to take, and the sooner it's over, the sooner you can go home. Of course, if you don't appreciate this artistic fate I've prepared for you, I have more immediate disciplinary measures available."

Zyid gestured towards a bottle of lighter fluid and a box of matches that lay over in a corner. Mr. Flint glared at the objects for a moment before slumping atop the stretcher.

"What do you want to know?" Mr. Flint asked in a resigned voice.

"Ah, ready to begin then?" Zyid observed. "Verbal responses will be acceptable, Mr. Flint, and you will be graded at my sole discretion. Question one, have the Educators briefed you on a group called 'the Truancy'?"

"The what?"

"The Truancy."

"You mean students that cut class?"

"I mean an organization."

"No, nothing about that."

"Are you sure?"

"Yes. I'd know what they told me."

"I'm sure you would. Question two, when and where is the next scheduled Educator meeting going to take place?"

"The school budget committee meets next Tuesday, in the Waterfront Hotel, top floor ballroom."

"Excellent. Question three . . ."

For the next fifteen minutes, Tack watched in amazement as Zyid covered topics ranging from attendance rates to the addresses of prominent Educators. Mr. Flint did not always have answers, and Zyid made a point of writing something down on a clipboard every time it happened. This, combined with the continued drops of water, seemed to slowly throw Mr. Flint into hysteria. Finally, Zyid reached the bottom of his list, and crumpled up the paper.

"You have a passing grade, Mr. Flint, but there's plenty of room for improvement."

"L-let me go now!"

"Oh, someone will, sooner or later, but you see, I have a busy schedule, and I've no time to cater to every one of my students' needs."

"You madman! You goddamn madman! *Get me out of here!*"

"I enjoyed this, Mr. Flint; perhaps we should do it again sometime," Zyid said, though there was definitely no trace of enjoyment on his face. "Come, Takan; it seems that you and Noni will be busy for the next few weeks."

Tack followed Zyid out of the rusty room, leaving the principal's anguished cries behind. As they climbed together out of the dusty construction site, Tack found a newly stoked anger boiling vaguely in his gut. No one deserved that. It would be days before the construction crew returned to work, and there Mr. Flint would lie, slowly losing his sanity until he died of thirst. But strangely, even as Tack mustered up the resolve to say something, the only way he found to express his rage in Zyid's presence was with a quiet question.

"What about the principal?"

"We leave him there," Zyid said, after only a moment's hesitation.

"For how long?" Tack demanded.

"Remember, Takan, act without mercy," Zyid said softly as they walked over to two waiting bikes, Noni having already taken the third. "He lies there for long as it takes for them to find him."

Zyid mounted his bike and silently rode away, leaving a horrified Tack to grip his handlebars tightly.

The boy sat on his cot in the darkness of the orphanage's dormitory, using a flashlight to illuminate the latest entry in the scrapbook that he had carefully assembled over the course of two years.

Two *years.*

For two long, boring years he had bided his time in this festering place, going to school every day, living amidst the other orphans, all of whom were nothing but stupid and ignorant. He didn't remember his parents, though before they had died they had at least left enough money to prevent their son from becoming a vagrant—enough to condemn him to life in a City orphanage. And now, after two dull years, he finally held in his hands that which he had been waiting for all along.

It was a newspaper clipping, whose headline read:

EDUCATORS SEEK BOY FROM DISTRICT 19

The boy felt his hands trembling with excitement, scarcely able to believe that at last he'd have a chance to realize his dark dreams.

At first he had believed the article to be about Umasi, his old mentor, the self-absorbed pacifist in voluntary exile, and he had cursed the paper for writing about the fool. But inevitably, curiosity had prompted him to read the article. Only when he had read the description of the boy they sought did he realize that it was *him* they were looking for. And he knew why—if they were bothering to search for him, it could only mean that they needed his help.

The boy was Edward, a sixteen-year-old child with a bitter history and a monstrous ambition.

Edward flipped back a few pages in the scrapbook, idly browsing through the countless other articles that he had gathered over the years. There were obituaries for Enforcers, stories covering the mysterious gas explosions, the power outage, the demolition of the District 1 School, and more. It was all there, and Edward knew the secret behind it. He knew of the Truancy. For the past two years he had studied them from the shadows.

And now the boy grinned wickedly, for he knew exactly how to destroy them.

17

The Taste of Blood

"So . . . er . . . nice day today," Tack said lamely.

Noni voiced no answer, but turned her icy, piercing eyes on him. It took Tack a few seconds to realize that he suddenly felt embarrassed. Tack quickly looked away; trying to make conversation with Noni was turning out to be harder than killing Enforcers. Unfortunately, there was nothing else to do up on the rooftop on which the two of them stood.

Zyid hadn't lied back at the construction site; Tack and Noni *had* been very busy for the past week, darting all over the City to act on the information that the principal had provided. As a result, the number of recently deceased Educators and Enforcers had steadily piled up. Up until now, Zyid had never asked Noni or Tack to work together, having observed the tension between them. This evening, however, he had insisted that the Educator meeting going on directly below them couldn't be handled by one Truant.

And so Tack and Noni now stood side by side atop the Waterfront Hotel under the blue sky. They wore heavy backpacks, waiting for the meeting to start, and doggedly avoided each other's gaze in the meantime. Tack was beginning to question Zyid's judgment in sending the two of them together; he couldn't see how he was supposed to work with someone he couldn't talk to, and he was sure that Noni was having the same problem. Nagging traces of guilt still began to tug at Tack's conscience, as they always did in Noni's presence. Suddenly, it occurred to Tack that he had an opportunity now to clear the air.

"I'm sorry about what happened in our duel," Tack said suddenly.

Noni's head snapped around, and this time Tack held her gaze as she probed him with her icy, glinting eyes. Suddenly, and entirely unexpectedly, Noni reached up and pulled her scarf down to her neck, revealing the long, ugly gash across her face. Tack only realized that he was staring when he noticed Noni glaring at him.

"Pretty horrible, isn't it?" she said bitterly.

"No, no, it's not!" Tack protested earnestly. "You look fine!"

Noni looked at Tack suspiciously, as if searching for some trace of mockery. Finding none, she seemed to relax slightly and even sat down on the hard roof.

"I owe my life to Zyid, you know," Noni said. "He saved me, a long time ago. I've been with him since before there ever was a Truancy."

"But you're still helping him now," Tack pointed out, simultaneously surprised and pleased that Noni was talking to him at all.

"It's not like before." Noni shook her head. "You're his new favorite now; you should know what it's like."

Tack grimaced. He did know what it was like, and he had a hard time tolerating it, and an even harder time imagining why anyone would want it.

"I didn't *mean* to replace you," Tack said honestly; if anything, he was regretting that he had.

"I know you didn't." Noni sighed. "When he found me, I was alone, scared, insecure, confused. I was weak, so I drew on his strength; I let him guide me so that I wouldn't have to worry about what to do."

"And so now he's not guiding you anymore?" Tack asked tentatively, amazed at what he was hearing.

Noni nodded and then averted her gaze again, looking as if she regretted having spoken at all. Tack let her alone and pondered what he'd heard. Tack hated his position as Zyid's "favorite," and yet Noni coveted it fiercely. Tack would've gladly given it up if he could, but that wasn't his decision to make. Cursing Zyid silently, Tack looked over again at Noni, who had withdrawn a water bottle from her backpack and was drinking from it, her scarf still around her neck. Noticing Tack looking at her, Noni turned and cocked her head at him.

"Are you thirsty?" Noni asked, looking sideways at Tack.

"Huh?" Tack blurted, shaken from his thoughts.

"Are you thirsty?" Noni repeated, looking curiously at him.

"Oh . . . yeah, sure," Tack replied, realizing that he *was* thirsty after all.

Noni screwed the top back onto the water bottle and tossed it over to Tack. Clutching the cool cylinder in his hands, Tack found himself wondering idly just how long it had been since he'd tasted lemonade. Looking up to find that Noni was watching him intently, Tack's face unconsciously flushed red. Removing the cap from the bottle, Tack hoped feverishly that she hadn't noticed anything. Tack gratefully tipped the bottle back and took a large gulp . . .

. . . and then promptly spit it out, gasping heavily. He looked at the bottle in shock, wondering if he'd gone crazy. The liquid he had spit out was splayed out on the ground, crystal clear, and yet Tack wouldn't have been surprised to see it turn dark red at any moment. The drink had barely touched his tongue for a second, but Tack was sure that it had tasted like blood.

"I take it you've never had mineral water before?" Noni asked, actually sounding amused now.

Tack looked up to find her smiling faintly, something that he'd never seen before. He shook off his shock and looked at the bottle again.

"Why does it taste like—"

"Blood?" Noni finished.

Tack nodded.

"It's the iron, I think," Noni said, looking away. "It's in our blood and the water too."

Tack looked at Noni. Her scarf had still remained around her neck, her ugly scar still clearly visible. Tack hesitated for a second, and then, though he was unsure of why, he spoke.

"You can't replace blood, Noni," he said quietly.

Noni's head snapped around to face him. Tack maintained his level gaze, wondering for a minute what he had actually meant and what she had interpreted it to mean. Noni brought her hand up to her scar, seemed to stiffen for a moment, and then slouched, nodding silently. Tack breathed a personal sigh of relief, then looked again at the bottle he held in his hand. Remembering how thirsty he was, Tack raised it to his lips and took another drink.

This time it didn't taste so bad.

"You hear that?" Noni said, suddenly tense.

Tack froze, listening intently. The muffled sound of conversation had slowly begun to drift up from under them. Tack nodded silently at Noni, who gracefully darted over to the large skylight on the roof and peered directly down into the ballroom below. Tack moved to crouch down next to her, and saw that a number of blurry figures wearing what looked like expensive suits had begun to sit down at the conference table conveniently located beneath the skylight.

"I count fourteen," Noni whispered, her icy eyes dancing around the room below.

"There may be some out of sight," Tack pointed out.

"Open with a smoke bomb then, if we don't know what we're dealing with?" Noni murmured.

"And one of the bigger pipe bombs at the same time," Tack agreed. "That alone should get most of the ones at the table."

"You deal with the explosives," Noni suggested. "I'll pick off the survivors."

Tack didn't argue; he was still adjusting to using guns, as they were the one weapon that Umasi had always made a point of not talking about. Noni quickly removed a semiautomatic from her backpack, while Tack unloaded a white brick of smoke bomb material, as well as a large section of concrete pipe sealed at both ends with a fuse sticking out of it. Tack knelt over the window, drew a lighter from his pocket, and clutched the heavy plastic pipe bomb in his arms as Noni checked her weapon.

"Ready?" Tack whispered, holding the unlit lighter to the fuse.

"Waiting on you." Noni nodded.

Tack clicked the lighter on, touched it to the fuse, then lifted the pipe bomb over his head and smashed it through the window before dropping it. Shards of glass sparkled and flew downwards even as the pipe bomb plunked down on the table below. The men in the room had only begun to shout when the bomb exploded, sending shrapnel flying outwards in all directions. There were screams, and then gunshots as Noni began determinedly firing down at anything that moved.

Tack heard the sound of doors below slamming open, and decided that reinforcements had entered the room. Tack grabbed the white brick, touched his lighter to its fuse, and then hurled it downwards quickly. It detonated, and thick white smoke began swiftly filling the room, but not before Tack caught a glimpse of dark figures running in, brandishing guns.

"Time to go," Tack said urgently, turning to Noni. "Before they figure out that we're up here."

Noni nodded, though Tack noticed that her eyes were once more brilliantly fierce. While the men below fired their weapons through the smoke, vainly trying to hit enemies that they couldn't see, Noni and Tack dashed over to the door leading to the stairs, where they paused briefly. They had both dressed casually and might stand a chance of blending in if they cast aside their backpacks and guns, but there was always the possibility that the guards might just shoot down any children they saw.

"Should we risk it?" Tack asked.

"We'll go without the guns," Noni said decisively. "If anyone tries to stop us, I have my knives and you have your sword."

Tack's hand unconsciously reached down to touch the hilt of his ceramic blade.

"All right," Tack said, dropping his backpack without regret.

Noni cast aside her rifle and dropped her backpack next to Tack's. Then they opened the door and dashed down the flight of stairs as fast as they could. Reaching the second-to-top floor, they exited the stairwell and made for the nearest elevator. As they did, three grim-faced men in black suits burst out of one of the hotel rooms. Two of them dashed for the stairs immediately, but one of them stopped to eye Noni and Tack suspiciously.

"You two, what are you doing here?" the man demanded, raising a pistol menacingly.

"We're trying to find our parents," Tack said, injecting a note of fear into his voice. "We heard the noises upstairs—what's going on?"

The man hesitated and looked them over uncertainly.

"What's that?" he demanded, pointing at Tack's sword.

"It's a toy; I got it for my birthday," Tack lied.

The man paused, then lowered his gun. The next thing Tack knew, Noni had plunged a knife into the man's throat. The hapless Enforcer gurgled and gasped horribly as blood sputtered from his neck, and Noni dispassionately relieved him of his pistol, threw it aside, and wiped her knife on his suit. The move had been so cold-bloodedly executed that Tack looked over at Noni, slightly horrified.

"There was no need for that; he was lowering his weapon," Tack said weakly.

"We can't take any chances," Noni said flatly, her voice so mechanically cold that she seemed like an entirely different person from the one Tack had spoken with on the roof. "We need to go, now. We cannot be seen here."

Tack gritted his teeth and looked down at the man, whose blood was still flowing freely from his throat. Noni was right; they couldn't be seen here. Deciding to pursue the topic later, Tack shook his head and followed Noni down the hall, around a corner, past countless doors until they reached the elevators. Noni quickly pressed the elevator buttons, and Tack was pleased to see one arrive quickly. Noni and Tack piled into it, finding that it was comfortably empty except for them.

The elevator took a few seconds to sink to the first floor, where it opened its doors, and Tack and Noni stepped out to find the lobby in chaos. Bellhops, janitors, managers, maids, and hotel guests all ran about screaming and crying while Enforcers did their best to sort through the commotion. Tack and Noni slipped into the frantic crowd, and slinked over to the door. As they did, Tack noticed that Noni had lifted her scarf back up onto her face.

Enforcers shoved past them without giving them a second thought, and they made it outside safely, where they vanished into the stream of fleeing people, running right past arriving Enforcer patrol cars. Sometimes it was good, Tack realized as they walked calmly over to the nearest subway, that people didn't take children very seriously.

So, bad news *and* good news?" the Mayor said, snapping his lighter shut as his cabinet sat nervously at the conference table. "That's a first. Give me the bad news; we've had so much of it around here that I think I've become numb to it."

The cabinet members looked at each other apprehensively.

"Well, sir, the school budget committee meeting was . . . interrupted," one cabinet member worded carefully.

" 'Interrupted'? Where do you come up with these euphemisms?" the Mayor said incredulously. "How many were killed?"

"Erm . . . five Educators dead, nine badly wounded," the cabinet member said tentatively. "An Enforcer was also killed; he tried to rush to the rescue."

"Any idea how the Truancy pulled this one off?" the Mayor demanded impatiently.

"They dropped a crude explosive through a skylight and picked off survivors through a smoke cloud," another cabinet member summarized quickly.

"And then they marched right out, did they?" the Mayor demanded.

"They did kill another guard during their escape," the cabinet member added helpfully.

"Great. I'm glad that all the extra security is worth something." The Mayor sighed tiredly. "Give me the good news, and quickly."

One of the cabinet members drew some papers out of a folder and flipped through them.

" 'On a routine foot patrol through District 13 at five twenty-seven P.M. this evening, two Enforcer officers spotted a number of Truants entering and exiting an abandoned movie theater,' " the cabinet member read out loud. " 'At least a dozen separate individuals were counted, and more are suspected to have holed up there. Under the circumstances, the patrol thought it best to report it directly to the nearest precinct and retreat.' "

"This is their main hideout?" the Mayor said, flipping his lighter open with unconcealed excitement in his voice.

"That's a possibility." The cabinet member nodded, flipping through the pages. "But it's just as likely that this is a cell or an outpost operating on its own. Either way, this is the first time we've been able to reliably locate a Truant shelter without being detected."

"Without being detected?" the Mayor repeated. "The Enforcers got away without being seen?"

"The officers believe so, yes." The cabinet member nodded, looking immensely relieved at the Mayor's reception of the news.

"It's about time that they did something right." The Mayor clicked his lighter shut. "Prepare a full assault immediately; give the Enforcers the authorization for anything they need. Move in on them at first light. I want these Truants dead or captured before they wake up tomorrow."

"It will be done," a cabinet member assured.

"Good," the Mayor said enthusiastically. "This may be the chance we've been waiting for. If this movie theater is the center of their operations, they'll be finished. If not, we'll still have paid them back for their actions at the budget meeting. Speaking of which"—the Mayor now turned to look grimly at his cabinet—"we need to discuss some of the so-called security measures you've put in place."

Do you have a body count for me?" Zyid asked curtly.

"No, sir," Tack and Noni said in unison.

"Very well," Zyid said. "I wouldn't have expected one under the circumstances, and you did accomplish the objective. Overall, a job well done."

Tack fidgeted uncomfortably. He still hadn't gotten used to Zyid complimenting him on how good his performance in killing was. Noni, however, looked pleased; her blue eyes sparkled as she stood at attention in the middle of the abandoned flower shop.

"By the way, I'd recommend that you two get some sleep now," Zyid suggested, turning around to face them. "You won't be getting much tomorrow."

"What do you mean, sir?" Tack asked softly, betraying none of the apprehension he felt boiling in his stomach.

"One of our cells contacted me earlier this evening," Zyid explained. "They believe that an Enforcer patrol spotted them." He raised his chin, surveying Tack and Noni imperiously. "I have ordered them to stand their ground."

Tack started, and quickly looked sideways at Noni, whose eyes had also widened.

"The Enforcers believed that they went unnoticed," Zyid continued, ignoring the looks on Tack's and Noni's faces. "They will wait to attack only when they are ready. In the meantime, I have directed several parties to reinforce their position, and additional reinforcements will be setting out tonight at midnight."

"But why?" Tack blurted, unable to stop himself.

"Because we now have the resources to make a stand," Zyid explained. "The Enforcers have constantly hunted us, never believing for a second that we could or would risk a full-scale battle. But this City cannot be won without them, and tomorrow will see the first one of this war."

"But we can't win a fight like that!" Tack protested suddenly, and out of the corner of his eye he noticed Noni jerk her head towards him in surprise.

Zyid raised an eyebrow.

"It is true that the Educators have greater numbers and resources," Zyid conceded. "It is probable that we will lose. It is even likely that many Truants will die, when their lives might otherwise have been spared."

"Then why?" Tack demanded, causing Noni to let out a small gasp.

"Because they are willing to lay down their lives for this!" Zyid hissed, his voice suddenly harsh enough to make Tack recoil. "Because they will make the Educators fear *them* before they die, instead of living the other way around! And because it is my decision to make, and their deaths will be on my hands, not yours, Takan!"

Zyid's dark eyes flashed menacingly, his teeth bared like some enraged beast. Tack didn't think he'd ever seen a more frightening expression, and he reflexively stepped backwards. A moment later, Zyid's sudden anger faded, and the Truancy leader relaxed back into his emotionless shell.

"The Educators will learn to take us seriously," Zyid said calmly. "Tomorrow will be decisive for us—win or lose. You two are dismissed. Be back here by midnight."

"Yes, sir," Noni said immediately, bowing her head.

"Yes, sir," Tack said.

Zyid turned away from them again and gave no sign of further acknowledging their presence. Tack turned and headed for the door, Noni following closely. As they stepped outside onto the street, the sun was setting far on the western horizon, allowing darkness to blanket the City once more. Tack took a deep breath of night air, then turned to look at Noni, only to find that she was already gazing at him. For a moment their eyes met, and then Noni turned and darted away into the growing darkness.

Tack watched her go, then contemplated going next door to the Truancy hideout to take a nap. Then he shook his head and began determinedly heading down the street, towards The Bar. The Bar was an establishment located a few blocks from the Truant hideout, where a number of Truants had restocked and repopulated an abandoned bar where they sold stolen alcoholic beverages cheap. The Bar was the only place Truants were able to get alcohol ever since the bulk of the Truancy had come under the direct supervision of Zyid.

The Bar wasn't approved of by Zyid, and no one was really sure that he even knew about it, though rumor had it that he did know but tolerated its presence anyway, accepting that sometimes Truants saw and did things that made alcohol necessary. Tack, for his part, always made a point of drinking after each kill to make sure that his memories wouldn't cause him too many problems. Lately his thoughts hadn't been filled with only images of Suzie, but also with flashes of bodies impaled upon a sword, blood streaming from gunshot wounds as a man's pale hands clutched desperately at his chest, a man bound to a table, screaming as drops of water fell upon his brow. They were victims, all of them.

His victims.

Tack shook the twinges of guilt from his head and resolutely pushed his way into The Bar, making his way towards an unoccupied stool. A number of Truants were there already, some of them slumped in corners, snoring loudly, as others slopped cheap beer down their chins or else engaged in raucous conversation with their companions.

Tack sat down on the stool and waved towards the bartender on duty.

"Beer, any kind," Tack said, pushing a wrinkled bill across the counter.

The bartender nodded and bent down behind the counter,

rising up to push a warm bottle over to Tack. Ignoring the temperature, Tack twisted the cap off and took a gulp, enjoying the sensation as the beverage ran down his throat. He was about to take another gulp when a voice called out to him.

"Takan! Hey, Takan!"

Tack turned to see Steve pushing his way through a group of Truants. Tack quickly scoured his memory; the last time he could remember seeing Steve was the day that they had fled the old hideout with Gabriel.

"Hey, Steve, what's up?" Tack asked with great effort, finding it difficult to talk normally after spending much time in Zyid's presence.

"Did you hear about tomorrow?" Steve asked excitedly.

"You mean, the battle?" Tack asked.

"That's the one!" Steve said enthusiastically. "Finally we get to show those Educators what we're made of. I'm set to leave with the midnight group!"

"Really?" Tack frowned. "So am I. Zyid just told me about it."

"That's great; I guess we'll be fighting side by side then," Steve said, rubbing his hands eagerly.

"Aren't you worried at all?" Tack asked, baffled at how ready Steve was to throw himself into terrible harm's way.

"You mean, about dying?" Steve laughed lightly. "Takan, if I were worried about that, I would never have joined the Truancy. There's not much else for me to live for, and if I die, I'll do it giving the Educators a piece of my mind."

It was in that moment, talking with Steve, that Tack realized that Zyid was right after all. Everything that had been said in that moment of anger had been true. Tack took another swig of beer as he continued his conversation with

Steve. As he drank his troubles away, chatting amiably, waiting for midnight to come, Tack suddenly wondered what sort of City it was, where a boy like Zyid could command such power and be so right . . . and yet so wrong.

Edward walked casually through the Grand Park, enjoying the luminous effect that the pale glow of the street lamps had on his dark surroundings as he traveled the paved paths. It was nighttime now, and he had sneaked out of the boring orphanage to be here. The orphanage was in District 18, where Edward had lived and attended school for as long as he could remember. It wasn't too far from the Grand Park of District 20, but it was still a lengthy trek, and he normally wouldn't have risked it—the orphanage staff was often more strict than the teachers at school.

However, tonight he was here with a purpose. He would take the first, small step towards realizing the dreams that he had cultivated for years—dreams of attaining power and vindication that others dreamed of but none ever achieved. He dreamed of having power over all those that had ever pushed him around or slighted him. Students, Enforcers, Educators, they would all answer to him before the end. None would escape his vengeance.

And there was one he would save for the end, Edward reminded himself as he inhaled deeply, savoring the rare smell of recently mowed grass. Umasi. Edward shivered slightly at the very thought of the boy. He had once tried to kill Umasi, only to be humiliated at his hands. Edward now knew better than to attempt another personal confrontation with his former mentor, at least until all the rest of the City was under his control. Only then would Edward have his final revenge.

Edward had dreams.

He also had memories.

And some of them were buried in this park.

Edward was whistling as he finally reached his destination—the great lawn of the Grand Park. The lawn had several trees placed intermittently throughout the vast green expanses of grass, but one stood out to Edward. It wasn't the largest, nor was it the most prominent, but rather the thinnest and lankiest of them all. Beneath it, Edward knew, was a personal treasure that he had buried two years ago.

Whipping out a small hand shovel, Edward set to work on the soil beneath the tree. It didn't take him long to expose an object wrapped in a plain white towel. Edward swiftly unwrapped the towel, seized the object within it, and turned it about in his hands nostalgically.

It was the sunglasses, the very pair that he had stolen from Umasi on that day when he had tasted defeat. It was a symbolic relic for Edward, evidence that he been in Umasi's lair, stolen something precious of his, and come out unscathed.

Edward grinned as he slipped the sunglasses into his pocket, feeling an intense excitement rise within him. His patience had paid off. His time was fast approaching. He could finally cease his dull act, and he would be free from his life entombed at the orphanage. He would help the desperate Educators and the Enforcers destroy the Truancy.

And then he would dominate them all.

"Umasi." Edward laughed darkly as he stood alone in the park. "You'll regret not killing me when you had the chance!"

18

The Heat of Battle

They will undoubtedly try to surround us," Zyid warned, crouching down over a map. "Accordingly, there are mines set here, here, and here, to cover our back." Zyid pointed at groups of dots etched on the map. "Snipers and RPGs have been positioned on the rooftops to the front. The RPGs have been instructed to save their ammunition for helicopters. As for ground assaults, the Enforcers have only two separate streets from which they can attack us head-on. We've formed wooden barricades on the western flank that will be burned if we retreat, and we've blown parts off of the buildings to the eastern side to form cover."

Tack and the eleven other Truants crowded around Zyid nodded. They were inside the entrance hallway of the movie theater, running over the plans one last time before they headed out to join the Truants already out there. Tack had indeed caught some sleep the previous evening, falling asleep at

The Bar, where he had lain sprawled over the counter until Steve shook him awake.

"The bulk of our forces," Zyid continued, "are positioned behind the masonry or the barricades. We have two parties covering our flank as well, in the unlikely case that they break through the minefield. Explosive barrels have been strategically placed all around to slow oncoming attackers. As a last-ditch resort, we've laid smoke bombs at the ends of the eastern and western streets which retreating forces will set off before falling back."

Zyid pointed at two squares imprinted on the map.

"In the case that they should reach the theater, we'll barricade the front doors and hold them off while we retreat through the back. There are a number of alleyways and abandoned buildings to flee to or hide in if we are routed. Also, as you can see"—Zyid now gestured towards the doors of the movie theater where two large cylindrical objects lay—"we have placed pipe bombs at the entrance, which should buy us more time."

Zyid stood up now, looking around at the apprehensive-but-determined Truants.

"As you know, a party consists of five people," Zyid said. "Each of you has been assigned to a party, and each of you has an officer to follow, with the exceptions of Noni and Takan. I would like them to stay for a moment"—Zyid looked at Noni and Tack in turn—"and everyone else to please head out to your assigned barricades."

There was a scramble as the Truants all filed out of the front doors, taking care not to tread on the pipe bombs as they went. Noni and Tack stood stiffly before Zyid, who waited for the last of the other Truants to leave and shut the doors behind him.

"Takan, you will be overseeing the eastern side," Zyid said. "Noni, you will be overseeing the western barricades. I myself will be traveling to whichever point needs me the most. If either of you is beaten back, it will be up to you to detonate the smoke bomb. This will serve as a signal to the other side and will also give you cover as you retreat. Understood?"

"Yes, sir," Noni and Tack said simultaneously.

"Good." Zyid picked up a shotgun from the ground and slung it over his shoulder, drawing his ceramic sword at the same time. "We've been lucky that they haven't attacked yet, but that won't last long. I think they expect to catch us asleep." Zyid let out a cold chuckle. "Let's disappoint them."

Zyid strode out the front doors of the theater, past the box office, and out into the dark streets. The sky was beginning to turn from black to deep blue, with the first traces of sunlight peeping over the eastern horizon. Noni sprinted off to the left with Zyid following leisurely. Tack steeled himself, shook off any weariness that clung to his body, and then darted to his right. He ran past a cluster of three explosive barrels, and up the street until it forced him to round a corner.

Tack boggled at what he saw; huge chunks of brick and masonry lay strewn all over the street, and behind each of them groups of five Truants crouched grimly, armed with guns. Barrels had been placed to the sides of the street, protecting the Truants' flanks. Above, on the rooftops, the dark silhouettes of still more Truants milled about restlessly. And only a few yards away from him, guarded by two Truants, rested a large, white cube that Tack instantly recognized as a smoke bomb. It was, perhaps, the most elaborate setup that Tack had ever seen.

"Takan, sir!" a voice called.

Tack turned to see a boy that he'd never met before run up to him, clutching a cell phone in his hand. Tack realized that he'd gained something of a reputation, having been Zyid's assistant for such a long time.

"Yes?" Tack asked as the boy halted in front of him.

"Word from the advance positions!" The boy waved the cell phone breathlessly. "Enforcer patrol cars and armored vehicles are close, heading this way by the looks of it. Helicopters too. We haven't been spotted yet though."

"So we have the element of surprise." Tack's mind began racing. "They can't drive over this mess; they'll have to fight us on foot. I'm headed for the front lines."

"Good luck!" the boy said earnestly, pocketing the cell phone and shouldering his rifle and running off to warn the other Truants.

Tack dashed past a number of chunks of masonry, slowing down slightly as he saw a few Truants crouched behind RPGs.

"Everyone with an RPG," Tack called out in a sudden burst of inspiration, "follow me!"

Tack was surprised and pleased to see a half-dozen Truants immediately leap up and run over to him; having a reputation had its perks. Tack continued running down the street until he reached the large chunk of a bank building that was at the front of the Truant positions. No Truants had yet been brave enough to take shelter behind this one, and Tack wasted no time in filling the vacancy, the six RPG-wielding Truants quickly following suit.

Suddenly, from far overhead, a faint buzzing noise reached their ears. Tack looked up to see a familiar black spot moving across the dawning sky.

"Ignore it," Tack whispered to the nervous Truants around him. "Leave the helicopters to the guys on the roofs. When the vehicles come into view, it's up to you to take them out."

The Truants nodded, which was all they had time for before the sound of speeding cars reached their ears. Then, at once, so many Enforcer cars burst around the corner and drove towards them that Tack was sure that every precinct in the City must have been emptied. The car sirens were off, and Tack, peering around the shelter of the masonry, was satisfied by the looks of surprise on the drivers' faces as they braked at the sight of the wreckage before them.

Tack wasn't about to give their surprise any time to wear off.

"Shoot, now!" Tack hissed.

The six Truants burst from around the shelter and hastily aimed before firing their rockets forward. Tack crawled above the obstacle and swung his rifle around towards the Enforcers. He was pleased to see that most of the rockets had done their job, demolishing the leading Enforcer cars and creating more obstacles for the others, though one rocket had gone awry and smashed into a storefront instead.

The Truants cheered, but not for long. The element of surprise was no longer theirs, and from the immense number of vehicles countless Enforcer officers poured forth like enraged bees from a damaged hive. At the end of the Enforcer column, a number of vehicles were already backing up, undoubtedly going around to attempt the western road instead.

"You guys, fall back!" Tack ordered, and heard the Truants all scramble for the nearest cover behind them.

Tack, for his part, stood his ground. Aiming his rifle, Tack fired through the smoke and flames rising from the wrecked cars and was pleased to hear a scream that meant he'd hit his mark. As dark shapes began to run through the smoke to emerge as grim and dangerous men, Tack quickly fired at as many as he could, downing a few before they could properly see him. But the number of Enforcers plunging towards him steadily increased, and soon Tack was forced to duck behind the masonry as a hail of bullets crashed into and around it.

Looking back desperately at the other fallen pieces of buildings, Tack saw other Truants poking their heads around them, firing shots at the onrushing Enforcers. One of the Truants waved furiously at Tack, and a moment later four other Truants came into view from behind their cover, firing furiously to keep the Enforcers' heads down. Tack didn't hesitate; he lunged and dived behind the obstacle, coming to a rest behind it just as the Enforcers overran his old position.

Tack swung his rifle around and fired repeatedly at the mass of blue uniforms surging towards him. All around him the ear-popping sounds of rifle shots hammered at his head, and Tack felt that he might go deaf if he stayed there. Still, he kept firing, and the Enforcers kept coming, occasionally pausing to fire back at the Truants.

Suddenly, over the din, the sound of a scream registered in Tack's numb ears, and he turned to see the Truant next to him sprawled on the ground, bleeding badly from the head. A few of the other Truants behind the cover pulled his body to safety and began examining him frantically. Tack ignored them and continued firing, knowing that their efforts were useless; the boy was obviously dead. Though a few more uniformed figures crumpled and fell to Tack's shots, more suddenly surged forward while Tack's companions were still busy examining their fallen comrade. Tack let out a snarl of frustration and drew his sword.

"Leave him; fall back!" Tack shouted at the other Truants.

"But—," one of them began to protest.

"*Do it!*" Tack roared.

Seeing the Enforcers draw dangerously close, the Truants looked at each other with frightened expressions, and then bolted, dashing for the nearest cover behind which other Truants were already waiting and firing. Tack again held his ground, crouching out of sight as reckless adrenaline shot through his veins. Obviously thinking that all the Truants behind the obstacle had fled, three Enforcers ran impatiently past it, unaware that Tack was lurking in wait. Tack lunged, plunging his sword straight through the first Enforcer's back, then bringing his rifle up to shoot another at point-blank range, promptly dropping him to the ground. The third Enforcer spun around and was about to raise his gun when Tack swiftly slashed at his throat, cutting a neat gash across it from which blood spewed, splattering Tack's clothes.

Another Enforcer appeared and aimed at Tack immediately. Tack dropped to the ground and slashed at the man's legs, crippling him and allowing Tack to follow up with a head shot with his gun. The other Enforcers seemed to hang back, wary now of this deadly adversary that lurked out of sight. Tack seized the opportunity and scrambled to his feet, dashing for the next nearest obstacle. As he did, Tack felt a bullet pass right by his ear, and then he was safely behind cover, with waiting Truants helping him to his knees.

By now a larger number of Truants had accumulated at each position that hadn't yet been overrun, allowing them to better resist the Enforcer advance. Wiping his sword on his pants, Tack peered around the obstacle to see the Enforcers now crouching behind the positions the Truants had abandoned. Tack swore loudly, but the sound was lost to the relentless, pounding sound of gunshots. Suddenly, Tack saw something fly through the air and land behind an adjacent obstacle where other Truants had taken cover. A moment later, a fiery explosion blossomed, and through the smoke Tack saw several bodies hit the ground.

"What the hell?" a Truant next to Tack exclaimed in horror.

"Bastards are using grenades!" Tack shouted furiously; somehow he felt that the Enforcers were cheating. "Fall back!" he yelled, gritting his teeth in frustration as he realized that it was the third time he'd said it.

The Truants didn't hesitate to obey, and this time Tack followed them, and not a moment too soon; as they dived behind the nearest cover, a grenade plunked down right where they had been hidden just a second ago. Suddenly, even as the smoke from the second grenade subsided, Tack's ringing ears were assaulted by a new, dreaded sound that struck terror into his heart. Looking up, Tack saw a black helicopter swooping down on their position, this one looking much deadlier than the one he had fled from before; it had two intimidating machine guns on either side of it that definitely looked like they meant business.

Tack and the Truants around him instinctively ducked down to the ground as the machine guns began snarling as they opened fire, sending a rain of bullets down upon the Truant positions. The only good thing Tack could see about the situation was that the Enforcers were now also hanging back, seemingly unwilling to approach for fear of friendly fire from the chopper.

Then there was another explosion, and Tack looked up to see the helicopter spiraling perilously towards the ground, smoke streaming from one side. Tack silently cheered whatever Truant that had been responsible for that hit. A moment later, the helicopter came crashing down right on top of the advancing Enforcers, most of whom dived aside in time; others, however, vanished in the resulting fireball. Taking advantage of the distraction, Tack leaped from behind cover and fired at an Enforcer that had paused to look back at the helicopter. The first shot caught the man in the arm; the next one brought him permanently to the ground.

Fresh Enforcers now began streaming from around the wreckage of the helicopter, and a sudden barrage of bullets forced Tack to take cover. Remembering the explosive barrels to either side of the street, Tack aimed around the obstacle and fired wildly in the left barrels' general direction. One of his shots hit, and the subsequent explosion sent Enforcers flying through the air.

"Fall back now, while they're busy!" Tack shouted to all the Truants nearby.

The Truants hastened to obey, and as he moved towards new shelter Tack spun around and fired a neat shot right into the explosive barrel on the right. Not waiting to see the results, Tack turned and dived behind a large piece of a deli rooftop as bullets whizzed by him. Suddenly, Tack felt an enormous tremor wrack the ground, and he spun around to see the burning wreckage of a second helicopter smoking in the middle of the street behind him. His ears were so numb that he hadn't heard the helicopter arrive or crash, something that vaguely frightened him. As his wits returned to him, however, Tack realized that the other Truants were already fleeing behind the wreckage of the helicopter without waiting for his word. Seeing a few of them get shot down before they could make it, Tack cursed and readied his sword.

An Enforcer leaped right over the piece of rooftop that Tack was crouched behind, and a moment later his mouth opened to emit what Tack knew was a scream despite the fact that his ears were too numb to hear it; it couldn't have been anything else, after all, since Tack had just plunged his sword into the man as he leaped overhead. Seizing the Enforcer's body, Tack slung it over his shoulder as a sort of morbid armor and swiftly retreated around the wreckage of the helicopter. As he made it to temporary safety, Tack threw the body away from him and dashed for the nearest obstacle. Once behind it, Tack looked back and saw with a sinking heart that they'd almost been pushed back to the end of the street; the white cube was in sight, its guards looking increasingly nervous.

As Enforcers once more poured from around the new helicopter crash, Tack made a quick decision that he knew would save the most lives.

"Retreat!" Tack bellowed. "Fall back!"

The Truants stared blankly at Tack, who decided to set the example and run. He dashed for the white cube, and as bullets flew at him and fleeing Truants screamed as they were hit, Tack drew a lighter from his pocket and touched it to the fuse on the cube. A few seconds later, a massive cloud of white smoke enveloped the area, eliciting shouts of confusion from the Enforcers. Using the smoke as cover, the Truants began to abandon the street completely, openly fleeing around the block and back towards the movie theater. Tack realized that the fight had been hopeless from the start; Zyid was able to outwit the Enforcers, but they simply outnumbered and outmatched the Truancy.

As Tack turned to fire at any Enforcers that had come through the cloud, he saw something that sent a wave of shock running through him, shortly followed by a surge of anger. A redheaded, unarmed Truant was standing on the sidewalk, deep in conversation with two uniformed Enforcers. The Truant pointed at the movie theater, the Enforcers spoke into their radios, and then they quickly ushered the turncoat Truant into an abandoned pizzeria.

Tack felt a righteous fury grip his mind, and the next thing he knew he was recklessly dashing towards the pizzeria, sword in one hand and gun in the other. Without looking twice, he shot down an Enforcer that emerged from the cloud, and then kicked open the door to the pizzeria as soon as he reached it. Plunging inside, Tack immediately brought his sword stabbing forward into the gut of the first Enforcer, who had been right by the door, and then brought his gun up to fire repeatedly at the second Enforcer until his gun had exhausted all of the rest of its thirty-two shots.

Loading a fresh clip into his rifle, Tack advanced into the dingy room, spotting the redheaded traitor cowering in a corner. As Tack grimly examined the boy's face, he found, with a jolt, that he recognized the Truant; it was Charles, the redheaded cigarette addict that he'd met the day he joined the Truancy. Tack raised his gun, and Charles let out a moan as he scrabbled to his feet. The ringing in Tack's ears had subsided just enough so that he could hear the boy's protests.

"Don't shoot me, please!" Charles begged, pressing his back against the wall. "Don't shoot; I didn't mean any harm; I just wanted out!"

"Why?" Tack held his gun straight, his voice filled with cold fury.

"Because it's too much! I don't want to die; I don't want anyone else to die; I just want out; I'll take the streets, the sewers, anything; please, let me go!" the boy wailed.

"You betrayed us," Tack said icily.

"I just wanted to leave! I hate school too; I like you guys; I just don't want to see any more death! I can't even calm my nerves anymore!" Charles wailed, sweating. "Please, Takan!"

"Why didn't you tell us?" Tack demanded.

"I couldn't!" Charles moaned hysterically. "You know Zyid! I was scared, and even if I asked he wouldn't let me; you know he wouldn't!"

"You were talking with the Enforcers about the theater," Tack pointed out. "You told them about the pipe bombs, didn't you?"

"I'm sorry; I swear I am! I just wasn't thinking; I just wanted out so bad, so *bad*! Please, man, don't screw me on this; I didn't mean any harm!" Charles slumped to the floor, crying.

Tack wavered. The boy's intentions were innocent. He didn't want to betray anyone. But still, he did betray someone—he betrayed them all. He put the entire Truancy in danger. If Tack hadn't caught him, who knew what he might have told the Educators? And if one kid lost his nerve and deserted, who could tell how many others would follow?

As the boy continued crying on the ground, Tack felt a sudden remorse welling up in his throat. Looking down at the blood on his clothes, he realized that he was being a monster. He didn't want to hurt a fellow Truant, no matter what. Since when had he become so heartless? Tack lowered his gun.

"Get up," he said hoarsely.

Charles looked up at Tack in terror, saw that he'd lowered his weapon, and then slowly got to his feet.

"It's okay," Tack said soothingly. "Don't worry, I won't do anything, but you are going to have to come back."

Charles' eyes ballooned.

"Back? I can't go back!" he screamed. "Zyid will make an example of me; you know he will; he'll have to! I can't, not back there, not with everyone around!"

"He won't kill you; the other kids would be disgusted if he did," Tack said, trying to convince himself just as much as he was trying to convince Charles.

"How can I look at their faces again? I ran away; I was a coward! I can't do it! They'll hate me!"

"This isn't school, damn it!" Tack yelled suddenly. "We don't fight each other!"

"I can't take that shame!" Charles insisted. "Please Takan, just let me go. I'll disappear. You won't regret it. No one will ever know."

Tack had opened his mouth to answer when suddenly another voice issued from behind him.

"I would know," Zyid said quietly.

Tack would forever remember the look of pure, bestial terror on the boy's face as Zyid spoke. Turning around to face the Truancy leader, Tack wanted to speak, to say something that might stop Zyid. But as Tack looked at Zyid, he found himself familiarly speechless, unable to say a word in that formidable presence. Zyid was again the judge, and he now the bailiff, with the defendant cowering in a corner. As Tack gazed at Zyid's face, he saw no trace of anger, but instead he was sure that, for the briefest of seconds, a great sadness had flitted across Zyid's face.

Charles, at least, seemed to know what this meant.

"No . . . no please no . . . no no no *no*!"

"My apologies," Zyid said quietly.

Tack froze. He could see it coming; he *knew* what was coming next. He wanted to stop it, he had told himself that he wouldn't allow it . . . but when the moment came, he couldn't even try. His own will had deserted him, and his sword lay motionless at his side.

Zyid drew his own sword swiftly, and then plunged it into the boy's heart in one fluid motion. The boy let out a final whimper before slumping against the bloodied wall. Zyid drew himself up slowly, as a great weariness now hung about his shoulders. Zyid straightened himself majestically, wiped his sword on the dead boy's shirt, then sheathed his weapon and turned to Tack.

"Takan, he died a hero's death fighting the Enforcers. Do you understand?"

Tack's face was emotionless even as he clenched his fist, gripping his pistol so hard that his hand turned red. How dare he. How *dare* he. He had no decency—he'd killed a defenseless boy like his life had meant nothing. It was murder in cold blood. Just like Suzie. At least this time Zyid was trying to do something for the dead person. Where was the heroism when Suzie died? Who had acknowledged anything about her? No one, least of all her killer, standing just three feet away!

"I understand," Tack croaked.

Zyid nodded solemnly, and then turned to leave. But this time, Tack was seized by a sudden madness and spun around to raise his gun, pointing it straight at Zyid's back. Breathing heavily, Tack could feel his face muscles twitch. Zyid might've stopped walking at that point, but Tack couldn't tell for sure. All he knew was rage. Dominating, blinding rage. It would be so easy. *So easy*. All he had to do was pull the trigger, and it would be all over. Thanks to Zyid himself, Tack knew the City better than anyone. He could avenge his sister's death and vanish in seconds. It would be easier than so many of his other kills. That was why he'd joined the Truancy, wasn't it? To kill this heartless *murderer*!

Tack blinked, then looked at Zyid again. The leader of the Truancy was standing quite still, listening to Tack's heavy breathing. Zyid made no move to run or turn around, but instead crossed his arms and waited. Tack struggled with himself for another second . . .

Then exhaled loudly, dropping his gun and his gaze.

Zyid didn't say a word, didn't turn around, but just walked away, leaving Tack shaking on the ground, supporting himself with his arms. Tack's head was swimming, anger giving way to nauseating confusion. Why couldn't he do it? Zyid had to die; Tack had known that ever since the day Suzie had died—so *what was stopping him*?

"Don't worry about it, Takan," Zyid called back. "The loss of a comrade is always difficult to accept."

Tack didn't know how long he had lain on the floor of that pizzeria, gasping as emotional spasms wracked his body. He didn't cry, though he certainly felt like it. The confusion and chaos in his head overwhelmed him, and all thoughts of war or killing or death left his mind, and he could have sworn that he saw Suzie smiling at him. Then the vision was shattered as a warm hand rested on his shoulder.

"Takan," a voice called gently. "Takan, are you all right?"

Tack looked up blearily, and saw a pair of icy blue eyes looking down at him concernedly. Tack shook his head violently and dropped his head to the ground, rubbing it against the floor as if it'd somehow relieve him of his painful confusion.

"That's not your blood, Takan," Noni said softly, and Tack felt her hands probing his body. "You're not hit anywhere. What's wrong?"

Tack froze at Noni's touch. Of all the people to see him at his weakest, she was the last that Tack would've wanted. Her concern burned him, as if he knew he were unworthy of it. These latest worries took their place at the top of Tack's pile of sanity, and then quite suddenly the whole thing came crashing down.

"Everything's wrong!" Tack wailed, thrashing wildly.

Tack felt the pair of hands firmly restrain him, pressing him down to the floor. He opened his eyes and saw icy blue ones staring back into his own, and their unblinking stare seemed to calm his troubled mind. Noni held his gaze, and then cupped his face in her hands.

"There are people counting on you, Takan," Noni said clearly, and Tack found himself nodding weakly. "Don't let us down."

Her words were like cool water dousing his feverish confusion, and with her help Tack shakily but determinedly returned to his feet. Tack steadied himself, and then felt his gun being replaced in his hand. Noni patted him gently on his back, and Tack realized that he didn't feel confused anymore, but perfectly sober. Without any further interruptions, the two of them emerged from the pizzeria together, and both brought their weapons up switched to full automatic fire. The gun vibrated in Tack's hands violently as it spewed out an endless stream of bullets, mowing down all the Enforcers that had just emerged from the smoke cloud and had been taken by surprise.

Once the last immediately dangerous Enforcer had crumpled to the ground, Tack and Noni reloaded their weapons. Tack took the opportunity to look over to the west, where he saw a second cloud of white smoke rising into the air. The theater, by the looks of it, had already come under assault; dead Enforcers littered the ground around it, and determined Truants had barricaded themselves inside the box office. Noni grabbed Tack firmly by the arm and ran for the theater with him in tow. As they ran, Tack felt one of his loose shoes fly off, but he could hardly afford to pay it any attention.

"Your side fell faster than we thought it would," Noni chided gently as they drew closer to the theater. "We burned the barricades on our side, and that seems to be slowing them down a bit."

Tack looked westwards. Small gray plumes of smoke did seem to be rising behind the white cloud. As they reached the theater, the Truants inside the box office spoke into a walkie-talkie, and the doors were swung open to admit Tack and Noni by several waiting Truants. Soon afterwards, the Truants from the box office joined them, firing a few parting shots at some advancing Enforcers.

"They know about the pipe bombs," Tack cautioned, pointing at the cylinders by the doors.

"I know." Noni nodded. "Zyid told me. They're expecting us to blow them up as they come in, so we're going to roll one out instead. The moment the second fuse is lit, we head for the back entrance and retreat."

"Are we meeting back at the hideout?" Tack asked feebly.

"Whenever we can, yes," Noni said reassuringly. "This wasn't a total loss, Takan. We got a lot more of them than they got of us."

"Yeah," Tack said vaguely.

"Help me with this," Noni said, grabbing one end of the cylindrical concrete pipe.

Tack grabbed the other end, and with one hand still on the pipe, Noni drew a lighter from her pocket and touched it to the fuse. Tack kicked the theater doors open, and in perfect sync Tack and Noni hurled the pipe bomb out into the midst of some wary Enforcers. Noni then touched her lighter to the second pipe bomb, and grabbed Tack's arm before running. They heard the first pipe bomb explode, which quickly set off the second. Tack silently hoped that the blast would block up the entrance, but those hopes were not high.

Still, the time it bought was enough, and they burst from the back doors and past the wreckage of Enforcer vehicles that indicated that the Enforcers had indeed tried sneaking up from behind through the minefields. As they ran however, Tack's bare foot slammed carelessly against the side of a concrete brick, and Tack felt a sudden, persistent pain shoot through his foot. He limped around frenziedly, and looked down to see that the nail on his big toe had been nearly torn off, blood flowing from the wound.

"Are you all right?" Noni asked worriedly. "That's a hell of a way to get injured, out here of all places."

"I'll live." Tack gritted his teeth. "We don't have much time; we'd better get going."

Tack looked up and met Noni's gaze, seeing concerned apprehension there. Tack understood, and knew that Noni also understood, that they would both logically stand a better chance of survival if they split up. Still, it was only with the greatest reluctance that Tack tore his gaze from Noni and limped as swiftly as he could for a side alley on his own.

• • •

Takan, Noni, you did well," Zyid said, gazing out the storefront window of the flower shop, giving no indication that the incident with Charles had ever happened.

It had taken Tack some hours to duck into a maze of back alleyways, through muck and filth, to shake off the Enforcers and return, on foot, back to the Truancy hideout. In the presence of both Zyid and Noni, Tack became very conscious that he was covered in grime and blood. Noni had been more fortunate, Tack had noticed; she had remained spotless, and was already waiting at the flower shop by the time Tack had stumbled in.

"Takan got himself wounded, though," Noni suddenly said condescendingly, tossing her braid behind her neck.

"Oh?" Zyid asked, turning around.

Tack could actually feel his face reddening. Noni was trying to embarrass him in front of Zyid, and apparently it was something that she was good at. Tack briefly wondered what had happened to the gentle, concerned Noni that he'd encountered during the battle.

"It was barely anything," Tack protested. "Just a stubbed toe."

"Yeah, right." Noni shook her head, her silky braid flailing in all directions. "Your entire nail was torn off."

"I've not heard of many deaths caused by toe injuries," Zyid conceded, glancing down at Tack's bloody foot. "However, you will be in for a nasty few weeks if it gets infected. I'm afraid that the few medics that know what they're doing are tending to more grievous injuries, so Noni, would you mind?"

Noni's head jerked backwards. Tack allowed himself a grin. Her plan had certainly backfired.

"No . . . not at all," Noni said, narrowing her icy eyes to make her displeasure obvious.

"Good," Zyid said, his voice suddenly chilling a few degrees. "I knew that you would have no objections to helping an ally. Friends must look out for each other, correct?"

Noni stiffened for a moment as she thought about it, then bowed her head.

"Yes, sir," she murmured.

"I'd be a fool if I attempted to end all the petty rivalries and personal quarrels in the Truancy," Zyid said, turning to look out the window again. "But that doesn't mean that anyone is allowed to get carried away by any. If one of you ended up sustaining unnecessary suffering or death because of the other, I'd imagine that that culprit would be feeling rather unpleasant—even before I got my hands on him or her."

"I understand," Noni said quietly.

"Yeah, okay," Tack said meekly.

"Excellent. Now get healed and get some sleep. Everyone's going to need some of that today."

Zyid clapped his hands behind his back, and Tack and Noni turned and left without another word. Walking next door, they entered through the revolving doors and strode over to a stairwell. Marching down to the basement, the two of them passed by a number of dimly lit rooms that had been converted to dorms and infirmaries, from which a tortured, heart-wrenching sound issued forth. Tack did his best to block out the crying and the moaning, and was only glad that there weren't too many voices for him to ignore—badly injured Truants couldn't be extricated from the battlefield. The only survivors were the ones who were well enough to make it back on their own. Still, judging from what Tack heard there in that basement, there weren't as many casualties as he'd feared. But the fact that there were any at all showed that Zyid was far from perfect.

Tack grimaced, an odd reaction to the memory of Suzie smiling at him. Yes, very far from perfect.

"What's wrong?" Noni asked, arching an eyebrow at Tack's angry scowl.

"Nothing," Tack muttered, looking at her stony, emotionless face. How could she show such genuine concern earlier, and now tolerate the suffering around them with such cold indifference? How could anyone walk so casually while friends were screeching in agony around her? Remembering how cold-bloodedly he had seen Noni kill, Tack began to wonder what made her any better than Zyid.

"If it's the noise that's bothering you, just ignore it," Noni suggested, a strange look of pain flitting across her face. "Either they'll get better or they'll die—nothing you can do about it, nothing to be gained by letting them bother you."

"If you ended up like them, wouldn't you want someone to be bothered?" Tack asked, glaring at Noni.

"No," Noni answered, after more than a moment's pause.

"So if I end up like one of them, you wouldn't be bothered?" Tack asked.

"I don't see what makes you any different," Noni said determinedly, looking straight ahead.

"Well, wouldn't you be concerned that someone *else* got to me before you did?" Tack asked, half-jokingly.

Noni let out a bark of laughter.

"You're not that important, Takan." Noni smiled and shut her dazzling eyes. "You got lucky and beat me once, but you're not that important."

Tack and Noni continued walking through the corridor in silence, until they finally reached an empty nursery. They walked inside and Tack promptly sat upon a stool, raising his injured leg. Noni rummaged around in a supply cabinet before returning with a bottle of iodine and a bandage.

"This might hurt a lot," Noni said dispassionately, opening the bottle of iodine.

"I can hardly wait," Tack said, gritting his teeth.

In truth Tack had probably felt worse, but the unique sting of iodine on an open wound is something that serves to erase all previous memories of suffering and literally causes pain like you've never felt pain before. Tack gritted his teeth and shut his eyes as it burned.

"Good, you took that without screaming," Noni said approvingly, spreading some sort of cream onto the bandage before crouching to apply it.

"Thanks," Tack said earnestly, as Noni stood up again.

"You're welcome," Noni replied, sapphire eyes glinting. "Don't get used to it, though. Next time, I'll use acid instead of iodine."

Tack snorted. "Acid can't possibly be much worse."

Noni shrugged. "Well, you can let me know how they compare."

"Well, now I'm really looking forward to getting myself injured again," Tack said, his voice laden with sarcasm.

"Not as much as I am," Noni commented, walking out of the nursery as Tack tested his step. "Oh yeah, and Takan?"

"Yes?" Tack looked up.

"Take it easy."

Noni left the room, leaving Tack feeling considerably better than he had when talking with Zyid.

19

His Most Dangerous Student

In the days after the Box Office Battle, as it had come to be called among the Truants, Tack began spending more and more time in Zyid's abandoned flower shop. Zyid kept him close like some sort of bodyguard, though Tack personally found the position to be pointless. Zyid had decided that the entire Truancy needed something of a break in the aftermath of the battle, and even the steady flow of assassinations had subsided. Morale had been seesawing of late; they'd done significant damage to the Enforcers, and yet many Truants had perished defending the theater, some of whom Tack had known. Aside from Charles, Tack heard that Steve had been cut down by a grenade on the western front.

Three days after the Box Office Battle, Tack sat cross-legged in one corner of the flower shop atop a moldy wooden crate that had once been filled with dried apples. Tack was grateful for the lull in the fighting, though he'd become so used to the constant action that he was actually growing bored. What really irked Tack was that he was alone in enduring this boring duty; Zyid no longer kept Noni around, and Tack found that he sorely missed her presence.

To pass the time, Tack was practicing throwing darts at a board hung from one wall of the flower shop. As dart after dart buried itself in the bull's-eye, Tack glanced at Zyid. Seemingly unconcerned with Tack, the Truancy leader was washing his hair in an old sink. Tack mechanically flicked his hand one last time, only to realize that he was out of darts. As Zyid began wringing his hair, his back turned to Tack, Tack was suddenly seized by an urge to whip out a real knife from his belt and hurl it at Zyid. Instead, Tack sighed and moved to retrieve the darts.

Meanwhile, Zyid had calmly finished drying his hair and now began to comb it violently. As Tack pulled the darts from the board, he noticed that Zyid's comb would get stuck when it encountered a particularly tangled knot of hair. Zyid retaliated by pushing the comb harder, until the hairs snapped and clung to the comb. Tack returned to sit on his crate, fingering his bandaged toe idly for a few minutes,

Tack looked up at Zyid. His head was beginning to return to its customary smooth and sleek state. But he couldn't notice the amount of hair that had been sacrificed during the grooming, and now what seemed like a painful effort was starting to pay off. Tack stroked his own hair lightly, wondering if Zyid really thought it was worth the trouble.

"Doesn't that hurt at all?" Tack asked suddenly.

"The comb?" Zyid said as a few more hairs snapped. "It's not as painful as you think it is. If you comb hard enough, the comb weeds out the weak, unruly hairs."

Zyid paused, took a strand of broken hair, and examined it. Then he grasped either end and tore it apart.

"There are no nerves in hair," Zyid explained. "Otherwise I'd be using haircuts in interrogations."

Tack forced a weak laugh. Zyid may have been joking, but Tack knew that he was deadly serious as well.

"So what are we, the comb or the hair?" Tack asked, feeling unusually philosophical.

Zyid looked at Tack with mild surprise. "We're neither, Takan."

"Then what are we?"

"The hand."

One of Zyid's eyes twitched as he shoved the comb through the last resistant patch of hair. With that regimen finished, he put the comb down and retied his hair into his customary ponytail.

"I will be absent for a while." Without another word, Zyid left the room, leaving Tack once again unsettled.

Tack frowned. Zyid always had a way of unnerving him. Lately he was feeling emptier and more confused than he had ever been in his entire life. The deaths he'd caused and witnessed were beginning to trouble him worse than ever. He was seeing blood and bodies now. Whenever he closed his eyes, he heard screams and explosions in his sleep, and he couldn't forget the look in an Enforcer's eyes before he died. But what troubled Tack even more was why, having killed so many others, he couldn't just kill Zyid and be done with it. Tack shut his eyelids. He wasn't so sure of anything anymore. It was a terrible feeling, to be doubting everything, especially himself.

Seized by a sudden, wild idea, Tack sat up and opened his eyes. Checking his watch, he realized that he'd have time. The battle was over, Zyid was gone, and no one would be looking for him for a while. They'd probably assume he'd be getting drunk somewhere. Why hadn't he thought of it before?

Tack got up and went for the door.

He had a sudden craving for lemonade.

"The investigation has concluded that the movie theater was not, in fact, their main hideout," a cabinet member informed the irate Mayor.

The Mayor groaned. He had waited three restless days in his office, just to hear this confirmation of what he'd already feared from the moment the initial reports had come back from the battle.

"Why did the Truancy defend that place so stubbornly?" the Mayor demanded; it was a question that had gone so far as to interrupt his sleep.

"We can only conclude that they wanted a battle, though we really don't know why," the cabinet member replied. "Perhaps they wanted to inflict damage; they certainly did manage to pile up a lot of Enforcer bodies."

"That they did." The Mayor frowned. "And the amount of equipment they destroyed was even more astonishing. But I am satisfied with the number of Truants that were killed. Forty-seven, I believe, at the last count? Much more than we've ever been able to bag at once."

"Yes, that's right," the cabinet member confirmed. "Additionally, we expect to uncover more bodies as we continue to search the area."

"I can't imagine that they can afford to lose that many people repeatedly," the Mayor said, sounding optimistic. "If they ever allow a full-scale battle again, I'll be happy to oblige them."

The cabinet members grinned at each other; it was very rare to get the Mayor into this good a mood.

"Anyway, you mentioned that you have some other news for me?" the Mayor said.

"That's right sir," a cabinet member said proudly. "Remember several weeks ago, you asked us to search for the boy that allegedly trained in District 19?"

"The blond kid?" The Mayor suddenly clenched his lighter tightly.

"He . . . says his name is Edward," the cabinet member explained. "And we've found him. Or rather, he found us."

"Where is he?" the Mayor demanded.

"Waiting outside at this very moment, sir," the cabinet member said.

"Waiting? Why didn't you tell me this before?"

The Mayor strode over to the door, seized the knob, and swung it open to reveal a teenage boy who stood in the hallway with his arms crossed. The Mayor looked the boy up and down. He had short blond hair and a soft, pale complexion. He might even have looked gentle, were it not for the long, thin eyebrows that gave him an unnervingly sharp appearance. He wore opaque black sunglasses that he had tilted down just enough to reveal striking green eyes, and he was clothed in a standard gray student's uniform.

"Edward?" the Mayor said.

"That's my name." The boy nodded. "I take it that you're the Mayor?"

"I am," the Mayor confirmed.

"I've heard a lot about you. And I've seen you on TV, of course." Edward's eyes narrowed as he swept the sunglasses from his face. "My old mentor used to talk about you all the time. I think he regrets that now."

The Mayor smiled as though contemplating a winning lottery ticket. He turned to face his cabinet, which had been staring at the pair intently.

"Leave us."

The cabinet members knew better than to protest. They quickly gathered up their assorted papers, clipboards, notepads, and briefcases and filed out of the room. Once the last of the cabinet members was out of sight, the Mayor beckoned to Edward.

"Come inside."

Edward walked into the Mayor's office and looked around. Spotting a padded armchair in one corner, Edward strolled over to it and seated himself in it comfortably, as though he were in his own house. The Mayor sat down behind his desk and surveyed the boy carefully.

"So, Umasi taught you?" the Mayor asked.

"Yes, that's right," Edward replied, holding the Mayor's gaze unblinkingly.

"What did you learn?" the Mayor pressed.

"A mixed bag. Strategy, personal combat, even some philosophy, though I ignored most of that," Edward answered with a grin. "I assure you, I am more than qualified for your job."

"Oh?" The Mayor flipped his lighter open. "And what job is that?"

Edward smirked, and his acid green eyes flashed as his sunglasses slid farther down his nose.

"I am not stupid, Mr. Mayor," Edward declared. "There's only one reason that you would seek me out. You need help against the Truancy."

"Yes, that's exactly right," the Mayor said. "I knew my son would not have mentored a stupid boy. But that leads me to wonder; what made you part ways with him?"

Edward's grin vanished.

"Umasi and I had a few . . . disagreements," he said guardedly. "He seemed to think I was too aggressive, if you can believe it."

The Mayor remembered the report of the Enforcer whose kneecaps had been shattered while scouting out District 19. Far from being repulsed, however, the Mayor was pleased; someone aggressive and violent was exactly the type of person who could fight the Truancy on their own terms.

"On one occasion he actually said that I was selfish," Edward continued. "He kept trying to fill my head with all sorts of pacifist nonsense, so in the end I ditched him." Edward ran a hand through his short, bristly hair.

"I will admit, however, that I underestimated your son. I tried to give him a piece of my mind before I left. I lost, and I have no intention of crossing him again, though I did get away with these." Edward pointed at his sunglasses.

The Mayor swelled with pride for his son, ignoring the likelihood that he was playing into the reaction that Edward had intended.

"So, it would not trouble you that Umasi wouldn't approve of you being here?" the Mayor asked.

"We left on bitter terms." Edward nodded. "And in any case, I never had much respect for his views. Respect for his talents, yes, but opinions, no."

"And what of your talents?" the Mayor asked, unable to keep the eagerness from his voice. "How do you compare?"

"Umasi once told me that I was his most dangerous student." Edward smiled at the Mayor. "He had two others before me, I believe, though he never talked about them much. I'm as good as you're going to get, unless you can get your son to come out of hiding and join you."

"That's not likely to happen," the Mayor said, shutting his lighter loudly. "So, you believe that you can help us against the Truancy?"

"That's right." Edward's voice now turned businesslike. "My first recommendation is that you need to stop trying to conceal the Truancy from the public, immediately. You're only doing their work for them."

"What?" the Mayor asked, taken aback. "If we give them publicity, then we look like we're not in control. It might incite more students to join them."

Edward's grin turned predatory.

"Not if you turn the students against them," Edward said. "You control the media; put a malicious spin on the Truancy. Make them look like the enemies of the entire City; make them hated and hunted."

"It's an idea," the Mayor conceded. "But there are other problems with that. There are . . . powers . . . outside this City, observing our progress. If they feel that our control of society is failing, it will mean even bigger trouble for us, all of us."

Edward frowned. "Umasi never mentioned anything about *that.* Would you care to elaborate?"

"No. Some secrets must be kept," the Mayor said firmly. "Umasi wouldn't and couldn't have told you either—he doesn't know. It is perhaps the best-kept secret in the City, and we should all hope it stays that way."

Edward seemed slightly troubled at not being let in on the secret, but quickly rallied.

"If you adopt all my other proposals," Edward declared, "the Truancy will surely fall long before any outside interference. This is why, at the same time you make the Truancy public, you must also form a Student Militia."

"A Student Militia?"

"Yes." Edward nodded. "Nothing would be a bigger blow to the Truancy's morale than to see students taking up arms against them. And not only that—there are hundreds of thousands of students in this City. Simply offer immediate graduation as a reward for service, and you'll have an instant army at your command."

"That would defeat the entire purpose of our school system." The Mayor frowned.

"But it will end the Truancy," Edward pointed out. "The school system can be restored after the war is won. Otherwise the Truancy will destroy it, utterly. They must be dealt with above all other concerns, and it would be prudent to use any tool you have available."

"What else do you suggest?" the Mayor asked with grudging respect.

"Offer amnesty to Truant deserters," Edward said without hesitation. "When faced with killing other children, I'm willing to bet that half of the Truancy will put down their weapons and walk away. From the information we might get from them, the Truancy could fall in a matter of weeks."

"I don't like the idea of letting them walk away without even a slap on the wrist." The Mayor clicked his lighter open.

"Then keep them tagged and kill them all after the Truancy is finished," Edward said dispassionately. "It's all the same to me."

"Is that so?" The Mayor shut his lighter and slipped it into his pocket. Though he approved of the boy's ruthlessness, he couldn't help but be suspicious of his motives. "And what would you want in return?"

"To assume a position among the leadership of this City," Edward said confidently. "A place on your cabinet, perhaps. And on the City Council, too."

The Mayor smiled. So, that's what the boy was after: personal gain. Here was someone with great ambitions along with the talents and intelligence needed to achieve them. The Mayor could relate to Edward, but was careful to remind himself not to let the boy get *too* ambitious.

"The position of Chief Enforcer is vacant," the Mayor said. "Would that interest you at all?"

"It's a start." Edward grinned.

"Yes, it is a start," the Mayor said, thinking fast. "Let us make a deal. You will lead the Enforcers for two weeks. If your performance impresses me, then the title becomes permanent and I will ratify every one of the suggestions you have made. And if your performance is not impressive—"

"You don't have to worry about that," Edward said lazily, leaning back in the padded armchair. "Shall I start today?"

"I don't see why not," the Mayor said briskly, standing up. "Let's go find you a uniform that'll fit."

It was like a dream, Tack decided. Yes, it was definitely a surreal sensation that he felt as he climbed over the wooden barrier and dropped down onto the other side, banging his shoulder against the hard, welcoming asphalt of the District 19 streets. Tack got up and began walking steadily along the route he had traversed in what felt like a different life. As he rounded a corner, his heart leaped at the sight of a familiar lemonade stand, and a familiar boy sitting behind it with his legs up on the table and a book in his hands.

Tack approached the stand determinedly. The boy shut his book, laid it on the ground, and looked up to survey Tack regally behind his opaque sunglasses. Tack drew up to the stand, and sat down on the same hard, metal folding chair that he had once been so familiar with.

Across from Tack, Umasi sat with arms crossed. Tack shuffled nervously, trying desperately to find the right words to say. As the silence stretched on, he cast his gaze towards the jug of lemonade. The ice in it had half-melted, and its glass surface was slick with perspiration. Looking back up at Umasi, who had remained motionless, Tack slowly drew a crisp bill from his jacket and placed it upon the table.

Almost mechanically, Umasi nodded and took a paper cup from the stack with one hand and poured the lemonade with the other. As he slid the cup towards Tack, Tack found that he could almost feel Umasi's eyes narrowing behind the black barrier of his sunglasses. Still unsure of what Umasi's reaction would be, Tack raised the cup to his lips and tried to drink, finding that out of nervousness he could only wet his lips. A slow smile stretched across Umasi's face.

"It's been a while, Tack," he said, with a trace of amusement in his voice.

Relief spread through Tack's body. "Yeah."

"You've certainly come a long way," Umasi observed. "An assassin of the Truancy now, I believe?"

Tack wasn't sure how Umasi knew about what he'd been doing, but somehow he wasn't surprised to find that he did. Tack swallowed, trying to figure out how to answer. Ever since he joined the Truancy, Tack had been wondering why he did what he did, but always an answer eluded him. Perhaps there simply was none.

"There come times in our lives when we do things that we don't understand," Umasi said suddenly. "We confuse ourselves, we might even logically oppose our impulses, and yet we act on them anyway."

Tack jerked up, suddenly realizing that his head had been bowed for the past few minutes, the lemonade forgotten. Umasi held up a hand, silencing him before he could speak.

"There are some things that we feel that we absolutely must do," Umasi said, leaning forward. "We might know that they're wrong, or pointless, or gravely punishable, and yet we do them anyway. These actions are not born of anger or emotion—we are perfectly sober. It's rather inexplicable. When the time comes, we can't stop ourselves, and so we cannot blame ourselves."

Tack found himself speechless, realizing why he'd returned. Umasi understood Tack better than he did himself.

"Zyid killed my sister," Tack whispered. "I swore to avenge her, but . . . I feel like I can't. I . . . sympathize with the Truancy, and Zyid is its heart and soul. Should I just give up and walk away? Leave the Truancy?"

"You swore to kill Zyid, but you feel that you can't?" Umasi repeated.

"Yes." Tack nodded.

Umasi leaned back in his chair, and seemed lost in thought. Tack took a sip of lemonade. It tasted the same way it always had, but now seemed blander, somehow, because of it.

"Your devotion to your sibling is admirable. I envy you for it," Umasi said finally, scrutinizing Tack more closely than ever. "Whatever you choose to do now, you won't accomplish it by running away from the Truancy, to which you now seem attached. Fleeing and leaving both your promise and the Truancy behind will tear you apart worse than anything you're doing now."

"So then . . ."

"You must end it as a Truant, one way or another," Umasi finished, pouring himself a cup of lemonade.

Tack took another sip from his own drink and pursed his lips. It was funny, Tack thought as he drank. He had never paid so much attention to the sourness of lemonade.

"You know what they say to do if life gives you lemons, right?" Umasi mused suddenly, glancing at the glass jug.

Tack found himself laughing at that, choking on his drink. As Tack coughed lemonade up his nose, Umasi reached out and slipped the bill into his pocket. Suddenly Umasi froze, then swung his head towards Tack.

"Someone is coming," whispered Umasi, who could now hear the distant echo of approaching footsteps. "I believe it is Zyid. It would be best if you aren't visible when he arrives."

"Zyid?" Tack blurted, sitting up in panic.

"Yes, I told you that we were acquainted," Umasi said casually. "Don't worry, Tack," he added, seeing the look on Tack's face. "You have nothing to fear from our conversing. Trust me. Now quickly, hide."

With no other options, Tack turned and darted as silently as he could over to an old Dumpster left in an alley. He crouched behind it just as Zyid rounded the corner, approaching Umasi's stand. Soon after, Tack heard the murmur of voices. He couldn't help but peer out from behind the Dumpster to watch, but to his annoyance he couldn't hear what was being said.

Zyid and Umasi seemed to be having an animated conversation. Now that they stood side by side, Tack for the first time realized just how much the two resembled each other. Before he could ponder that, however, Tack felt a sudden jolt of confusion as he realized that Zyid held a scabbard in his hand, though one already rested at his side. Tack rubbed his eyes and looked again; there was no mistake: Zyid was carrying two separate swords. Tack's head was spinning; if the Truant leader always had two, why couldn't he have given one to Noni, when she had wanted it so much?

Then Tack saw Zyid hold the sword out, offering it to Umasi, and Tack somehow understood that Zyid had saved the sword for just this purpose. In response, Umasi said something that obviously annoyed Zyid, and Zyid withdrew his arm, letting the second sword rest limply at his side. The two exchanged some more words, and then Zyid turned to leave, a look of unmistakable disappointment on his face. Tack shifted his gaze to Umasi, who now seemed to be more expressionless than ever before.

Tack pondered what he'd just seen. Zyid had come to give a sword to Umasi, who had refused it, and Zyid had left. Apparently Umasi and Zyid had a closer relationship than he'd realized, but even before Tack could worry about what that implied, he remembered what Umasi had said.

Don't worry, Tack. You have nothing to fear from our conversing.

Tack believed him.

Trust me.

Tack did.

You must end it as a Truant.

And Tack would, for their cause, though not their leader, had become his own.

PART III

TRUANT

20

A Treacherous Threshold

"What the hell happened?"

"Are there people still in there?"

"This guy's not dead; somebody help!"

"Water, we need water!"

"Someone get Zyid!"

At first Tack didn't pay the shouts and screams much attention as he approached The Bar, but as he slowly realized that these were not the usual outcries of mirth, a sudden dread gripped his gut. Breaking into a run, Tack rounded the corner and froze, transfixed upon the nightmarish sight that greeted his eyes. His right hand unconsciously clenched tightly upon a red rose, and Tack ignored the pain as one of the thorns pierced his skin.

All he could see was fire. A mocking, dancing, laughing fire that engulfed The Bar and was spreading eagerly to neighboring buildings. A flickering sickly orange glow cut through the dimming dusk, casting long, shifting shadows down the street. Shards of glass and brick were strewn across the sidewalk as if they had been blown from the building by some great force. Bodies lay writhing and burning on the ground, and as Tack took a deep breath, the horrifyingly familiar stench of burning flesh filled his nostrils.

Tack wasn't alone; the street was filled with Truants. Some, like Tack, could only gaze in horror, transfixed by the growing flames. Some were bloody and charred to various degrees, struggling to run or crawl away as best they could. Some had remained healthy and were frantically trying to help those that were less fortunate, crouching over any Truants that still stirred as they lay on the ground. And others, too many others, were lying on the sidewalk, and Tack knew just by looking at them that they would never stir again.

"Takan!"

Tack tore his gaze from the flaming building and turned to the two figures running up to him. Tack quickly recognized the first as Gabriel; the second was a pale dark-haired boy that Tack had seen before but didn't know by name.

"Wha-what happened here?" Tack asked, still not quite able to believe what he was seeing.

"We were attacked," Gabriel said gravely.

"Attacked?" Tack said faintly. "Someone . . . did this on purpose?"

"Yes." The pale boy nodded grimly. "A kid, no less."

"A kid . . ." Tack felt overwhelmed.

"This is a bad time for introductions, but Takan, this is Alex. Alex, this is Takan," Gabriel said, hastily indicating Tack and the pale boy in turn. "Alex and I used to work personally with Zyid."

"I know Takan by reputation." Alex nodded; it was a comment that would've bothered Tack under normal circumstances, but at the moment barely registered.

"How did this . . . who?" Tack asked distractedly.

"We don't know." Alex shook his head. "Some of the survivors said they saw a blond kid with sunglasses walk in with a camera around his neck. From what we can gather, the guy had a drink, walked out, and dropped a brown paper bag on the way. Then there was an explosion, and then . . ." Alex waved his arm to indicate the fiery mess behind him.

"None of the survivors ever saw the boy before," Gabriel said grimly. "Not that there were many survivors."

"Was he . . . one of ours?" Tack sputtered.

"We don't know." Alex frowned. "Personally though, I don't see how it could be anyone else."

"Wait to see what Zyid thinks before we start blaming each other," Gabriel cautioned, looking at Alex. "You're sure you called Zyid, right?"

"Yeah." Alex nodded.

Tack did not participate in their conversation. All he could concentrate on was the dancing flames licking at the blackened skeleton of The Bar. Tack watched helplessly as Truants suffered and died when they least expected to. He suddenly realized that this was what the Educators must feel like. Tack looked down at his hand still clenching the rose, and grimaced at the blood now dripping through his fingers and onto the ground.

Tack made no move to release the rose, even with its thorns; all he could do was wonder who had so rudely opened his eyes to the horrors of his own work.

• • •

First day on the job, and already dramatic results?" The Mayor clicked his lighter open and shut excitedly.

"That's right." Edward nodded, leaning back comfortably in the padded armchair that he'd claimed as his own, clothed in a blue uniform not unlike a suit, though with two parallel sets of buttons running down alongside a prominent gold badge. "The first thing I did as Chief Enforcer was review all the juvenile robbery cases. What you must realize is that to support bigger crimes, the Truancy must surely commit minor ones."

The Mayor nodded; the idea made sense to him.

"What I found was that one liquor store bordering on an abandoned district had complained several times that kids were making off with unguarded crates," Edward continued. "I personally went down to the store in more casual clothing—this uniform is excellent, by the way—and arranged for some goods to be left lying around. When the kids showed up to take them, I followed them, and found that they were operating their own little bar, of sorts."

The Mayor raised an eyebrow. "And you didn't call for backup?"

"Nah," Edward said dismissively. "I wanted to be seen. It'll confuse them, make them suspect each other. And in any case, what I did made more of an impact than anything a full Enforcer team could have done."

"Oh?" the Mayor asked, leaning back in his chair as if enjoying a bedtime story. "And what did you do?"

"I had a drink," Edward said, grinning. "And I tipped them a few explosives as thanks."

The Mayor flipped his lighter open. "You gave them a bit of what they've been giving to us," he observed delightedly.

"Yes, I doubt they'll enjoy being on the receiving end of their own tactics," Edward said. "They'll also spend a lot of time wondering who did it and why. An unknown adversary is more intimidating than any familiar one, or so your son used to say."

"Why didn't you follow the Truants leaving the bar?" the Mayor asked. "You might've found their main hideout that way."

"Their main hideout will come in time," Edward said patiently. "We have to take this in steps. Trying to assault the hornet's nest straight up will only get us stung badly."

"Well, one attack on a Truancy installation is more than any of your predecessors managed to do in a month," the Mayor conceded. "Do you think you can keep up the good work?"

"Naturally." Edward flashed him a venomous grin.

"Do you know how many you killed?"

"I'm afraid not, though I did snap some pictures, before and after," Edward said. He tossed a few photographs onto the Mayor's desk.

The Mayor looked down at the pictures. There were three of an old, run-down bar with a door hanging on one hinge and of its interior, which housed happily chatting children. The fourth looked hastily taken and was of the outside of the bar, with flames and smoke pouring from the shattered windows and bloody bodies lying on the street. The Mayor was disappointed with the quality of the picture; it was blurred, as if the cameraman had been running when the shot was taken. Still, he could hardly complain under the circumstances.

"Excellent," the Mayor said, clicking his lighter shut.

The Mayor looked up at a gloating Edward. As the boy's

green eyes glinted in the office's dim lighting, the Mayor suddenly remembered something.

"By the way, what happened to your sunglasses?" the Mayor asked.

Tack turned the pair of sunglasses over in his hand. They were very familiar, even to Tack's dazed eyes. He was sure that they were Umasi's—or at least the same as the ones Umasi always wore. Wondering if this were all a bad dream, Tack looked back up at the smoking building, saw Truants grimly piling their dead fellows into a pile, and realized that it was too terrible to be a nightmare even after the fires had been silenced—a pickup truck filled with fire extinguishers had been parked beside the ruins of The Bar, and several Truants were now walking through the remains, dousing any last remnants of fire.

Zyid had arrived on the scene with the truck, but hadn't had any time to talk with Tack yet. The Truancy leader was now busying himself by interviewing all of the survivors. He'd shown no surprise about The Bar, which indicated to Tack that Zyid had indeed known about The Bar all the time, though he had certainly kept that knowledge well hidden. Tack reflected uselessly on the fact that the whole thing wouldn't have happened if the Truancy had just given up on alcohol like Zyid had suggested.

Tack looked over at the growing pile of bodies. Even before Zyid had arrived, Tack had personally examined each of those corpses. Some of them were burned beyond clear recognition; others were only horribly maimed. For a few panicked moments, Tack's mind had entertained the fear that Noni might have been among the dead, despite the fact that he'd never seen her at The Bar. After examining all the bodies, Tack was able to assure himself that none of them was Noni.

Tack looked up to see Alex and Gabriel, who were now picking through the burned remains of The Bar, looking around for anything that might be helpful, and as Tack watched them, he gripped the pair of sunglasses, hard. He'd found the sunglasses on the sidewalk, where they had apparently fallen from their owner's face. The sunglasses were made of plastic, and so far from breaking, they were actually in good condition. Remembering that the survivors had blamed a blond boy with glasses, Tack wondered why he didn't rush to Zyid immediately with the evidence.

As he thought about facing Zyid, however, Tack frowned, remembering something that he'd decided about Zyid earlier in the day, before he had come to The Bar, before the rose's thorns had pierced him. His day had been very busy, and Tack reflected that it was lucky that it was. Looking up at Alex and Gabriel, now lifting another hopelessly charred body from the remains, Tack realized that he'd had a close call. If he hadn't taken as long as he did doing the things he had, he too might've been nothing but ashes by now.

Tack's hands clenched tightly as he remembered what he had spent his day doing, and a few more drops of blood fell to the ground.

Hey!"

The dark-haired girl spun around to see who was calling out to her from the crowd of students leaving the District 20 summer school program. Tack could tell at once that she didn't recognize him, which was for the best.

"You're Melissa?" Tack asked, slightly out of breath.

"Yes," Melissa answered, her wide eyes searching Tack.

"I'm Suzie's . . . cousin," Tack said, swiftly picking an appropriate lie—something he was growing increasingly good at. "I heard that you were her best friend."

There was a suspended moment of silence while the sounds of the chattering students around them seemed to recede. Then Melissa burst into tears.

"I k-killed her," Melissa sobbed.

"Huh?" Tack frowned confusedly.

"If s-she hadn't gone and t-taken the blame f-for me she'd still b-be alive," Melissa wailed, doubling over with grief.

It took Tack a moment to understand, but as soon as he realized that Melissa was blaming herself for Suzie's death, he almost felt like laughing bitterly. Melissa hadn't seen Zyid or heard his remorseless words. But Tack's dark urge was quickly stifled by Melissa's increasingly pronounced sobs. Tack vaguely noticed that students were turned to stare or even point, but this did not bother him as he knew it would have, back before he'd become a Truant. Tack attempted to calm Melissa down.

"It wasn't your fault," Tack said soothingly. "You weren't the one who blew up the car."

"She was in the c-car because of m-me," Melissa said through her sobs.

"No." Tack shook his head and patted Melissa on the back. "She made her own decisions. She was in the car by her choice, not yours."

"If I'd s-stopped her—," Melissa began.

"Anyone might've stopped her," Tack said patiently. "None

of them did. She made her own choice." *And I made mine,* Tack added silently.

"You really think so?" Melissa asked, looking up at Tack through red eyes.

"Yes," Tack said firmly. "Let's talk about something else. How's summer school been for you?"

"It's been okay, I guess," Melissa said, drying her eyes.

Meaning it's just as bad as normal school, Tack translated silently.

"Suzie and her brother Tack used to tell me about this teacher, Mr. Niel, all the time," Tack said casually. "Have you seen much of him lately?"

"All I know is he was being as nasty as usual," Melissa sniffed. "Except to his favorites."

"Sounds like him." Tack nodded sagely. "By the way, did they ever get the bathrooms fixed?"

"No, the third floor one is still closed. They say they might not have it open in time for the new school year."

"About that Zero Tolerance Policy . . ."

For the next fifteen minutes, Tack and Melissa walked slowly to the subway, chatting about school. Tack had thought that it would be painful to delve into his past, but all he found was comforting familiarity. He had spent the better part of the morning watching his old school from afar, looking in through the windows with binoculars, watching the students sitting grimly at their desks, obeying their teachers like slaves would a master. Seeing the life that he'd left behind, and speaking with those that still lived it, Tack was reminded of what he was now fighting to change. He and Melissa parted ways at the subway station, and Tack was left to ponder where he would go next.

Tack made a decision and headed for the first flower shop that he saw. This flower shop was not abandoned, dim, or moldy like the one he had spent so much time lurking in. It was lively, with a veritable forest of color blooming throughout the shop, all of it brightly lit. A wonderfully fresh, perfumed scent permeated the air, and Tack found himself smiling back at the cashier as he paid for a bundle of fresh-cut, thorny red roses.

Tack next entered the subway, which he found to be something of a novelty now that he hadn't traveled out in public for so long. There was something reassuring about losing oneself among an endless crowd of commuters in a giant network of rattling trains that stretched from underground to far above the City. Tack sat in his rattling seat aboard the subway, taking care to read all of the advertisement posters in the train car with interest as the world sped by. Eventually, the train reached the stop Tack desired, and as the doors slid open, Tack followed the steady flow of people out of the train.

Once on the station platform, Tack scaled the stairs and made for the surface, passing through the turnstiles as if they didn't exist. Pleased to be up in the fresh air again, Tack found that he was looking out upon his old acquaintance, the West River.

"How've you been?" Tack called out to the river, which flowed contentedly in response.

It didn't take Tack long to reach the Riverside Cemetery, where he knew that his parents had always talked about being buried. It was a dismal place, despite the blue sky and bright sun above. It was deserted by the living, and only the occasional photograph or bouquet showed any sign that anyone had been there to visit the dead. Tack only assumed that Suzie would be buried here, and after he'd climbed the fence and searched through the sea of plaques and tombstones, he wasn't disappointed. What took Tack completely by surprise, however, was finding a second tombstone next to Suzie's with his name on it.

As he stood there, looking at those two solid, inanimate tombstones, Tack found that they somehow forcefully drove home the fact that his old life really had died away with Suzie. Tack laid the bouquet of roses down onto Suzie's grave and, after only a moment's consideration, withdrew a single rose from it and held it loosely in his right hand.

"This one's for someone who's still alive," Tack explained to the river, which was gurgling at him questioningly.

Tack regarded the graves carefully, and before he noticed it, a single tear had dripped down his cheek and fallen upon the hard ground. And with that, he felt as though a great burden had been lifted from his shoulders, and he cried no more. Tack stood up tall, enjoying for a second the cool breeze sent his way by the river, and then he knelt down before the tombstones. He no longer felt anger, or grief, nor was he plagued by painful memories, but as he stood atop those graves, he did feel the empty sensation that he recognized to be an unfulfilled promise. Tack brushed his hand over Suzie's grave, and imagined that he was touching her face as he remembered why he'd joined the Truancy in the first place.

"I will kill him," Tack said softly, addressing Suzie now while the river gushed in the background. "I promised you I would, so I will."

Tack stood up now, and looked out at the river, as if it were to be his witness.

"You hear that?" Tack yelled at the river. "I'm gonna kill him! Remember that!"

And with that, Tack had turned his back on the graves and on the river, which seemed to splash loudly in approval.

What's that in your hand, Takan?"

Tack snapped out of his remembrance and looked up to find himself face-to-face with Zyid. Tack immediately resisted his first urge, which was to jerk backwards, and quickly suppressed his second urge, which was to draw his sword and cut Zyid down where he stood. Tack reminded himself that he had to be practical; he had resolved to wait until he and Zyid were alone, somewhere when Zyid's death could be explained away. Despite the fact that he'd finally determined to kill Zyid, Tack still found himself unwilling to part with the Truancy that he had truly become a part of.

"A rose," Tack said quietly.

"Yes, and a bloody one too, but I meant your other hand," Zyid said sardonically.

Tack said nothing, and Zyid reached down and removed the sunglasses from his clenched hand. As Zyid examined the glasses, Tack was certain that he could see a flash of recognition flit across the Truancy leader's face. So, he hadn't been imagining the resemblance to Umasi's sunglasses. As Zyid's gaze shifted from the sunglasses over to Tack, he remembered that he had an act to keep up. Tack searched around wildly for something to say.

"How many dead?" Tack seized on the first question that came to mind.

"Thirteen at the last count," Zyid said impassively, still studying the sunglasses. "The attacker happened to hit at the busiest time of day."

"Do you think it was a Truant that did it?" Tack gestured towards the remains of The Bar.

"No, Takan." Zyid turned the sunglasses over in his hand. "I think it was someone far more dangerous."

Tack briefly wondered if Zyid was talking about Umasi, but he instantly dismissed the thought as he remembered that the attacker had been blond—Umasi's hair was black. In addition, knowing that Umasi always preached peace and patience, Tack found it impossible to believe that his old mentor could be responsible. But on the other hand, Umasi's plain, simple sunglasses weren't popular in the City, especially not at dusk. To find a pair just like them here seemed to be too much of a coincidence. As he contemplated this, Tack remembered something.

Three of them were former friends of mine. About two years ago, I worked with them one by one in a manner similar to how I am working with you now.

The last one betrayed me. He attempted to kill me, though I'm pleased to report that he failed.

Zyid slid the sunglasses into his pocket and bent his head, seemingly deep in thought.

Tack's mind began reeling. He had never given those nameless three any thought before. But now . . . now it seemed horribly possible that Tack might have to face one of them. Tack frowned uncertainly; when he passed Umasi's final test, he had felt like he could take on anything at all, but who knew how he would compare against another who had done the same?

The only thing that Tack knew for sure as the sun slipped over the horizon was that the war had just crossed a treacherous threshold. Tucking that worrisome thought into the back of his mind, Tack turned away from Zyid and headed off into the night in search of Noni; the rose remained to be delivered.

21

The Definition of Love

How we have deceived ourselves, Takan," Zyid murmured.

"Huh?" Tack looked up, sensing that Zyid had more to say.

Ever since the Bar incident, Zyid had been growing increasingly moody. Lately he'd been given to strange pronouncements that Tack found difficult to understand and vaguely unsettling. Still, on the whole, Tack found it easier to endure Zyid ever since he'd determined to kill him, and so he waited patiently for Zyid to elaborate.

Instead of doing so, the Truancy leader stood up, reached into his pocket, and unfolded a sheet of paper. From what Tack could see in the dim lighting of the flower shop, it looked a lot like a report card. Zyid looked the card over carefully, as if examining a precious yet hated artifact. Zyid folded the paper, returned it carefully to his pocket, and turned to Tack and sighed.

"You and I, Takan," Zyid said, indicating the two of them

and then sweeping his arm around to encompass the world. "All of us—the Truants, the students still left in the schools. We all entered the classrooms confident that we would be rewarded. We were shoved into the school system, promised that if we worked hard enough, we could have anything we want.

"We were taught that we could earn anything we wanted so long as we sacrificed enough of our dignity to do so. We sold ourselves to the Educators, Takan, from the moment we stepped into the classrooms." Zyid's face darkened. "Security and happiness are by no means guaranteed to graduates, but the Educators would have us believe that they are. They school us into believing that their way is the only way."

"But what about those that drop out? There are some," Tack pointed out, gesturing toward the wall next door behind which was the Truancy's main hideout.

"There are more than anyone would like you to believe, Takan. The Truancy has allowed them to make their presence known, but before, things were very bad for them." Zyid frowned, the lines on his face becoming so pronounced that it looked like he had wrinkles. "They were the vagrants, the homeless, and they suffered more than anyone else in this entire City."

"So, about dropouts . . . is it because—"

"It has nothing to do with intelligence," Zyid said sharply. "Some people are not meant for school. All kids are branded as a single faceless mass and herded through school like cattle. Some of them may be as smart as you want, and yet still recoil at their freedom and dignity being stolen from them by the Educators. The Educators will make them beg and sweat for an abstract grade just as a dog might perform tricks for a bone—except that the dog might chew on the bone and taste something concrete while the student is left only with a bitter taste in his mouth."

Tack was silent, brooding on Zyid's grim speech.

"So . . . where does all that leave us?" Tack asked, though he already knew the answer.

Zyid looked at Tack piercingly. "Those of us who were never meant to be in school? We are offered few options. For us, all we have to choose from is death or revolution."

"How . . . how many choose death?"

Zyid smirked bitterly. "Not as many as have chosen the Truancy, but also more than I would like . . . more, even, than the Educators would like."

Tack frowned. He didn't bother asking Zyid how he knew what he knew—he seemed too sure of himself to be wrong. But still, this was Tack's sister's murderer. He would love to hear Zyid's explanation about what justified *that,* but he couldn't exactly ask him.

Zyid's words were weighing Tack down now, and he decided that he needed some balance. He rose to his feet and made for the door.

"Where are you off to now, Takan?" Zyid asked calmly.

"I'm thirsty; I'm going to go grab a drink," Tack said. It was the truth, after all. Part of it, anyway.

"All right, Takan, but be back by tonight at eight." Zyid inclined his head. "I have another job for you."

Tack managed to nod and left the flower shop. Walking down the street, head bent, Tack was startled when something bumped into him. Snapping back to his senses, Tack looked up to see a pair of icy blue eyes searching him. An unreasonable nervousness gripped his stomach as it had before when Noni had beamed at him after he'd given her the rose.

"He's been giving you the talk, hasn't he?" Noni said, flicking a strand of loose hair behind her ear.

"Huh?" Tack responded dumbly, still entranced.

"Yeah, that's always how I felt afterwards," Noni said wistfully. "You know what I'm talking about. It's kind of enlightening and confusing at the same time."

"Yeah . . . yeah exactly," Tack said slowly.

"I always used to enjoy it. Made me feel better about . . . about being kicked out . . . and everything else." Noni cocked her head. "But Takan, now that you're Zyid's protégé, how are you liking it?"

Tack wasn't sure how to respond to that. It wasn't entirely bad to be in a position where he could fight for a cause he believed in, and yet there was the inescapable fact that he had to kill Zyid. Noni, however, took his hesitation to mean something else.

"Don't worry; I'm not bitter anymore," Noni said, pulling down her scarf to reveal a faint smile. "I don't think I'm even jealous."

"How come?" Tack asked, perplexed and yet pleased.

"After some time on my own and with you, I learned something," Noni said, flashing Tack a grin. "I don't have to rely on Zyid's strength anymore."

And with that, Noni clapped Tack on the shoulder and walked past him, pulling her scarf back over her face as she did. After a moment, Tack resumed his walk, grinning and feeling very pleased with himself.

Do you want anything, Gabe? Soda? Chips?"

"No, no, I'm fine, Alex; just buy quickly and get out."

Gabriel's eyes darted around the pharmacy, scrutinizing

everything that moved. One elderly man stood in front of a rack of greeting cards, another was in the soda aisle inspecting some bottles of sparkling water, and a third had filled his arms with boxes of batteries. Gabriel knew that another also lurked out of sight behind a display of painkillers. Except for the four men and the clerks, the five Truants milling about the snack aisle seemed to be alone in the pharmacy.

"Are you sure you don't want anything? These corn chips are great, I swear," Alex said, nudging Gabriel in the side.

"Yes, I'm sure, Alex," Gabriel muttered, still looking vigilantly around the room.

"Lighten up, Gabriel; we're in the middle of the living City," Alex said exasperatedly. "I don't think that we're going to find any Enforcers hiding behind the popcorn."

"Keep your voice down!" Gabriel hissed as the old man briefly looked up from the greeting cards towards them. "And you're right; we are in the living City; that's what I'm worried about."

Alex looked at Gabriel in surprise.

"Well, we've been here all the time before, haven't we?"

"Yeah, but you can't be too careful nowadays," Gabriel cautioned. "Remember what happened to The Bar?"

"What's that got to do with corn chips?" Alex asked brightly.

"The word is that the Enforcers have a new chief," Gabriel said as the elderly man vanished down an aisle with his greeting card.

"That'd be for what, the twentieth time?" Alex snorted. "He'll be just like the rest of them—old and stupid."

"Maybe," Gabriel conceded, now staring at the man who seemed to be comparing brands of sparkling water. "But maybe not. In any case, I think it was a bad idea to come here."

"There's not much else to do on patrol," Alex pointed out, piling his arms full of corn chip bags. "And anyway, wouldn't we look more suspicious if we just walked around all the time?"

Gabriel scowled; Alex had a point. Regular Truancy patrols had resumed since The Bar incident, and patrols in the living, inhabited parts of the City were especially dangerous—a task Zyid usually assigned to Alex and Gabriel, both capable officers. With all the Enforcers on the lookout for suspicious children, walking around looking for Enforcer stations could be suicidal if Truants failed to blend adequately with students. Telling himself that corn chips could be part of their disguise, Gabriel waited in silence as the four other Truants picked out their snacks.

"Got all your stuff?" Gabriel muttered to Alex, who alone seemed to still be examining the rows of snacks while all the other Truants gathered silently around Gabriel.

"Yeah, I guess this is enough," Alex said, lifting his arms up so that a mountain of snacks obscured his head. "Let's go pay for this stuff."

Gabriel didn't argue, and all the Truants quickly headed for the checkout counter. Once there, however, they found that all of the cashiers had vanished. The Truants froze for a second, and then Alex stepped cautiously forward, dumping his snacks onto the counter to free his arms.

"Where did they go?" Alex whispered, suddenly alert.

"I don't know, but I have a bad feeling about this," Gabriel murmured, suspicion in his voice.

Before Alex could voice his agreement, something crashed

to the ground and the Truants looked around in alarm to find an old man pointing a gun at them, a greeting card lying at his feet. Before they could react, the three other men in the pharmacy swiftly emerged, forming a semicircle around them, backing them against the counter.

"Get on the ground, with your hands where we can see them!" one of the men barked loudly.

There was a suspended moment of silence as the Truants weighed their options. It wasn't long, however, before Gabriel opened his mouth.

"To hell with that, you bastards!" he snarled, whipping a pistol out from a back pocket.

The four plainclothes Enforcers opened fire. Two Truants went down instantly, while Gabriel, Alex, and the other dived for cover. Gabriel landed behind the counter and quickly brought his gun up to fire at the nearest Enforcer. The first bullet caught the man in the arm, and the second finished the job. At the same time, Alex drew his own gun and leaned around a display of deodorant to aim a shot at another Enforcer, cleanly landing a head shot. By then the third Truant had managed to draw his gun and leaped out from cover, which proved to be a mistake. One of the Enforcers turned at the first sign of movement and fired, catching the Truant in the shoulder. The Truant squeezed the trigger by reflex, and his gun sent a bullet into the belly of his attacker before his partner unloaded three other shots into him, killing the Truant on the spot.

Taking advantage of the Enforcer's distraction, Alex and Gabriel simultaneously aimed and fired. The Enforcer crumpled to the ground with two holes through his head, and suddenly the only sound that could be heard in the pharmacy was Alex's and Gabriel's heavy breathing. The previously white linoleum floor was now covered with blood from the seven bodies that lay sprawled upon it. Alex and Gabriel looked at each other, wondering how things had gone so horribly wrong.

The sudden, sharp sound of clapping cut through the silence, and Alex and Gabriel turned to the entrance to see a kid standing there, ominously framed in the sunlight of the open door. The boy was grinning widely, clapping enthusiastically as if he'd just finished watching an impressive play.

The boy was wearing what looked like a bulletproof vest over an Enforcer uniform, and was armed with two pistols. Alex and Gabriel instantly bared their teeth as they saw the boy's hair—platinum blond.

"Well, what have we here?" the blond boy said loudly, stepping forward as the doors slid shut behind him. "Five children wandering around the City with guns, and two of them apparently know how to use them. Would you care to explain yourselves?"

"Shoot first, ask questions later, is it?" Gabriel snarled.

"I know better than to negotiate with the Truancy. My name is Edward, by the way—nice to meet you," he said casually. "No, really, it is; you have no idea how many unfortunate and innocent groups of five children we had to arrest before you came along."

"Why are you helping the Enforcers?" Alex demanded. "Haven't you ever been to school?"

Edward laughed coldly. "Yes, I have been to school. But I've put that behind me, and now I have my own future to think about. Speaking of which, why don't you surrender? It'll look good on my report if I take two Truants alive. Hell, I just might even get you amnesty in return."

"We won't sell out like you, traitor," Gabriel growled.

"Who, me? Oh, I'm no traitor." Edward grinned. "I was never loyal to anything to begin with."

"That so?" Gabriel raised his gun. "Well, we aren't surrendering; what're you gonna do about it?"

"There is a SWAT team and several Enforcer patrols waiting outside right now, on the off chance that you manage to kill me," Edward said. "But if you do resist arrest, I'd prefer to deal with you myself."

"Without calling for help?" Alex said skeptically.

"That's right." Edward grinned.

"I've had enough of this!" Gabriel said loudly, gripping his gun tightly. "If we're gonna die, let's take this bastard with us, Alex."

Edward regarded Gabriel for a moment with venomous eyes, then without warning darted sideways into an aisle, swiftly drawing his guns. He fired off two shots at the pair of Truants before they could react. Both bullets missed, one sinking into the linoleum floor and another smashing into a refrigerator behind them, shattering the glass and sending shards scattering everywhere.

Gabriel leaped forward and cautiously moved down the aisle Edward had vanished into. Alex drew his gun and darted left and then down the beverage aisle. For a minute there was only the squeaking of sneakers on linoleum, and then, as Gabriel reached the middle of his aisle, four shots rang out in quick succession, smashing bottles of shampoo and conditioner that had been right next to Gabriel's head. Gabriel ducked and wildly fired back, causing jets of shampoo to spew outwards as bullets passed through their containers.

"You should thank me; you can wash your hair now!" Edward called out from behind several rows of shelves.

"I would if I had any to wash, blondie!" Gabriel retorted as a bullet passed right over his shaven head.

Meanwhile, Alex stealthily crept towards the middle of his own aisle, aiming to get adjacent with the source of the commotion. More shots rang out, this time piercing bottles of soda all around Alex. Colorful jets of soda spewed from the pierced bottles, and Alex almost slipped on the resulting puddles as he fired back blindly.

"I think thirst must be affecting your aim!" Edward yelled. "Relax! Here, have a drink!"

Before Alex could respond, there was a great upheaval and the shelves began toppling like dominoes towards Alex. He had nowhere to run. Alex could only swear loudly as the shelves came crashing down on him, along with dozens of bottles of soda. Alex let out a pained yell from under the shelves, and then groaned as he worked to extricate himself from the mess.

Seeing what had happened, Gabriel decided to imitate Edward and kicked the shelf nearest him, letting out a grunt of satisfaction as it fell and started a chain reaction of toppling shelves. Edward, however, wasn't one to fall prey to his own tactic. He climbed up onto the shelf he was hidden behind, and with perfect timing leaped down from it as the next shelf came crashing into his own and tipped it over. Even as he jumped, Edward aimed up at the ceiling and fired, shattering the lighting directly above Gabriel. Parts of the lighting fixture came crashing down upon Gabriel, who fired wildly at

Edward and missed. Edward smirked as he leisurely approached Gabriel, who now lay on the ground bleeding from a dozen cuts. Edward kicked the gun from Gabriel's hand, and then raised one of his own to finish the job. But before he could pull the trigger, there was the sound of soda cans clattering, and Edward spun around.

Alex had finally extricated himself from the shelves, but seemed to have lost his gun in the process and was now soaking wet with soda. Unarmed and bedraggled, Alex clenched his fists and glared at Edward defiantly. Edward regarded the Truant for a moment, then flashed him a predatory grin and tossed both his pistols aside. Alex gaped slightly as Edward broke into a run, dashing towards him with the ferocity of a wolf. Alex stood his ground, but Edward leaped up into a powerful kick that caught him completely unprepared. Alex was sent reeling backwards, while Edward himself landed safely among the bottles of soda.

Gabriel, having shoved the remains of the fluorescent lighting off him, saw what was happening and rushed forward to join the fight. Edward was back up in an instant after his fall, and Alex too had managed to rise shakily to his feet. Gabriel wasted no time in snapping a kick at Edward's thigh, but Edward seized Gabriel's leg as it swung towards him and twisted forcefully, spinning Gabriel's entire body and sending him crashing to the ground. Alex rushed forward in an attempt to land a punch, but Edward delivered a firm kick to his stomach that knocked him backwards. Gabriel lashed out at Edward from the floor with his legs, but Edward simply jumped to avoid the blow, landing a forceful kick to Gabriel's back. Alex lunged forward again, but was in no shape to compete with Edward, who drove a fist into his belly, bringing him to the ground where Edward finished off with a kick to his temple. Alex went limp.

"Ready for your turn, darkie?" Edward called, turning to face Gabriel, who was getting up with blood dripping down his face.

"What did you just say?" Gabriel demanded.

"Are you ready for your turn, darkie?" Edward repeated loudly.

Gabriel let out a snarl of rage and lunged forward, swinging a punch at Edward's head. Edward ducked, but even as he did, Gabriel executed a forceful kick to his stomach that caused Edward's green eyes to widen in surprise. Gabriel followed up with another punch, but Edward dodged to one side, seized Gabriel's arm, and then hurled him over his head so that he went flying into the snack stand. Something crunched beneath him, and Gabriel tried to assure himself that it was only corn chips and not bone. Meanwhile, Edward dusted his hands off and walked forward.

"I got overconfident," Edward said. "But that was still impressive; I didn't expect you to manage to land a hit."

"I'll manage a lot more than that, you bastard," Gabriel hissed, rising to his feet and wiping blood from his eyes.

"Oh, I doubt it." Edward crouched down to pick up Alex's gun from amidst the soda bottles. "You were lucky that you managed to do anything at all. It was fun though, while it lasted."

"Cheating son of a—," Gabriel roared as Edward raised the gun.

A single shot rang out through the pharmacy, and Gabriel dropped to the floor with a neat hole in the center of his forehead. Edward nodded in satisfaction, then tossed the gun aside. Strolling casually over toppled shelves towards the exit, Edward turned his head to admire the scene of total carnage. He let out a cold chuckle and then shouted out, addressing no one in particular:

"Cleanup in all aisles, please!"

So, what brings you here today, Tack?" Umasi asked, sliding a cup of lemonade across the table. "Aside from your thirst, of course."

"Nothing in particular," Tack murmured. "Zyid was just giving me a lecture about school."

"Ah yes, he does go on like that sometimes." Umasi rubbed his chin thoughtfully. "Did what he said bother you?"

"I guess." Tack shrugged. "Some of it's true though."

"Well, you certainly look like something's on your mind, and I don't think it's Zyid's speech," Umasi said omnisciently, pouring himself a cup of lemonade.

Tack hesitated. He did actually feel like talking about it, and if there was anyone he could talk to, it was Umasi. After all, who else knew him better than he did himself?

"There's this girl," Tack said tentatively.

"Oh." Umasi raised his eyebrows. "Attractive?"

"Yeah, very." Tack nodded. "She's . . . well, it's Noni."

Umasi seemed momentarily speechless, something that Tack had never witnessed before.

"Well, now that's interesting," Umasi murmured at last. "The two of you get along?"

"Yeah, we do," Tack replied firmly.

"Do you love her?" Umasi asked, setting his cup down on the table.

The question broadsided Tack, who almost jumped out of

his seat in surprise. After the initial shock wore off, Tack dropped his gaze, uncomfortable with the subject.

"I don't know," Tack said honestly.

"You loved your sister, isn't that right?" Umasi asked.

Tack looked up sharply. Then he slouched in his seat, nodding.

Umasi stroked his chin. "Perhaps you are uncertain because you do not know what love means."

"Yeah," Tack murmured.

"Would you like my thoughts on the subject?" Umasi asked.

Tack was taken aback. Umasi never asked his permission to talk about anything, no matter what it was. Tack frowned, deciding that he had probably become too used to Umasi telling him anything he wanted. The topic didn't seem as important as others they'd discussed, so Tack couldn't imagine why Umasi had extended him the unusual courtesy.

"All right, why not?" Tack offered, glad the subject had shifted away from Noni, specifically.

"I believe that love is when you are willing to value someone's or something's existence above your own," Umasi said simply. "Take Zyid for example. Zyid loves the Truancy very much."

Tack frowned. It was difficult for him to imagine Zyid loving anything, and he could tell that it showed on his face. But Umasi, as always, ignored his expression.

"While Zyid is readily willing to kill for his cause, and for the Truancy, he is also willing to die for it. I think, in fact, he hopes that he will," Umasi mused.

Tack had nothing to say to that. It was probably true, after all, though ever since he'd visited Suzie's grave, Tack expected that Zyid wouldn't die quite in the manner Umasi described.

"Back on topic, Tack," Umasi said with a grin. "Do you love her?"

Tack shook his head helplessly. "Let me get back to you on that."

"Oh, I don't expect that you'll figure it out all at once. It's probably something you'll discover gradually."

"Thanks," Tack said, not entirely sure what he was thankful for.

"Anytime." Umasi picked up his book from its resting place on the sidewalk and began to read as Tack pushed his seat in and walked away down the empty street.

22

A Student Militia

"Is there something wrong?" Tack asked tentatively.

Tack's words shattered the fragile silence, and Zyid looked up at him sharply. The Truant leader had been poring over a map of the City while Tack stood motionless in a dim corner of the flower shop, which had become his routine these days. With little else to do, Tack had noticed that Zyid looked uncharacteristically troubled as he traced invisible routes on the map with his finger. Seemingly displeased at being disturbed, Zyid glared reproachfully at Tack. The anger passed almost instantly, however, and Zyid straightened up, looking and sounding impassive.

"Party One is long overdue," Zyid explained. "Yesterday they were sent on a routine scouting mission in the living City, and were supposed to return by nightfall. As you may have noticed—" Zyid gestured towards the show window of the flower shop, through which brilliantly pale sunlight poured in—"it is now morning."

Tack frowned. Party One was co-captained by Alex and Gabriel, both skilled, experienced, high-ranking Truancy lieutenants. Tack hadn't known Alex very well personally, but Gabriel had been there ever since Tack joined the Truancy. Gabriel had struck Tack as the strong, unyielding type, though extremely fierce and dangerous when angered. He was the type to fight to the death.

To the death.

Tack's frown deepened.

"Do you think they were killed?" Tack asked Zyid, who had resumed inspecting the map of the City.

"Yes, Takan," Zyid said candidly. "That is my belief. I hope, however, to be proven wrong—it wouldn't be the first time."

Tack was surprised to find that news of Gabriel's presumed death didn't seem to bother him very much, especially since he'd counted Gabriel as one of his friends. Sure, Tack was disturbed that such an able Truant had been killed, but on a personal level he felt almost nothing. Perhaps he'd cried every last tear he had over Suzie's grave—maybe those emotional scars ran so deep that he couldn't feel for others anymore. It was a vaguely frightening thought, and one that Tack decided not to dwell on.

"How do you think it happened?" Tack asked, sure that Zyid must've come up with some sort of theory after all the time he'd spent thinking.

"It is possible that they were spotted, tailed, ambushed, and slaughtered," Zyid said dispassionately. "If the Educators have picked up on the fact that parties consist of five Truants, and I now suspect that they have, then they'd have been on the lookout for Gabriel and Alex's team. I shall have to vary the number of Truants per party from now on."

"How could the Educators have known about the parties in the first place?" Tack asked blankly.

"Perhaps through observation," Zyid mused. "If one is methodical enough, he can discover much that is hidden about his opponent."

Tack looked at Zyid curiously. The Truant leader was speaking as if discussing a formidable and respected adversary, something that Tack had never heard before. Suddenly, he remembered a rumor that he'd heard several days ago while eating a soggy tuna salad sandwich two doors down in the abandoned burger shop.

"They say that the Enforcers have a new Chief," Tack said carefully.

"They do." Zyid nodded. "And I suspect that I know who he is, or at least what his background is. Though, as before, I hope to be proven wrong."

Remembering the sunglasses he'd found the night The Bar was destroyed, Tack recalled his own suspicions. So far he'd seen nothing conclusive that could confirm his fears about one of Umasi's other disciples now working against the Truancy, but he had to admit that the war that had at first seemed to be going so well for the Truancy had recently and inexplicably turned against them.

The door to the flower shop swung open, and Zyid and Tack turned their heads around to see Noni standing in the doorway, her slim body casting a disproportionately huge shadow against the morning brightness. Tack could feel his heart start to beat faster, and consciously willed himself to remain impassive as Noni glanced at him before turning towards Zyid.

"There is something you should see, sir," Noni said respectfully.

"Oh?" Zyid straightened up. "And what's that?"

"The Mayor is holding a press conference in a few minutes," Noni said. "The news said . . . it said it's about a criminal organization threatening the City."

Zyid stiffened, and Tack saw his dark eyes narrow very slightly. When Zyid spoke, his voice was carefully controlled, though Tack could sense his apprehension; Tack himself didn't like the sound of what Noni had described.

"Well then, we'd better have a look," Zyid said, striding towards the door immediately. "Come, Takan."

Tack followed acquiescently, and as he reached the door, he turned for a second to see Noni staring at him. They locked gazes for a moment, and Tack could see fear flickering in her infinitely blue eyes.

And that, more than anything, scared him.

The room was utterly dark, save for the light that crept in from the slit under the door. They were in Zyid's office, the one he kept his private television in. To Tack's annoyance, Zyid had dismissed Noni and sent her off to squat before one of the public televisions. She'd taken the order stoically, though Tack knew that she'd be irked at sharing a television with the dozens, maybe hundreds of Truants that would be crowded around the other television sets, each of them just as eager for the news as Tack was.

Zyid strode over to the television. A moment later, something clicked and the television sprang to life, illuminating the room with its faint glow. After a second of fuzziness, the

Mayor's familiar face swam into focus, instantly capturing Tack's attention like no teacher ever could.

"Dear citizens," the Mayor was saying gravely as he stood at a podium on the steps of City Hall, "I come before you today to address a real and growing threat to our City. But before I do, I would like to take this opportunity to discuss the incident that occurred downtown yesterday and left nine dead."

Tack felt Zyid stir next to him, and knew that they were thinking the same thing; Gabriel and Alex's party had taken four Enforcers down with them. Tack was about to speak when Zyid held up a hand for silence as the Mayor continued his speech.

"I will be succinct; the deaths were the result of the actions of a youth-oriented criminal organization that calls itself the Truancy," the Mayor declared. "It is our belief that the Truancy has been acting among us for quite some time, and is now preparing to initiate an all-out war against this City. Indeed, for the first time, circumstances allow me to reveal that many fatal incidents in the past that appeared to be accidents were actually cleverly disguised, cold-blooded murders and sabotages performed by the Truancy. A full list of these horrible crimes will soon be made available to the public."

It was Tack's turn to be disturbed. The Mayor seemed to describe both Suzie's death and what Tack had been doing for the Truancy with brutal accuracy, though admittedly none of it had exactly been cleverly disguised. Tack had no time to feel guilty or vengeful, however, as the television was still blaring.

"The Truancy seems mostly to be comprised of expelled and rejected students that turned to crime after failing to live honest lives," the Mayor continued. "I ask the City to remain vigilant and strong in the face of these despicable criminals.

There may well be tough times ahead, as this Truancy has recruited enough misguided members to pose a very real threat to the entire City. And now, here to address that fact is a very courageous young man that we should all applaud for his initiative and loyalty."

The Mayor stepped down from the podium, and Tack's heart skipped a beat as a blond-haired boy with acid green eyes came into view. As the boy turned to look into the camera, Tack heard a sudden intake of breath next to him, and he suddenly knew that he was looking into the eyes of their mysterious adversary.

"My name is Edward," the blond boy said. "I was once a student, just like many of you out there are. I once sat next to my classmates as a normal child. I was content to stay idly among them . . . until I heard of the Truancy." Edward's voice now turned harsh, and his emerald eyes flashed theatrically.

Tack knew it was acting, but it was *good* acting.

"When I heard of the horrors that this Truancy has been perpetrating against our City, I was so outraged that I knew that I had to do something. And so I decided to quit school." Edward paused, allowing his words to sink in. "I decided to quit school," Edward repeated, "and do everything I could to oppose these Truancy thugs. Soon afterwards, I approached the Mayor with an idea of mine."

Edward grinned, and Tack felt the familiar sensation of dread fill his stomach.

"I proposed the creation of a Student Militia," Edward said dramatically. "I believe that we, as the children of this City, have every bit as much right and obligation to defend it as any adult does! Why should we have to stand by and watch while brutes commit murder in the streets?" Edward's voice was now raised, growing more excited with every syllable. "My fellow students, the Truancy threatens the *entire* City! Not just the adults, but us as well! If our lives are endangered, why shouldn't we be allowed to fight back? And we *can* fight!"

Tack gritted his teeth, his fears confirmed. It didn't make any sense that Edward could've heard about the Truancy before the press conference, unless he was working with the Educators all along.

"Fortunately," Edward now continued, "the Mayor is a great and understanding leader. He greeted my proposal with enthusiasm, and has even agreed to make it an official program. What's more, he has promised that every individual brave enough to enlist with the Student Militia will be granted instant graduation upon the defeat of the Truancy." Tack could see something triumphant and malicious flickering in Edward's venomous eyes.

"That's right," Edward said. "Instant graduation. Join us, and if we as students stand united with the Educators, together we can destroy this mutual threat."

Zyid's silhouette moved, and a moment later there was another click as the television died, and the room was plunged again into darkness. In the resulting silence, Tack realized that he was gaping in horror at what he'd just seen and heard. He slowly closed his mouth, and felt Zyid turn to face him in the darkness.

"I must address the Truancy," Zyid said wearily. "There are dark times ahead."

That went well," the Mayor observed as Edward stepped into his office and promptly made himself comfortable in the cushioned armchair.

"Yes, I do pride myself on my acting," Edward said smoothly.

"I think you convinced a good many students with it," the Mayor complimented, setting his lighter down on his desk.

"And perhaps a few Truants along with them," Edward added.

"Hopefully." The Mayor nodded, toasting Edward before tilting his glass back and downing the whiskey in one gulp. "Speaking of which, good job with those five Truants yesterday."

"It was rather fun, to be honest," Edward said wolfishly. "I haven't had a good fight since your son bested me."

"I'm glad you enjoyed it," the Mayor said, flicking his lighter open. "By the way, you remember that Truant that was taken alive?"

"Ah, so he was just knocked out?" Edward said idly, inspecting his knuckles. "I thought he was dead."

"Well, he is now," the Mayor said, and Edward looked up at him in surprise. "He was sent to the hospital, where his wounds were treated. He was then moved into a cell, where he promptly hung himself the first chance he got."

"Stubborn bastard." Edward chuckled.

"Indeed." The Mayor nodded. "Never even got the chance to interrogate him."

"A waste," Edward reflected. "But not much of a loss, really."

"He won't be missed," the Mayor agreed. "Especially now that things are heating up."

"We'll have plenty of Truants to interrogate when they surrender in the face of my Student Militia," Edward said dismissively.

"Ah yes, the Student Militia," the Mayor said, his lighter

snapping shut. "How soon do you really think we can expect to have a sizeable Militia prepared to fight against the Truants?"

"The size will be no problem," Edward assured him. "With the promise of instant graduation? We'll have hundreds, if not thousands, of volunteers by tomorrow, guaranteed. Preparation and training isn't something I'll agonize over either—the Student Militia's main purpose is simply to demoralize the Truancy. I doubt very much that the majority of the Truancy would be willing to kill their peers."

"So then, Student Militia patrols will be going out in what, a week? Two?"

"Give me four days and I'll personally lead the first five-person team against the Truancy," Edward promised.

"That's a tall order," the Mayor observed.

"And one that I can meet."

"Very well." The Mayor nodded approvingly. "You've lived up to your promises before. We can only hope that the trend continues."

"And if it does?"

"Then your position as Chief Enforcer will become public," the Mayor said, smiling at the boy's unquenchable ambition. "And you will be given a spot on the City Council, as well as in my cabinet."

"That *would* be nice," Edward admitted.

"Noni!" Tack called desperately. "Hey, Noni!"

Tack had been searching all throughout the Truancy headquarters for her, leaving Zyid behind to address the Truancy. Tack wasn't sure why he needed to see her so urgently. Perhaps he simply couldn't face the dread of what lay ahead alone. After nearly half an hour of looking, Tack had finally found her lurking in a basement corridor. The moment she spotted him, however, she had begun to walk away at a fast pace.

"Noni, please!" Tack called out again.

The figure in front of him stopped abruptly, standing completely motionless. Tack sighed with relief and ran to catch up to her. When he reached her, however, he let out an involuntary gasp. Noni's face was ashen and paler than normal, and her blue eyes had dulled to gray. Her scarf hung loosely around her neck, and her mouth was slightly open as she stared blearily back up at Tack. It seemed as though the weight of a hundred years had gripped her by the shoulders, pulling her down.

"Noni . . . ," Tack whispered weakly, finding his throat suddenly very dry.

"I'm . . . I'm going to have to . . . to kill them," Noni mumbled, averting her gaze.

Tack froze, knowing instantly what Noni was talking about, since the same fears commanded his own attention. Tack looked around desperately for any words of comfort that he could find.

"You won't have to kill them," Tack said. "We can talk to Zyid. I'm sure he'll understand—"

"He'll . . . he'll need me to kill them," Noni said, still looking away from Tack.

"No." Tack's voice hardened. "I'll kill them for you. I'll kill enough for the both of us!"

Tack regretted the words as soon as they left his mouth, wondering what sort of madness had made him say them. He knew full well that killing other kids wouldn't be anything like fighting the Enforcers—he'd be a murderer, no better than Zyid.

"... I owe him everything," Noni muttered.

"Zyid?"

"If he needs me to kill them ... I will."

Tack felt a sudden anger surge through him.

"Why do you feel that way about him?" Tack demanded. "He doesn't even respect you; the moment I came along he tossed you aside like a dirty rag!"

"He saved my life," Noni said softly, one hand coming up to touch her scar. "If I had to ... I'd die for him."

I believe that love is when you are willing to value someone's or something's existence above your own.

Umasi's words struck Tack like a hammer blow to the head, and he reeled backwards. Noni would die for Zyid.

Would he die for Noni?

No, Tack realized, he had unfinished business on Suzie's behalf.

Would he die for Noni after Zyid was killed?

Yes, Tack told himself, *yes.*

"All right, you'll have to kill them," Tack conceded reluctantly. "But so will I, and I don't want to any more than you do! Why are you so down?"

"I ... don't want to burden you with my troubles," Noni murmured, though Tack had the sense that she was reluctantly yielding.

"You don't have to," Tack said firmly. "But you don't have to bear them alone. I'm counting on you, Noni. Don't let me down."

And then, seized by recklessness, Tack stepped forward and swept Noni into a tight embrace. Tack could feel Noni stiffen against him in shock, but a moment later she relaxed, and her arms snaked around his waist. Noni looked up at Tack, who could see color return to her eyes, just before they shut firmly. Noni buried her head in Tack's shoulder, and he felt simultaneously relieved and elated as he gently patted her on the back, feeling her warmth melt away his own dread. For the briefest of moments, he was reminded of embracing Suzie, and the comfort that had brought him.

"Takan?"

"Yes?"

"Thank you."

23

Backed into a Corner

"We're almost there," Tack said hoarsely, shuffling forward as he supported Noni.

"I've never . . . never fought anyone like that." Noni coughed, and flecks of bloody spittle landed on the ground.

"Neither have I," Tack said grimly, feeling Noni's steady grip on his bare shoulder weaken slightly.

"He can't be human." Noni gasped as Tack's supporting arm lifted her up and forward.

"He's a monster," Tack agreed. The door to the flower shop was steps away, and Tack had never been gladder to see it.

"Are you all right?" Tack asked as Noni coughed up more blood, though he knew very well that she wasn't. He wasn't either, come to that.

"No," Noni said, wiping her mouth with her free hand. "But I'll live. What about you?"

"I'll live too, I think," Tack said evasively, ignoring the

pains stabbing his body as he heaved himself to the door, scrabbling for the knob with a burned hand.

As he pulled the door open, Tack forced himself to stagger forward, dragging Noni along inside. Overcome by relief, Tack and Noni released their grip of each other and crumpled to the floor. Tack managed to catch a glimpse of something dark sweeping towards them before he felt a powerful arm raising him to his knees.

"What happened to you two?" Zyid demanded, his dark eyes darting back and forth between Noni and Tack, noting their ugly bruises.

It was Noni who spoke. "Edward," she said, unable to meet Zyid's eyes.

As Zyid let out a sound halfway between a snarl and a hiss, Tack slumped over. It was growing hard to focus, and he could hear the dull thump of his heart pound in his chest.

"Did you kill him?" Zyid asked.

"No." Noni shook her head wearily. "We barely got away."

"Unfortunate, but not unexpected," Zyid muttered. "You two need to lie down." The next thing Tack knew, he was lying dazedly on his back on the hard wooden floor.

"Relax," Tack heard Zyid say, though his voice sounded strangely distant.

Tack squirmed as he felt something cool but stinging being poured over a gash on his leg, and then he felt his head being propped up by something soft. Zyid was saying something, but Tack was finding it harder than ever to concentrate, nearly exhausting all his reserves of mental energy just to decipher Zyid's words.

"I need to know what happened," Zyid was saying. "It's important that you tell me if you can."

Noni would have to relate the story, Tack thought. For him, it was a chore just staying awake. If it weren't for the sharp pains assaulting his body, he'd have drifted off to the sweet sanctuary of unconsciousness long ago. As Noni's steady recital of the morning's events drifted through the air, Tack was himself brought to remember those painful and embarrassing events with vivid clarity.

It's hopeless; we have to go!" Tack shouted.

Noni's head snapped around, blood dripping off her knives. She had cast aside her gun a while ago, having exhausted her supply of ammo firing furiously around the corner of the alley where they had taken cover. They were on the border of Districts 13 and 14, helping to slow an Enforcer push while the Truancy evacuated a riverside warehouse. Unfortunately, not only had the Enforcers shown up in force, but the first Student Militia squad the Truants had ever faced had also deployed ahead of them, causing many to hesitate.

In less than half an hour, the Truants had been pushed back five blocks, suffering heavy losses all the way. Tack and Noni alone now crouched in the alley, though other survivors were doggedly firing back from behind other cover. The Student Militia was still advancing, however, and now two young bodies lay at Noni's feet, dead from stab wounds as they attempted to rush the alley. Noni didn't look sorry as Tack knew she was, as she seemed to be shielding her emotions with a sort of cold, mechanical efficiency.

Though her eyes flashed angrily, she accepted the logic of Tack's suggestion.

"Split up," Noni said decisively, sticking her knives back into her belt.

Tack frowned, reluctant to part with her, though he too was forced to accept the logic of *her* suggestion as bullets flew by, chipping bits of brick off the wall behind them. Without another word, Noni leaped up and darted out of the alley, running from the approaching Enforcers. Tack immediately bent around the corner and fired wildly at the uniformed enemies, covering Noni's fleeing back.

A short, youthful figure crumpled to the ground, and Tack felt a slight twinge of regret, though it quickly faded as he was forced to duck as the Enforcers opened fire again. Hoping that Noni had gotten to safety, Tack decided it was time to make his own escape. Rising to his feet, he turned and darted down the shadowy alley, but not before he heard a vicious voice shout out an order behind him.

"Go after the other one; I'll take him myself!"

Something in that voice filled Tack with a primal fear, and he pumped his legs harder than ever. As Tack neared a wire fence blocking his way, he heard a gunshot, and a moment later he realized that his ear was bleeding. Seized by a sudden panic, Tack ignored the pain completely and jumped on top of some trash cans, knocking them over as he leaped forward, his feet connecting briefly with the wall of the alley. With all the strength in his legs, Tack pushed off the wall and flew forward, landing behind the wire fence as bullets flew just over his head.

Falling onto the filthy ground of the alley, Tack felt his gun slip from his hands. Knowing that he had no time to retrieve it, Tack rose to his feet despite the newly acquired pains from the fall, and swiftly lunged forward and out of the alley. More gunshots rang out from behind him. Thinking quickly, Tack turned and ran left towards what looked like an abandoned library. Yanking the front doors open, Tack darted inside, realizing his mistake too late; the doors were slow to close, making his hiding place obvious to any pursuer.

A sudden calm stole over Tack as he flattened himself against the wall next to the entrance. If he was to die here, there was nothing more for him to do but put up the best fight he could. Tack steadied his breathing and studied his surroundings. Rows and rows of dark bookshelves told Tack that his first impression had been right; it was a library. It wasn't the type of place he'd have chosen to make his last stand, but he couldn't be picky.

Suddenly, Tack tensed as he heard the doors swing open and slow, cautious footsteps enter the library. Knowing that he had just one chance to disarm his enemy, Tack gritted his teeth and prepared himself. A moment later, a darkened figure stepped forward, and Tack lunged, tackling the boy to the ground. Acting instinctively, Tack first seized the boy's gun arm, and then brought his other fist back for a punch.

Reacting with a swiftness Tack never thought possible, the other boy caught Tack's hand as it rushed towards his head, his green eyes glinting predatorily. Only then did Tack realize whom he was facing. A confident, malicious grin, platinum blond hair, acid green eyes, these could belong to no one but Edward, founder of the Student Militia, Umasi's former pupil, and the only enemy Tack had ever dreaded.

Taking advantage of Tack's surprise, Edward lashed out and head butted Tack in the face, hard. Blood started flowing from Tack's nose, yet he stubbornly held on to Edward's arm, struggling to keep the gun facing away from him. Then suddenly Edward's arm went still, and the blond boy let out a laugh.

"So, you're afraid of my gun?" Edward jeered. "I see you've lost yours. How about I make this fair for you?"

Edward wrested his arm from Tack's grip and tossed his gun behind him. Completely shocked at this new development, Tack wasn't prepared as Edward drew his legs back so that his feet connected with Tack's chest. The next thing he knew, Tack found himself flying backwards into the librarian's desk. Edward was up in an instant, and reaching for his belt produced a painfully sharp-looking knife. Tack acted almost reflexively, drawing his sword and swinging it forward horizontally, nearly slashing Edward across the chest.

"Interesting weapon," Edward observed, showing no concern about having been nearly cut open. "Ceramic, I take it? The Educators never did find out what you Truants wanted from that ceramics facility."

Tack snarled and rose to his feet, infuriated that Edward was getting any information from him, involuntary or not. Before he could attack, Edward lunged forward with startling speed, one foot raised to execute a kick that pinned Tack's sword to the desk while his arm brought his knife plunging towards Tack's neck. Tack had no choice but to release the sword and slide to the ground as the knife stuck in the wood above his head. Seemingly expecting this outcome, Edward withdrew his foot and his arm, letting the sword clatter to the ground as he brought his knife forward for another thrust.

Seeing that his life was in danger, Tack lashed out suddenly and violently with his legs, successfully catching Edward in the stomach. Edward staggered backwards a few steps, and Tack leaped to his feet and picked up his sword, swinging it furiously at Edward's head. Edward stepped backwards to avoid the sword's superior reach. Undeterred, Tack lunged forward, aiming a stab this time. Edward merely continued backing up in short leaps, infuriating Tack as slash after slash narrowly missed his blond adversary. As Edward reached the first aisle of bookshelves, he seized a thin storybook and hurled it at Tack.

Tack struck the book down with his sword before it reached him, and shredded pages spewed into the air, floating gently to the ground. Another book flew through the air at him, and Tack slashed at it as well, only to have yet another streak towards him. Edward laughed as he hurled book after book at Tack, filling the air with bits of paper like confetti. As Tack slashed at a book particularly violently, Edward lunged forward without warning, sweeping his knife in an arc at Tack's thigh. The attack drew blood, cutting through Tack's clothes and skin, though the Truant had backed up at the last minute just in time to avoid serious injury.

Tack snarled and swung his sword at Edward in retaliation. Edward, however, seized a thick leather-bound book and blocked the blow with it. Lashing out with his feet, Edward kicked Tack in the belly, forcing him backwards. Edward took the opportunity to turn and dash down the aisle, sweeping as many books as he could onto the floor as he ran.

Tack immediately gave chase, leaping over the piles of books that Edward had dumped onto the floor. But as soon as Edward was in striking distance, he spun around and dived, passing right between Tack's legs and slashing with his knife as he did. The blade cut a gash across Tack's right leg, and Tack let out a roar of pain as he spun around to bring his sword down on Edward. Edward raised his foot to block the blow, and Tack's sword sunk into the thick sole of Edward's boot, biting the footwear but not penetrating it.

A growing suspicion that he was outmatched sneaked to the surface of Tack's mind, and as Edward kicked the sword off his boot and jumped to his feet, Tack turned and ran, sheathing his blade and reaching into his jacket as he did so. Drawing a lighter from his pocket, Tack whipped a bottle out of his jacket, spun around, and lit the cloth stuck in the neck of the bottle. Edward skidded to a halt, and his green eyes widened as Tack hurled the firebomb at him. As the bottle flew through the air, Edward lashed out with his foot and kicked the bottle up and over the shelf to another aisle. A moment later, there was a loud noise and a burst of flame, and Edward still stood before Tack, grinning triumphantly.

"Nice try, Truant." Edward laughed.

"Lucky bastard," Tack snarled, lunging forward recklessly.

Ignoring the growing flames that hungrily lapped at the dry wood of the shelves and the crisp pages of old books, Edward repeated his dodging routine while Tack slashed repeatedly at him. The fires became steadily larger, spreading to adjacent shelves, filling the dark library with flickering orange light and gray smoke. Soon Edward and Tack were fighting between two flaming bookshelves, coughing while they struck and dodged.

Suddenly, Edward reached out and seized a book that had only just caught fire, and threw it at Tack. Taken by surprise, Tack didn't see the heavy volume, which struck him, lighting his shirt on fire. Batting at the flames furiously, Tack had no choice but to remove the shirt and cast it aside, but while he was distracted Edward tackled him to the floor and brought his knife to Tack's neck.

"Well fought, Truant," Edward breathed. "Yours will be a death worth remembering."

• • •

Tack was painfully snapped back to the present as he felt a bandage being tightened over his leg. He blinked, and then realized that his head was feeling much clearer, and the pains had dulled, though they were still very much present. Tack sat up to see Zyid applying a bandage to Noni's limp arm. Tack gingerly rubbed his bruised chest as the Truancy leader stood up, muttering under his breath.

"Did I miss anything?" Tack asked.

"Eh?" Zyid looked distractedly over at Tack. "Nothing much. Noni passed out while relating her part of the story to me."

Tack immediately felt guilty. Tack looked over at her still figure, her scarf pulled down to her neck as she slept. Noni had saved his life, risking and nearly losing hers in the process. Tack was sorry about that, and yet couldn't help but feel pleased at the same time.

"We have a problem, Takan," Zyid said, spreading some papers out on the table sitting in the corner.

"Yeah," Tack said, agreeing with the obvious.

"This Edward has forced my hand," Zyid declared. "We will have to end this war quickly, much more quickly than planned."

"Can we?" Tack asked, sitting up in surprise and wincing.

"It's risky, but possible," Zyid said, shuffling through the papers. "We have to execute a series of strategic strikes on Enforcer targets, power stations, Educator facilities, and also incite a larger revolt by hijacking the City-wide loudspeaker system. We throw the City into chaos, and pick up the pieces when the dust settles."

"How could we pull something like that off?" Tack asked.

"Half of the Truancy refuses to fight against students, and even if they didn't, with Edward leading the other side we'd still probably lose."

"Yes, this Edward and his Student Militia does pose a problem." Zyid frowned. "The Student Militia will have to be dissolved, and Edward must be killed."

"Can you kill Edward?" Tack asked, knowing that if the answer was "yes," he would never be able to avenge Suzie. "Me?" Zyid mused. "Perhaps. I'm not sure. Why don't you tell me?"

"How would I know?" Tack said, taken aback.

"You've fought him," Zyid pointed out. "Noni didn't tell me much, and I know nothing of what happened when you actually fought Edward." Zyid turned to eye Tack. "Perhaps you should tell me."

Tack nodded, and began recounting his duel with Edward. Zyid listened, motionless. Tack got all the way up to the point where Edward had held his knife at his throat before Zyid interrupted.

"How did you get away?" Zyid inquired.

"Noni," Tack said simply.

"Ah." Zyid nodded. "So, she fought him off while you fled?"

"No." Tack shook his head. "We both fought him together."

"And lost?" Zyid asked incredulously.

"And lost," Tack agreed grimly as he began to recount how it had happened.

Tack looked up into Edward's venomously green eyes, staring death in the face. So, this was how he would die. He'd made his last stand; he'd fought as best he could. His only regret was that he'd never fulfill his promise to Suzie.

"Hands off!"

"What the—" Edward spun around, bringing his knife away from Tack's neck.

Noni barreled into Edward with tremendous force, knocking him off Tack and onto the floor behind him. Tack shakily rose to his feet, and stared as Noni furiously wrestled with Edward, struggling to restrain his knife arm.

"N-Noni?" Tack sputtered in shock.

"How about some help?" Noni demanded.

Coming to his senses, Tack gripped his sword and lunged forward between the two burning shelves. Unfortunately, he chose to do so right when Edward had brought his feet up to kick Noni off him just like he had done to Tack before. A moment later, Noni was sent flying through the air right into Tack. Both Truants crumpled to the ground, and Edward rose to his feet.

"So, female Truants do exist!" Edward breathed. "I was beginning to wonder."

Noni said nothing as she rolled off Tack and stood up, glaring menacingly at Edward, her icy eyes reflecting the flames. Tack followed suit, and Edward surveyed the two with interest.

"There's no way you can beat us both, Edward," Tack challenged.

"Of course there is, Truant." Edward sneered. "Unless you'd care to surrender now."

"You can't be serious," Noni muttered.

"Sorry, girlie, no chivalry today." Edward laughed. "Don't take me for a fool; I'm not afraid to hit girls."

"Good, because she's not afraid to hit you," Tack warned.

"Oh, excellent, a feisty one," Edward jeered. "Too bad she's covered up that pretty face."

Somehow it was Tack, not Noni, who struck first, lashing out at Edward with his sword out of pure rage. Edward parried the powerful blow with his knife, and retaliated with a kick that sent Tack sprawling. Noni aimed a powerful punch at Edward's exposed head, but Edward ducked and head butted Noni, knocking her backwards. Ignoring Tack, Edward lunged forward at Noni, slashing furiously at her waist.

Noni leaned backwards to avoid the attack, then seized the opening and kicked at Edward's stomach. Edward blocked the blow with his palm, then brought his knife behind his back to parry Tack's sword, which had been swung at him. Edward then shoved her seized leg forward, knocking Noni off-balance. At the same time, he kicked backwards violently, catching Tack in the chest, sending the wounded Truant staggering backwards.

Noni kicked up at Edward, who sidestepped and slashed downwards, cutting her across the knee. Noni didn't scream, but leaped to her feet with surprising grace even as blood trickled down her leg. Tack lunged forward and arced his sword down at Edward's back, but Edward likewise lunged forward, avoiding the blow and tackling Noni, violently punching her in the stomach before turning her around like a human shield against Tack's attacks.

Tack snarled in frustration, having barely stopped himself in time from slashing Noni's back. Noni, though dazed by Edward's blow, managed to slam her head into Edward's forehead, forcing him to release his grip. Noni rolled aside onto the floor, gasping and coughing up blood. Now with a clear shot, Tack lunged forward again, aiming to stab Edward. Edward knocked the blow aside with his knife, then delivered a forceful punch to Tack's stomach, knocking the wind out of the Truant.

None of the three combatants had had the leisure to observe how the flames had grown, but by then nearly the entire library had succumbed to fire, the dry books serving to spread it quickly and efficiently. The fighters were now near the entrance of the library, and the entire building was heating up like an oven as the flames licked at the wallpaper and even the librarian's desk.

Mindful of the intensifying heat, Edward drove his knee up into Tack's belly and twisted his hand until the ceramic sword clattered to the ground. Edward then brought his knife up to pierce Tack's throat, hoping to end the fight before they all went up in flames. Before he could thrust, however, a strong arm gripped his steadily, and then bent it behind his back in a painful position. Growling in annoyance, Edward drove his head backwards to slam into Noni's face. Her scarf slipped down to expose her face. Far from letting go, however, she seized his other arm and locked both behind his back.

Seeing his opportunity, Tack drove his fist forward to punch Edward in his unprotected chest, and then his face. Tack felt a vicious satisfaction as his fists connected with Edward, but before he could land a third blow, Edward lifted his legs and violently kicked off of Tack, pushing himself backwards so that he fell on top of Noni. Edward instantly leaped to his feet as Tack staggered backwards, and snapped his foot to Noni's neck, stepping down to crush her windpipe. Over the now-roaring flames, the sound of desperate gurgling filled the heated air.

"My, what a hideous scar," Edward commented, looking

down at Noni's exposed face. "I guess she's not so pretty after all."

In a sudden fit of reckless fury, Tack seized a burning book from the librarian's desk, heedless of the flames that bit at his hand. Hurling the book into the air, Tack sent it flying towards Edward. The book bounced off Edward, but not before setting his uniform alight. Roaring in outrage, Edward stepped off Noni and backed up, batting at his flaming uniform. Spotting a fire extinguisher near the entrance, Edward ran for the red cylinder and seized it, dousing himself thoroughly with the white foamy spray.

Tack had picked up his sword and had half a mind to attack Edward that instant, but feeling the pains of his injuries, having seen what he was up against, and seeing Noni half-alive on the floor convinced him not to pursue the fight. Sheathing his sword, Tack helped Noni up from the ground and was immensely relieved when she slung an arm around his neck and gripped his shoulder firmly. Sliding his arm under her armpit, Tack supported her as they hobbled out of the doomed library and onto the streets.

Tack guided Noni towards the nearest alley, looking back only once before they slipped into it. As he did, Tack was sure that he saw a weary but very much alive figure emerge from the library.

He is more formidable than I thought," Zyid mused, his back to Tack as he continued examining the papers on the table. "If we allow him to proceed unchecked for much longer, he may very well defeat us."

"Yeah," Tack said, examining one of his colorful bruises. "So, do you think you can beat him?"

"Like I said, Takan, it's possible," Zyid replied. "But by no means is it a sure thing. I do not wish to risk such a fight."

Tack was at once simultaneously relieved and disappointed to hear that. On the one hand, it meant that Zyid was mortal; Tack could stand a chance against him when the time came to kill him. On the other, it meant that the Truancy's future was very grim indeed.

"Isn't it hopeless as long as Edward's alive?" Tack said, voicing his fears.

"Quite possibly," Zyid affirmed, creasing his brow.

"So, he has to be killed," Tack pressed.

"Yes, he does." Zyid nodded.

"Well, isn't there *anyone* who can stop him?" Tack said in exasperation.

Unexpectedly, Zyid froze, and then turned to look at Tack pensively. His eyes misted over for a moment, and then a strange look of sadness flitted across his face.

"Yes, Takan," Zyid said mournfully. "There is one."

24

At the Hands of a Pacifist

The sun was high in the sky over District 19, bathing the City in bright daylight that managed to lighten even the stubbornly black asphalt, when the tranquil brightness was suddenly marred by a dark figure moving smoothly across the illuminated ground, casting a long shadow behind him.

The figure moved with a purpose, marching across a street to approach a lemonade stand behind which waited another figure, this one observing the other serenely from behind opaque sunglasses. His persistent shadow trailing behind him, the dark figure drew up to the stand and unceremoniously dropped a sword down onto it. A pair of glinting sunglasses glanced downward at the sword, inspecting it for a moment before rising to look back up at the dark figure.

"I thought I told you last time." Umasi frowned, the light

casting his features into shadow as he firmly pushed the sword away with one hand. "No thanks."

"Circumstances have changed since last time," Zyid said grimly, squinting against the harsh sunlight that struck his eyes. "Have you been keeping up with the news?"

Umasi folded his arms and sat motionless, though Zyid knew very well that he was being scrutinized by those hidden eyes.

"No. I've decided that I don't even want to know what unsavory things you've been up to," Umasi said dryly. "I've been sticking to books lately."

Zyid frowned and looked distastefully at Umasi, who indeed seemed to have several piles of books resting around him. He couldn't help feeling annoyed at Umasi for burying himself in books at such a crucial juncture.

"I'll cut to the point," Zyid said brusquely. "Do you know a boy named Edward?"

Umasi's composure abruptly slipped. Very slowly, he uncrossed his arms and leaned forward. As he did, his dark sunglasses slid down his nose, and for an instant Zyid was sure that he'd caught a glimpse of dark eyes widened in shock. Zyid inclined his head slightly, the only sign of his pleasure at having provoked a reaction.

"What if I do?" Umasi said guardedly, carefully pushing his sunglasses back up to cover his eyes. "There are a lot of Edwards."

Zyid snorted, and in response plunged one hand into his black jacket and withdrew it clutching a folded newspaper. Zyid slammed the newspaper down onto the lemonade stand, watching imperiously as Umasi picked it up. Umasi unfolded the paper, and then stared at it from behind his sunglasses, his arms going rigid as he did.

"A Student Militia?" Umasi said quietly. "Edward did this?"

"This Edward is already responsible for dozens of deaths," Zyid said harshly. "Students, Truants, and Enforcers alike. Hundreds more may die at his hands."

"Oh, this is no good," Umasi murmured sadly.

"Is he one of your little experiments?" Zyid demanded.

Umasi sighed at Zyid's choice of words and bent his head, his face cast into deeper shadow than ever. Zyid waited with rigid patience as Umasi hesitated to respond.

"Yes. He was," Umasi said finally.

"Then he is your responsibility," Zyid asserted.

"He is my mistake," Umasi admitted, looking back up at Zyid.

"Then correct it," Zyid demanded. "If you value life so much, he must be stopped, and quickly. Tonight we will attack his headquarters—a warehouse on the District 13 docks. It will be a distraction. You will have your chance."

"I can't do that," Umasi said unconvincingly. "You are capable of handling him. This is your war; he is your enemy. You should do it."

"You created him. You're the one who must destroy him," Zyid said firmly. "He took on Noni and Takan together; who's to say that I'd fare any better? I seem to recall that it was *you* who bested *me* two years ago."

There was a heavy silence as Umasi pondered Zyid's words. And then, with only the slightest hesitation, Umasi reached out to grasp the hilt of the sword and lift it up. Umasi raised the sword up to the sun, whose pale light reflected brilliantly off the white blade. Bringing the gleaming weapon down to his side, Umasi looked ruefully at Zyid's shadow.

"Congratulations, Brother," Umasi said reproachfully. "You've turned me into a hypocrite."

"I'll try not to lose sleep over it," Zyid muttered, and spun around to leave as if Umasi's very presence burned him.

Umasi didn't watch him go. Instead, he bent his head again and sat in silence, motionless in his seat behind the lemonade stand. He didn't even notice that even as Zyid slipped out of sight, the bright skies were being steadily encroached upon by a growing cloud of gray. Umasi's head remained bent for a long time, so that by the time he looked up again, the cloud had devoured the light and cast the City into shadow.

Umasi got to his feet, and as the first tentative drops of rain began to dot the ground, he turned his head towards the glass jug of lemonade resting upon the stand. Without warning, he swung his arm through the air, and the jug flew from the table and crashed to the ground, shattering as it scattered glass and lemonade across the ground. With that, Umasi turned his back on the lemonade stand and strode off into the growing shadow, gripping the sword tightly in one hand.

I don't understand," Tack said, gingerly rubbing a bruised spot as he stood before Zyid, trying to make sense of the Truancy leader's orders.

Zyid didn't answer at first, but stretched leisurely as he glanced out the show window of the flower shop. Outside, the muted sun's last rays had been vanquished, giving way to a pitch-black night accompanied by a steady patter of rain that poured down rhythmically, relentlessly showering the City. Water sloshed everywhere in sight, washing the streets and sweeping down the gutters in small streams. Wet trickles of water flowed down the show window itself, oddly distorting the dark world outside.

"It's very simple," Zyid said finally, turning to look condescendingly at Tack. "I've raised fifty volunteers willing to fight against the Student Militia. I want you to lead them all in a frontal attack on their base."

"But you don't want us to actually take their base," Tack pointed out.

"No, nor do I want you to overexert yourself, especially wounded as you are," Zyid agreed, picking up his windbreaker and buttoning it around his neck. "Just keep them focused on you."

"But why?" Tack couldn't help but ask.

"Because this way, we spare the most children on both sides," Zyid said, attaching his sheathed sword to his belt.

"But what do we accomplish by just setting up camp in front of their headquarters?" Tack demanded.

"What we'll accomplish is going a long way towards ending this war," Zyid said impatiently, turning to look at Tack with a strange gleam in his dark eyes. "Tonight, Edward will die."

"How do you know?" Tack asked, taken aback. "The bastard fights like a monster."

"He will die," Zyid repeated simply, pulling the hood of the windbreaker over his head.

"Is that where you're going?" Tack asked, wondering if Zyid might get killed before Tack could get the chance to do it himself.

"No, Takan, I'll be helping Noni keep the Enforcers busy," Zyid said, clapping Tack on the shoulder as he headed for the door. "You had better get going. The advance parties will already be setting up their attack positions. They await only your leadership."

And with that, Zyid swept out of the room, his black windbreaker swishing behind him, leaving Tack alone in the dark. Tack remained just as confused as ever, but quickly realized that there was nothing he could do but follow orders. Tack placed his hand on the hilt of his sword, and then pushed the door of the flower shop open, ignoring the aches and pains it cost him to do so. As he stepped out into the cool, solemn wetness, Tack felt the rain wash away his apprehension and replace it with the excited anticipation of battle.

Tack flicked a wet strand of brown hair out of his eyes. Zyid had just been too sure of himself to doubt. Tack didn't know how, but Edward *would* die that night.

Umasi ran gracefully through the streets, feeling his warm breath contrast harshly with the cold rain. Drops of water from his soaked hair trickled down his face, and his sunglasses were hopelessly fogged. Still, blind or no, he ran through the rain, his sneakers becoming increasingly soaked as they splashed into the puddles on the street, until they let out a soggy squish each time they touched the ground. Flecks of water sprayed behind him as Umasi ran, and he could feel his clothes grow heavy, clinging to his skin as they became soaked with water.

"What are you doing, Umasi? You swore you would never kill anyone," he muttered aloud, his words instantly lost to the rain.

But if you don't, how many others will die?

"I survived my ordeal two years ago without becoming a murderer. Why start now?"

Because only you can undo your own work.

Umasi frowned. He had always regarded Edward as his greatest mistake, his most dangerous student. Umasi had been naïve when he had met the boy. He had ignored all the signs of ruthlessness, greed, and malevolence, only appreciating how brilliant Edward was. Umasi had been eager to teach, and Edward had been eager to learn, and so Umasi had unwittingly placed powerful weapons, originally intended for good, into dangerous hands. And now his mistakes were claiming lives, returning to punish him for his errors.

Umasi pushed his legs to run faster, and felt his muscles start to burn even as his flesh was chilled by the unrelenting rain. Every death suffered at the hands of Edward would rest on Umasi's conscience, when only Edward's death should have. Edward had attacked him, the day that he left. Edward had learned all he needed, and coveting sole possession of that knowledge, he had tried to kill his mentor. Killing had never come easy for Umasi, and so he had spared Edward, content to believe that he would never see his monstrous pupil again. That day Umasi should have seen what Edward was. Umasi could have ended it then, he should have ended it then . . . but he didn't.

He had *never* been able to bring himself to kill.

"But this time, I'll set things right," Umasi promised, with only the rain to witness his vow.

As the sound of gunshots suddenly became audible over the relentless rain, Umasi clenched his fists, his knuckles growing white from gripping his sword so tightly. Raising his head up to the sky, he smiled ruefully at what he knew would come next, and all the while the rain continued to cascade down onto his face.

• • •

"Send two teams of six to either side. Use the parked cars as cover—seek to flank them at all costs," Edward ordered, his brow creased in frustration. "Update me in case of any significant developments—otherwise I'm not to be disturbed."

His lieutenant, a boy whose badge declared that he'd been recruited from the eighth grade, nodded and left, his eyes wide in shock at all that had happened. Edward wasn't exactly sure what the boy's name was—he'd been called in only an hour ago to replace Edward's old lieutenant, who had been, most tragically, shot as he tried to meet the Truants head-on.

Edward shook his head and locked the door behind the boy. Right now Edward needed privacy to think. He'd have plenty of time to learn names later—at the moment there was a battle that wasn't going to win itself. As a matter of fact, so far it was going against them. His Student Militiamen had been operating out of one of the Truancy's abandoned warehouses when they'd been attacked without warning. So far the assault had only come from one direction, which happened to be the front. Edward honestly hadn't been expecting such a crude attack from someone as crafty as Zyid was reputed to be. Edward had wondered idly if Zyid himself would show up to challenge him.

Edward's basic training programs had managed to produce a good number of Student Militiamen in a short period of time, sixty-seven of whom were under his direct command at the warehouse. However, the Truants were far more formidable than his inexperienced and hastily trained Militia—the previous day's encounter at the library had convinced him of that—and their simple tactic was proving effective. They were throwing explosives, bullets, and lives at Edward like expendable ammunition. Edward had called for Educator reinforcements, but was sardonically informed that they had their own hands full and that he was a big boy who could take care of himself. Edward had vowed that the officer he'd talked to would pay when he ascended to the City Council.

That had been a while ago, and now even Edward's steady confidence was wavering as he looked over the list of casualties. So far seventeen had been killed or incapacitated, which was actually quite outstanding considering what they were up against. Still, seventeen losses were seventeen too many—morale was plummeting, and he only had fifty more lives to spend.

Fifty-one, including my own.

Edward brushed that thought aside. This battle was far from lost—indeed, he was certain that he could win it. He would survive this, help the Educators wipe out the rest of the Truants, and assume his rightful position among the leadership of the City. His current strategy was a sound one—if he could hit the attacking Truants from all sides, it would make his soldiers' numbers appear larger than they were, and force the attackers to divert their attention while he prepared a more permanent solution. The Truancy warehouse still had stocks of various flammable liquids, and if he could figure out a way to safely deliver them to the Truancy lines, they could wreck havoc on the Truants that had barricaded themselves right in the middle of the street, rain notwithstanding.

Edward took a deep, calming breath, and ran his fingers through his blond hair absentmindedly. This was manageable. It was difficult, no question, but Edward's life had hardly been easy. Even with that comforting thought in mind,

Edward shivered despite himself—something he quickly attributed to the cold draft that had made its way into the room. Rising to his feet, Edward was about to go examine some of the explosives when he heard something over the steady sound of rain.

Edward paused. It sounded like footsteps, echoing throughout the walled-off portion of the warehouse that he'd claimed as his own. He spun around, peering into the gloom that masked the stacked crates and other paraphernalia. Edward grinned; if someone was snooping around, they'd certainly picked the wrong guy to disturb.

What Edward heard next made his blood run cold.

"I see you've come a long way, Ed."

The voice struck Edward like a lightning bolt. Shaking slightly, Edward found that he couldn't move—the shock of hearing that voice that he'd all but forgotten simply overwhelmed him. Slowly, he found that control of his jaws returned to him.

"M-Mr. Umasi?" He didn't dare turn towards the sound of the other boy.'s voice, afraid of his fears being confirmed.

"Such formality, Edward!" The voice chuckled coldly. "And I thought we were friends. Please, plain 'Umasi' will do fine."

Edward felt some more of his shock wearing off. Turning abruptly, he faced his old mentor and shuddered despite himself. Umasi was just like he'd remembered, albeit completely soaked—plain khaki jeans, beige vest, mushroom-style haircut, and that pair of enigmatic sunglasses that argued against its owner having a soul. Edward's former mentor leaned against a large wooden crate, arms crossed, completely relaxed, managing to look somehow majestic despite being dripping wet. Edward also noted that he carried a suspiciously white sword at his side. Ceramic, Edward realized. Just like the ones the Truancy was using.

"You don't look pleased to see me," Umasi observed, not stirring an inch. "But me, on the other hand, I'm very glad to see you."

Edward ignored the cryptic statement.

"How did you get in here?" Edward demanded, his voice quivering.

Umasi's lips curled into the vaguest of smiles.

"I *know* you, Edward. You always considered yourself above others, so I knew you wouldn't be fighting alongside those you lead. Even when battling to make an example, you'd take any excuse to work alone. Secure in your headquarters, you would choose a private space to work in, like this one."

Umasi looked around casually. "There was an old broken window in the back—surely you've noticed the draft in here? Scaling the exterior wall wasn't particularly difficult, especially with your woefully unprepared militia focusing all of their attention elsewhere."

Edward managed a confident sneer, though inside he was churning with panic at his oversight. He had never dreamed that this particular ghost of his past would come out of hiding just to hunt him down. It was actually an honor, in a way, that Umasi had gone to such lengths to find him. After all, the dripping sword at Umasi's side could only mean one thing. . . .

"You've joined up with the Truancy to take me down, eh?" Edward asked.

Umasi regarded him coldly for a moment before responding.

"No, Edward. I know what you want to hear, and you won't hear it," Umasi said slowly. "You'd gain a lot of self-satisfaction,

I think, were I to confess that I allied with the Truancy because of you—that I'd considered you a threat."

"What? Are you saying that you don't?" Edward shouted, anger replacing any traces of shock.

"Yes, that's exactly right." Umasi smirked. "I'm not going to eliminate a threat—I am merely going to settle a grudge. You see, you rather offended me the day we parted ways. That was a mistake, and one that you repeated when you turned my methods towards the murder of other children for greedy, selfish reasons."

Umasi unfolded his arms, holding the sword steadily in his right hand.

"I'm not here to kill you, Edward, not right away, at least," Umasi declared, taking a confident step forward.

"Is that right?" Edward demanded, taking a cautious step backwards. "You say that you don't see me as a threat, but you will!"

Edward grabbed the pistol from his desk and pointed it at Umasi. Umasi regarded the weapon carefully, and halted before speaking.

"Before you die, Edward, I'll have to humble you."

Umasi suddenly lunged, and Edward instinctively fired. The bullet buried itself firmly in the warehouse floor, as Umasi had, with almost inhuman agility, feinted to Edward's left, landing as a blur behind some crates.

"Hiding again, Umasi?" Edward laughed.

"When your opponent is overly aggressive, your best offense is a good defense," Umasi recited one of his old aphorisms.

"Your silly words won't save you, Umasi, not from bullets!" Edward shouted as he leaped, rolled, and brought himself into a crouch, aiming behind the crates where Umasi had been hiding just moments ago.

"Do not seek out an elusive opponent—let him reveal himself to you," Umasi suggested, his voice this time coming from far to the right.

Edward growled and pointed his gun towards the source of the noise. He hadn't noticed any sign of Umasi moving, but there was a clear trail of water that seemed to be leading right behind his own desk. Edward's observations were not unanticipated; a second later, Umasi swiftly leaped and, with greater speed and grace, executed the same roll Edward had performed a moment ago, coming to a rest behind another crate as Edward fired and, predictably, missed.

"You can't keep this up forever." Edward forced a laugh.

This time Umasi's response was different. Edward's letter opener—which resembled half of a pointed scissor and had been thoughtlessly left on his desk—flew through the air, burying itself in Edward's shoulder before he realized what was happening. For a moment Edward stared in disbelief at his right shoulder, and then he let out a roar of pain and outrage as he plucked the letter opener and cast it aside.

"Nothing hurts a foe more than his own devices," Umasi declared, smugness creeping into his voice.

Edward tore off a strip of his shirt and applied a makeshift bandage onto the bleeding wound. Reckless fury taking ahold of him, he charged at the crate Umasi was hidden behind like a truck bearing down on roadkill.

Umasi, however, leaped on top of the crate and snapped a powerful kick to the charging Edward's injured shoulder. Edward let out a scream of pain as his arm jerked to the right, and his third shot missed Umasi. Before Edward could recover, Umasi drew his sword back, then plunged it neatly into Edward's uninjured shoulder. Another scream of agony echoed throughout the room, and Edward's soldiers, finally realizing that something was wrong, began pounding at the locked door.

"We don't have much time, Edward," Umasi said softly as he dropped behind Edward and deftly twisted his right hand to break his wrist. Edward screamed as the gun he had held fell to the floor.

"Screw you!" Edward shouted, attempting to head butt Umasi, who easily dodged.

"Language, Ed," Umasi admonished as he grabbed hold of Edward and swept his legs out from under him.

The banging and shouting at the door increased in intensity as Umasi applied a judiciously calculated kick to Edward's groin, which produced an expected shriek. Bleeding from both shoulders and clutching his privates with his one good hand, Edward still managed a look of pure hatred as he glared at Umasi.

"Are you going to kill me already, or do you have something else to prove?" Edward hissed.

"I never had anything to prove, certainly not to you, at any rate," Umasi said lightly, wiping his sword on Edward's pants.

"Then why come here without a gun?" Edward gasped as Umasi placed a dripping foot on Edward's chest, applying just enough pressure to cause discomfort.

"Like I said earlier, Edward," Umasi mused. "I came here to humble you."

"Well, then you've succeeded; is that what you wanted to hear?" Edward spit. "Now kill me, or leave me alone!"

"I'll do the former, of course," Umasi said quietly, causing

Edward's eyes to widen in genuine fear. "It'll be quick. And probably less painful than this little encounter proved to be."

"No, wait . . . ," Edward protested feebly.

"Yes?" Umasi inquired, shooting a glance at the door, which now seemed to be in danger of collapsing at any moment.

"I . . . there's so much . . . left for me to do," Edward sputtered.

"You must die so that others may live," Umasi explained quietly.

"I don't want to die at the hands of a *pacifist*!" Edward hissed, some of his old venom seeping into his voice again.

"I'm not your killer." Umasi shook his head. "Remember, I once told you. Unbridled ambition leads to self-destruction."

"You're giving me a headache," Edward protested.

"Then it's time for me to put you out of your misery." Umasi sighed. "Beforehand, I'd like to apologize. I always deplore ending lives, and yours is no exception."

Umasi removed his foot from Edward's chest and brought him to his knees, grabbing his blond hair to bend his head forward.

"There are other ways of curing a headache." Edward gritted his teeth as he closed his eyes, awaiting the inevitable.

"If something harmful is attached to you . . ." Umasi raised his sword.

". . . sever it," Edward finished breathlessly.

Umasi brought his sword down in one quick stroke, striking Edward's neck at a joint. Edward's head rolled across the floor, utterly lifeless. Blood splattered Umasi's drenched clothes as he stood there, contemplating the magnitude of what he had done, of the life he had taken. Killing had never come easy for him. And yet kill he had. As water dripped down from his clothes and mingled with Edward's blood, the pounding at the door brought him back to his senses.

"You wouldn't want anyone to see you like this," Umasi murmured, swiftly taking a sheet from a corner of the room and draping it over Edward's body. He glanced around the room, and his eyes fell upon a container of gasoline the Truancy had left behind. Moving quickly, Umasi seized the container and poured all of its contents over Edward's covered body.

Producing a lighter from his pocket, Umasi hung his head in a moment of briefest mourning, speaking only one word.

"Farewell."

The lighter clicked on, and dropped onto the drenched sheet. Flames leaped up instantly, and Umasi turned away, telling himself that he had done the right thing. Knowing it was too late for second-guessing, and determined to save as many lives as he could, Umasi steeled himself for what would come next.

Walking over to the door, Umasi flung it open and came face-to-face with a group of frightened Student Militia members. Some peered over his shoulder, staring at the fire, searching for their leader, though most simply stared at the soggy stranger before them.

"Edward is dead," Umasi said wearily. "There is no longer any reason for you to be here. You can run home, you can join the Truancy, or you can stay and die. If you go outside now with your hands up, I'm sure that the Truancy will welcome you with open arms. If you flee, you might be able to hide with your family until this is all over. Either way, no other child needs to die tonight at the hands of another."

Umasi's fellow children continued to stare at him, though none of them went for their weapons. He hadn't expected them to, though he couldn't help but feel slightly relieved nonetheless.

"Go," he ordered, this time adding a note of urgency to his voice. "Get out of here."

Snapping out of their stupor, the small crowd that had gathered outside the door began to disperse as the children ran to let their fellows know what was happening. Half an hour later, they had all safely left the warehouse, which had by then become a massive funeral pyre, with angry flames stabbing upwards into the night, defying the rain as a plume of smoke rose to join the clouds in the sky.

Eventually, most that were present at that battle would come to forget the brilliant boy entombed in the smoldering wreckage. But for Umasi, the mistake known as Edward would always haunt his conscience. He had accepted this as a consequence at the same time he'd accepted the sword from Zyid, and now that his grim task was done, Umasi returned to his quiet stand, where he mixed for himself a particularly sour glass of lemonade.

He drank unflinchingly, and there, alone in the darkness and the rain, he cried for the first time in years.

Killing hadn't come easy for him. And it never would.

25

No Regrets

The morning after the battle with the Student Militia found much of the Truancy overcome by giddy disbelief. Few had dreamed that things could have possibly turned out as well as they had, and their greatest enemy seemingly vanishing in a fire that defied logical explanation seemed nothing short of miraculous. Truants who had been in the battle returned to the hideout to relate increasingly fantastical stories of how the Student Militia's headquarters had spontaneously burst into flame, killing Edward and forcing the students to surrender. Explanations for the phenomenon had grown steadily wilder, to the point where it was suggested that the warehouse had been crisped by a series of righteous lightning bolts. No matter what they believed, however, one persistent and unanswered question rose to the forefront of the mind of every Truant.

"How did you do it?" Tack demanded the moment he entered the flower shop.

Having led the attack on the Student Militia, Tack had been repeatedly subjected to that very same question, and certainly didn't have an answer to it. Being exhausted, he had gone to sleep early the previous night, though he had awoken that morning feeling both more curious and more rested than he had in weeks.

"Pardon me?" Zyid raised an eyebrow, looking up from his seat at the table. "What did I do?"

"Set a fire inside the warehouse. Scattered the Student Militia. Killed Edward." Tack ticked off each deed on his fingers.

"I did nothing of the sort, Takan." Zyid smirked.

"That fire didn't start itself," Tack accused.

"One of the students must have set it by accident." Zyid yawned.

"You told me that Edward would die," Tack pointed out. "You *knew.*"

"Call it a lucky guess," Zyid said smoothly. "In any case, Takan, this is the opportunity that we've been waiting for. The Enforcers will be in disarray after the loss of their chief, and Edward no longer stands in our way. Morale has never been higher, and the entire Truancy is prepared to fight."

"We're going to launch those big attacks you were talking about?" Tack asked, distracted from his questioning. "Today?"

"Tonight, actually," Zyid said, turning back to the papers on the table. "It will be messy, and destructive, but it's our best chance of ending this war. And there is a particularly important part that I want you to play."

"What's that?" Tack asked curiously.

"The Mayor's grip on the media has given him the opportunity to shape the public image of the Truancy. Naturally, we have been unable to contest this, unable to plead our case."

Zyid paused to scribble something onto a sheet before continuing. "Tonight, that will change."

"Wait." Tack's mind was suddenly racing. "So you want *me* to 'plead our case' to the City?"

"Of course not." Zyid smiled ruefully. "I will do that myself. Your job will be to help me get into Penance Tower so that I can spread the word."

Everyone in the City knew about Penance Tower. Named after its designer, it was by far the tallest building in the entire City. Located in District 1, it stood at the very center of the City so that its ominous silhouette could be seen from just about every other district. It was a prominent Educator building, and contained controls for everything from the City's drawbridges to its school speakers. Tack suspected that Zyid would make use of the latter in order to "spread the word."

But it wasn't the mention of Penance Tower that had caught Tack's attention. "Just me?" he asked, unable to believe that he'd be so lucky.

"Yes, Takan," Zyid repeated lightly. "Just you."

Tack willed his face to remain impassive, but his thoughts were churning. Tonight the Truancy would deal a decisive blow against the Educators, and afterwards Tack would have as clean a shot at Zyid as he could possibly hope for. There would be no other Truants to witness it, and if Tack returned alone, it would be easy to say that Zyid had been killed by an Enforcer.

Tack knew that he might not succeed, and that even if he did, Zyid's death might very well throw the Truancy into chaos. Still, it was a chance that Tack had to take. Everything came after Suzie, and from that standpoint, he had never felt more hopeful than he did as he stood in the flower shop, listening to Zyid begin to relate the risks of what he hoped would be the Truancy's decisive battle.

"You've got to be joking," the Mayor said disbelievingly, his lighter falling from his hand onto the carpeting where it lay forgotten.

"I'm afraid not, sir," the Enforcer officer replied, clasping his hands behind his back as he stood in front of the Mayor's desk.

"Edward, dead?" the Mayor breathed, standing up.

"Presumed dead," the Enforcer corrected. "The Student Militiamen under his command have been scattered, and their headquarters have been burned."

"But . . . but Edward had over sixty Student Militiamen with him!" the Mayor sputtered. "The Truants slaughtered their own kind to get to Edward?"

"We actually don't know how many were killed, and Edward's body still hasn't been recovered," the Enforcer pointed out. "That's not surprising though, since the fire was quite thorough."

"So Edward might be alive?" the Mayor said desperately.

"There is a slight possibility," the Enforcer conceded. "But if he were alive and still interested in aiding us, he would have contacted us by now."

"So . . . ," the Mayor began weakly.

"We cannot rely on the boy anymore," the Enforcer said firmly. "Apparently *he* sent *us* a call for aid when he came under attack. Of course, our forces were all occupied at the time, dealing with the other Truancy attacks."

The Mayor stiffened and narrowed his eyes dangerously at the Enforcer.

"You mean to tell me," the Mayor breathed, "that Edward called for help and was refused?"

The Enforcer frowned. "Yes."

"Imbeciles!" The Mayor groaned. "He was the Chief Enforcer! He was to be denied nothing!"

"I'm aware of it," the Enforcer said silkily. "But as you know, his status was not made public. There are still some in uniform that are unaware that a child was chosen to lead the Enforcers."

"Find out who received the message," the Mayor snapped. "And have him imprisoned indefinitely for treason."

The Enforcer hesitated, but quickly wilted under the Mayor's furious gaze.

"It will be done," the Enforcer assured him.

"No one can know about this," the Mayor hissed. "You hear? No one else finds out that the Student Militia is leaderless! I want whatever is left of the Militia out there on the front lines. Find them a new leader. And while you're at it, arm a few dozen more students and send them out there, today!"

"Today?" the Enforcer repeated cautiously.

"Yes, today," the Mayor snapped. "I don't care how little training they get; if they can stop a bullet, that's one bullet more that we won't have to worry about." The Mayor kicked at his lighter and missed. "Speaking of which, did you deal with those other Truancy attacks?"

"We've forced them into a full retreat," the Enforcer said quickly. "We've suffered heavy losses, of course, but so did they. And we have men to spare, while they don't."

"Did they all retreat at the same time?" the Mayor demanded.

"Yes," the Enforcer replied, frowning.

"Before or after the attack on the Student Militia?" the Mayor pressed.

"Shortly after," the Enforcer said uncomfortably, seeing where the conversation was going.

"So would it be a fair assumption that these other attacks were nothing more than diversions to keep us busy while they murdered our most valuable officer?" the Mayor snarled; he was no fool.

"Well . . . yes, I suppose so," the Enforcer replied.

The Mayor shut his eyes in exasperation and leaned on his desk wearily. Of course the Enforcers had arrived at that conclusion before, and had tried to hide it from him. Not stirring from his position, the Mayor felt something inside him snap as he opened his mouth to address the Enforcer before him.

"*Get out!*" the Mayor roared.

"But sir, shouldn't we prepare to—"

"*Out!*"

Not inclined to argue, the Enforcer swiftly turned around and left the Mayor alone to brood in his dimly lit office. Even without the Student Militia, without Edward, the Truants were still outnumbered by the Enforcers. Really, it was far from hopeless. But then again, why did it suddenly feel that way to the Mayor?

And then the Mayor remembered why, though he kept that greatest of secrets to himself as he stamped his foot in frustration. His expensive black boots hammered his dropped lighter, driving it deeper and deeper into the thick carpet.

• • •

Tack carefully buttoned up the blue Student Militia uniform, admiring the quality of the fabric. The uniform had been taken from a deserter, and Zyid had provided it as a disguise that they would use to sneak into the television station. Tack thought it looked good on him, though it did have a sort of uncomfortably formal fit that Tack hadn't been accustomed to since his days as a student. Taking a deep breath, Tack straightened his cuffs and tried to mentally prepare himself for what he knew lay ahead, but somehow he just couldn't manage it.

Giving up on mental preparation, Tack sighed and strapped his sheathed sword to his belt, idly wondering if it would be the weapon to kill Zyid or if he would simply end up shooting the Truancy leader in the back. Tack decided that he'd figure it all out later. In the more immediate future, he had to worry about the attack on Penance Tower. If Zyid accomplished what he set out to do with his broadcast, the Educators might well fall even if Zyid died afterwards, which would be the best-case scenario for Tack.

Through the flower shop window, Tack could see what looked like the entire Truancy spilling out into the darkening City streets, climbing into or atop vehicles, arming themselves, wishing each other good luck. There were more of them than Tack had ever seen at the same time, though Tack knew they were much fewer than there had been a week ago. Tack also knew that Zyid was walking somewhere among them, probably already dressed in his Student Militia uniform, giving last-minute instructions as he waited for Tack to finish. Tack silently vowed that this night would be the last for at least one of the two of them. The pieces were all in place.

The Truancy was poised for victory. And Zyid would be out there in the chaos, with no one but Tack to witness his death.

The door swung open and Tack spun around, expecting to see Zyid standing in the doorway. Tack's heart leaped up into his throat when he saw it was not Zyid but Noni, looking oddly at him with unusually warm blue eyes. Tack immediately noticed that she had done away with her scarf completely, leaving her scar in plain sight. Try as he might, he couldn't find anything to say as she walked forward, letting the door swing shut behind her.

"So," Noni said quietly. "This is it."

"Yeah," Tack said.

"The last battles."

"Hopefully," Tack agreed.

"I heard you're going along with Zyid," Noni murmured.

"Yeah." Tack nodded. "Where are you going?"

"Nowhere so dangerous," Noni replied quietly. "I'm leading an attack on a power station."

"Good luck," Tack said sincerely, suspecting that her assignment was more dangerous than she'd have him believe.

A few moments passed during which the two stared at each other, and Tack could feel an excited tension begin to build up inside him as they locked gazes.

"Takan," Noni said suddenly in a voice that instantly drew Tack's undivided attention.

"Yes?" Tack asked breathlessly.

"In case one of us doesn't survive," Noni said hesitantly, "there's something I wanted to do."

Noni slowly drew closer to him, and as if controlled by a puppeteer's strings, Tack moved forward to meet her. The next thing he knew, Noni had flung her arms around him and pressed her lips to his. Tack didn't remember his arms sliding around her waist, but once he found them there he hugged her tightly to him, as if there were some danger of her being wrested from his grip. It seemed awkward at first, but after a few seconds all Tack could think about was how good it felt to be wrapped around her body, how tender her lips were, how sweet her fragrance was. It was like conscious thought had abandoned him, replaced by a primal rush of excitement.

"Ahem."

Tack and Noni sprang apart instantly, turning to see Zyid standing in the doorway, a massive shadow in the growing dark. Tack knew that he must look embarrassed, and he chanced a quick glance at Noni, whose cheeks had reddened slightly, though her expression made it clear that she had no regrets. That was good, Tack thought, because he had none himself . . .

except for one.

Tack suddenly felt a mad urge to confide in Noni now, at the last minute. He wanted to tell her what he planned to do to Zyid, to apologize in advance for killing someone she so obviously cared about. But Tack knew that he couldn't—ever since he first joined the Truancy, he had worked under his own agenda. His was a secret that could be shared with no one, a secret that he'd even buried from himself, and one that could never come to light.

And in that respect, Tack realized that he was truly alone.

"It's time to go," Zyid said briskly, as if he had not just walked in on two of his lieutenants kissing. "We're behind schedule."

Noni nodded reluctantly, and as she made for the door, she turned to look at Tack once more, and though she said nothing, in an instant Tack read all he needed to in her glittering blue eyes. Then she broke eye contact and darted out the door, leaving Tack alone with a uniformed Zyid, who gestured wordlessly outside. Tack picked up his gun from the table, and then followed Zyid out into the bustling street, where cars filled with Truants were already departing, roaring down the streets and around the corners.

"How are we getting there?" Tack asked as Zyid led him away from the vehicles.

"We're taking the subway," Zyid said, setting a quick pace towards the living City. "We have no reason not to. To commuters we'd look like nothing more than two foolish students fighting to keep ourselves in chains."

"I thought the Student Militia was routed, though," Tack said cautiously, walking faster to keep up with Zyid.

"You were there, not me," Zyid pointed out.

"Won't they know that the real Student Militia is routed? And notice us?" Tack asked, gesturing at their uniforms.

"Unlikely," Zyid said dismissively. "There's been nothing on the news. The Mayor wouldn't want to make that public anyway. Edward and the Student Militia were among his greatest assets, and were their loss to become known, Enforcer morale would plunge. Besides," Zyid added as they slipped over a short wire fence and into the living City, "there are doubtless hundreds of students still lined up to earn that instant graduation. If we allow it to, the Student Militia will soon revive and perhaps even thrive, though likely under less competent leadership."

"So we don't allow them," Tack said logically as they strode down the dark and empty avenue towards the moving lights of traffic.

"Of course we don't," Zyid agreed. "I have decided to stake everything on tonight's events. The entire Truancy will face the Enforcers. It will be a battle that encompasses the entire City. If we succeed, we'll come very close to winning this war."

"So why even bother spreading your message?" Tack asked as they turned a corner to join the nighttime pedestrians walking along the noisy and unnaturally bright street.

"Because, Takan, I hope to incite a larger revolt," Zyid explained.

"A larger revolt?" Tack repeated uncomprehendingly as they walked down the stairs to the subways below the City.

"Yes." Zyid nodded. "There are thousands of students still in this City who are neither Truants nor part of the Student Militia, and there may be dozens of Student Militia members-in-training that are armed and might be swayed."

"And you think that you can convince them to turn against the Educators?" Tack asked skeptically.

"That remains to be seen," Zyid said as they each slipped over the turnstiles without scanning their student bar codes. "And, incidentally, there's something else I'd like to talk to you about."

"What's that?" Tack asked curiously.

"Noni."

Tack nearly tripped over his boots in surprise, grabbing ahold of a railing to prevent himself from tumbling down the stairs that they had been descending to reach the actual subway platform. Tack straightened up and looked suspiciously at Zyid, who was now regarding him with a raised eyebrow. The way that Zyid had ignored his intimacy with Noni made him assume that the Truancy leader would have nothing to say on the subject, and Tack didn't enjoy the prospect of taking fire from this unexpected direction.

"What about her?" Tack asked defensively.

"I'm pleased that she's found someone she might be able to open up to," Zyid said, resuming his descent. "I helped her cover up her scar, but you helped her overcome it."

Tack was utterly speechless at what he was hearing, and could barely force his legs to move him down the stairs in pursuit of Zyid, who wasn't waiting for Tack's input before continuing.

"She's had a very difficult life," Zyid said as he reached the platform. "More so than you can imagine, and perhaps more than even I know. It is immensely difficult to gain her trust, and yet you have done so. She deserves to be loved, and I think that she expected it of me. Obviously, I disappointed her in that regard."

Tack felt his voice returning. "Why's that?" he asked.

"Because, Takan"—Zyid turned around to smirk at Tack—"I'm a heartless bastard."

Tack certainly couldn't argue with that.

"There is one thing I must warn you about, however," Zyid said casually. "Noni is dangerously attached to me. Should I die, Noni might become . . . unpredictable."

Tack froze, feeling a sudden panic welling up in his chest. He forced himself to appear calm as he studied Zyid's face carefully. It was as if he knew; it was as if Zyid *knew* what Tack intended to do. Tack waited with bated breath, but as seconds dragged on in silence and Zyid gave no indication of suspecting an attempt on his life, Tack allowed himself to believe that it was just a coincidence.

"Unpredictable?" Tack repeated.

"Like I said." Zyid glanced at Tack. "She's had a hard life. I think that only she knows just how bad it was."

Tack couldn't find anything to say to that, and so when the train pulled into the station with loud screeching and shuddering, he silently followed Zyid through the nearest automatic sliding doors. As they moved to occupy a pair of empty plastic seats, the doors slid together behind them, and Zyid made no effort to continue the conversation, crossing his arms and legs and shutting his eyes, as if in meditation. This left Tack to ponder what Zyid had told him in silence.

Umasi had once asked him if he loved Noni. Tack didn't have an answer back then, but were the question to be posed to him again, he wouldn't hesitate to answer with a resounding "yes." They understood each other so well, and yet knew so little about each other. And though Tack was loathe to admit it, even to himself, Zyid did seem to know a lot about Noni, and Tack didn't like the sound of what Zyid had said.

Tack shook his head violently like a dog shaking off water. He wouldn't, couldn't believe Zyid. Zyid was probably just trying to make his life seem more valuable, make himself seem more important. Besides, Umasi had also asked Tack if he had loved Suzie. Tack had been able to say yes back then, and nothing had changed since. Still feeling discomfited, Tack nonetheless managed to steel his resolve with that thought.

The rest of the ride passed without incident, though several passengers who came and went cast interested looks at the pair of uniformed boys with guns and swords. None of them, however, questioned their boys' right to have such weapons, merely showing mild interest. The Student Militia had served one good purpose after all, Tack reflected grimly.

When the train shuddered to a screeching halt for what seemed like the tenth time, Zyid rose to his feet without warning and walked swiftly out of the car and onto the platform. Tack hastened to follow him, and moments later they were again aboveground, feeling the cool night air. Zyid led Tack around a street corner and down several blocks until they stood at the base of a monstrous skyscraper with a front wrought entirely of stainless steel and glass—Penance Tower. Standing outside the doors was a veritable platoon of guards.

"We've been ordered to patrol the interior of this building," Zyid said crisply, snapping a salute to the guards.

"Why's that?" one of the guards asked curiously.

"Edward believes it to be of strategic importance, and we're here to review its security on his behalf," Zyid explained smoothly. "We were told that you should contact the Mayor himself if there was any question about Edward's authority."

The guards exchanged glances, then looked back down at Zyid.

"That won't be necessary," one of them said accommodatingly, opening the doors wide. "Go right on in."

Zyid thanked the guard and strode confidently into the building, Tack following in his wake, almost unable to believe that the guards were so easily fooled. Clearly Edward had built up a far more formidable reputation than Tack had known.

"The Mayor has not properly grasped the importance of this building," Zyid told Tack quietly as they headed for an elevator. "Otherwise it'd have occurred to him to protect it with an army of Enforcers rather than just a herd of regular guards."

"Would it have occurred to Edward?" Tack asked pointedly.

"It would likely have crossed the mind of our late adversary, yes." Zyid nodded as the elevator doors opened to admit them.

"So how exactly are we going to get this message out?" Tack asked as Zyid pressed a button; he certainly seemed like he knew where he was going.

"I have it recorded already," Zyid explained, patting a lumpy spot on his uniform. "I will hijack control of the City-wide speaker system. Every loudspeaker in every school and Educator building will hear the message. It's only a matter of dealing with anyone in the appropriate room and then setting the tape to loop constantly."

"Won't someone just come along and take the tape out?" Tack asked.

"Before we leave, we will barricade the door," Zyid explained. "By the time they get in, the message will have repeated itself several times, and I think it likely that word of mouth will handle the rest."

The elevator doors opened with a *ding*, and Tack followed Zyid out into a nondescript white hallway with a lot of doors. Zyid seemed to be right at home, marching over to a door that was slightly ajar. Tack could hear voices coming from within, and Zyid hesitated for a moment.

"Takan, you stay out here. If you see anyone, kill them," Zyid said curtly.

Without waiting for a response, Zyid took a deep breath and plunged into the room. Tack briefly wondered why he had been asked to come along if it was going to be this easy, but those thoughts were quickly interrupted by confused inquiries, then panicked shouts, the sound of a scuffle, a scream, and then sudden, heavy silence. Several moments dragged on as Tack stood helplessly outside the door, and then there was the sound of something heavy being dragged across a floor. A second later, Zyid emerged from the room holding a string in one hand, his blue uniform partly stained dark red. Zyid tugged hard on the string, and something crashed into the door from the other side, slamming it tightly shut.

"I upturned one of their desks," Zyid explained.

Tack nodded, finding that the murders of whoever had been inside that room didn't bother him at all. Perhaps it was because the end was in sight, because Tack knew that Zyid would very soon be made to pay dearly for *all* of his crimes. Or maybe Tack had simply become accustomed to death; he really couldn't tell. All he could think about as they entered the elevator again was how he would kill Zyid as soon as they left the building.

Now that the moment was so close, Tack felt excitement and apprehension build up in his gut at the same time. If he botched it, he would be in for the fight of his life, which could easily turn into the last fight of his life. And yet there was an undeniable pleasure of knowing that this promise that he'd been dreaming of fulfilling for so long would at last come to a conclusion, one way or another.

As Zyid and Tack stepped out into the lobby of the building, they saw that the guards hadn't moved from their posts, their backs facing the Truants through the glass. Zyid nodded at Tack, and moved behind them. Tack followed suit, and a second later both of them opened fire at once, shattering the glass and swiftly sending the hapless and confused guards dropping to the ground like leaves from a tree. The boys heard screams from behind them, but paid them no attention, instead stepping through the gaps they'd broken in the glass and out into the night.

Tack could barely contain his righteous enthusiasm, and had half a mind to shoot Zyid down where he stood, but hearing the persistent screams behind him, he decided to wait until they were away from the building, where there would be no witnesses. Before Zyid set out, however, he looked for a moment at his wristwatch and then turned to look solemnly at Tack.

"It's started, Takan," Zyid said quietly. "The City will finally learn what Truancy really means."

In the nightmares of children and adults, in the darkest imaginations of Truants and Educators alike, there had existed no images as horrible as those that eyes of both young and old now witnessed throughout the City. The once brilliant, lively lights of the City had been extinguished in many Districts, surrendering to the darkness of the starless night, a darkness disrupted only by the fires that now blazed unchecked throughout the City. The sounds of gunshots, of screams, of sirens and explosions mingled to create a hellish rancor. The whole City had been plunged into madness, and in the space of a few hours, anarchy had replaced any semblance of order, wreaking damage of an unimaginable scale all throughout the urban landscape.

In the streets, it was now not only Enforcers and Truants engaged in combat but every man, woman, and child of the City tearing and ripping at each other with whatever they could lay their hands on. Looters fearlessly pillaged stores and houses, while delighted arsonists set fires for no purpose other than the joy they derived from destruction. The innocent cowered inside their homes, praying that the chaos that had interrupted their lives would pass them by, while the guilty celebrated the fall of law. And everywhere, in the street, on the sidewalk, sprawled over cars and hidden behind trash cans, lay the dead, with more and more of the living dropping to join them.

Occasionally a Truant or an Enforcer would look around and see what they, together, had wrought. Often they would not be able to tear their eyes away from the horrors, and they would stand and forget the war, only to fall dead at the hands of a more apathetic foe. Neither side was willing to yield, not even if it meant the destruction of themselves and all around them. What had once been a struggle founded on the noblest intentions had spiraled out of control into an unending conflict of hatred.

Zyid's gamble had succeeded. He had finally incited the uprising that he had always dreamed of. But Zyid had never believed that in doing so, he would blindly sacrifice everything decent that the City had to give . . .

And if Tack got his way, Zyid would never find out either.

26

A Guilty Conscience

Tack could feel his heart thumping in his chest as he followed Zyid into a secluded alleyway. The time had come at last. Everything Tack had waited, worked, and hoped for would culminate in this moment. As Tack brushed past some garbage cans, he reflected that the setting seemed so normal, their actions so routine, that for the briefest of seconds he wondered if this could really be the defining moment of his life. Then Zyid stopped in his tracks, and instead of wondering why, Tack decided that *this* must be the moment he was meant to do it. In a most surreal fashion, Tack silently raised his pistol and pointed it at Zyid's motionless back.

"It won't bring her back, Tack."

The shock of hearing those words stunned Tack senseless, and all he could do was stare openmouthed at Zyid. The Truancy leader didn't even turn around to face him, but rather crossed his arms and waited.

"Wha-what?" Tack stammered.

"Killing me won't get you your sister back," Zyid said calmly. "But if it'll put your mind at ease, then please proceed."

Tack made no motion to pull the trigger, and so Zyid slowly turned around to look at him.

"I know that it won't take you long to make up your mind," he said. "But if I may make a suggestion, you shouldn't do it that way." Zyid gestured at the gun in Tack's shaky hands.

"Why not?" Tack demanded.

"Because you'll feel guilty," Zyid said. "You'll feel guilty that you never gave me a chance to fight back, guilty knowing that you stooped to my level to gain your revenge."

"You don't deserve any better."

"No, Tack, I don't," Zyid admitted. "But you have a conscience, Tack, and it would bother you."

"How do you know?" Tack snapped.

"Because"—Zyid smiled solemnly—"even I have one. And it bothers me more every day." His expression grew sad. "I regret what happened to your sister, Tack, and I'm sorry for what I said that day. If it's any consolation, her death at my hands likely haunts me more than it does you."

"No, it doesn't," Tack snarled. "It can't. And you're a heartless bastard; you said it yourself."

"Yes, but I do have a conscience," Zyid said quietly. "I once thought that my emotions had deserted me completely—but they haven't. Do you think that I sleep easily nowadays, knowing that I've left hundreds of children dead, and even more without parents?"

Zyid's voice grew simultaneously harsh and somber. "I must lead by example, so I always keep my emotions masked. But let me tell you, Tack, over the last two months I've often cried myself to sleep."

Tack looked disbelievingly at Zyid, whose expression was one of unmistakable pain and remorse. It seemed as though during all the time that Tack had known him, Zyid had been wearing an emotionless mask, which he had suddenly allowed to slip from his face. Suddenly remembering all the times Tack had thought he'd seen pain, regret, and sadness on the Truancy leader's face, Tack found that he believed Zyid, though he sure as hell wasn't going to let that change anything. Gripping his gun steadily, Tack decided to voice another question that he had to have answered.

"Did you always recognize me?" Tack asked.

"No, as a matter of fact, I didn't." Zyid shook his head. "You were vaguely familiar, but I never recognized you."

"Then how—"

"Umasi."

Tack shut his mouth and clenched his jaw, feeling an entirely new and highly unpleasant sensation stab at him. It didn't take him long to identify the emotion as betrayal.

"Before you judge him too harshly, Tack, you should know that he made me promise not to act on what he told me," Zyid said wearily.

"And he trusted you?" Tack hissed disbelievingly.

"You're still alive, aren't you?" Zyid pointed out. "In fact, did you know that I brought you along just to give you this chance? I could've handled the mission myself. But I wouldn't break a promise to Umasi, Tack. After all, we are . . . or at least were . . . brothers."

Tack spent several seconds trying to wrap his mind around this revelation. It did make sense, and the more he thought about it, the more Tack wondered why he hadn't figured it out himself before. Zyid and Umasi did share a resemblance, and they did know each other from way back. But their philosophies were firmly planted at either end of the spectrum, and their dress had made them look so different that it had never crossed Tack's mind that they might be related.

"What exactly is the history between you two?" Tack demanded. "Umasi mentioned something about two years ago. That's when you started the Truancy, isn't it? What happened back then?"

"Some stories we take to our graves, Tack," Zyid said solemnly. "That, I'm afraid, is one of them."

"Then at least answer this," Tack said fiercely. "Why didn't you kill me when you had the chance?"

"Like I said, I owe Umasi that much," Zyid repeated. "And I owe you more than that."

"You'd let me shoot you down in cold blood?" Tack asked skeptically.

"Oh, I doubt that you'll shoot me down in cold blood," Zyid said quietly.

"Oh yeah?" Tack challenged. "Why's that?"

"Because you know that what I said earlier is true, little though you'd like to admit it, even to yourself," Zyid said. "You have a conscience. But you can also have revenge without the guilt."

"How?" Tack demanded.

Zyid suddenly grinned and spread his arms, letting his own gun drop to the dirty ground of the alley.

"A duel to the death. You and me. Fair and square," Zyid said. "No guns. Just our wits, and our swords."

Without hesitation, Tack turned his gun horizontally and released his grip on it. The pistol clattered on the ground, and Tack drew his sword, glaring at Zyid, waiting for him to make the first move. Zyid casually removed his Student Militia uniform to reveal his usual outfit underneath, complete with the black windbreaker buttoned at his neck like a cape. Shoving the uniform aside with his foot, Zyid then drew his sword and turned to look majestically at Tak.

"Are you ready?" Zyid asked.

"Oh, yes." Tack bared his teeth.

"Since I know who I'm really fighting," Zyid said formally, "it's only fair that you know the same, Tack. *My* true name is Zen, the brother of Umasi . . . and adoptive son of the Mayor of this City."

Before Tack could fully register what he had just heard, the Truancy leader lunged forward, moving faster than Tack had believed possible. Tack's mind barely had time to register a sword swinging horizontally towards his chest when instinct took over, and his own blade darted up to parry the blow. Undiscouraged, and moving with the same calm, inhuman speed he had already displayed, Zyid seemed to almost glide around to face Tack's flank, his windbreaker billowing behind him as he swiftly lashed out with his sword. Tack spun to face the oncoming blow, blocking it as it came within millimeters of his neck.

"So, you're the Mayor's son, huh?" Tack grunted as they leaped apart.

"Of course!" Zyid said, bowing low to sweep his sword at Tack's legs, an attack that Tack tactfully jumped over. "How do you think we found out what the Educators were doing?"

"Your father told you?" Tack guessed as he aimed a diagonal slash at Zyid.

"Hardly." Zyid snorted, leaping aside to avoid Tack's attack.

"We pieced together things we overheard during his little cabinet meetings."

"And Umasi didn't help you?" Tack asked, slashing more forcefully at Zyid's head.

"No, in fact he did his best to thwart me," Zyid confessed as he parried the blow and snapped a kick to Tack's shin. "He didn't even willingly surrender any of his . . . allowance."

"Allowance?" Tack asked uncomprehendingly, rubbing his shin with one hand while swinging his sword at Zyid with the other.

"How do you think Umasi and I got our money?" Zyid asked, leaping backward calmly as Tack's sword clipped the front of his shirt.

"What?" Tack asked carefully, suddenly remembering Umasi's seemingly inexhaustible funds.

"Our dear father provided each of us with money that he believed to be enough to last our entire lives," Zyid explained as he suddenly lunged forward to stab at Tack.

"And the Mayor lets you spend it fighting against him?" Tack asked skeptically as he knocked Zyid's sword aside with his own.

"Of course not." Zyid recovered quickly, launching another vicious assault. "He believes *me* to be dead."

Tack would have said that the Mayor's belief would soon be true, but at the moment Zyid's actions, not words, commanded his undivided attention as their swords locked together. Tack and Zyid stared each other down, teeth gritted and muscles strained as each attempted to break the deadlock in his own favor. It very quickly became apparent to Tack that Zyid outmatched him in brute strength, and so in an effort to cut his losses he suddenly sprang backwards. Zyid seemed surprised for one fleeting instant, then decisively charged forward.

Tack braced himself for an attack, but as Zyid drew near, he suddenly and swiftly spun around so that his black windbreaker snapped impressively towards Tack. Acting reflexively, Tack struck, slicing through the thin fabric—and nothing else. As Zyid completed his spin, his foot lashed upwards, striking Tack's hands with shocking precision. Tack's sword flew up out of his hands just as Zyid's sword arced towards Tack's waist.

Tack had no choice but to stagger back clumsily—unarmed—as Zyid's blade came an inch from cutting him open. Losing his balance, Tack fell backwards, crashing into a cluster of trash cans. Zyid seized his opportunity and jumped forward with his sword raised high above his head, aiming to bring the blade crashing down upon Tack with the full force of gravity.

The reflexive action that put Tack in his unenviable position now saved his life, closing his hand around something metallic. As Zyid's blade descended on him, Tack swung the garbage-can lid that he'd grasped above him as a sort of makeshift shield. Zyid's sword crashed upon the lid with a tremendous clatter, but did it no noticeable damage, and Tack was back on his feet in an instant, clutching the lid tightly.

"Interesting improvisation," Zyid complimented, nodding at the trash-can lid.

"Why, thank you," Tack said with mock politeness, lunging forward to swing the lid at Zyid.

Zyid laughed as he easily dodged the attack and struck at Tack with his sword. With similar ease, Tack blocked the sword with the lid, and then proceeded to attempt another zealous but ineffective swing. The problems of fighting with a trash-can lid soon became obvious to both combatants; it was easy to block blows with, but it was simply no good as a weapon. Even Zyid began to show signs of frustration as his sword clanged off of the lid for what seemed to be the umpteenth time. Acting decisively, Tack leaped back a few paces, and then hurled the lid towards Zyid.

As Zyid knocked the lid out of the way, Tack dived for his sword, sliding it into his hands as he gracefully rolled to come up into a crouch. A twinge of annoyance flitted across Zyid's face, but even so, he darted towards Tack without any hesitation or sign of weariness.

"Getting tired?" Zyid asked shrewdly as he slashed swiftly at Tack's neck.

"Never," Tack lied, parrying the blow and lashing out with his foot.

"Well then, it looks like we have a long fight ahead of us," Zyid observed, sidestepping the kick and swinging his sword at Tack's legs.

"Definitely," Tack agreed, leaping backwards to avoid the attack.

Now that they were locked in combat, Tack felt a reckless confidence and daring that he wasn't familiar with, motivating his muscles even as weariness set in. He found it unusually easy and even encouraging to accept conversation in battle, and the more that Zyid's talents were shoved into his face, the greater Tack's willingness to respect those talents grew. None of this, however, prevented Tack from doing his best to cut Zyid to pieces.

As Zyid leaped sideways to avoid a particularly fierce attack, he suddenly froze and stared at the mouth of the alley.

Wondering what could possibly be distracting the Truancy leader, Tack paused as well. Then he heard it: the sound of hushed voices and heavy footsteps approaching the alley. Tack and Zyid glanced at each other and lowered their swords, instantly coming to a nonverbal agreement; they would not allow their duel to be interrupted.

As the footsteps drew closer, Zyid swiftly moved to an unturned trash can, positioning it so that it faced the mouth of the alley. Waiting until the voices sounded like they were right around the corner, the Truancy leader gave a forceful kick, and the trash can shot down the alley, clattering noisily every bit of the way. A second later, three tall, dark figures came into view—just in time to have the trash can slam into one of them.

Surprise. "What the hell—"

Revulsion. "Truants!"

Anger. "Shoot them, you idiots; shoot them!"

By the time the first shots rang out, Tack and Zyid were already a good distance away, not even having waited to watch the progress of the trash can. Tack had become quite experienced in running during his life as a Truant, and he sped down the alley faster than he'd ever thought he could. Tack quickly passed Zyid, who didn't seem to be quite so concerned; the alley was extremely dark, and they had a healthy head start. Only an extremely lucky shot could hit them, and, as it turned out, the Enforcers were not lucky.

"Where to?" Tack panted.

"The subway," Zyid said decisively. "There's nothing they can do once we board a train."

Tack wasn't in a mood to argue, and followed Zyid down

the street towards the subway station that they'd exited before. As he ran, Tack looked up at the sky and found it to be pitch-black, with the orange glow of the dim street lamps serving only to cast the shadows of their surroundings. It was an impressive and frightening feeling, to be under an endless blanket of vast darkness, with only the most subdued light to illuminate the rough concrete beneath their feet. Unfortunately, the light was not subdued enough.

"There they are!"

"Bastards are heading for the subway!"

"Damn," Zyid breathed as gunshots began echoing throughout the empty street.

Tack was feeling fairly worried himself; they were as good as unarmed, and one of the pursuers had already managed to hit a mailbox that Tack had just run past. Tack chanced a look backwards, and saw three figures a fair distance behind, though still too close for comfort. As the three passed under a street lamp, Tack thought he caught a glimpse of blue Enforcer uniforms, which really didn't tell him anything that he hadn't already assumed. Turning forward again, Tack almost fell down the subway stairs before he skidded to a halt; they were already here; had they really been running that fast?

Zyid, however, hadn't looked back and didn't pause at all, instead sliding smoothly down the silver handrail without hesitation. Cursing, Tack leaped down the stairs two at a time in pursuit. They soon reached the turnstiles, where both boys found themselves absentmindedly scanning the bar codes on their arms. The turnstiles quickly and predictably refused to grant them access, informing them that they were both truants. Tack and Zyid spared each other a mutual grin, and then Zyid planted his hands on either side of the turnstile and swung himself over while Tack crouched low to duck underneath. Behind them, the familiar sounds of gunshots rang throughout the ominously empty terminal, and Tack could hear bullets ricocheting off of the bars that separated them from the stairs.

Reaching the second flight of stairs leading down to the platform, Zyid again smoothly slid down the handrail. Tack attempted to imitate him, but couldn't quite pull it off, crashing gracelessly to the ground at the bottom of the stairs. Picking himself up and rubbing his bruised shoulder, Tack dashed after Zyid, who was now running along the platform. Suddenly, a growing rumbling and a pair of increasingly bright lights in the dark tunnel ahead brought a smile to Tack's lips; this would be the first time he actually got lucky with subway arrivals. Sure enough, a moment later a train clattered into the station, sliding its doors open.

Zyid darted inside the nearest car, and Tack quickly followed suit. Behind them, they heard furious shouting as bullets slammed into the exterior of the train and shattered one of the windows in the car, but the doors had already slid shut, and the train was already in the process of lurching forward. Tack grasped one of the vertical metal poles in the car to steady himself as the train picked up speed, and as he caught his breath, he felt his heart rate return to normal. Watching patiently in front of him stood Zyid, who had opted to hold on to one of the handlebars hanging from the ceiling.

"We seem to have lost them," Zyid observed, turning to gaze at Tack with a glint in his eye.

Knowing what was about to come next, Tack straightened

up stiffly and gripped his sword tightly. Looking steadily over at Zyid, Tack nodded grimly.

The next thing he knew, Zyid had released his handlebar, lunged forward, and swung his sword horizontally in one fluid motion. Tack released the pole and leaped backwards as Zyid's sword slammed into the pole but missed its target. Tack was about to lunge forward himself when the train suddenly lurched to a halt, flinging him onto his back. Zyid used the train's momentum to push himself forward past the pole, slashing downwards at Tack as the doors to the car slid open.

Tack rolled aside as Zyid's blade struck the filthy floor, and then looked up in surprise as he saw several adults and even a few children rush into the car, promptly freezing in their tracks to stare at the sight of the two Truants. There was a moment of suspended shock as the newcomers gaped stupidly, a moment that was soon shattered by Zyid's angry voice.

"Get out!" he barked.

Silence.

"It's a madhouse out there; we'll be killed!" a man protested, protectively gripping the shoulders of a girl that appeared to be his daughter.

"If you stay here you'll be killed," Zyid snarled pitilessly, brandishing his sword.

The message got through, and the civilians reluctantly backed out of the car as the doors slid shut. As the train lurched forward again, Tack took the opportunity to spring to his feet, aiming a slash at Zyid's head. The blow was parried almost lazily, and Zyid followed up with a swift stab. Tack sidestepped the assault, then turned to dash towards the pole. As Zyid pursued, Tack suddenly sheathed his sword, grasped the pole, and used it to swing himself around, kicking out with his feet to catch a surprised Zyid in the chest.

Zyid staggered backwards, and Tack followed up by grasping the ceiling handrails on either side to swing himself forward, lending his next kick tremendous momentum. This time Zyid was sent sprawling across the floor, and Tack lunged forward, drawing his sword and bringing it forward in a diagonal slash at the ground. Zyid used his own sword to parry the blow, then leaped to his feet and grasped the left handrail to swing himself forward as his right hand brought his sword around in a powerful arc at Tack's neck. Tack was forced to leap backwards to avoid the blow, and Zyid tightened his grip on the handrail as he raised his feet to plant them firmly on the side of the car. Zyid now hung menacingly from the ceiling, looking as if he were in the process of literally walking up the wall.

Tack lunged forward, aiming a slash up at Zyid. Zyid knocked the blow aside with his sword, and stabbed downwards at Tack, who tilted his head aside just in time to avoid being skewered. Tack slashed upwards again, but Zyid steadily parried the attack and swept his sword downwards with enough reach to force Tack to drop onto his back to avoid the blow. Zyid seized his opportunity and released the handrail, bringing his sword down upon Tack's vulnerable figure. It would have been a clean kill . . . had the train not shuddered to another sudden halt at that same instant.

The sudden stop drove Zyid backwards as he released the handrail, sending him crashing to the floor with his sword inches away from Tack. Tack rose to his feet as the doors slid open, suddenly finding himself staring at stunned and frightened faces. In no mood to argue with civilians, Tack swung his sword fiercely in their direction, coming nowhere close to hitting them but feeling a sort of grim satisfaction nonetheless as they tripped over each other in their haste to back up.

"And stay out!" Tack called.

The doors slid shut again and Tack turned to find Zyid facing him grimly. Without a word or warning, Zyid lunged forward just as the train lurched forward, swinging his sword at Tack's chest. Tack parried the powerful blow with some difficulty, then barreled forward elbow-first, slamming forcefully into Zyid. Zyid staggered backwards first, and then leaped backwards again as Tack slashed furiously at him. Tack was beginning to feel the strain of weariness pulling at him as the fight dragged on, and was resolved to end it as soon as possible.

Zyid had other ideas, however. As Tack slashed at him repeatedly, he didn't even bother to parry, instead leaping steadily backwards until his back was to the manual sliding door that separated this car from the next. Reaching behind his back to slide the door open, Zyid backed up to stand on the dangerously unstable and exposed juncture between the two cars. Tack hesitated for only the briefest of moments before he plunged forward. Zyid forcefully moved to shut the door so that it slammed into Tack's already-bruised shoulder, and then swung his sword at Tack's exposed head.

Tack was forced to fling himself backwards to land on his back inside the car. The door slid shut again, but not before Tack caught a glimpse of Zyid turning to dart through the door to the next car. Tack growled and rose to his feet, sliding the door open to follow. As soon as he stepped out, however, the train hit a curve and nearly flung him off the edge onto the speeding tracks below. Looking at the door to the next compartment that still remained shut, and wondering what kind of greeting Zyid was preparing there for him, Tack decided to withdraw into his car, where he promptly flung himself into the nearest seat to catch his breath.

Moments later, the train came to another halt, and Tack leaped to his feet and over to the closest doors, which promptly slid open. Tack dashed out onto the platform and rushed towards the next car, only to see Zyid dart out of it and run towards him, his sword drawn back in preparation to swing. Tack gritted his teeth and met the attack head-on, bringing his own blade around in a powerful arc as the train doors slid closed. The swords clashed forcefully, though the noise was soon lost to the sound of the train leaving the platform, and the two Truants upon it, left behind.

As Tack and Zyid parried and slashed at each other, they soon became aware of strange, disturbing sounds that seemed to flit down from the street. Tack swore he could hear screaming, and gunshots, and the distant, horrible roar of flames. Remembering the dire words of the man in the train who had been with his daughter, Tack suddenly felt a chill shiver up his spine, and he was seized by a sudden dread. Leaping backwards to avoid a horizontal slash by Zyid, Tack turned and ran for the nearest stairs.

Tack rushed up the stairs, leaping up three at a time. He heard Zyid following behind him, but for the moment all thoughts of the battle had left his mind. Tack leaped right over the turnstiles and dashed up the second flight of stairs towards the darkness of the surface, the terrible sounds growing louder all the while. As Tack burst up aboveground, he froze still, looking around in horrified disbelief. The district that had housed the news station hadn't been attacked, and had remained relatively unscathed. The district that Tack now stood in, whatever district it was, had received the full force of the blow, and Tack thought that the word *madhouse* seemed to describe it well.

The blanketing darkness in this part of the City had been thoroughly pierced by dozens of flashing stoplights, glowing street lamps, upturned cars with their headlights still glaring, and hungry, insatiable fires. Blackened skeletons of once-great skyscrapers now blazed ceaselessly, yielding a dark smoke onto the darker skies. Gunshots rang out continuously, and dark figures silhouetted by the flickering flames moved about, fighting, shooting, dropping motionless to the ground. The stench of burning flesh that had come to permeate Tack's nightmares now drifted freely through the air, and Tack was almost glad that the darkness concealed much of what he knew daylight would reveal to be a slaughter. The screams that burst through the night belonged to children, adults, the elderly, and the newly born; bullets and fire had no regard for age.

Frozen in a horrified trance, Tack sensed rather than saw Zyid draw up to stand behind him, but the Truancy leader made no motion to attack him. On the contrary, Zyid soon seemed to be even more rigid than Tack himself. The two Truants gazed around in the horror of their design, and slowly, Tack turned to look at Zyid.

"Was this what you wanted?" Tack asked bleakly, his voice barely audible over the screams.

Zyid made no answer, but the flickering light of flames revealed a face that Tack could see was wracked by horror, shock, and pain. But above all, as Tack glared at Zyid, it was as if a twisting, growing, parasitic guilt was eating away at the Truancy leader's conscience.

Zyid didn't respond, and so Tack looked back at the unfolding scenes of horror. Suddenly, something caught his eye: past four lanes of traffic a vast area that seemed oddly secure from the madness surrounding it. No ominous skyscrapers burst from the ground to flirt with the sky, no hellish screams yet emanated from it, and the fires had left it untouched. Distant, twinkling pale streetlights, entirely unlike those that lined the sidewalks, seemed to beckon Tack forward, which was when Tack realized, with a jolt, that the lights illuminated a trace of green.

Trees. So it was a park, and judging from the size, not just any park. It was the Grand Park, which could only mean that Tack and Zyid now stood in District 20 . . .

Or at least what had become of it.

27

The Fall

In better times, and under the full light of day, the four lanes of traffic that Tack and Zyid now stood by were crammed with honking cars as citizens went about their business around the City. The only people in uniform were the students traveling to and from school and the unarmed officers who peacefully directed the vehicles at this crucial traffic juncture. The skyscrapers reached up not into gaping darkness but into cheery blue as the images of clouds reflected off of the buildings' windows. The emerald sheen of the park was clearly visible under the bright sun, and pedestrians flocked towards it looking for nothing more than peaceful recreation.

Knowing what District 20 had once been and seeing what it was now filled Tack with a hopelessness and sorrow that he hadn't thought he was still capable of feeling. It took every ounce of conscious effort that he still possessed to keep from sinking to his knees under the gloating darkness of the heavens. As Tack heard Zyid shift next to him, his despair gave way to anger, and Tack turned to glare at the Truancy leader.

"You. You did this," Tack accused over the sound of gunshots.

"Yes, Tack," Zyid admitted resignedly. "I did this."

"Why?" Tack demanded as a few more silhouettes dropped to the ground.

"I didn't think that it would come to this," Zyid said quietly. "And in any case, when the sun rises, I think it will reveal that the Educators are no longer in control of this City. The Truancy will be in a position to take over."

"Is that all you care about?" Tack snarled. "At this rate, there won't be anything to take over."

"I'm not infallible," Zyid said.

"You're supposed to be a leader!" Tack shouted over a burst of fresh screams.

"You don't know what it's like to lead, do you, Tack?" Zyid said, suddenly sounding angry. "Do you think I can just wave my hand and make things happen the way I want?"

"No, but you sure as hell waved your hand and sent people who believed in you off to die, destroying the very thing they're trying to save!" Tack shouted.

"And could you have done better?" Zyid challenged.

"I probably could have!" Tack roared. "You've been a complete failure!"

Without warning, Zyid drew his sword to slash at Tack. Tack swiftly leaped backwards, snarling furiously as he drew his own sword, his face a mask of outrage.

"Perhaps you're right. Perhaps I am unfit to lead the Truancy," Zyid said in a deadly voice as he advanced upon Tack. "The thought has often occurred to me before.

"To tell you the truth, Tack . . ." Zyid thrust his sword at Tack's head, forcing him to leap aside.

". . . this has all become tiring for me. . . ." Zyid swept his sword sideways at Tack before he could recover. ". . . It's almost as if leading drains the very life from me . . . ," Zyid said as Tack ducked low to avoid the attack.

". . . If you want to shoulder my burden . . ." Zyid slashed downwards at Tack, who skillfully parried the blow.

". . . if you can do better at leadership . . ."

Tack leaped to his feet and cautiously backed up into the street.

". . . then come and *take it from me*!" Zyid shouted.

Zyid lunged at Tack with such ferocity that Tack stumbled backwards. Zyid's sword clipped a button off the front of his uniform. Zyid aimed slash after slash at Tack, forcing him farther backwards into the street. Tack attempted to parry only once, and the sheer force of Zyid's attack shook his sword so hard that his hands ached. Tack had never before seen Zyid as wild as he was then, lit by the distant flames. Strands of hair from the Truancy leader's ponytail had come loose. His nostrils were flared and his eyes were wide and bloodshot. But while his blows were monstrously strong, Zyid no longer moved with his customary grace and accuracy, but with all the elegance and refinement of a tank.

He'll wear himself out in no time at this rate, Tack realized as Zyid's sword swept past an inch from his face, clipping strands of brown hair. *He's serious. He* wants *to die.*

Fresh gunshots rang out, and Tack looked down to see that bullets had struck the asphalt that they now stood upon. That moment of distraction was enough for Zyid, who struck with every bit of force he possessed. With no time to dodge, Tack raised his sword to block the blow, bracing himself. The force of the attack slammed Tack's blade aside completely. Before Zyid could take advantage of the opening, Tack turned and sprinted towards the park, bullets nipping at his heels.

But if he wanted to die, Tack wondered as Zyid pursued him through the open gates to the park, *then why didn't he just let me shoot him down?*

He must have a purpose, Tack decided, leaping over a low fence to run across a sea of short, wavy green tendrils, with the gentle glow of the nearest street lamp reflecting off their lush surface. *But what?*

And then a strange, dark suspicion took root inside Tack's gut. Spinning around suddenly, Tack swung his sword at the pursuing shadow. Zyid halted just in time, the sleeves of his windbreaker billowing forward as he eyed Tack warily.

"You planned this all along," Tack said.

Silence. No trace of anger or madness now remained on Zyid's face. Instead, the soft light of the lamp revealed something that looked oddly like pride.

"You wanted me to take your place all along," Tack said, now understanding why Zyid had kept him close all that time. "You planned this."

"Very good, Tack," Zyid said. "You have an intuition befitting a leader."

"You bastard," Tack snarled. "If you wanted to quit so bad, why did you drag me into this?"

"You dragged yourself into this, Tack," Zyid said. "You want to kill me. What do you think will happen if you succeed? The Truancy will find itself leaderless, and will look naturally to my second in command for guidance."

"Which was Noni, until you made me it!" Tack shouted.

"Would you really wish that upon Noni?" Zyid asked quietly.

Tack scowled. Zyid knew his weaknesses.

"No," Tack said grudgingly. "I wouldn't."

"I wouldn't either," Zyid said. "I love the Truancy, Tack, as I know that you do as well. If through my own death I might escape and leave behind an able replacement, free from blinding hatred, then so be it."

"Don't try acting noble," Tack snapped. "You just want out. You're being selfish."

"That's one way to look at it, Tack," Zyid agreed. "But you must admit that even if that were wholly true, I've played my cards well."

"What do you mean?" Tack demanded cautiously.

"There are three ways you can go from here," Zyid explained quietly. "You might die at my hands, and your death will be the latest to rest on my conscience. You might kill me, and abandon the Truancy to whatever fate awaits it. Or, if you care about the Truancy—which you do—you will kill me and lead the Truancy to victory."

Tack would not have been so infuriated if Zyid had been wrong, but try as he might, he couldn't discover any fourth option. It was unspeakably frustrating, to be in the power of one he hated, even as he was poised to kill him.

"Is it really that bad?" Tack asked quietly.

"Come and find out," Zyid suggested, slinging his sword over his shoulder.

Tack looked up at the sky, and saw with some trepidation that the darkness was beginning to lift. The pure, infinite blackness that had seemed to reach down to choke the City itself was giving way to a twilit midnight blue, rendering the skies distant and unthreatening once more. Bringing his eyes back down to Zyid, Tack gripped his sword tighter than he ever had before, and then held it evenly in front of him. For a brief moment, both Truants were completely still, motionless silhouettes against the omnipresent light of the street lamp.

And then, as one, they lunged. His windbreaker billowing behind him, Zyid arced his sword at Tack's neck. Tack swung his blade up to meet the attack, and both swords crashed together only to be knocked apart by the force of the impact. A moment later, Zyid and Tack slammed into each other and fell to the ground, both of their swords but none of their momentum having been deflected. Neither Truant was willing to show any sign of weariness or injury, and both of them were back on their feet in an instant.

Tack struck first, swinging his sword diagonally at Zyid's chest. Zyid parried the blow neatly, then lashed out with his hand to grasp Tack's shoulder, shoving him sideways and off-balance. Tack swiftly recovered and ducked to avoid a slash aimed at his head, then backed up to evade a subsequent thrust. Feeling his back press up against something, Tack looked up to realize that they were now directly under the boughs of a tree. Zyid slashed at Tack again, but Tack quickly flipped himself around to the other side of the tree trunk, and felt a certain amount of satisfaction as he heard Zyid's sword bite into the wood. As Zyid withdrew his blade from the tree and rounded the trunk to get at Tack, Tack slashed upwards, severing a branch right above Zyid's head.

As Zyid ducked to avoid the falling branch, Tack quickly grasped a sturdier one and hoisted himself up to stand atop it. Zyid came at him again, aiming at his legs. Tack knocked Zyid's sword aside with his own, then slashed upwards again, slicing through more branches and leaves. Prepared this time, Zyid leaped forward to dodge the falling limbs and aimed a swift slash at Tack's unprotected back. Seeing the danger, Tack instantly leaped to the ground, and Zyid's sword again buried itself in wood.

As Zyid worked to retrieve his sword, Tack staggered forward, finding himself at the edge of a broad knee-high flower patch. The faint light of the street lamps couldn't do the colorful petals justice, but even under the circumstances Tack couldn't help but pause to admire the delicate texture, the subdued though distinct whites, reds, yellows, and purples. A rich, familiarly seductive fragrance hung in the air, and for a moment Tack almost forgot what he was doing.

And then the grass behind him rustled in agitation, and Tack spun around to see Zyid rushing at him, sword over his head in preparation for an attack. Tack planted his feet firmly in the ground and braced himself, swinging his sword in a half circle as Zyid brought his blade vertically down upon Tack. Tack's maneuver managed to sweep both his and Zyid's swords into a deadlock, pointed diagonally at the ground. Zyid, however, was first to seize the advantage, snapping a kick to Tack's thigh. Tack staggered backwards into the flower patch, and Zyid followed up with a horizontal slash.

As Zyid's sword passed above Tack's head, he fell amidst the flowers and all of a sudden he was surrounded by sweet scents and lush petals. Even the breeze created in the wake of Zyid's slash seemed to gently caress Tack, to lull him to inertness. But then survival instinct kicked in, and as Zyid's sword swept down at him, Tack rolled aside, crushing the flowers beneath him as Zyid's blade severed the petals he'd admired a moment ago, casting them into the air. Tack sprang to his feet and swung his sword at Zyid, who raised his blade to parry the attack. Knowing that he had to, and yet regretting every moment of it, Tack swiftly slashed again, aiming at Zyid's legs. Zyid leaped deeper into the flower patch to avoid the attack, and as Tack's sword swept by, the tops of flowers fell to the ground as neatly as if they had been cut by a lawn mower.

As Zyid and Tack continued to fight, the air soon became filled with gently fluttering petals. Flashes of color would occasionally become visible to the two Truants as petals were struck by the lamplight, but these moments were fleeting, and appreciation for such beauty had long since become second to their appreciation for battle, and though both of them breathed heavily and deeply of the perfumed air, neither of them gave a thought about its source.

Finally, having beaten a destructive path through the delicate flowers, Tack found himself backed up against a fence. As Zyid slashed at him again, Tack brought his sword around to engage in a deadlock, and then pivoted on one foot to swing his other around to plant a forceful kick in Zyid's belly. Zyid staggered backwards into a cluster of thorny roses, and Tack seized his opportunity, quickly turning to scale the fence. As he dropped onto the other side, he found himself at one end of an immense rectangular area paved with gray stone and lined with bright street lamps. Various paths led away from the area, and at the other end of it Tack could see a wide opening leading out into the streets, with massive buildings that looked less ominous than they had all night as the skies steadily lightened. But most noticeable of all was the massive large rectangular fountain that ran the length of the area, jets of water forming liquid arches across its surface, light reflecting off of the rippling surface and foamy spray.

Without hesitation, and without fully knowing why, Tack leaped into the fountain with a splash, and quickly found the water to be ankle deep, as his boots and socks were instantly soaked. The bottom of the fountain was littered with coins that passersby had cast aside in exchange for good luck. As Tack waded through the water, he heard a loud splash behind him, and turned to face Zyid. Tack held his sword at the ready, and Zyid ran forward to oblige him, splashing and disturbing the surface of the water with each step.

Zyid's sword was held at his side, its tip slicing a trail through the water as he ran. As he drew close to Tack, Zyid swung his sword upwards, drops of water falling from the blade as it swept towards Tack's neck. Tack took a step backwards into the wet spray of a watery jet and parried the attack. Tack then swung his sword around through the jet, water momentarily crashing against its surface as it passed through. Zyid ducked the blow, but was splashed by drops falling from Tack's blade. Zyid thrust his sword forward, and Tack leaped backwards with a splash, Zyid's blade cutting through the resulting spray.

Zyid plunged through the jet of water and emerged, shaking his head to dislodge flecks of water. Tack backed up into another jet, and kicked the surface of the fountain, splashing more water into Zyid's face. Zyid never stopped charging, even as he shut his eyes against the wet spray. Zyid's sword arced through the jet of water and towards Tack, who parried the blow so that both blades met in the midst of the powerful torrent, spraying the both of them thoroughly.

Feeling the sogginess begin to weigh down on his uniform, Tack backed up steadily and wiped his face to clear his eyes as water trickled down his drenched brown hair. Zyid took a moment to follow suit, and then lunged forward swiftly, drops of water now splaying off of his billowing windbreaker. Tack swung his sword up at Zyid, passing through the water of the fountain as it did. The drops it sent into the air splattered against Zyid's windbreaker, but the Truancy leader splashed aside to avoid the blow, then swung his own blade at Tack's waist. Tack fell backwards into the fountain as Zyid's blade scattered drops into the air above him. Zyid seized his chance and swung his sword down upon Tack, who suddenly remembered something Edward had done against him.

Tack jerked his foot up suddenly, splashing water into Zyid's eyes as his sword sank into the sole of Tack's drenched boot. Rising to his feet, Tack turned and dashed to the end of the fountain, leaping through a last jet of water to land upon the dry pavement. Suddenly faced with the exit to the park, Tack found that he recognized where they were and, more important, what lay nearby. As he heard Zyid plunge after him, an ironic smile came to Tack's lips.

"Catch me if you can!" Tack shouted, breaking into a run.

Zyid said nothing, which Tack suspected to mean that Zyid understood exactly where he was going. Still, the squishy footsteps behind him that refused to relent told Tack all that he needed to know; Zyid was following. Tack ran as if passing through a memory. He spotted the once-lively pizza shop that he had eaten at with Suzie so often, now boarded up and empty. He ran down a sidewalk so familiar that he recognized each patch of cement. And as he looked up to the steadily lightening blue of the sky, he felt as though even the air was familiar to him.

As they rounded a corner, Tack saw it: his old school. The

street was empty of all cars and people, and the school itself seemed dark and abandoned. They passed a patch of street that was irreparably scorched, and Tack grimly remembered the first time he had met Zyid, when the both of them had stood upon that scorched spot, the sole witnesses to Suzie's death. With thoughts of how far he had come dominating his conscience, Tack reached the doors to his old school and was pleased to find them unlocked. Swinging them open, he plunged through them, hearing Zyid close behind him.

Tack immediately ran to the stairwell and dashed up the steps two at a time, hearing Zyid's chasing footsteps like an echo to his own. Coming upon the third floor, Tack pushed the stairwell doors open and emerged into a dark hallway, a set of large windows barring the way to the bare roof of a room below. Without hesitation, Tack seized a desk lying on one side of the hallway and hurled it against the window. Tack leaped through the resulting opening even as the glass flew through the air, feeling gashes being cut across his skin by the sharp shards.

Standing atop the small roof, Tack spun around and swept his sword at the hole in the window just as Zyid came plunging through it. Zyid ducked his head and rolled as he hit the ground, rising gracefully to his feet away from Tack. Tack let him do so, watching impassively all the while.

"Your old school?" Zyid asked as he rubbed his back.

"Yeah, this is the one," Tack said casually, as if talking with a close friend. "What do you think?"

"I never thought I'd enter any school again," Zyid admitted as he eyed Tack warily.

"Well, where better to end this than here?" Tack asked, laughing.

"It's as good as any other," Zyid conceded, raising his sword. "So, let's finish it."

"Let's."

Tack lunged forward, and swung his sword around to meet Zyid. Their blades clashed again, and for a moment it looked like they would be engaged in yet another deadlock. Then Zyid twisted his sword around in a circle, shaking Tack's blade off and scratching Tack's hand. Tack dropped his sword in surprise, and Zyid quickly kicked it backwards. Tack backed up a respectful distance as Zyid moved to stand by his sword, which had skidded close to the edge of the roof. Zyid trapped the blade beneath his boot, and then looked at Tack disappointedly.

"Perhaps I was wrong," Zyid said quietly. "How can you lead the living if you cannot even avenge the dead?"

Tack shut his eyes as a surge of anger threatened to overwhelm him. Remembering tedious hours of concentrating and sorting through salt, pepper, and sugar, Tack forced himself to focus, and he quickly felt his anger fade away.

Tack didn't remember breaking into a run; he only knew that he did. Unarmed, with blood running down one arm, he charged at Zyid, who now stood stoically as the object of all the controlled hatred that Tack could muster. He saw Zyid bring his sword back to strike, and he kept running, fearless now, even of death. He saw Zyid swing his sword around at his head, and Tack reached out with both of his flattened hands, trapping the blade between them even as it swung through the air. As he held tightly on to that sword, in that split second before he reached Zyid, he saw, for the first time, fear in Zyid's black eyes.

We must act without mercy.

And then Tack realized then that he wasn't really Tack the student, who had died with his sister, nor was he Tack the confused miscreant, but rather Takan the Truant. The Truant raised his leg and kicked Zyid squarely in the chest, releasing the sword as he did. There was a moment of shock as Zyid realized the position he had put himself in, and then suddenly peaceful acceptance swept over his face. His windbreaker billowed around him as he was knocked from the edge of the roof where he had placed himself precariously, and he outstretched his hand towards the new Truancy leader as if in blessing . . . and then he fell.

He fell, the greatest prodigy the City had ever known.

He fell, the worst student that had ever graced a classroom.

He fell, away from the school, a Truant to the end.

He fell, and the darkness fell away with him as the waking sun crept over the horizon.

He fell, with no one to see him fall, for Takan had turned away and never looked back. As Takan climbed back through the window and into the school without remorse, he felt as though he were suddenly freed from an old burden, only to have a new, greater one fall upon his shoulders. His personal struggle had ended at last. The Truancy's struggle, which had now become his own, still lay ahead.

He came, as Zyid somehow knew that he would. Slowly, mournfully, a lone figure walked up the sidewalk with the dawning sun to his back, halting as he cast his shadow over his brother. As the familiar shadow fell over him, Zyid found that, despite the deep bitterness that had once existed between them, he was glad that Umasi had come. In fact, now that the two brothers were together again, it felt as though they had never been apart. Zyid smiled faintly, feeling completely at peace with the world.

"Hey," Umasi greeted softly, crouching down so that the sun struck Zyid's eyes anew.

"Hey," Zyid replied, shutting his eyelids against the light.

"How did it go?" Umasi asked, after an apologetic pause.

"He will take my place," Zyid said, sighing as if suddenly having been relieved of a great burden. "I've cleared his mind. He is as ready as I could've hoped. And I . . . now I can rest."

Umasi tried to smile, to be as pleased as Zyid was, but he just couldn't manage it.

"You're dying," Umasi observed in a strained voice.

"I know." Zyid nodded resignedly. "But I believe death is not unlike a long nap, and I've not had enough sleep lately."

There was no question of saving him. Umasi had known from the moment that he laid eyes on his brother that Zyid was doomed, but his death was a fact that both brothers had already accepted without complaint. There followed a moment of heavy silence, and then Zyid's eyes suddenly snapped open, and he stared pleadingly up at Umasi.

"He'll need your help," Zyid said urgently. "You'll help him, won't you?"

Umasi sighed. He had feared that Zyid would ask exactly that, though it wasn't unexpected. What did surprise him was how easily the answer came to his lips.

"Yes," Umasi said quietly. "I'll help him."

Zyid let out a pained, rattling breath that he had been holding, managing to sound relieved even as he bled his life out of his shattered body and onto the City streets.

"Promise," Zyid said hoarsely.

"I promise," Umasi swore without hesitation.

Zyid's eyes seemed to mist over, and his entire body relaxed. There followed several moments of silence, and Umasi saw Zyid's lips moving, though no sound came forth. It seemed as if Zyid were in a waking dream, and as the seconds passed by, Umasi looked backwards distantly at the brightening horizon. Neither brother stirred an inch, lost in their own remembrance. Then Zyid's eyes cleared, and Umasi looked back down at him.

"When death lies ahead, it's natural to look back," Umasi said quietly as Zyid looked up serenely.

At that, Zyid shut his eyes and went very still. For a moment, Umasi believed that his brother had died at last, but then Zyid opened his eyes resiliently and looked up, and Umasi understood that his brother had been recalling all that they had gone through two . . . no, nearly three years prior now.

"You looked, didn't you?" Umasi whispered.

"Yes. Yes, I did," Zyid replied.

"So did I." Umasi smiled wryly.

Zyid closed his eyes again, and his chest heaved more violently, his entire body rattling. Umasi understood that his brother was now on the verge of death, and knelt down to grasp his hand. It came as a surprise when Umasi felt Zyid return his grip, and it was an even bigger surprise when Zyid opened his eyes one last time to speak.

"You were right in the end, Brother," Zyid said weakly.

And then his grip loosened, his eyelids slid together, and his chest stopped heaving. Tears dripped down from behind Umasi's black sunglasses, and he released Zyid's limp hand, which fell motionless to the ground.

"Only now I wish that I were wrong," Umasi murmured sadly.

And with that, Umasi reached down and slung Zyid's lifeless body over his shoulder, then steadily rose to his feet, stoically bearing the morbid burden in silence. Slowly, solemnly, the two brothers turned as one to face the warm, beckoning glow of the rising sun, together for one last time.

All throughout the City, in hundreds of schools, Student Militia barracks, Educator facilities, and Enforcer stations, a clear message repeated itself, inspiring hope or fear depending on who heard it. Some of the schools were empty, while others were filled with terrified refugees or smug criminals. Many who heard the message were grim Educators or proud Truants. By the time the sun had risen, few remained that had not heard the message that repeated itself without fail.

But even as the night had faded, and the message outlived the interest of those that heard it, the voice relating it stubbornly spoke on. For the first time, there was no carefully controlled announcement blaring on the loudspeakers of the City. There was only the memory of a Truant whose dream had refused to die with him.

"Children of this City," Zyid said solemnly. "For most of our waking lives, all of us have suffered in academic shackles. Our parents, our teachers, the Mayor—adults of all kinds—have all worked to keep us in these invisible chains. They tell us that we have no rights. They tell us that we are not equal. If we argue, we are disciplined. If we resist, we are punished. We are driven like cattle into the classrooms to obey and feign respect for teachers that treat us like wayward beasts. The Educators have always patiently taught us of our own inferiority, to the point where many of us had begun to believe their words.

"Tonight, we've changed the curriculum," Zyid proclaimed. "No longer will we beg for their favor. No longer will we fear their displeasure. No longer will we hide from failure. Tonight, my friends, students and Truants alike, we have shown them *their* great failure—their failure to wholly subjugate our generation. They did not believe in our intelligence, or our wisdom, or our strength. And we taught them how wrong they have been.

"But now that we have already proven our willingness to fight"—Zyid's voice softened—"let us prove our willingness to have peace. Lessons have been learned by all, the most important of which is that a cycle of escalating violence can only bring us to mutual ruin. Educators, Enforcers, adults of the City, you were once what we are, and you know that you cannot stop your own future. Together, let us end the cycle of bloodshed, and let us end the cycle of oppression.

"In their place, let truancy live forever."

Wherever there is school,
there will always be truancy.

—Zyid

Tor Teen Reader's Guide*

Questions for Discussion

1. Why do you think the author chooses to begin *Truancy* with a prologue entitled "Follow Instructions"? In what ways does the question of whether or not to "follow instructions" play an important role throughout the novel?
2. In the City, students are educated to become unquestioning adult citizens. Do you think education has the same purpose in our society? Why or why not?
3. Describe Tack's relationships with his parents and with his sister, Suzie. How does Suzie contribute to Tack's first foray into District 19?
4. What does Umasi offer Tack to encourage his return to District 19? Is Umasi's offer the only thing drawing Tack back? If not, what else entices him?
5. What actions are Zyid and the Truants taking against the Mayor's Educators and Enforcers? Do you think the Truants' level of violence is acceptable? How does the Mayor respond? Compare the strategies of the Mayor and the

Truants in terms of their effectiveness and of their moral correctness.

6. When details of the Truants' attacks against the City threaten to reach the public, the Mayor orders a news report on a possible outbreak of "Pig Flu" to be released. Why does he think this will control the people? What is Tack's reaction to such news? Does this recall news reports of your own experience? In what ways?
7. Why does Umasi tell Tack that "curiosity is a dangerous beast" (page 108)? How might the Mayor explain this phrase to those in his employ?
8. What are the results of Tack's "final exam" from Umasi? What other meanings does this phrase take on as the final events of part I unfold?
9. Whom does Tack meet on the banks of the West River as part II begins? How does he identify himself to these characters and for what reasons?
10. Where do Truants sleep and eat? In what unhealthy behaviors do they indulge and why? How do they obtain food, clothing, and weapons? Were you to live in Tack's city, would you join the Truants? Why or why not?
11. How did Noni become so closely allied with Zyid? How does Tack succeed Noni as Zyid's protégé? How does the character of Noni help readers better understand the mentality of Truants in general?
12. Are the attacks made by the Truancy against the Educators in part II reminiscent of modern, real-world terrorism? What contemporary news stories seem to have parallels with the events taking place in *Truancy*? Explain your answer.
13. In chapter 16, Tack struggles with his allegiance to the teachings of Umasi and Zyid, ". . . trying to figure out how to fit 'do not seek to take life' alongside 'restraint is a weakness.'" Can this paradox be resolved? Why or why not?

14. What is Edward's plan to defeat the Truants? What makes him qualified to do so? What does he want in return? How does the Mayor feel about Edward?
15. In the chapter 18 battle, what does Tack do when he discovers Charles has betrayed the Truants? What does Zyid do? Does this change the dynamic between Tack and Zyid?
16. How does Tack's relationship with Noni evolve toward the end of the novel? What is important about their friendship? How does it affect Tack's choices?
17. In chapter 21, Zyid suggests that "some people are not meant for school." Do you agree? What are the choices left to those "not meant for school" in the City and in your community?
18. Is Edward's Student Militia successful against the Truancy? How is it counter to the Mayor's overall strategy for controlling his population? Explain.
19. How does Zyid finally persuade Umasi to take action against Edward? How do Umasi's actions change the course of the Truancy rebellion?
20. What is especially appropriate about the name of Penance Tower in terms of the novel's themes? What does Tack plan to do when he escorts Zyid to the tower? How does Tack react when Zyid tells him he knows his true identity and history?
21. As Tack and Zyid do battle, what do they discover has happened to the City? Where does Zyid finally meet his end? Is Tack responsible? Has he been able to "act without mercy"?
22. Who comes to the dying Zyid and how does his presence change your understanding of the story? Do you think Tack will take on the role of leader of the Truancy? What did Zyid mean in saying, "Where there is school, there will always be truancy"? Do you agree?

Writing and research activities are available online at www.tor-forge.com/truancy.